THE

Sweetwood

SERIES

THE
Sweetwood
SERIES

DANIELLE HINES

Maitland, Florida

Orange Blossom Publishing
Maitland, Florida
www.orangeblossombooks.com
info@orangeblossombooks.com

First Edition: June 2023

Library of Congress Control Number: 2023907467

Edited by: Arielle Haughee
Formatted by: Autumn Skye
Cover design: Sanja Mosic

Print ISBN: 978-1-949935-67-7
eBook ISBN: 978-1-949935-77-6

Printed in the U.S.A.

Dedication

For Kimmy

Table of Contents

SWEETWOOD CHRISTMAS

Sweetwood Secret

Chapter 1

*H*olly Blake slumped back against the wooden booth of her local café with a sigh. That was the last signature. With the final stroke of her Holiday Inn pen, she was now officially divorced. It didn't feel real. Daniel Kinsey had been the most important person in her life for two years. He'd been her world. And now... Now he was soaking up the sun and surf in Puerto Vallarta with "Mitzi" while she was freezing her butt off in the early-October chill of the Big Apple.

Daniel, at forty years old and ten years her senior, had the quintessential mid-life crisis. Yes, Mitzi was indeed his secretary. And just to rub salt in to an already nasty wound, she looked exactly like Holly—medium height, medium build, bright blue eyes, and dirty blonde hair—only she was twenty-two.

Holly's coffee was cold. She had not anticipated the process would take so long. Gabe, her lawyer and longtime friend, had lost interest after five minutes and was chatting up an elderly lady at the next table about her grandson's rights to the matrimonial home.

"Tell him not to leave or do anything until he calls me, Norma. I mean it," he said as he handed the woman his card.

Holly watched in amusement. Gabe was ever the hustler, but not in the ambulance-chaser sense. He was a workaholic. His life was the gym, work, maybe four hours of sleep, repeat. Tall, fit, and always impeccably groomed, he was forever being approached by women, though he claimed to not have time for a relationship.

They met in college. He was pre-law. She was majoring in English, hoping to shift her focus to journalism. They had spotted one another at a party wearing the same No Doubt concert t-shirts and became instant friends.

"You okay, Holls?" he asked, turning back around to face her.

Holly pushed the papers towards him and sighed again. "Yeah, I think so. Or I will be at least."

Gabe reached out and patted her arm gently. "It was intense. I know."

That was one word for it, thought Holly. Intense, chaotic, a roller coaster. But she didn't want to think about any of that right now. She wanted to get herself another coffee and then get on with her life. Gabe read her mind as he picked up her old cup and, with a wink, told her the next one was on him.

The kindness of that small act was almost too much to bear. How many times had she wished Daniel could be considerate like that? Her eyes welled up at the thought but she sniffed and pushed it away. She had already shed far too many tears over that man.

Holly fished through her purse for her phone to find she had eight missed calls from her younger brother, Lucas, and just one text. Odd. Lucas despised using the phone. And the number of times he called in such a short period of time was alarming. She switched apps and checked the text.

Lucas: Disappearing for a while. Can you feed my dog?

She read it over and over, searching fruitlessly for a clue. And then she scrolled up to compare it to the last time they had texted five days ago. They had been reminiscing about their dearly departed parents who had died a year ago in a boating accident.

Mom's belly laugh and Dad's Christmas shortbread, she'd said.

Mom's singing voice and Dad's Hulk Hogan impression, he'd replied.

Gabe returned to their table, coffees in hand. "What's the matter?" he asked. Holly's face was white, and she was frantically scrolling through her phone.

"It's Lucas. Something is wrong. He called... and then he texted. He... he..." Her hands were shaking.

Gabe took a deep breath and calmly reached for her phone. "Okay, it's okay. Let me see," he said. Scrolling to the bottom of the screen, he read the text aloud. "'Disappearing for a while. Can you feed my dog?' Doesn't seem so bad, Holls. You know Lucas. He takes off every now and then."

Holly nodded and then shook her head, trying to gather her thoughts. "Yeah, but there's just one problem," she said.

"Oh?" replied Gabe. "And what is that?"

She took the phone back and stood up from the table. "Lucas doesn't have a dog."

Sheriff Max Cooper leaned back in his worn-in leather office chair, rubbed his stubbled chin, and ran a hand through his dark brown hair. This was it. This was what he'd been working toward for the past ten years and now it was all his. He was, as of today, Blairsville's newest and youngest sheriff ever to hold the title. Granted, the honor was bestowed upon him because his mentor, Sheriff Jim Brown, had suffered a massive heart attack and had been made by his loving wife, Janet, to retire.

But still. Here he was. This was now his chair, his desk, his office, his nameplate...Whoops. Nope. That still had Jim's name. Max pulled out his iPhone and added a voice note: "Have Carly order a new nameplate," he said slowly and succinctly.

Just then, the aforementioned deputy sheriff popped her head in the door. "Yes, boss?"

Max attempted to dismiss her with a wave. "Oh nothing, Carly. I was only making a voice note."

She looked puzzled. "With my name?"

"Yes, that's right. It's a voice note for you."

She squinted at him. "But I'm right outside. You could just call me."

Max took a deep breath. "Yes, but this is more professional. I record the voice notes, then send you the file so you can receive them all at once."

"Right, but I'm literally just outside your door," she said. And it wasn't clear if she was still confused or was just having fun with him.

Max lightly slapped his hands on the arms of his office chair. "Okay, Carly. I hear you, but we're gonna do things my way. Now, is there something else you wanted?"

She gave the slightest roll of her eyes but then broke into a smile. "No, boss. Not a thing," she declared, turning to leave and then, "Oh! I almost forgot. Holly Blake called...twice, actually."

Max colored. "Holly?"

"Yes."

"Blake?"

"That's right."

"Called twice?"

Carly sighed. "Like I said..."

Max began nervously tapping his desk with a pen. "Why didn't you put her through?"

She clucked her tongue. "You said you weren't to be disturbed."

Now it was his turn to squint. "But you just disturbed me two minutes ago."

"Yeah, but you called my name."

"I didn't," he began heatedly, but then calmly reconsidered. "Did she leave a message?"

Carly bit her lip slightly to hide a smile, not unlike that of the Cheshire Cat. "No, but she left her number. I'll send you a voice note," she replied and shut the door.

———

Holly couldn't say why she did it. Habit maybe? A masochistic desire to be reminded of one's lot in life? Whatever the reason, she hated that Daniel's voice still provided comfort. Yes, he'd cheated, but it wasn't at all surprising. They had been growing apart as a couple almost immediately after the wedding. It still hurt; she would never deny that. But she decided it wouldn't do her any good to hate him.

"He called eight times?" he asked, his tone calm and even.

She pictured him sitting in his hotel room—tanned and slightly buzzed—probably getting ready for dinner. And then she remembered he wasn't alone and how that wasn't even her business anymore. "Right? So unlike him. But it was the dog thing that threw me off completely. That's when I knew it was more like a cry for help, or a warning at the very least."

"So, are you going down there?"

"Yes," she replied, slightly out of breath from frantically packing her suitcase. "My flight leaves in two hours."

"And did you call him?"

Holly stopped. "Him who?"

Daniel let out a breath. "Holly, you know who. Your ex-fiancé, the big-time sheriff. That's who."

That made her smile. "Checking up on old Max, are we, Daniel?" She could just see him rolling his eyes at that comment, and it made her smile even wider.

He cleared his throat pointedly. "You insisted we become Facebook friends, remember? Anyway, did you call him?"

She zipped up her bag and ran to the bathroom to retrieve her toothbrush. "I left him two messages. In any case," she started, but was interrupted by a call waiting signal. "Oh, Daniel?"

"Yeah?"

"That's him on the other line."

"Him who?"

She laughed. "Okay, I'll call you later. And Daniel?"

"Yes, Holly?"

"Thanks for listening."

He was wearing a self-satisfied smile at that. She knew it but didn't care. She truly was thankful. "Anytime, Holly."

Max waited a full ten minutes before picking up the phone to call Holly back. His heart had been racing, blood pumping voraciously in his veins. If he didn't calm himself down, he'd betray the anxiety in his voice. How long had it been since he'd seen her? A year, he decided—her parents' funeral.

Gosh, that was a terrible day. Carl and Stefie Blake were wonderful people, always kind and welcoming. And they had been nothing but gracious toward him when Holly had broken the engagement. When he approached her at the reception following the funeral, she stepped forward and pulled him to her with such force, it took his breath away.

"They loved you," she whispered in his ear, her voice heavy with emotion. "They thought I was a fool to let you go. Not that they said it; I just knew."

He said thanks, and then moved on down the line to give his condolences to Lucas, her younger brother. Max kicked himself. He had all these words of wisdom and comfort planned out in the truck on the drive over. But he had no idea she'd be the one to speak up first. And he especially had no idea that she'd say something so meaningful. So, in the end, all he said to the woman he loved since he was sixteen years old was, "Thanks."

Back then, she had that jerk of a husband of hers in tow. They were divorced now. Facebook told him that. Of course, he could have simply asked her brother Lucas for an update on Holly at any time. He was always at The Fox and Fig Pub, the local bar Max's sister, Nancy, owned. Max could tell Lucas looked up to him. And part of the way he ingratiated himself was to act as a direct line to Holly, because he knew Max was still in love with her. But, hell, everyone in Blairsville knew that.

Taking a deep breath, he dialed Holly's number. And after four full rings, she picked up.

"Max?" she asked, out of breath. "Is that you?"

She sounded like she was in distress. He cleared his throat. "Hey, yes. Are you okay?"

He could hear her opening and shutting drawers. "I am fine," she replied. "It's Lucas."

Holly recounted the calls and the mysterious text. Max had to admit it was strange behavior—even for Lucas. "Okay, it's not enough for a missing person's report," he began.

"I know that, Max. I just need you to go down to the hunting cabin and see if he's there. Can you check on him? I mean, he's not answering his phone, but who knows? He may actually be fine, and this is all some massively stupid prank. I don't know. Either way, I'm catching the next flight into Chattanooga."

Max's breath caught. "You're coming here?"

"Yes," she replied. "I'll be there before midnight. So, I just need to know if you can check on him in the meantime."

He finally pulled himself together. Holly was worried. She needed him. There was something he could do—right now, for crying out loud—to help her. It took all the strength he could muster to sound cool. "Of course," he said. "You can count on me, Holly."

Chapter 2

*I*f Holly hadn't known that she crossed state lines from Tennessee into Georgia, she would now. The roads were strewn with billboards for "Sweetwood Syrups" every five miles or so. Patricia Sweetwood, the wife of patriarch and billionaire Bill Sweetwood, looked wide-eyed and overly eager to consume her sorghum syrup-laden biscuit. The ads were corny as all get-out but apparently did the trick.

The Sweetwood Syrup Company was a big deal in Blairsville, employing half the town at its processing plant. Bill Sweetwood hit the jackpot in the 90s when he was able to pass off his sorghum syrup as the "healthier sweetener." The company was still riding high. From what Holly could gather, Bill Sweetwood was an aloof yet shrewd businessman who valued business over everything. His wife, Patricia, was a lonely attention-seeker who often drank too much. Their eldest son, Jacob, was keen on inheriting and taking over the business, while the younger son was a partier who spent money like no tomorrow. And then there was Zena—the daughter who wanted nothing to do with any of them. She ran a small art gallery in the middle of town and mostly kept to herself.

Holly was vaguely familiar with the family having attended high school with Jacob and Zena. Lucas had been closer with the Sweetwood clan. He and the youngest son, Keith, had played football together.

Hmmm, thought Holly. Keith. Whenever Lucas got into trouble, Keith was somehow involved. She made a mental note to track him down the next day.

As soon as Holly landed in Chattanooga, she took out her phone to text Max.

Holly: Anything?

Max: He's not at the cabin, Holly. And I didn't see anything suspicious.

Holly: Okay. Thanks for looking. I appreciate it.

Max: Are you still coming out here?

Holly: Yes, of course. There might be something you're not seeing. I'm his sister, after all. And he's still missing...

Holly had lost so much this past year, first her parents, then Daniel. How could she ever bear losing Lucas too? She sniffed back the tears and told herself it was much too soon to think that way. Her brother was out there somewhere—he had to be.

As Holly merged onto the interstate that would bring her back to her hometown, things started to look familiar. Her chest tightened up, and she forced herself to take a deep breath. It was strange to not be in New York. She had tried so hard to shake the sweet Georgia-girl persona she'd acquired growing up here. It certainly would not serve her in her career as a journalist. And yet, she had to admit she missed this place. She missed the landscape, the fresh air, and the food. Her mother's cooking had been incomparable—turnip greens, pulled pork, and peach pie. But Holly? She'd never deigned to learn, though she felt deep regret about that now. There were so many things she had taken for granted, wishing instead for sushi bars, authentic New York pizza, and glamorous parties with important people.

Her mind drifted back just then to the butterflies she felt upon hearing Max's voice over the phone. That had been unexpected. She'd come so far in pushing the memory of him way, deep down. It wasn't until the day of her parents' funeral that everything she ever felt for him came rushing back in an instant. It seemed Daniel had noticed too, because he grabbed her elbow to steady her.

She had reached for Max as soon as he was close enough. And though she couldn't recall what she said to him, she knew it was the truth. It was from the heart. But it made him uncomfortable. A wave of embarrassment washed over her as she recalled how he pulled back, thanked her, and went on his way. Holly knew she couldn't do that to him again. So, whatever these butterflies meant, she would have to get ahold of herself.

Chapter 2

Looking up, she saw a sign for the Meeks Motor Inn and briefly considered sleeping there for the night but then quickly shook off the notion. No matter how difficult it might be, she needed to stay at the hunting cabin. That's where Lucas would show up if (and when) he did.

Just then, her phone rang. She scrambled to connect it to the Bluetooth of her rental. Why hadn't she done that back at the airport? Pushing buttons, plugging cords, she nearly veered off the side of the road in a frantic state. What if it was Lucas? Finally, she heard it connect.

"Lucas? Is that you?"

The caller cleared his throat. "It's Max, Holly."

She was panicked. "What is it? Did you find him? Just give it to me straight."

Max made a shushing noise and kept his tone even. "No, Holly. Nothing yet. I would have texted, but I knew you were driving and figured you probably hadn't set the Bluetooth up to read your texts."

Holly winced a little at being so easily known.

"Anyway, I just wanted to let you know I'm still here at the hunting cabin, and I'll stay here as long as you need—on the couch that is. I wanted to give you a heads-up so you didn't freak out when you saw the sheriff's truck in the driveway."

She was speechless. Max was going to sleep there? He didn't ask her. He was telling her. And just like that, she was twenty-three again, feeling stifled and claustrophobic because of an overbearing boyfriend.

"Holly?"

She took a deep breath. "I'm here," she said.

His voice was wary. "Okay, and do you have a response?"

"We'll talk when I get there," she managed to say. "I'm about twenty miles away."

Sheriff Max Cooper poured himself a bourbon from the bottle above the fridge. Maker's Mark? How on earth could Lucas afford this? It must have been a gift. And yes, he probably should not have been helping himself to someone else's liquor—perhaps especially when they were most likely a missing person—but he needed some liquid courage before facing Holly again. The effect that even hearing her name had on him was overwhelming. His shoulders clenched, and his mind raced. Just when he thought he was over her, something would occur to show him he wasn't.

It didn't help that Max never left Blairsville. This is the town where they grew up together. They fell in love by the bleachers of Union County High School, got engaged by Helton Creek Falls, and broke up in front of the county courthouse. And then there was Lucas who was a fixture at Nancy's bar. Holly was everywhere—all the time.

The problem was Max was in love with a ghost. Holly had spent the past seven years in New York. She had become a successful journalist, and rubbed shoulders with people Max could never even dream of meeting. And she had fallen in love with someone else, then married him. Holly had a whole other life of which Max was only distantly aware. It was intimidating. Even if she had divorced that Daniel guy, there was still most likely a lineup of other Daniels just waiting to take his place.

Holly had moved on fully. She knew herself and what she wanted. Max did, too. He knew he belonged in his hometown. He loved the people here, and it was his deepest wish to do his duty to protect and serve them. So, what a lousy bunch of luck that their paths were meant to diverge in such a significant way. She was out there shining like she should. And he was still the same old guy he'd always been. Only now, he wore a sheriff's uniform.

Max checked his watch. She should be here in about a half hour. He thought back to the way she sounded on the phone, and it occurred to him she may have been annoyed. There was something in her voice almost like... exasperation. Did she not want him to be here? Of course, he only wanted to ensure she was safe, but should he have asked her first? Max recalled this was often an issue between them when they were a couple. He'd act first, ask later, and Holly hated it.

He pulled out his phone. He may be a slow learner, but by golly, he learned.

"Geez, boss. It's eleven thirty. My radio didn't go off so I know there's no emergency. This better be good," said Carly with a yawn.

"Yeah, sorry about this. No emergency, but it is important," he said, dumping his bourbon down the sink.

"Let me guess," she said with a sigh. "This involves Holly Blake."

"That's right. I'm at Lucas Blake's hunting cabin just off Kittle Road. You know it?"

Carly laughed. "Know it? I was at a party there two weeks ago. Unlike you, sheriff, I have a life and see actual people in person on my days off." This was a reference to Max's hobby of online gaming. He let it slide.

"Okay, get here ASAP. I need you to stay the night so that Holly feels safe."

"What? Why me? Why can't you do it?"

Max let out a breath. "I... I don't think she wants me here."

"Well, that makes sense. I don't know that I'd want to play hostess to my ex-fiancé while my brother was missing, even if he is the town sheriff."

He swallowed hard. "So, you'll do it?"

"Yeah, yeah," she replied. "I'll be there in ten."

———

Holly pulled down the long, tree-covered driveway to her family's hunting cabin at precisely midnight. She hoped to see her brother's old Jeep Cherokee parked there, but no such luck. Her heart sank. The more time passed without seeing or hearing from Lucas, the more real the possibility became that he was, in fact, missing.

She parked beside the sheriff's truck in front of the garage and turned off the engine of her tiny rental car. Resting her head on the steering wheel for a moment, she took a deep breath. The truth was, she was a little more fragile than she would have liked. The divorce, while inevitable, had taken a heavier toll than she had anticipated. And then Lucas's text. And now Max and his... expectations. Holly rubbed her temples and sighed. There was nothing to do but face it all. She grabbed her purse and duffle bag and headed into the cabin.

As she approached the front door, she realized she heard music. Was that...? Wait. Could it be? Was that Jewel?

Yup, it was Jewel.

And some woman whom Holly didn't recognize was dancing in the kitchen.

"Hello?" called Holly.

The woman spun 'round and greeted her with a smile, arms open wide. She was petite with short black hair and wide brown eyes. "Oh, hey! Holly!" She walked toward her holding out a hand to shake. Holly took it warily.

"I'm Carly Watie, the deputy sheriff. I'm a friend of Lucas's too." She paused. "I'm really sorry he's taken off."

Holly nodded. "Thank you," she said, looking around, surveying the cabin.

Carly caught her eye. "Max isn't here," she said, a slight smile on her face. "He asked me to stay with you; he figured you wouldn't want the full Max experience quite yet."

Holly's eyes went wide. "I beg your pardon?"

"You know, his dishes in your sink, his socks on your floor, his body on your... couch." Carly didn't miss a beat.

"Right," she replied flatly, not wanting to betray any feelings.

"I'm messing with you, Holly. All he said was that you sounded like you might need some space. But he wanted someone watching over you."

Hm, thought Holly. *So, maybe he's learned a little something over the years.* How many women had it taken to teach him? Had this deputy sheriff been one of them?

Carly danced back into the kitchen. "Now, I can skedaddle if you want to be alone. You're a grown woman. And I spotted the Smith and Wesson underneath your sink two minutes after I got here."

Holly gasped. "Lucas has a gun in the house?"

Carly narrowed her eyes. "This is a hunting cabin, right?"

"Well, sure. There are a few rifles locked up in the loft, but a handgun? And in the kitchen? That's not like Lucas. That means something."

Carly shrugged. "I'll have to take your word for it. Everyone I know has a handgun in the kitchen." She took a small notepad from her purse and wrote down a few points.

Exhaustion hit Holly hard just then, and she knew she couldn't handle anyone being at the cabin. Carly seemed nice enough, but her energy was too much. Kind? Sure, but also way too cheery for what Holly was navigating. "Carly, I'm honestly just going to sleep, so you can go. I'll be all right. Besides, if Lucas has done something illegal, I wouldn't want him to be scared off of coming back to the cabin because there's a sheriff's truck in the driveway."

Carly cocked her head in consideration then nodded. "You got it," she said, putting her coat on and grabbing her purse. "I'll leave you my card. It has my cell on it. Call me anytime, day or night. And I'll be back here first thing tomorrow."

Holly took the card from Carly's hand and smiled gratefully. "Thank you," she said, letting out a breath she hadn't realized she'd been holding.

As soon as she heard the truck backing out of the driveway, Holly went straight to the cupboard beneath the sink. Sure enough, there it was—her grandfather's old Smith and Wesson.

"Lucas Shepherd Blake," she said aloud. "What the hell have you gotten yourself into?"

Chapter 3

*L*ucas Blake surveyed his surroundings with a mix of grogginess and alarm. His mind was attempting to process many things at once. He was in a motel room—a cheap one at that. It smelled of mold and cigarettes. Outside, he could see that it was dark, but the moon was bright and visible through a small slit between the curtains. The pain in his head and the bump on his temple told him he'd been hit, possibly knocked unconscious. The brain fog indicated that he may have been drugged. He was tied to the bed, his arms bound and tethered to the headboard.

Lucas tried to yell but his mouth and throat were too dry. Where was he? A motel, yes, but where? He took a deep breath and attempted to bring to mind the last thing he could remember. He had texted Holly. But wait, he'd tried to call her first. Why did he try to call her? And then he got in his car. Where was he going? He could recall being angry, so very angry.

As he shifted in the bed, he felt something in the crook of his arm. It was a sports water bottle, and it was full! Gingerly, he maneuvered the spout toward his mouth and lifted his head to take a sip. It was water. He prayed it was only that. With his thirst now quenched, he shouted out again.

"Help!" he yelled. "My name is Lucas Blake, and I've been kidnapped!"

Lucas shouted these words, over and over, for what felt like hours but was most likely only twenty minutes. He concluded he was alone in the room at the very least, possibly in the entire motel, too. It seemed likely, given the state of the place, that the building was abandoned.

But someone had brought him here. Someone had tied him up and left him water. That probably meant that someone was also coming back for him. His head was throbbing, and the pain was almost unbearable now. It made remembering that much more difficult. And just then, his eyes felt heavy again.

The water... he thought.

Damn.

Max watched from inside his old Ford Expedition as Carly's truck pulled out of the cabin driveway, and he felt grateful for his foresight. Okay, so maybe Holly didn't want to be watched over, but that didn't mean she was right. He hadn't mentioned it to her when he called her earlier but, even though there was nothing overtly suspicious about the state of the cabin, there was something off about it. Max's gut had felt it as soon as he'd crossed the threshold.

This wasn't just Lucas taking off on a bender or chasing after some girl he'd fallen for. Lucas had left with purpose and resolve. But what had happened after that? And who knew what he was looking for in the first place? Whatever was going on, it wasn't good. Max had decided to file a missing person's report in the morning.

Trusting his gut instincts like this had not made him popular among his colleagues over the years. He was constantly being called out for drawing out investigations or giving perpetrators the benefit of the doubt based on nothing but his intuition. But, nine times out of ten (literally—he'd kept track), he was right.

Max was parked catty-corner from the Blakes' hunting cabin, camouflaged by night and pine tree branches. With his binoculars, he could see into the kitchen window. Holly was standing over the sink; Lucas's gun was in her hand. He saw her shake her head and put the gun back in the cupboard. What was she thinking? He wanted so badly to talk to her, to be near her. She looked beautiful—exactly as he remembered her. She wore her hair up in what Nancy referred to as a 'messy bun.' But the worry on her face hurt his heart. It made him feel helpless, and he didn't like that.

What if Lucas was dead? Or was it worse if he had disappeared, and they never found him at all? Max hated that he couldn't protect Holly from disaster. It had been bad enough when her parents died. Of course, Max had called Lucas and given him the news. The Blakes had been out on their pontoon boat. It was reported they were preparing to dock when the engine suddenly cut off. While Mr. Blake was trying to restart the engine and gain control of the boat, it drifted into a dead tree on the lake's edge. A huge branch from above broke off and came crashing down. It crushed them both—killing them instantly.

Lucas asked if Max could call Holly and tell her. Max agreed. It was the worst phone call of his entire life. She asked him to repeat it three times. He obliged. Then she let out the most primal cry he ever heard. It was a wail from the gut—a mixture of shock and despair. Max's chest went tight, and he kept saying softly, "I'm so sorry, Holly," until someone (Daniel was the most likely candidate) took the phone and hung up. Max was left with nothing but his own tragic sense of helplessness. Holly was devastated, and there was nothing he could do.

Holly knew that despite what she told Carly, she'd never get to sleep right away. So, she busied herself with cleaning the place. Lucas was fine with making sure everything was tidy, but he rarely cleaned things properly. Years back, an old girlfriend had left behind some patchouli-lavender-vinegar concoction that was supposed to pass as a 'cleaner.' It did not. And he was still evidently using it when he did decide to clean.

It occurred to Holly that she had no idea what was going on in Lucas's social life these days. Who were his friends? Was he dating someone? Why had she never heard Carly's name even though she called herself his friend? Holly was beginning to feel like a lousy sister. She'd been so caught up in her own chaos, she rarely checked in with her little brother anymore.

Holly finished up with the kitchen, and as she gave the sink a final wipe-down, she felt the strangest sensation that she was being watched. It briefly alarmed her until a thought crossed her mind. Testing her theory, she turned off the light above the kitchen sink and looked out across the road. Sure enough, just beyond a set of branches, she could make out the lines of an old SUV, and she knew exactly who was inside.

Butterflies again.

Max was giving her space but still watching over her, making sure she was safe. Knowing this made her feel so many things. But most of all, it made her feel protected after having felt so vulnerable these past months. He cared. Someone who knew her and had once loved her actually cared. Holly could feel the tears in her eyes and decided to let them come. She was in her family's cabin, closer in proximity to her brother than she'd been in years. And in light of all that had gone on in the past few hours, she was finally safe enough to feel.

After a few minutes, she went to her purse and fished out her phone, typing out a message to Max.

> Holly: Thank you. Everything is happening so fast, and yet, I feel like I'm in slow motion not knowing where he is. I miss him. I'm beyond worried about him. But knowing you are outside right now watching the cabin... Max, I'm just so grateful. You were always so good. Thank you for being the calm within my storm again.

Holly read the message twice. She imagined him sitting there in his truck, reading her words and maybe even congratulating himself on doing the right thing. And though Holly could not exactly say why, she put the phone back in her purse and did not press send.

Chapter 4

*M*ax woke with a start. Someone was banging on the window. It took him a moment to remember he had fallen asleep in his truck across from the Blake family hunting cabin. He looked up to see Carly smirking at him. At least she was holding two coffees. He so badly needed one.

"Hey," he said, rolling down the window. "How did you know I was here?"

Carly rolled her eyes. "You really think you're some mysterious genius, don't you?" she said, handing him his large, black coffee.

"No, but I did think I was more well-hidden than this."

She laughed. "I'm not knocking your skills at camouflage, boss. But your transparency when it comes to matters of the heart is something else altogether." She reached in and punched him lightly on the shoulder. "I knew you wouldn't be able to leave her tonight, so then it was just a matter of finding out where you parked."

Max took a long sip of coffee and tried his best to ignore how utterly predictable he apparently was. If Carly knew, did Holly know too? He shook off the thought. They had work to do.

"What time is it?" he asked.

"It's seven," she replied. "I'm sure Holly is up."

They crossed the road and walked up the driveway. Sure enough, Holly was sitting on the front porch scrolling through her phone. Her hair was wet, and she was wearing an oversized Georgia Tech hoodie (her dad's) and silk pajama pants (her mom's). Max's heart clenched. The amount of loss she had experienced over the past year was mind-blowing. He wanted to pick her up and carry her away as far as he could run, just to keep her from having to feel one more awful feeling. She looked up at them and smiled wearily.

"Any word from Lucas?" Max asked.

Holly shook her head. "I've been going through my texts with him as far back as three months, but I cannot find any clues. We talk about Daniel, baseball, missing mom and dad..." her voice trailed off, pained. "I should have been checking in with him more."

No one said anything for a moment. Max wanted to interject and give her a hundred reasons why this wasn't her fault, but it wasn't what she needed. She needed to find her brother.

"Can we sit inside and ask you some questions, Holly?" he asked finally.

She nodded and led them through to the kitchen table. Max had always loved the Blake's hunting cabin. It was a log home, typical in these parts, with a large vaulted ceiling. The kitchen was to the right, a bedroom and bathroom to the left, a cozy sitting area complete with a broad, tall stone fireplace in the middle, and a loft overhead with the other bedroom. The place was warm and welcoming and always smelled of cypress and smoke.

Max turned his head toward the fireplace and was instantly transported back to all the nights he and Holly had snuck off and spent here. He turned back to see her observing him.

"It's been a while since I've had you here," she said softly. The look on her face was unreadable.

Carly cleared her throat, looking from Max to Holly, and then back to Max again. "So, we should probably get started. Right, boss?"

"Right," he replied, rubbing his forehead in an effort to shift his thoughts back to the task at hand. "Now, Holly, I know you said you weren't too aware of who Lucas has been spending his time with lately, but I think Carly and I can help with that."

She blinked hard and let out a long-held breath. "That's so good to hear," she said.

Carly piped up. "I said to Max last night that I'd like to head over to The Fox and Fig today and interview the regulars. Nancy, too."

"Yeah, I told my sister one or both of us would be over there today," said Max.

"What about Keith Sweetwood?" asked Holly. "It occurred to me on the drive here last night that whenever Lucas was in serious trouble, Keith was never far behind."

"Yes," said Carly. "He's on our list. He's been hanging at the bar a lot more lately. And then there's..." her voice trailed off as she locked eyes with Max. He nodded, prompting her to continue.

"What?" asked Holly. "What is it?"

Carly turned toward Holly and softened her tone. "There's a rumor going around that Lucas has been seeing someone."

Holly knit her brow. "Okay," she said carefully. "Is this someone I know?"

Carly nodded. "Yes, you know of her at least. The rumor is that he is having an affair with Patricia Sweetwood."

Holly gasped and covered her mouth, eyes going wide in shock. It was well known that Patricia Sweetwood was unhappy in her marriage. It was equally well known that Bill Sweetwood didn't give a damn. He was as cold and mechanical as she was needy and ridiculous.

"How could he do it? Patricia Sweetwood? He grew up going to their house, swimming in their pool. How does he go from that to an affair?"

Max looked at her, his tone gentle. "People get lonely, Holly."

She tucked a stray lock of hair behind her ear and nodded slowly. "Okay, you're right. This is no time to be judgmental. So, does this mean you'll be questioning her, too?"

"Yes," answered Max. "Seeing as it's been more than twenty-four hours without word from Lucas, we definitely need to question her."

"Good," said Holly. "That's good. So, how can I help? What can I do?"

Max smiled warmly. "I'd like you to go back to the station with Carly to file a missing person's report. Are you okay with that?"

She nodded but then looked concerned. "Not you?"

Carly reached out and touched Holly's arm reassuringly. "Max is going to start the interviews. He's good at it, Holly. Let's, you and I, go do the paperwork, and then we can check in with him later today."

Holly visibly relaxed and took a long sip of her coffee. "I've been calling him, by the way—off and on since yesterday. His phone is either off or dead. I couldn't remember if I mentioned that or not."

"That's great, Holly," said Max. "That's helpful to know." He stood to leave, and it took every ounce of his strength to stay still. He wanted to lean down and kiss her or, at least, place a comforting hand on her shoulder. In the end, he knew only words were appropriate. "I'll meet you back here this afternoon, okay? I'll let you know what I find out."

She smiled weakly. "Thank you, Max," she said.

———

The Fox and Fig Pub had been a Blairsville fixture for over thirty years, but it had been the last five years since Nancy Cooper took it over that it had finally been restored to its original glory. With gleaming cherry-wood tables and booths, green velvet upholstered chairs, Civil War-era paintings, and soft candlelit lighting, it was perhaps a touch more elegant than its clientele required. But Nancy had always wanted to own something nice—something tasteful and inviting.

Max was proud of his little sister. After spending half a decade learning the tricks of the trade in various bars and restaurants across Atlanta, she'd brought her expertise back home and added a little sophistication to their sleepy little town.

Pulling up to the parking lot, he was surprised to see cars other than Nancy's there, and none that he recognized. He wanted to talk to her privately, to see if she'd seen or overheard anything within the bar recently. She tolerated Keith Sweetwood as a paying customer, but he knew she'd always had a soft spot for Lucas. Whether it was a kind of pity or genuine care for him, Max couldn't tell. And because Lucas was such a ne'er-do-well, he didn't want to encourage Nancy either way.

It was always strange visiting the bar before noon. The air was stale—smelling like a mix of spilled beer and Pine-Sol—and it was dark except for the odd beam of sunlight seeping through. Max settled himself at the bar. He could see his sister sitting at a corner booth with two men he'd never met. They appeared to be discussing business. Nancy caught his eye and flashed him her right hand with all fingers spread, indicating she'd be with him in five minutes.

True to her word, she bid the men goodbye with handshakes and then came to the bar and wordlessly poured him a coffee.

Max thanked her before beginning his inquisition. "Who were those guys?"

Nancy smiled. "Just business, big brother. They're trying to sell me on piña colada and daiquiri mixes."

He laughed, nearly spitting out his coffee. "Did they not do their research before they came here?"

"I know, right?" said Nancy with an eyeroll. "You should have seen their faces when I told them ninety percent of my female clientele were either beer or whiskey drinkers and that I go through a magnum of Chablis maybe every four weeks."

Max raised his coffee mug and clinked it with hers. "Here's to trying."

Nancy winked at her brother in appreciation. "So, what can I do for you, Max? This about Lucas Blake?"

Max's face turned serious. "Yes," he answered. "Lucas is missing. Holly called me yesterday. She's really concerned." He went on to update his sister on the last twenty-four hours. And by the end of the story, Nancy was as troubled as the rest of them.

"That doesn't sound good at all," she affirmed.

"So, can you tell me anything? Any arguments at the bar recently? Or even just weird behavior involving Lucas somehow?"

Nancy nodded, answering right away. "Oh, yes. Lucas and Keith Sweetwood totally got into it the other day."

Max pulled out his phone, opened the voice note app, and pressed record. "When exactly?"

"Um, let's see. It was the night before last, October 4th. We're busier lately as people begin to pile in for the festival, but I noticed them because Lucas rarely raises his voice."

In less than a week, Blairsville, Georgia, would be in the throes of the event of the year, the Sorghum Festival run by its largest sponsor, Sweetwood Syrups. Every Autumn, during the second and third week-ends of October, folks would come from miles around for good food, square dancing, and of course, sorghum making. It was a big deal, bringing in tons of cash for the town and, in turn, Sweetwood Syrups.

Nancy herself had been crowned Miss Sorghum Festival 2007—a pageant judged every year by Patricia Sweetwood, the mayor, and the sheriff. Max had politely declined this year. Jim Brown had been more than happy to resume his duties and take his place.

"Did you hear any of their altercation?" Max asked.

She sipped her coffee and wiped her mouth with the back of her hand. Max loved how much she looked like their mother, right down to her delicate hands with long, graceful fingers. She was tall and fair with large green eyes and often drew comparisons to Uma Thurman. "Yeah, I did. Pretty sure Lucas didn't even finish his beer that night. As soon as he saw Keith, he cornered him in that booth over there." She pointed across the room to a secluded booth at the back of the bar. "And then a few minutes later, I heard him yell, 'Well? Is it true? Is it?' He yelled it over and over until some guys pulled him back. Keith looked really upset. But more than that... He looked worried."

Max raised an eyebrow. "Worried? How so?"

Nancy shrugged. "I don't know. Like all the color had drained from his face as if he'd been caught or found out. He looked guilty and afraid. Anyway, Lucas left right away and said something along the lines of 'This is far from over.'"

Max considered this. It didn't add up. "Did he mention anything about the affair?"

"Who? Lucas?"

Max shook his head. "No, Keith. You have heard, haven't you?"

Nancy rolled her eyes. "Of course, I have. I'm not living under a rock. But that's been going on since July, Max. And everyone knew. Keith never seemed to care. His mother does this all the time. The men just keep getting younger and younger."

"Yeah, I know. It just doesn't make sense is all. Why should Lucas be upset with Keith?"

"Who knows? Keith is constantly screwing up. In fact, that's all he does. Who's to say this latest mistake didn't affect Lucas in some way?"

Max nodded in agreement. "True," he said. "But Lucas is working at the quarry these days, right? That doesn't have anything to do with Keith. Other than Patricia Sweetwood, I'm not sure where their lives would intersect."

Nancy rubbed her forehead. "Me either, big brother," she said, standing to her full height. "Listen, all the regulars should be here tonight if you wanna ask them your questions. I've got a truckload of beer getting delivered so I have to jet."

He took a deep breath. "Yeah, I'll send Carly," he replied. "I'm going to have to talk to Mrs. Sweetwood. That much is clear."

Max's sister took one last swig of her coffee and set it down on the bar with a flourish. "Be careful," she said, looking him up and down. "There's only one thing that woman loves more than a handsome, young man."

"Oh yeah? What's that?"

"A handsome, young man in a uniform."

Chapter 5

$\mathcal{F}$iling the report with Carly took less than an hour. It helped Holly to know she was doing something, but now what? She couldn't just stew at the cabin. A job opportunity graced her phone that morning—a story on illegal horse breeding—but there was no way she could focus on that right now. She wanted to be tagging along with Max, to be gathering information, figuring this whole thing out, so they could find her brother and bring him home safely. The thought of him out there somewhere helpless and alone made her throat tighten and her eyes well up. Sure, he was a grown man. But in Holly's mind, he was still her little brother.

She thought back to what Lucas was like as a young boy. He was always so observant and thoughtful, a sensitive soul for sure. One day, he'd been playing in their sandbox with his Tonka trucks, perfectly happy to construct a make-believe system of roads by himself, when he unearthed something small and shiny. It was a ring—a mood ring—probably belonging to their babysitter. He held it up to the sky inspecting it, and then spat on it, drying it off on his t-shirt. He stood up and ran over to where Holly was laying in the sun reading her Archie comic book.

"Haw-wee," he called sweetly. "I found this."

He knelt beside her, grabbed her hand, and rolled the ring onto her middle finger, the only finger big enough to wear it. Then he kissed her hand quickly and ran back to the sandbox.

The memory caused a wrenching in her heart so great she could barely breathe. Her brother had always been big-hearted. The world didn't necessarily appreciate men like him and often didn't treat them well. Holly had always hoped he'd pursue something artistic and take off to the West Coast where, God willing, he'd find some kin. But he never did.

Instead, Lucas fumbled and flailed, taking odd jobs, never keeping a girlfriend for longer than a few months. He went through periods where he drank too much, and then he'd sober up for a while. Sometimes he would text her long accounts of his regret, as if he thought he'd disappointed her and longed for her forgiveness. But Holly would always reply in the same way.

"Just take care of yourself, Lucas," she'd say. "You deserve to be happy."

Holly decided to go for a drive both to get her out of the cabin and to look for Lucas. Even if the latter was fruitless, at least it was something. Maybe it would help to clear her mind and recall something that might lead them to him.

October in Blairsville was like something out of a postcard. The trees with their changing leaves set against the mountains and big sky were breathtaking when a person was willing to put down their phone and look. New Yorkers drove hours out of the city for what was right here. Shades of crimson, gold, and sienna graced either side of the road for miles ahead. The beauty of nature in these parts was effortless. Skies of blue and fresh mountain air filled the senses and reminded a person to be grateful. This was God's country.

Holly decided to hop on Old Smokey Road and go from there. When she was in her late teens, she did this all the time. She'd borrow the family minivan, hook up her mp3 player, and drive for miles and miles. Back then, she dreamed of skyscrapers and fame. Now, all she wanted was her family. She turned on the radio and tuned to the local station. Unsurprisingly, Lucas's disappearance had made the news. The broadcaster echoed the description she had given to Carly earlier that day.

Twenty-eight year old male, five-foot-ten-inches tall, one hundred ninety pounds, with light brown hair, blue eyes, and the tattoo of a crow on his right shoulder.

Somehow, hearing it in this way made it all the more real.

Holly rounded a bend in the road and spotted a bright red sports car on the shoulder with its four-way flashers on. The license plate read: SWTWD5. *Keith Sweetwood*, she thought. What on earth was he doing at the side of the road in the middle of the day?

She decided to pull up behind him and approach the car. He appeared to be alone, and it looked as though he was shaking. As Holly bent down to knock on the window, she could see he was actually crying.

The stereotypical baby of the family, Keith Sweetwood was spoiled and enabled, had been all his life, and never had a job his daddy didn't give him. Of course, he was reckless—whether it be racing his speedboat down the river or cliff diving after too many beers. He was also mostly harmless, never malicious. He was too soft for the Sweetwood family though, certainly too soft for his father Bill's liking, and his way of coping was to get so high he forgot who he was.

Holly tapped the window lightly so as not to shock him completely. Keith looked up at her with what could only be described as unbridled fear, but then he quickly masked it with an unconvincing smile.

"Hey, Holly," he said, rolling down his window and sniffing back tears. "You're back."

She eyed him suspiciously. "Keith, what are you doing at the side of the road? And why are you crying?"

He made a noise that was half-laugh, half-cry. His eyes weren't just red, they were bloodshot. "Oh, you know me, Holly Blake. I'm always doing something worth crying over."

Holly leaned in closer, sniffing. The smell coming from his car was like a noxious gas. If she had to guess, it was a mixture of vodka, beer, cigarette smoke, and cotton candy-scented vapor. "Sweet Jesus, Keith!" she exclaimed. "Are you drunk?"

Keith hiccupped then belched. "Maybe."

She rolled her eyes and took out her phone. "Carly?" she said. "It's Holly. Listen, I'm on Old Smokey Road by Benson's farm. Keith is here pulled to the side of the road. Drunk. Can you send someone to come get him?"

"No, no, no," he protested, waving his hands. "No, I'll just sober up here."

"Not happening, Keith. Someone is already on their way."

He banged his head against the steering wheel over and over causing the car horn to blow. Holly reached in and pulled him back.

"Just breathe, Keith," she said gently. "It's gonna be okay."

Keith shook his head fervently. "You don't understand," he said. "If he finds out I've messed up again, he's gonna cut me off."

Holly observed him with pity. "Your dad, you mean?"

He nodded.

She took a deep breath. "Listen, I can't leave you here. Just ask the officer to drop you at a friend's place. Or you can even stay at the hunting cabin with me, if you like."

"You shouldn't be nice to me. No one should be nice to me," he said, swaying slightly. And before she could ask him why, he slumped to the side.

Holly heard a truck pulling up alongside them. It was Max.

"Hey," he shouted. "He okay?"

"Yeah," she answered. "Just wasted. He's passed out and snoring already."

Max pulled up ahead and got out of his truck. For a moment, Holly allowed herself to remember how good he looked in uniform. Tall, broad, and fit with piercing brown eyes, Max had always been nice to look at. She instantly felt guilty for the thought. This was not the time nor the place for that.

"I heard the call on my radio, and I was close by," he said, then looked puzzled. "What are you doing out here?"

"I was out for a drive to clear my head, and I spotted him here. He's not exactly easy to miss."

Max laughed. "Yeah, 2019 Mercedes A250 in Jupiter red—all the Sweetwoods have one, except for Zena. She refused hers so it just sits in the garage at the Sweetwood mansion."

"Wow, good for her."

Max nodded in silent agreement. "So, did he say where he wants to go?"

Holly paused before answering. If he stayed with her at the hunting cabin, she could question him as soon as he came to. "He's going to stay with me until he sobers up."

Max raised an eyebrow at her, but didn't protest. "Okay, then," he said. "I'll have his car towed to the impound lot. Meet you back at the cabin?"

"Meet you there," she said.

After installing Keith into Lucas's bed at the Blake family cabin and receiving a promise from Holly that she'd call as soon as he awoke, Max went back to work. He headed out to the Sweetwood mansion to interview its matriarch, Patricia Sweetwood.

The house itself was a sprawling monstrosity that had only recently been completed after nearly five years of construction. It sat upon twelve acres of land and with two pools, a tennis court, stables for a half dozen horses, and a gazebo that could shelter fifty people. It was by far the most lavish home for miles around. Max gave his name at the front gates and watched them open slowly. In wrought iron, "Sweet" was written on the left gate and "Wood" was on the right. He shook his head and laughed to himself. Bill Sweetwood didn't do subtle.

Max was greeted at the front door by an attractive woman in her sixties wearing modest heels and a black business suit. Her grey hair was in long dreadlocks and dark-rimmed glasses framed her contoured face. She was the Sweetwoods' house manager, Anita Bayu, and she'd been with them for as long as Max could remember.

"Well, if it isn't Max Cooper!" she exclaimed with a wide smile, ushering him inside. "Or should I call you, Sheriff Cooper?"

Max blushed, removed his hat. "Max is fine, Anita. And how are you doing?"

"I'm good, sugar. You know, doing my thing here. It's never boring; I can tell you that much. I sure do miss the days when all you kids were running the halls and having your pool parties. The old house was great for gatherings, wasn't it?"

Max nodded. "It sure was."

Anita's lips went tight. "Now, we have this," she said, gesturing around vaguely. "Kids move out so he builds himself a bigger house. Don't make any sense to me."

"Keith lives here though, right?" asked Max.

Anita laughed. "Oh, Keith will never leave. But he has his own quarters. There's a guest house on the east side of the property; he lives there." She paused and winked at him. "But I think you knew that."

Max blushed again. She was referring to his having recently, briefly dated Zena Sweetwood. "I suppose I did know that, Anita. But

Zena and I aren't seeing each other anymore. I haven't spoken to her in months."

She clucked her tongue. "Well, that's a shame, honey. That child could use a man like you, someone down-to-earth and gentlemanly."

"I appreciate that. Zena's great, though. She'll find someone."

Anita smiled and led him through the massive foyer to a sitting room with floor-to-ceiling windows overlooking the dense woods to the west. "What brings you by then, Max?"

"It's Lucas Blake," he answered, taking a seat. "He's gone missing. His sister is worried sick."

"Lucas? Oh, dear."

Max paused, cleared his throat. "Anita, I need to speak to Mrs. Sweetwood about this."

Her eyes went wide at first, but then she nodded knowingly. "Does she know you're here?"

Max shook his head. "No, this isn't anything official, but I do need to find out the last time she saw Lucas."

Anita stood to leave. "Wait here. I'll let her know you need to see her."

Ten minutes later, Patricia Sweetwood entered the room. She wore a navy blue one-piece bathing suit with a plunging neckline, a white satin robe, and gold sandals to match the gold costume jewelry on her ears, wrists, and neck. Her auburn hair looked professionally styled and framed her fair, freckled face perfectly. Max had to wonder if she always looked like this—fully prepared for company. Though in her fifties, she didn't look a day over forty and clearly took her job as the resident model for Sweetwood Syrups very seriously.

She sauntered past him, walking over to the bar on the other side of the room. "Drink?" she asked.

"Uh, n-no, ma'am," he stuttered. "I'm on duty." *That and it's two in the afternoon*, he thought.

She poured herself what appeared to be vodka and came to sit down across from him. "Now, what can I do for you, sheriff?" Her voice was heavy with a tone Max was sure she'd used many times to get what she wanted.

"It's about Lucas Blake," Max said plainly, trying to gauge her reaction.

Mrs. Sweetwood didn't bat an eye. "What about him?"

"He's missing. His sister hasn't heard from him for over twenty-four hours. He left her a mysterious text and well, she's worried."

She took a graceful sip of her drink. "I assume next you're going to tell me what this has to do with me."

Max sat back, put his hat beside him on the sofa, and folded his hands in his lap. "It's probably best for both of us, Mrs. Sweetwood, if we're honest with one another from the start," he began, and noticed she did not move a muscle. "The word around town is that you and Lucas have been seeing one another, that you're having an affair."

"My, my, Sheriff Cooper," she said with mock sweetness. "I wouldn't have pegged you as the type to listen to idle gossip. How terribly disappointing."

He cleared his throat. "To be more accurate, my deputy knows Lucas personally. She said he had mentioned the affair to her." True, Carly had not given him explicit permission to share this, but he needed to make some progress with this line of questioning.

Mrs. Sweetwood took a moment before replying. "My husband already knows, you know. He doesn't care. So, please don't think you're going to threaten me."

Max was getting annoyed. "Mrs. Sweetwood, I have no intention of doing anything of the kind. This is a missing person's investigation. I am trying to locate Lucas Blake. Now, can you tell me the last time you saw him?"

She swirled the clear liquid in her glass and took a sip. "You must think I'm cold and uncaring," she said. "I'm not, you know. I actually care a great deal about Lucas."

Max gave a curt nod but said nothing. As an adult, he had never really interacted with Patricia Sweetwood. The experience was proving to be a frustrating one. She appeared to be far more concerned with how he perceived her than anything else. And, at this point, he was perceiving her as selfish, secretive, and difficult.

She pursed her lips. "The last time I saw Lucas was two days ago," she said finally. "We met at the Meeks Motor Inn and made love. I left at eleven p.m. I think he left shortly after."

"Do you always meet there for your... encounters?"

Mrs. Sweetwood smiled wryly, enjoying some unknown advantage she seemed to think she had. "For sex, you mean? Yes. It keeps things...tidy."

Max took out his phone and asked if he could record. She agreed.

"So, you saw him two nights ago. Did he seem different to you at all?"

She shook her head, brushing a lock of hair from her eye. "No, he seemed his usual self. But then, we never do much talking."

Max was unconvinced. "Mrs. Sweetwood, you just finished telling me that you care a great deal about Lucas. Now you want me to believe your relationship is purely physical?"

Her eyes flashed. "Believe what you want!" she shouted. "What should I care? No one knows the real me. No one has ever even taken the time."

He took a deep breath, deciding to change tacks. "Can you recall any conversation at all from that night? Or any text messages that stick out in your mind? Truly, Mrs. Sweetwood, you never know what could help us figure out what's happened."

Again, she shook her head. "No," she said. "Nothing sticks out. Like I said, it was a regular night for us."

"He argued with your son, Keith. Were you aware of this?"

Max thought he saw a glimmer of something in her eye, some small admission of worry or guilt or fear, but it was gone almost instantly. "No, when was this? Where?" she asked, her tone almost robotic.

"The night of October fourth," he replied. "At The Fox and Fig."

She recovered her earlier nonchalance and shrugged. "Oh. Well, I know nothing about that."

Max's gut was loud and clear: she was lying. But he had no way to prove it. Not yet, anyway. Turning off his voice note recorder and picking up his hat, he stood and offered a short bow.

"Thank you for your time, Mrs. Sweetwood," he said, turning to leave. There was no sense wasting another minute on someone who was only out to deceive.

"Of course," she replied sweetly, a look of relief washing over her. "Anita will show you out."

"That's all right. I know the way."

"Oh, Max?" she called, his given name dripping like honey from her lips. "I meant to ask. How is my Zena?"

He turned back and flicked the brim of his hat. "I don't know," he replied. "Maybe you should call her some time."

———

Lucas woke up again, and this time the sun streamed in through the windows. The room was muggy, and he felt warm. His mouth was pasty and dry, but he remembered this time to not drink the water. As his vision started to clear, his surroundings came into focus, and he could make out some of the furniture. There was a cracked mirror across from him, a green love seat with a tear down the middle, and a coffee table littered with old, yellowed newspapers. It was at this moment he began to sense he wasn't alone.

He looked to his right, but no one was at the door to the outside. Turning to his left, he could see the bathroom door was shut, but there was light pouring out beneath it—a shadow moving back and forth. Someone was in there.

"Hello?" he croaked. "Who's there?"

The toilet flushed and then the faucet was running. Lucas's chest clenched tight with a mixture of excitement and panic. There was a living, breathing person here with him. And it was either someone who could help or someone out to harm him. His pulse raced as his instincts told him it was the latter.

The light switched off and the door opened to reveal a tall, bearded man with broad shoulders in his late forties. His head was shaved, and his forearms were covered in tattoos. The man wiped his hands with a white hand towel and threw it to the ground. He didn't even blink, simply stared right at Lucas with no expression.

"Who are you?" asked Lucas. "Why are you keeping me here?"

The man grunted but made no answer. He took out his cell phone and, after a moment, said, "Yeah, it's me. He's awake."

Chapter 6

*H*olly toweled off in the bathroom and slipped into a pair of her brother's sweats. She had brought her own clothes, of course, but this helped her feel closer to him somehow. It comforted her. She peeked in on Keith who was still out cold, snoring loudly. It was dinner time, but Holly could not bring herself to eat. This had been her second shower of the day, and it was nothing more than a means of distracting herself, a way to pass the time.

Taking out her phone, she began to dial Daniel's number out of habit. His face flashed before her eyes, and she felt a millisecond of ease. She was anxious and scared. And even with everything that had happened, her mind was still programmed to reach for him. The problem was he was no longer hers to hold and hadn't been for quite some time. In a quick decision, Holly changed his contact info to 'Daniel Notyourhusband.' Then, taking a deep breath, she texted Gabe instead.

Holly: Still no word. I'm kinda freaking out.

Gabe: Oh, Holls. I'm sorry. Is there anything I can do?

Holly's eyes welled up. Gabe's sympathy was enough to break her.

Holly: You're doing it.

Gabe: I'm always here for you. But let me know if you want me there with you, okay? I'll hop on the next flight.

Holly smiled and took a deep breath, relieved. She hadn't even realized that this was what she needed to hear. She needed to know that someone from her life back in New York was willing to come help her in her old one.

Holly: Thank you, Gabe. I promise I will.

There was a knock at the door. Holly was briefly excited thinking it could be Lucas, and then she quickly realized he'd never knock at his own door. She felt silly and wanted to cry, but she pulled herself together and answered it.

It was Max. He was standing at her door in plain clothes carrying a pizza box and a bottle of wine. "I took a chance that you hadn't eaten and were in need of a good wine buzz," he said.

Without thinking, Holly walked straight to him and wrapped her arms around his neck. She pulled him tight and breathed him in, his scent like limes and sandalwood. God, why did he always smell so damn good? She took a step back and apologized.

Max stepped closer, bridging the distance. "Don't ever be sorry for needing a hug," he said.

She wanted to hold him again and let him hold her. But it wasn't right. She was just needy and lonely and upset. Using Max was unfair. "Thanks," she said quietly, bowing her head. "Come in."

He stood for a moment. She could feel him staring at her, almost daring her to keep ignoring him. "Holly..." he started.

She spoke up quickly. "Uh, so, Keith is still sleeping. I'm not sure he'll be awake before morning."

Max smiled. "So, I get you all to myself for the evening."

Holly gave a short laugh in an attempt to cancel out the incessant butterflies in her stomach. "Yes, in all my grey cotton glory," she said with a mock curtsy.

"You'd look good in a potato sack, Holly, and you damn well know it."

With that, she blushed and turned, leading him to the kitchen table. She grabbed the plates and wine glasses and lit a candle. As she did, she thought about how different Max seemed. He acted so calm, so sure. This was new. When they were a couple, he'd always been the chaser, the people-pleaser.

In the end, it had been the thing she rejected. His love had been almost overwhelming at times. And as she had begun to realize she was going to need space and room to grow, it became increasingly clear that she could not have that and be with Max.

But now... Now he wore a quiet confidence. He was still kind and thoughtful, but there was no expectation attached anymore. Holly was mildly surprised at how attractive this was. He was like the Max she knew but more himself than he'd ever been. And for someone feeling as lost and unsure as she currently felt, that was incredibly comforting.

Max poured them each a glass of wine and made a toast. "To finding Lucas safe and healthy as soon as possible."

Holly's throat went tight. She tried to thank him, but no sound came, so she smiled gratefully instead. The wine was good. It left a warm and pleasant trail down her throat that allowed her to finally speak again. "How did it go with Mrs. Sweetwood?" she asked.

"All right, I guess," he replied. "She admitted to the affair, but she's definitely hiding something. After we talk to Keith, I want to speak to Zena. I'm hoping she can fill in some gaps."

"Can I come with you?" she asked.

Max looked momentarily uncomfortable. "Um, well, I don't know, Holly. I should probably just go myself to keep it professional."

Holly wanted to press him, but decided to leave it for now. She could always insist tomorrow. And depending on what Keith had to say, it might be moot anyway. She realized she was heavily banking on Keith knowing something. His whole demeanor seemed guilty, albeit drunkenly so.

They polished off the first bottle of wine, and Holly opened another one from the cupboard. She was beginning to feel bolder now, caring less and less about doing the 'right' thing. She invited Max to join her on the sofa and noted to herself that it was nice to feel somewhat relaxed for a change. A thought of guilt tried to creep in, telling her she had no right to feel good while Lucas was out there somewhere. But she pushed it aside. There was nothing she could do in this moment.

Max took some kindling and a few logs from the old crate beside the hearth and started a fire. Holly, meanwhile, took out her phone and searched for a very specific playlist. Soon enough, they were reminiscing as Patsy Cline sang sweetly.

"Do you remember the party out at Gibson's Farm?" asked Holly. "We were nineteen, I think. Robbie Gibson told everyone to bring a bottle of something—vodka, whiskey, gin... But do you remember what you decided to bring?"

Max laughed out loud. "Oh my gosh, yes! My parents had an old bottle of absinthe in a closet in the crawlspace. I had no idea what it was. I only knew it was some kind of alcohol."

Holly leaned over and poked him in the stomach. "You were so innocent," she said teasingly. "Poor Lucas ended up with it. He had two shots and promptly fell to the ground and stayed in the fetal position all night singing 'Puff, the Magic Dragon.'" She giggled and then sighed. "He's always been so sensitive—to alcohol, drugs, just life in general. He's too good for this world."

Max nodded. "Agreed. Lucas is one of the good ones," he said. "But to be fair, it was absinthe."

Holly threw a pillow at his head. "You know what I mean!"

He smiled at her. "Yes, Bo-Bolly," he said. "I know what you mean."

She stopped. "You haven't called me that in years," she said. "Not since..."

"Not since we were engaged," he replied, finishing her thought. "It feels nice to say it again."

Holly swallowed hard. "It's nice to hear it again." And just then, a new track started playing, and it sounded louder than the one before it. "True Love." It was their song. Holly colored instantly and looked away.

Max reached for her chin, turning her head towards his face with a gentle touch. "You know, I wondered what you were doing putting on a playlist of only Patsy Cline," he said softly. "I wondered if you'd forgotten or remembered."

She was flustered. "I-I can't say," she began.

"You can't say? Or you won't say?"

"I-I don't know, Max. I just wanted to hear Patsy Cline."

His eyes never wavered from hers. "I see," he said finally. "Well, will you dance with me?" he asked, rising and offering his hand.

Her entire body was buzzing now. She wanted nothing more than to be close to him, to feel his heat and strength. She wanted the look he'd been giving her all night to transmute into their bodies swaying together, into his hand at the small of her back, and into his mouth full and warm on hers.

Holly rose to meet him and melted into his arms. Everything about him was both familiar and new. It was intoxicating. She felt him hug her tighter, his breathing growing heavier. Here was a man who knew her, who cared for her, maybe even loved her still. And he was good. She was safe with him.

Holly raised her head from his shoulder and looked up to see he was already looking down at her. Max kissed her without hesitation, deep and slow. She felt all the tension leave her body, her head going light. Instinctively, she pressed her body closer to his and heard the most exquisite moan escape his lips.

"Holly," he whispered as he placed his hands on her hips, pressing his fingers into her flesh.

Just then, a loud shuffling and a bang came from the second bedroom. "Guys? Guys!" shouted Keith. "I've fallen off the bed."

Max buried his head in Holly's shoulder. "Can I kill him?" he asked.

"After we find out what he knows." She gently pushed back and winked at him.

The sofa at the Blake's hunting cabin was a pull-out and a massively uncomfortable one at that. Max didn't sleep a wink. He had a more restful sleep in his truck for crying out loud. But it was a step closer with Holly. He had ended up spending most of the night thinking about their past. It didn't take much searching of his mind to have a memory pop up. Max guessed that all these little stories of their relationship had been there at the surface all along, no matter how good he thought he was at keeping them at bay.

One such story was from mere days after their engagement. Max had texted Holly that he was going to pick her up and take her to dinner. At first, she'd said yes with tons of exclamation points and happy faces. But then, she messaged back saying she was tired and just wanted to stay in. When Max pushed her for more information, she was vague, and that wasn't like Holly at all.

Then, Max got a strong feeling. At first, it showed up as a fleeting thought: she's lost her ring. It made Max chuckle because that was absolutely something Holly would do. But the thought didn't go away. It soon took hold and demanded to be taken seriously. So, Max deliberately calmed his mind. He took a deep breath and followed the feeling. He knew Holly had been gardening with her mother earlier in the day, and she hated wearing gloves—said she liked the feel of the earth in her hands too much to wear them. Max figured this is where she had lost her ring.

Jumping into his car, he drove to the Blake's home. When he pulled in the driveway, it was clear they had gone out. Max remembered it was their euchre night with friends from church, and that meant they would be gone for hours. He got out of the car and headed for a bed of echinacea that looked as though it had just been planted.

Feeling the earth with his hands like Holly had done hours before, he pulled out her modest diamond solitaire ring and felt an easy satisfaction. He realized in that moment that helping Holly was the thing that made him feel most connected and alive. And though he wasn't an especially devout man, he looked skyward and gave thanks for having her in his life.

Ten minutes later, he had texted her a message with a picture of the ring:

> Max: Is this what made you tired?
>
> Holly: How on earth did you know????????
>
> Max: I just had a feeling.
>
> Holly: You're incredible. I love you. Thank you.

Max brought his thoughts back to more pressing matters, back to the present. The night before had gone so much better than he had anticipated. They had flirted and danced. He'd kissed her, and she'd kissed him back. If it hadn't been for Keith, he might even have spent the night in her bed.

Who was he kidding? Even if the sofa bed had been more comfortable, he still wouldn't have slept. How could he? Too much had happened. A reconciliation with Holly was now a possibility. This was something he hadn't let himself even consider for years. She was single. She was here. And she wasn't pushing him away.

And then there was the memory of how she felt in his arms last night, how she pressed in close and almost begged him to kiss her. She played Patsy Cline. That was their music. When they were younger, they used to sneak up to the attic at her parents' old place to be alone. There was a dusty record player in there with exactly one record: *Showcase* by Patsy Cline, featuring the Jordanaires.

Max wanted to talk to her, to find out if she still loved him. He wanted to tell her that he never stopped, that he dated women since she'd broken their engagement, but no one ever measured up. Of course, he knew now was not the time for any of this. She was heartbroken. Still grieving the death of her parents, the end of her marriage, and now worried sick about her brother, Holly was in no state of mind to recommit to him.

The thoughts of doubt began to creep in now. What if she had simply clung to him last night because of who they used to be? What if it had just been wine and despair that had influenced her? Holly's life was in New York. His was here in Blairsville. That had not changed.

Max rubbed his eyes and looked at the clock. It was five in the morning. Only six short hours ago, he had been so full of hope, and now it was sinking in that nothing was different. Not a thing had truly changed. He was going to have to bury his feelings for Holly back down deep today. The focus had to be on finding Lucas.

Keith's rude awakening last night hadn't led to anything. He and Holly helped him back into bed, and he'd fallen asleep instantly. As they closed the door to let him rest again, Max reached for her in an attempt to continue what they started.

"I think we should get some sleep, Max," she said gently.

And so, he let her go again.

Yes, today he would ignore every feeling that had been brought to the surface. It's not as if he wasn't a pro at that already. He would do it because he had to in order to survive and to be the man Holly needed him to be—the man who would find her brother and bring him home.

Chapter 7

*H*olly awoke at seven and cursed herself. She had slept right through her alarm. Time was a-wasting. She needed coffee and to question Keith Sweetwood. Her head ached slightly—too much wine last night. But it had been so nice, she could not bring herself to regret it. Max was helping to make an unbearable experience bearable. And though she hesitated to encourage him in any way, she had to admit he was exceptionally good at offering comfort and distraction.

She walked into the kitchen to find Max standing at the sink, staring out the window and had to stop herself from winding her arms around his waist like she used to do. A long list of all the things they used to do had been filling her mind the past few days. A part of her wanted to indulge the impulses. But reason won out and instead, she said hello.

He turned to her and smiled. "Hey, beautiful," he said. "Did you sleep okay?"

Holly nodded and poured herself a coffee. "You?" she asked.

Max blushed and hung his head. "Not great, Miss Blake. And it's all your fault."

She smiled shyly, shuffling her feet. "I see," she said. "I'm very sorry, Sheriff Cooper. How can I make it up to you?" This was a dangerous play on her part, but she couldn't help herself. Max was bringing out a part of her that had not seen the light in such a long time.

He made a low growl. "Oh, Holly. You shouldn't ask such things..."

Keith appeared just then wearing Stefie Blake's pink cotton bathrobe. His eyes were puffy, and his face was beet red. He was shorter than the other men in his family, and stouter too. But he was always

41

well-groomed with a shaved head and a trimmed beard. The confidence with which he sported the bathrobe was admirable.

"Oh my God," he exclaimed in a scratchy voice. "Please tell me there is coffee."

Max rolled his eyes and handed him a mug. "Yes, princess. There's coffee."

Keith laughed. "Oh this? It's all I could find. My clothes smell like a barn."

Holly gritted her teeth. "It's my mother's," she said.

Keith's eyes went wide. "Shoot. I'm sorry, Holly. I'll—"

She waved her hand dismissively. "It's fine. Just, please, cinch it a little tighter."

He gathered the pink material with his hands and sat down at the kitchen table. "Ay, ay, captain."

Max pulled out his phone, put it on the table, and sat down. "Okay, Keith. Let's get started. And I'm recording this, just so you're aware."

Keith looked flustered for a moment. "Oh, uh, okay."

"When was the last time you saw Lucas Blake?" Max began.

Holly sat down with the guys, not wanting to miss a thing.

Keith scratched his head and sat back in his chair. "It was three nights ago, I guess. We were at your sister's bar. He came at me as soon as he saw me."

Max didn't look surprised. "He was upset?"

"Yeah, he kept asking me if it was true."

Holly interjected. "If what was true?"

Keith shrugged and swallowed hard. "I don't know, guys. He was real upset, but I don't know."

Holly watched Max. His expression didn't change, and it puzzled her. Keith was so clearly lying, but Max didn't call him on it. Instead, he mimicked Keith and shrugged back. "If you had to guess," he said casually. "What do you think he meant?"

Keith nervously tapped his foot. "I mean, like you say, if I had to guess... Maybe it had something to do with my mom?"

Max kept his gaze on Keith, nodding. "Right, your mom. See, the thing is, Keith, I spoke to your mom yesterday. She said she had no idea why Lucas would have gone missing. So, that leaves me with two people who saw him within hours of his disappearance who claim to have no knowledge of the reason."

Keith shrugged again, and Holly decided if he kept doing it, she would leap across the table and slap him. How could he do this? How could he sit there at her family's table and lie?

"How do you feel about the affair your mother is having with Lucas?" asked Max.

Keith gave a short laugh. "I don't feel anything about it. They're both grown-ups."

"And what about your father?"

Keith's face went white at the mention of Bill Sweetwood. "H-he knows she does this," he said, his voice cracking. "He's always known and has never seemed to care."

"Are you close with your mother?" asked Max.

Keith gave that same sarcastic laugh. "Max, you know damn well I'm the black sheep. My parents couldn't care less if I lived or died."

Max narrowed his eyes. "That's a bit extreme, don't you think? They clearly care about you."

"Have you met Bill and Patricia Sweetwood? All they know is extreme. My mother only cares about getting attention and pissing off my father any way she can. And my father cares about exactly two things: his business and the image of his family."

Holly was confused. "But doesn't having a wife who continually cheats tarnish that family image?"

Keith shook his head. "Not to Bill Sweetwood. It means he has a hot wife. Happiness is not part of his equation of success. It's all about how things look."

"That is messed up," she whispered.

"Tell me about it," said Keith.

Max continued his questioning. "Okay, so, if you're not close with your mother, why would Lucas come to you about her? Why wouldn't he go to your dad or Jacob or Zena?"

Keith rubbed his temples. "Lucas would never get past security to see my dad, same with Jacob. As for Zena, the only person in my family who dislikes my parents more than me is my sister." He added, "You should know that."

Max fumbled. "I-uh, suppose..."

Keith looked at Max, then to Holly, then back to Max. His face fell, as if realizing he had made a mistake. "Shoot. Sorry, man. I had no idea she didn't know about you and my sister."

Holly's entire body went tight. She was a fool! Of course, he would have dated Zena, maybe they were still a thing. She was beautiful, smart and, most importantly, she was local. So, this was why he didn't want her tagging along. "It's fine, Keith," she said. "Max's private life is his business. He's single and can see whomever he chooses." She stopped there, realizing she had said too much.

Max gave her a puzzled look and then turned back to Keith. "You still haven't answered my question. Why would Lucas come to you?"

"I don't know, man, okay? And I'm starting to think I need to call my lawyer. Am I under arrest?"

"Of course not," Max replied. "Keith, relax. We can stop now, if you like. But I want you to promise me you won't leave town until we find Lucas. You may know more than you think."

Keith visibly relaxed and nodded. "Yeah, man. No problem." He raised both hands as if in surrender. "Listen, I couldn't leave even if I wanted to. The festival is next week. My dad would never let me get out of that."

The two men stood and shook hands. Max offered to give Keith a ride to the impound lot—after he got changed, of course.

Holly couldn't bring herself to move out of the chair. She felt frustrated that they were no further ahead, that Max had been so easy on Keith. And then the business about him dating Zena. It all left her feeling emotional and even more helpless than before.

Max put a hand on her shoulder, and she winced, pulling away. He narrowed his brow.

"Holly, what's wrong?"

Her throat was too tight with overwhelm to answer him. She took out her phone, pretended to busy herself in an email, and ignored him.

"Okay, well, let's talk when I get back. I have to go interview Zena after I drop off Keith."

"Hmpf," she uttered, surprising even herself at the level of immaturity she was displaying.

Max bent down to meet her eyes. "Holly, I—"

She put her hand up in protest. "I don't want to talk about this now."

He looked dejected but said nothing—only nodded, took his keys, and left.

———

The Sweetwood Gallery was mere steps away from the historic Union County Courthouse. It was prime real estate in Blairsville that only a Sweetwood or some foreign investor could afford. Zena may have turned her back on her family in many ways, but she kept the name and at least some of the money.

Max couldn't say he blamed her. Their hometown wasn't an especially culturally diverse place. Running something like an art gallery in these parts meant one couldn't be too concerned with turning a profit. Of course, the festival was coming up which meant more visitors. It was Zena's busiest time of year, but even that didn't mean much. Most people just came to take a gander and that was about it.

His thoughts turned to Holly as he parked outside the gallery. Damn Keith and his big mouth. Naturally, Max had no intention of keeping his former romantic relationship with Zena a secret from her. But there was such a thing as timing. The look on her face made his chest go tight. She'd been hurt. And the last thing he ever wanted to do was hurt Holly.

As for Zena, he couldn't be sure how she felt—not ever. She had always been very kind and sweet, but when he'd asked her to slow things down last summer, she gave him mixed messages. At first, she told him he was making a big fuss, they'd always been casual anyway. But then she would randomly send him heart emojis out of the blue. When he asked his sister, Nancy, what that was about, her answer struck him.

"She's lonesome, Max. She's simply too proud to say so. Can you imagine what it would be like living in this town, with that last name, but not having anything in common your family? Zena Sweetwood is lost and lonely, and you're truly the perfect guy for her to reach out to."

Zena always came across as having it all together. But sometimes, usually after they'd both had some whiskey, she would let her guard down a little and do things like thank him for caring about her or reach out and squeeze his hand for no reason. Their relationship, it seemed, meant something to her. But eventually, they just stopped trying, stopped texting altogether. For Max, it had been a relief. What it meant to Zena, he simply couldn't say.

Max stepped into the gallery and spotted Zena at the back. She looked impeccable, just like always. Her hair was the most lustrous shade of chestnut he'd ever seen, but Zena always wore it up in what she told him was called a French twist. She wore a fitted black, sleeveless dress, impossibly high heels—the ones with the red soles—her trademark pearl choker, and had a pen in her mouth in a way that made men salivate (and of this she was well-aware). She smiled at Max when she saw him walking toward her.

"Sheriff Max Cooper," she swooned in an exaggerated Georgia drawl. "As I live and breathe."

Max offered a sheepish smile, never able to match her intensity. "Hey, Zena. The place looks great."

Zena looked around and nodded. "Thanks. It's getting there." She led him to her tiny office in the back of the store and sat behind her desk piled with file folders. "I'm sorry about the mess. It's just me running things, and I'm so behind."

"No problem. I didn't even tell you I was coming."

She smiled. "Yes, but word gets around fast. I assume this is about Lucas Blake?"

Max updated her on all they knew, realizing again as he spoke how little progress had been made. He hated missing person's cases. The inherent hope was almost always more of a curse than a blessing. Lucas had his fair share of running with the wrong crowd. And this intimate association with the Sweetwoods only made things worse because now money, power, and reputation were involved.

Zena listened attentively, watching him closely as he spoke. "I'm not surprised my mother didn't tell you anything," she said, almost apologizing. "She's gonna love all the attention this brings her, even if it's negative. I wish I knew something. But I'm keeping my distance from all of them, as you know. Have you spoken to my father yet?"

Max shook his head. "No, I hope to today—your older brother, too."

Zena scratched the spot beneath her nose. "Jacob is in New Zealand. I'm surprised no one told you that."

That surprised Max, too. But then his focus had been on Keith and Patricia for obvious reasons. "Okay, then. Bill Sweetwood it is."

She raised a hand in warning. "Don't expect much from him, Max. If anything, he'll make a game of this. He likes to give a show of not caring at all what my mother does. So, even if he does know about Lucas's disappearance, he probably won't let on."

Max shrugged. "Be that as it may, I still need to touch base with him. And hopefully I can gather something from his demeanor even if his words won't reveal much."

Zena smiled wide, leaning toward him. "It's hot seeing you like this—all decisive and in charge."

He didn't know how to respond to her. This was why he hated not tying up loose ends. None of this was her fault, of course, but now he was so uncomfortable. Zena, for her part, was no fool. She could read a room and picked up on his awkwardness right away.

"You're back with Holly," she said coolly.

Max felt his whole body tighten. "No," he said.

She cocked her head, taking him in. "Yes, you are. It's written all over your face. I mean, I always knew you weren't over her—"

"Zena," he interrupted. "With all due respect, this isn't helpful. Holly wants her brother found safe and sound. The rest doesn't matter right now."

She nodded. "You're right. I'm sorry." Zena sat back in her chair, crossed her legs. "I'm surprised though, that you didn't get any information out of Anita. She knows all the goings-on with the Sweetwood family, even when she politely pretends not to."

Max narrowed his eyes in confusion. "Anita? Your family's house manager?"

Zena laughed. "She's our everything-manager. Are you kidding? She has a law degree from Emory. She's basically Dad's right hand. How did you not know this?"

He felt foolish. That was a good point. How did he not know this? Could it be he'd been seeing much of this family and its associates through the lens of his teenage self still? "I—uh, I don't know. I guess I just thought she took care of you guys and the house. I had no clue she was involved in the business."

"She's basically Dad's other wife—the wife he wishes our mother could have been maybe? I don't know. But she runs the house, yes, and helps him run Sweetwood Syrups, too. She mostly works from the house, so maybe that's what threw you. Mark my words though, Sweetwood Syrups wouldn't be worth half of what it is now without Anita Bayu."

Max ran his fingers through his hair. "I didn't ask her anything. I told her that Lucas had disappeared."

"Did she look surprised?" asked Zena.

Max tried to recall. "Yeah, I think so."

"Talk to her again," she advised. "And before you talk to my dad, if possible."

"I'm scheduled to see him right after I finish with you."

Zena shrugged. "All right then. I hope you get something helpful out of it."

Max's phone buzzed. It was a text from Carly: Call me.

"I've got to go," he said, standing up to leave. "Thanks for your help, Zena. Please let me know if you hear anything."

"Of course," she replied. "And Max..."

He peeked his head back around her office door. "Yeah?"

"Good luck," Zena said. "With everything." And Max could tell she meant it.

He tapped the door jamb twice, attempting a cool exit. "Thanks, Zena."

Chapter 8

*H*olly could not stop thinking about Max, and it was making her feel like the worst sister in the world. Last night with him had been incredible—confusing, but incredible. She hadn't felt like that in years. But there was so much going on around them. How true could it all really be? He was familiar and safe in a time and place that felt so scary and unstable. And she had intruded on his life, expecting him to drop everything for her. It was presumptuous to say the least.

But Max had always been there for her. There was never a time, not since they'd met, where he hadn't been completely and utterly available for her. She was spoiled by his devotion. Yet, he had a life here that was separate from her, from all they'd been together, and he was doing good things. He fulfilled his dream and became the town sheriff. He moved on with a beautiful, intelligent woman. Goodness, was she a home-wrecker? Had she unknowingly cashed in on Max's old feelings for her to the detriment of a serious relationship?

No, that couldn't be. Max could never betray someone like that. He simply didn't have it in him. But obviously, he and Zena were at least seeing each other. Holly had to admit the thought of him with another woman was enough to make her nauseous. And she knew it was unfair. After all, she had been the one to take off to the big city, leaving him behind, and marrying someone else—someone older, more worldly, and successful. And through it all, Max never stopped being there for her.

Enough. Holly decided she had to distract herself. She remembered the shed at the edge of the property. She and her mother never went out there. But her father and Lucas did. It was a tiny man-cave complete with tools, fishing gear, some hunting paraphernalia, and a CB radio. Maybe Lucas still hung out there and maybe there was a clue worth following.

She pulled on her mother's rain boots and made the trek west toward the stream. How long had it been since she'd been out here? Ten years? Her mother had asked her to go fetch the boys for dinner. She had been cooking venison stew with biscuits. Holly could still smell it—the earthy scent of carrots, potatoes, and meat mixed with the sweet, warm scent of freshly-baked biscuits. It made her miss her mother so much her eyes began to well up.

Of course, "the boys" back then meant her dad, her brother, and her fiancé. The thought of this caused what she had come to call "love-ache." It brought a smile to her face and throbbing pangs to her chest. There was no way around grief—Holly knew this. The only way was through. So, she walked on with the memories wrapped around her like blankets.

The shed was in good shape—the outside having recently been repainted, a new light fixture added, and the long grass surrounding it trimmed. Lucas was clearly using it. Holly looked under the doormat and retrieved the key. The door opened easily and once inside, she could see this space was a kind of refuge for Lucas. Holly had to wonder if spending time here was a way for him to feel close to their dad.

Flicking on the light, it was plain that not much had changed on the inside. It still bore the pungent smell of moth balls and gasoline. But there were three new barstools and a makeshift desk. The desk had papers spread out over it. Holly moved to have a closer look and was surprised at what she saw. The thing that caught her eye was her parents' obituaries—both written by Holly. The sight of them, complete with pictures of her dear mother and father broke her in that moment.

It hit her that Lucas had taken down nearly all the pictures of them in the cabin, but here they were alongside the words she'd written. Holly let out a wail, a sound so intense in its feeling and fervor, she frightened even herself. Her parents had been so good, so kind. Many times, Holly wished to be more like her mother—devout, thoughtful, and a proponent of the simple life. Not once had she shamed Holly for wanting something more. No, she always supported her with loving encouragement and only a hint of motherly concern.

Holly cried a few minutes longer, not able to move from the spot she was in. Eventually, she gathered up all the papers, piling them in a folder that sat opened on the desk. She couldn't bring herself to look at anything else. Selfishly, she decided she was unable to. Max would though. He would help, just like he always had.

The fog in Lucas's brain brought on by whatever this guy used to drug him was finally starting to lift. As soon as his captor ended the call, he went back into the bathroom and, an hour later, still hadn't come out. At first, Lucas panicked and yelled for help, hoping the guy would either take pity and help him or at least let him know what was going on. After about five minutes, it was clear neither was going to happen so, Lucas decided to use his energy to remember what happened leading up to waking up here in this godforsaken motel room.

The problem was he was hungry. It was difficult to concentrate while his stomach hurt, and his body felt so weak. But he remembered the car following him on the highway. And how he knew in his gut it wasn't good. He recalled dialing his sister's number many times and her not picking up.

Then, he was run off the road. Someone big grabbed him, took his phone. Was it this guy here with him now? It could have been. Then Lucas remembered thinking quickly, asking the guy to text his sister to feed his dog. And the guy did it, or at least he said he did. So, if this was the same dude who kidnapped him, he could be reasoned with. He had a heart. This was good.

Finally, Lucas couldn't take it anymore. He yelled out that he was hungry and had to use the washroom. He could not bring himself to think about how his bodily functions had been handled up until this point. After a minute, bald guy with the beard came out and sat down on the bed beside him. He reached into the bedside table and pulled out a granola bar, unwrapped it, and fed it to Lucas.

"Thank you," said Lucas taking a grateful bite. "What's your name?"

The man looked dubious, but then answered, "Todd."

Lucas smiled, deciding a slow but sure approach would be best. "Thanks, Todd."

He finished the granola bar and used the washroom while Todd stood guard beside him. It was humiliating to say the least, but Lucas was determined to keep a cool head. He asked Todd if he could be restrained with one hand free so he could read the Bible (thank God for the Gideons!). Fortunately, Todd said yes.

Having his hunger and bladder both satiated, Lucas was now in a much better place to remember details. Just then, Todd spoke up.

"Have you accepted Jesus Christ as your lord and savior?" Todd asked.

Lucas decided he would have to tread carefully. Who knew what side of the fence Todd was one, after all? "I was raised Christian, but really lapsed in my teens and early twenties. Trying my best to do better these days."

Todd nodded. "I respect that."

This turn of events made Lucas feel brave, so he asked, "I don't suppose you know how long I'll be here, do you?"

Todd swallowed, looked away. He was quiet for a moment but eventually replied, "My instructions are to keep you here until after the festival."

Lucas narrowed his brown in confusion. "The festival? Why? That's a week away. What does the festival have to do with any of this?"

It was instantly clear he had gone too far. Todd got up without a word and went back into the bathroom, slamming the door behind him.

Damn, thought Lucas. *So close!* All he could do was hope Todd would come around. But that divulgence had left Lucas with even more questions. While it was good to hear this was most likely a temporary thing, he needed to know who wanted him out of town during the festival? And why? He would have to try his best to remember more. The answer was there in the back of his mind. All he needed to do was retrieve it.

But then Todd reappeared with a syringe. And before Lucas could even protest, he was out like a light.

Max sat in his truck in the parking lot of the Skillet Café and wolfed down a roast beef sandwich. His phone lit up, and he answered it right away. It was Carly.

"Talk to me," Max said into the phone, pumped with hope and adrenaline that they might finally have a lead.

"Okay, Uncle Jesse," she replied dryly. "I'll start with the bad news. We've had no luck tracking Lucas's movements. There have been no cell phone pings, no credit card use at all. I've interviewed all the patrons of the bar who were there the night Lucas and Keith got into it. No one remembers what was said, just that they argued. But there is one guy left to track down, the one who actually pulled Lucas off of Keith that night. Nancy's ex, Thomas Grange, remember him?"

Remember him? How could he forget? Thomas Grange had been an absolute jerk to Nancy when they dated in high school. They fought constantly and publicly. To this day, Max ignored him if he saw him. In his opinion, the guy was useless, and Max had nothing to say to him. "Yeah, I remember."

"Right, well, I guess he's back in town for the festival."

Max gave a resentful laugh. "I didn't even know he'd left."

"Yeah, he took a job in Atlanta as a lighting assistant in the studios at CNN. Apparently, he's really cleaned up his act."

That is odd, though Max. How come Nancy had not mentioned any of this to him?

Carly read his mind. "I'm sure Nancy didn't mention it because you so clearly hate the guy."

"If you knew that, why did you ask me if I remembered him?"

"Keeping you on your toes, boss! Anyway, I'm going to meet with him in an hour at your sister's bar if you want to join."

Max considered this. While he didn't especially want to see Thomas for any reason, it would be good to hear what he had to say about the skirmish with Keith and Lucas. Anything helpful Max could bring to Holly would ease her mind a little. "Okay," he said. "I'll try. I'm off to meet with Bill Sweetwood right now."

"Oh man," said Carly. "Good luck. You'll need a mental shower after that one. He's a total sleazeball."

"Really? I always thought he was a snob."

"Don't worry," replied Carly. "He's that, too."

Chapter 9

The Sweetwood Syrups head office was located at the edge of town, adjacent to the processing plant. Both the plant and the office building had been completely updated and overhauled two years prior and now everything was state-of-the-art. Max felt out of his element. Other than his grandmother baking biscuits and slathering them with butter and some sorghum syrup (the Sweetwood brand, of course), he had very little idea at just how successful the business was.

Max flashed his badge at the security gate and was waved on through by a yawning, young man in his early twenties. He parked at the west side of the complex, closer to the office building and realized he had never even been here before. He had driven past it, read about it, spoken to people who worked here, but he'd never actually seen Sweetwood Syrups up close and in person.

When Max entered the main building, he was greeted by a woman in her mid-forties wearing a headset and carrying a tablet. She introduced herself as "Meg," told him he was expected and asked him to follow her. They rode the elevator up to the top floor, and she whispered to him to take a left as the doors opened up. Apparently, the entire floor belonged to Bill Sweetwood.

Max opened the only door he could see and was greeted by another woman in her mid-forties who could have been Meg's twin. She asked him to have a seat, and he obeyed. All of the office furniture was dark cherry wood. The walls were a rich navy blue, and there were lit antique lamps everywhere. Max removed his hat, kneading it between his fingers somewhat nervously. There was a lot riding on this interview. He wanted so badly to get it right. If Bill Sweetwood was involved in

Lucas's disappearance, then let that come out today. Time was passing by all too quickly.

There was a rustling down the hall to Max's left, and then some voices. A minute later, a door opened and out came Anita. She smiled widely when they made eye contact and then wordlessly squeezed his knee as she walked past him. So, it was true. Anita was much more than a house manager. Not that he'd ever doubted Zena's word. It was just a bit jarring to have this whole new version of Anita confirmed. What was it Zena had called her? Their everything-manager. Now, Max wanted to know just how far that management went.

Meg's twin popped her head into the waiting room and instructed Max that Mr. Sweetwood would see him now. He thanked her and made his way down the corridor to the room at the end.

Bill Sweetwood greeted him cordially. "Sheriff Cooper. It's a pleasure. I haven't seen you since the pool party days when y'all were in high school," he said, shaking Max's hand. He was medium height with broad shoulders and wore what looked like a very expensive, very tailored suit. He had a full head of hair that was graying at the sides and was well-trimmed. His moustache was full—a man's moustache as Max's grandfather would have said.

Max had not anticipated a warm welcome, much less outright folksiness. "It's good to see you again, Mr. Sweetwood."

"Call me Bill, please," he replied, motioning for Max to take a seat in front of his massive antique desk.

"Bill, thank you. I think Anita probably explained why I'm here."

Bill smiled. "Well, you did, son—when we spoke on the phone."

Max noted the deflection but proceeded. "Right, so Lucas Blake is missing. I'm here to see if you recall seeing or speaking to him in recent days."

Bill sat back in his brown leather chair and said nothing. Instead, he opened a drawer to his right and pulled out a long cigar and ran it beneath his nose. "I received a box of these from the mayor of Havana last year as a thank you for opening up a sorghum processing plant there," he said.

Max nodded but did not reply.

Bill then pulled out cigar cutters and cut off the tip. "And these," he began, "were a gift from Ted Turner after I gave a sizeable donation to his foundation's fight against climate change."

Max did not blink.

Finally, Bill pulled out a gold-plated lighter and lit the cigar taking a few brief puffs before that long, first inhale. "And this, son," he said brandishing it like a weapon, "was a present from Jack Nicklaus for hosting our annual golf tournament in support of children's charities."

Max coughed in spite of himself, unused to cigar smoke as he was.

Bill leaned forward, placing the cigar in an ashtray on his desk. "Do you understand me, boy?"

"What I understand, sir, is that you still have not answered the question," replied Max, determined to keep his cool.

Bill smacked the desk, his eyes wide in mock excitement. "That's right. And I never will. I don't dally with people below my station. My wife has different philosophies. But I decided long ago to let a woman do as she pleases, so long as she comes home to me and does what I need her to do when I need her to do it. Aside from that, I don't speak to or commiserate with people who are only a waste of my time."

"So, you're saying you have not spoken to Lucas Blake, and you know nothing about his disappearance."

Bill Sweetwood was clearly incensed but was doing his absolute darnedest to hide it. He was red-faced, and the tiniest beads of sweat were beginning to pool at his hairline. Without breaking eye contact, he rose and held out his hand to Max. "Sheriff Cooper," he said. "Always a pleasure."

Max sighed, stood, and shook the older man's hand, finally resigning himself to what he should have known all along: this interview had been over before it had even begun.

Holly held the folder of papers in her hands as she sat at the kitchen table. She still had not been able to bring herself to look through what was in there. Her parents' deaths seemed like a lifetime ago, yet the pain was still so fresh. She missed her mother's hugs, the way she'd call her baby girl. She missed her father's whistling, and the way he'd catch her eye when she was pouting and make funny faces until she laughed. Daniel always told her to focus on the good stuff and she would not be as sad. But it was more complicated than that.

The good was good, yes, and had always been good. But it was the "never again" of it all that weighed so heavily. Daniel had never been comfortable with her being anything other than okay. He was a fixer. And grief was not something to be fixed. It needed to be lived out, never holed up, but respected all the same.

Yes, she had been grieving, but there was more to it that she had not faced. There was guilt for not being here in Blairsville when it happened. And there was shame for not doing more to help and support her brother through everything. But she couldn't go down that emotional road right now.

Holly considered calling Max to tell him about her discovery, but the truth was she was still feeling weird about the whole Zena thing. It was now an elephant in the room, and that was just annoying. She hated that it bothered her and that she couldn't pinpoint why. Was she really so petty to be jealous when they had barely reunited? The answer appeared to be yes. But in an effort to be gentle with herself, Holly chalked it up to feeling so vulnerable after all that had occurred in the past while.

In the end, she decided to wait until he got back to the cabin. There should be a lot to discuss with any luck. He was meeting with both Zena and Bill today. Someone had to know something. It made Holly so angry that Patricia Sweetwood could both claim to care for Lucas and then offer no help or insight into finding him. The relationship between them could not have been serious. Mrs. Sweetwood was notorious for having these affairs, but she was equally renowned for staying married. Holly knew her brother. He wanted more. He wanted a real partner, someone to share his life with, to give him children. Patricia Sweetwood could offer none of these things.

Max walked into The Fox and Fig Pub feeling dejected and small. Why had he let Bill Sweetwood treat him like a scared little boy? While he knew it would have done no good to try and bully the man, Max could not help but feel that he'd squandered a chance to stand up for himself and earn some of the older man's respect in doing so. And it wasn't that he needed his respect, he simply wanted his rank acknowledged. Max had earned his sheriff's badge fair and square.

Nancy spotted him right away. "Hey, big brother," she said with a smile. "Carly and Thomas are in the corner booth."

Max wondered briefly about Nancy's thoughts on Thomas's apparent new life, but that conversation would have to wait. When he approached their table, he noticed that in spite of a shift in job and location, Thomas looked exactly the same: an average guy with an average build and shaggy brown hair with the slightest hint of a beard. Max concluded he would always be unimpressed with this dude.

"Well, hey there, boss!" greeted Carly. "I'm glad you could make it. We were just talking about the night of Lucas and Keith's little argument."

Thomas, to his credit, stood and shook Max's hand before the latter sat down beside Carly. "Good to see you again, Sheriff Cooper," he said. "I was just about to tell your colleague here that whatever was going on between those two, it wasn't little."

Max raised an eyebrow in question. "Oh? And what makes you say that?"

"Lucas was angry, like passionately angry. This was personal," said Thomas.

Carly leaned in. "What exactly do you recall them saying to one another?"

"Um, well, I remember watching Lucas make a bee-line for Keith, almost like he had just seen he was there. He walked up and just grabbed the guy by his shirt, and he shouted, 'Is it true? Is it true? Were you there?'" said Thomas. "And then Keith was like, 'Man, I don't know what you are talking about.' And then Lucas said, 'The boat, Keith. I know about it. Your mother told me.'"

Max paused a beat, unsure if he'd just heard what he thought he'd heard. "Wait, what?"

Thomas repeated, "Yeah, he asked him if it was true over and over, but I only heard him mention the boat part once."

"Okay, yeah, because you're the first person we've interviewed to mention anything about a boat," said Carly. "What happened next?"

Thomas shrugged. "I pulled Lucas off of Keith, told him to cool down. And then Keith ran right out of here."

Max was scratching his head. "What boat though?"

"How the hell should I know? I'm just telling you what I heard." Thomas got up, agitated. "Guys, are we done here? I have to get ready for a date."

"Yeah," said Carly. "Just don't leave town, all right? We may need to ask you more questions."

Max gave Thomas a serious look.

"Hey, now," Thomas protested, his hands up in an innocent gesture. "It's not with your sister. Don't worry."

After Thomas left, Carly turned to Max. "Are you thinking what I'm thinking?"

Max knit his brow. "I don't know."

She rolled her eyes. "Seriously? Max, come on. This must have something to do with the Blakes' deaths."

Max felt the possibility of that hit him straight in the gut. "But how? That was ruled an accident. Sheriff Brown himself investigated the whole thing. If there was foul play, he would have known or at least followed up on a suspicion."

Carly narrowed her eyes. "Max, I know you have always admired Jim Brown, so I've just kept this to myself, but that man is as crooked as a barrel full of fish hooks."

Max was flabbergasted. "I beg your pardon?"

"Do you know what he asked me during my job interview?"

Max shook his head.

Carly cleared her throat. "First, he asked what tribe my parents belonged to."

Max made the universal cringe face.

She continued. "Then he asked if I was healthy, followed by an inquiry as to the ticking of my biological clock. And then, lastly, he brought it back to my Native heritage asking if I had any relatives in the casino business who could quote-unquote 'hook him up.'"

Max rubbed his forehead, taking in this new information. "Okay, that makes him pretty terrible. But it doesn't make him dishonest."

"Right, well, he was having an affair last year before his retirement."

Max sighed with disappointment. "Oh, man. I hate hearing that. His wife is a good woman. Do you know who with?"

Carly paused before looking Max in the eye. "Anita Bayu," she said.

Max spotted Holly cooling her tea on the front porch of the hunting cabin, a folder filled with papers on her lap.

"Looks like Keith knows more than he's admitting to," he said, standing in front of her, trying to assess her mood. It was unreadable though, and Max decided to not inquire. Instead, he went on to tell her what Thomas had said about the fight between Lucas and Keith.

Holly was incensed and suggested Max track Keith down and beat the bejeezus out of him. Out of all the Sweetwoods, Keith was by far the weakest link and their best chance at finding out the truth. Problem was, of course, it was against his sworn oath to serve and protect to do such a thing.

"I have had it with this family," she said, seething. "All they do is cover their own asses! And they don't care who they hurt. Keith is a moron. Patricia is a liar. Bill is a narcissist. Jacob is nowhere to be found. And Zena is..." Holly paused. "Well, I don't know what Zena is, but I am so angry right now!"

Max took the chair beside her, leaned forward, and put his hand on her knee. "For what it's worth, I don't think Zena knows anything."

Holly gave a resentful laugh. "Yeah, sorry, Max. Your opinion on what your girlfriend knows isn't worth anything right now."

He pulled back. "My what?" he began and then thought better of it. "You're upset so, I'll just let that go."

And with that, Holly broke. "Upset? Are you kidding me? I'm beside myself! This is all taking way too long, and I am really starting to wonder if you are up to the task of finding my brother. I know Blairsville is a sleepy town and all, but I need you to wake the heck up! Lucas is missing. He could be dead. And all you care about is defending some woman you sleep with?! I'm better off hiring a private investigator."

Max was in shock. He had never seen Holly like this. "Holly, Zena and I—"

"Don't finish that sentence," she shouted. "You know what? I need you to leave. Send Carly over or keep your watch outside—I don't care. But I cannot look at you right now."

A thousand words descended from Max's brain to the tip of his tongue, all of them defensive. He wanted to tell her how she knew nothing about how to run a missing person's investigation, about how frustrating it was, and how long it often took with rarely a happy ending in sight. He wanted to remind her how few leads they'd had up until now, and how being lied to certainly didn't help. He wanted to say that he cared for Lucas too and considered her family his family, and he was committed to finding him—no matter what it took. And then he wanted to tell her how much he still loved her, how he had never been able to get her out of his heart, how there had never been anyone else like her, and he knew there never would.

In the end, he swallowed every last one of those words. She was not herself. No, she was angry, confused, and grieving. She didn't need his sentiments; she needed his deeds. "I'll sleep in the truck tonight," he said. He stood, kissed the top of her head, and left.

Chapter 10

*H*olly sat before the fireplace and stared at the dancing flames. She had been crying for hours and finally decided to make herself a cup of tea and build a fire. Her heart and mind were at the height of grief and helplessness, and frankly, she did not want to feel or think anymore. All she wanted right now was sleep, but that would not come easy. Chamomile and a fire would help.

There was a knock at the door just then. Holly raised her head to see Carly peeking through the window, waving at her with a smile. Then she held up her hands to reveal a takeout bag of Chinese food.

Carly wore gray sweats and a rhinestone fanny pack. "You already know who sent me, but what you don't know is I wanted to come. I need this as much as you do. I don't want to be alone," she said as Holly opened the door to let her in.

Holly instantly felt guilty of her own dark mood. "I'm poor company tonight, I'm afraid."

Carly put down the food and turned to Holly with her hand on her hip. "Well, it probably helps that I don't know any different of you! Don't worry. I won't make you entertain me or spill your guts. Let's just eat crappy Chinese food, gossip, and go to bed."

Two hours later, both women were full and feeling a little better. They both stared into the hearth, each lounging on their own sofa, and kept their conversation to celebrity breakups. Holly was relieved to not be alone tonight, even if this was all manufactured by Max.

"I wish you could have known me before this whole mess," she said unsteadily. "I-I'm normally stronger and much funnier."

Carly sighed. "Yeah, grief, a divorce, and a missing brother can really do a number on your comedy routine."

Holly threw a cushion at her. "I'm serious. You seem so cool. I want to be friends."

"We are friends," Carly said, smiling.

Holly shook her head. "No, you're my babysitter."

"Oh, stop! I told you I wanted to be here. Anyway, Max has told me a lot about you, so I already liked you."

"I'm really pissed at him, you know," she ventured, unsure if Carly knew anything of her most recent discussion with Max.

Carly nodded but didn't move her gaze from the fire. "You're allowed to feel how you feel," she said finally.

"Do you know he actually defended Zena even in spite of what we're learning about the Sweetwood family?" Holly's cheeks were flushed both from the heat and her own feelings of frustration.

"I did not know that. But I'm not super surprised. Max is a defender-of-the-innocent-until-proven-guilty kind of guy. It's part of what makes him such a good sheriff."

Holly sat up, intrigued. "You think he's a good sheriff?"

Carly kept her eyes fixed on the fire. "Yes, I do. You don't?"

Holly let out a sigh. "I'm not sure. I just... I expected more by now. It seems like he's not doing enough, like he's too soft or something."

Carly sat back and, looking at Holly now, curved her legs beneath her. "The waiting is awful. I know. My cousin went missing a few years back."

"Really? Oh Carly, I had no idea. I'm so sorry," said Holly.

"Thanks, yeah, it was incredibly difficult. He'd been hiking with some friends and went off on his own. He told them he had to follow a certain kind of bird—a cerulean warbler, whatever the hell that is—but he never came back. It took nearly two weeks to find his body. Max was the one who found him."

Holly gasped. "Oh no..."

Carly cleared her throat and wiped her eyes. "It took two weeks—and that's with knowing where he'd been lost, with witnesses who were helpful and forthcoming. Now, I am not saying that Lucas has succumbed to a similar fate. I actually have a strong feeling he's alive. But I am saying that while it seems like it's taken forever, I want you to know that Max is doing everything he can, following every protocol—all while being worried sick about you and your well-being, not to mention trying desperately to hide his being head over heels-in-love with you still."

That did Holly in. She fell sideways and buried her face in the faux fur blanket, crying the ugly cries. "Carly, I can't," she wailed. "I'm too... it's just...I'm so concerned about Lucas. I'm not thinking straight about anything."

Carly got up and sat beside Holly, rubbing her back. "I know. But just so you're aware, Zena and Max were never really a thing. Both of them were only trying to get over their exes. It was never going to go anywhere."

Just then, Carly's phone went off. She answered it. After five minutes of nodding her head and saying "okay" over and over, she hung up. "That was Max," she said gently. "He found Lucas's car out on Rockridge Road, and he's had it towed to be examined. So far, there is no evidence of foul play."

Holly let out a sigh of relief. "Thank God. Anything else?"

"He found out that Patricia caught a flight to New Zealand a few hours ago. Keith is also nowhere to be found, but Max thinks he's got a lead on his whereabouts. Apparently, Zena told him to check the family houseboat on Lake Blue Ridge, and he's asked the local police to knock on the door. He's interviewing the old Sheriff, Jim Brown, in the morning. Oh, and he told me to tell you he'll be sleeping in his truck across the road tonight as per your wishes."

For what seemed like the millionth time in the last few days, Holly attempted to process the massive amount of information she had just been handed. Things were happening. Lucas's car had been found not too far away. Max was handling things like he always said he would and maybe like he'd been doing all along.

She realized she had become accustomed to the way her ex-husband handled things. Daniel was often a bully when it came to making things happen. He was entitled and rich and thought mostly of himself and his immediate circle—all was well as long as you fell within the circumference. Max's approach was different. She was wrong to assume it was less effective.

Thankfully, Carly's tone was confident and reassuring—that helped more than Holly could say. She reached out and squeezed her new friend's hand. "I cannot thank you enough," she said.

Carly winked at her and gestured to Holly's phone. "It would mean a lot to him," she said.

Holly picked up her cell and sent him a text: I'm so glad it was you.

Back in her bedroom, finally having brought herself to open it, Holly stared at the contents of the folder, her mouth agape. Lucas had collected all of the newspaper clippings and the accident report from their parents' boating incident.

Why was he looking at this? It had been over a year. What could he possibly hope to glean from it at this point? Holly gathered all the papers into one pile and put them inside the manila folder of the accident report. Maybe Max would have a better idea what this was about. But something tugged at Holly: If Lucas had been obsessing about the details of their parents' deaths recently, why on earth had he not shared it with her?

Why was Lucas revisiting their parents' accident? Did this have something to do with his disappearance? It didn't make any sense though. The report had been clear, and Sheriff Jim Brown himself had told them what had happened. No, if anything, Lucas was more than likely reminiscing, maybe even questioning why this had all occurred at all. Lord knows, Holly had similar thoughts. Her parents were such good, kind people. Why them? An accident was random by nature and, in some ways, more difficult to accept.

Chapter 11

*L*ucas woke up to his captor, Todd, speaking on his cell phone in a hushed tone. It appeared that he was receiving instructions as he kept saying "Mm hm." Lucas's brain was, again, a fog but he did have some clarity. There was an empty soda can to his right that he could reach with his mouth and, with some careful determination, use to cut the rope that currently bound his wrists. Todd had only let him read the Bible that one time.

In order for this plan to work, he would have to pretend he was still out cold until Captor Todd went to sleep. For some unknown reason, Todd spent most of his time in the bathroom and appeared to sleep in there, too. The curtains were closed in the motel room, but Lucas could discern enough to know that the sun had gone down. It shouldn't be too long before Todd did, too.

In the meantime, Lucas closed his eyes and tried to recall the last night he had spent with Patricia. That woman had been nothing but a distraction and really, nothing but trouble. Their time together had been fun; she was hot and always up for some chaos. But she was also worldly, adventurous, intelligent, and so damn rich. Did it bother Lucas that she was married? Yes. It bothered him a lot, in fact. Every time he saw her, he swore to himself it would be the last. But he had been so incredibly lonely these past few months. The loss of his parents had been immense and left a void that he could not fill, no matter how hard he tried.

His parents...

The last time he and Patricia hooked up, he brought up his parents. It was the first time he mentioned them to her, and he realized it was the first time he'd talked about them out loud to anyone other than Holly since the funeral. He remembered thinking how that probably wasn't healthy. Their names felt heavy in his throat. He barely got through the first sentence without crying. And the effect it had on Patricia was strange.

They had been drinking. It occurred to Lucas now that this was most likely the reason he felt safe talking about his parents because Patricia was not exactly the kind of woman you confided in. For all her worldliness, she was actually quite shallow and very uncomfortable with any sort of vulnerability.

Lucas breathed deep, clearing the cobwebs. He recalled Patricia stood up clumsily from the bed they'd been sharing. She walked over to the mini bar and grabbed herself a tiny bottle of gin. She chugged the entire thing in one swig, and that's when Lucas noticed she had tears in her eyes. He asked her what was wrong.

Patricia stood there, swaying a bit and sniffing. "I want you to know I am truly sorry," she said finally.

Lucas remembered feeling confused. "What? Why?" he asked her. "Patricia, what do you mean?"

She sat down on the edge of the bed, but could not bring herself to look at him. "Keith knows what happened. And I'm...just...I'm so sorry..."

The words floated around the edges of his mind. *Keith knows what happened.* And then it clicked. She was trying to tell him about his parents' accident.

Though he couldn't recall exactly what he said, Lucas remembered yelling at Patricia with everything in him. It was a primal scream of pain and confusion. Her face went ashen, and she seemed to sober up almost instantly. She ran from the room without even grabbing her shoes. That was the last time he saw her. But whomever she had confided in after that had clearly been involved in kidnapping him. Of course, it could have been Patricia herself, but he didn't believe she had it in her. She was too frail, too superficial. No, this had the imprint of Bill Sweetwood all over it.

Max had been caught in a loop of thought ever since Holly had asked him to leave. It was more like a memory loop, and he could only shake it by taking action to help find Lucas. The memory was a dark one, something he had tried to push down and forget about for nearly a decade: the day Holly broke their engagement.

When Max let himself see the past clearly, he could recall some signs that she was unhappy, signs which he had brushed off as wedding jitters. She changed the venue three times, going from an outdoor wedding in June, to a holiday celebration in December, then to a spring shindig in early April. And then there was the fact that Holly could not find a dress she liked or how she wanted a new engagement ring because rose gold clashed with all her silver jewelry.

It seemed impossible to get her to focus on their actual marriage and their future together. She spent every waking moment obsessing about the wedding. Nancy told him at the time that this is what women did, and he so wanted to believe it.

When Holly would spin out in high wedding anxiety, Max would grab her and hold her close, whispering in her ear: "Let's go to Vegas, Bo-Bolly. Just you and me. Let's just do you and me." Sometimes she'd melt into his arms and thank him, others she'd push back and tell him he was a distraction. This confused Max to no end. The whole point was supposed to be spending their life together, wasn't it?

The turning point was when he surprised her for a lunch date. She had been working for the local paper and was often the only one in the office. That day, however, they had an editorial meeting. Max walked in with a paper bag of burgers and fries and a rose between his teeth. Holly's co-workers smiled and clapped. But Holly was mortified. Max apologized over and over until finally, he seemed to win her over.

What he did next, though, is something that he regretted every day since. In an effort to get her to focus on something positive, he sat her down and showed her a website where you could upload a picture of yourself and your partner and receive back an image of what your future child would look like. Max always wanted a big family. Holly did too, before they were engaged. But in that moment, looking at a picture of their potential future child, she broke down completely in what he could only describe as emotional pain and exhaustion. She heaved and cried out. Max reached for her, attempting to comfort her, but to no avail. Holly shook him off and bolted from the building.

By the time he caught up with her, she was in front of the courthouse completely out of breath.

"Hey, hey," he said, approaching her with caution and speaking gently. "I didn't mean to freak you out. I'm sorry. You okay?"

Holly bent over, clutching her stomach. "It's just a cramp," she said.

"Okay," he replied, taking a step closer to her.

"Max, I know you didn't mean to freak out," she said slowly, trying to catch her breath. "I know... I know that everything you do is with the best of intentions. That's never the problem."

That made him feel good for a second. She saw him, saw the good in what he did. But then he thought about what she wasn't saying. "Okay, so what's wrong then?"

Holly walked over to the closest park bench and asked him to sit down next to her. Her breathing was slowly returning to normal. "That picture should not have freaked me out. It should have made me laugh or smile or tackle you to the ground right then and there to make that baby. Instead, I felt absolute terror."

Max felt like he'd been punched in the stomach. Terror? What could she mean by that? How could the idea of their baby make her feel something so awful? "I-I don't understand."

She ran her fingers through her hair and shook her head. "I know. I know I'm not making any sense. This... it's all been coming on so gradually. But lately, I have...I just..." Holly paused, looking skyward for the words. "Max, I'm sorry. I am just so unhappy."

He reached for her wrists, held them tight. "Why? What am I doing wrong? What can I do differently?"

Holly seemed to instantly calm at his words. "Nothing, Max. I mean, we've talked lately about you smothering me or not honoring my boundaries. But I'm seeing now that even if you changed those things, it wouldn't help. I-I don't want this. I don't want to get married and have kids right now. I don't want to live here in Blairsville. I need more."

"I'll go with you!" he protested. "We don't have to break up. I can just go where you go, and we can build a life wherever that is."

She took a deep breath, took his face in her hands. "You have wanted to be the sheriff of this town since you were three feet tall. No. Your life is here."

Max's throat closed up; tears threatened to sting his eyes. "My life is you," he said.

Holly hugged him so tight at that. "I know. And my life has been you, too. It's just, I need more right now. And what I need to do means we can't be together. I'm so sorry."

Max withdrew from her then and wiped his eyes. He looked at her, knowing she meant every word. There was no convincing, no negotiating. This thing they called love was done. All the hopes and dreams he'd held so close were now going up in smoke. It was too much to think about. He couldn't handle what it all meant.

"I have to go," he said finally, standing and turning to leave. But then he stopped for a moment. "You know," he began. "I normally have an instinct on things, but I missed this. I missed it completely."

Holly smiled, wiping away tears. "It's amazing what we can miss when we don't want to be hurt. And I'm sorry I hurt you."

He nodded. "Yeah," he said and walked away from her.

Holly stood. "Wait!" she called. And his heart hoped for just one moment she had changed her mind. "Here," she said, removing the ring he'd given her, placing it in his hands and curling his fingers over it to hold it safe. "My first love... I'm so glad it was you."

Chapter 12

*L*ucas heard Todd's snoring from the bathroom and knew the man was finally asleep. Now was the time. Carefully, he leaned over and grasped the can's pull-tab with his teeth. Then, using his chin and neck, he crushed the can to push the opening up. Now the sharp edge was more accessible. Raising his hands to meet the edge, he slowly cut through the rope that bound his wrists. If Lucas had to guess, it took about twenty minutes and ten, tiny cuts to his wrists to make any progress. Finally, he made it through and his hands were freed.

It took everything in him not to shout out loud. He was going to get out of here! Bending forward, he untied the ropes that bound his legs. The bed was creaky and made a noise every time he shifted his weight. He would have to keep his movements small. Slowly shuffling to the side of the bed, he made it to the edge and put his feet on the floor. Now, all he had to do was stand. Lucas heard Todd suddenly stop snoring, and his heart skipped a beat. He was so close! Five seconds later, the muffled breathing resumed, and Lucas carefully rose to standing.

His legs were stiff and unreliable at first. He took a moment to shake them out quietly. After a minute, he made his way to the door, slowly unbolted all the locks, and removed the chain. Opening the door slowly, wary of any creaks, he slid his way through the narrow opening, closed the door behind him, and bolted into the midnight darkness.

The next morning, Max woke up in his truck with a start. It was Holly, knocking on the window with a cup of coffee in hand.

71

"Oh my gosh," he exclaimed as he rolled down the window. "Thank you. I overslept."

She smiled, and her voice was soft when she said, "I know."

Max accepted the mug and took a grateful sip. "I'll be out of your hair in a minute," he said. "I'm heading over to see Jim Brown."

"Oh, okay," replied Holly. "I just wanted to show you something." That's when he realized she had been holding a file folder in her other hand. "I found these in the old shed. You remember?"

Max nodded, not looking up at her, just staring at the folder.

"Well, I guess Lucas still uses it. The shed itself and everything around it had been cleaned up and is taken care of. Anyway, these papers were inside. I was so upset yesterday that I forgot to give this to you. But I opened it last night. Lucas had been looking into my parents' accident and knew Keith was involved somehow."

"Can you leave this with me for now?" he said more curtly than he intended. She looked taken aback but said nothing, only smiled and thanked him again. He realized in that moment that he had not responded to her text. It wasn't that he held anything against Holly. It was simply that he didn't have much to say until he could finally bring her brother home. That was his goal, and he had to keep focused on it.

Twenty minutes later, he was pulling into the driveway of his old mentor, Sheriff Jim Brown. Max had been to the house many times at the behest of Jim's wife, Janet, who had always seen fit to endear herself and her cooking to her husband's co-workers. This time, of course, Max was approaching their home with a heavy heart.

The rumor that Jim had an affair with Anita Bayu was troubling to say the least. Jim had always been a gentleman from what Max had observed, but who knew what went on in the hearts of men and women anyway? Carly's revelations about Jim's character had been shocking. She basically painted the picture of a chauvinist. And while this may have fit with a man of his generation, Max wondered at his own inability to see Sheriff Brown clearly. Had he just seen what he wanted to see all this time?

Max knocked on the front door, and the man himself opened it with a welcoming smile.

"Max, my boy! It's great to see you, son," he said, pulling the younger man in with a hug. "You look good—healthy and strong. How the heck are ya?"

It was always strange for Max to see Jim in regular clothes instead of his uniform. The former Sheriff had worn it like a second skin, it suited him so well. Six-foot-four with a barrel chest and legs like tree trunks, Jim Brown was an intimidating presence. "I'm good, Jim," he replied. "Thanks for agreeing to see me."

Jim slapped Max on the back with a generous: "Of course!" and led him to the backyard where he had a couple Adirondack chairs set up in front a good-sized fire pit that was pleasantly ablaze. "Janet's gone to town for groceries, so we can talk, just us guys," he said. "What's up? How can I help you?"

Max updated his mentor on the situation with Lucas's disappearance as best he could, leaving out the information given to him by Thomas and Carly for now. He watched Jim carefully as he spoke, but was not entirely sure what he was looking for. The connection with Anita could be nothing at all as far as this case went. There were a lot of dots, but not many of them connected yet.

Jim cleared his throat when Max finished. "Son, I'm just gonna go ahead and say the obvious thing here, if you don't mind?"

"Of course."

"Isn't it possible that Lucas has just left? Heck, maybe the boy took off with a woman closer to his own age. Or maybe he had been running with the wrong crowd."

Max narrowed his eyes in confusion. "Sir, I looked into that last possibility. Like I said, the shadiest character I could find in Lucas's recent history is Keith Sweetwood. As for a woman, the only one that's come up is Patricia."

Jim leaned forward and put his hands to the fire, warming them. "But you don't have his phone. There is so much potential information that you're missing just with that."

Max paused, observing his old boss closely. His gut was telling him something was not right here. Without thinking, he asked, "Sir, do you know something about Lucas's disappearance?"

The older man appeared taken aback. "I beg your pardon. Just what are you implying, son?"

Max sat back, rubbed his chin, never taking his gaze off of Jim Brown. "Something doesn't feel right is all. Are you protecting someone?" Max surprised even himself at his gumption.

Jim stood up. "Now that is a step too far, Max Cooper. You are at my home. You are my guest. For you to throw out allegations like this is...well, it's ungentlemanly. I'm going to have to ask you to leave."

This was abrupt to say the least. Why was the man so defensive if he was innocent? Call Max rude, sure. But to flat-out ask him to leave? Without hesitation, Max stood and looked Jim in the eye. "I'll go, sir. But first, answer me this: Does this have anything to do with Anita Bayu?"

Jim went white as a sheet. He stuttered but no words came.

"I know about the affair, Jim. Carly told me."

The older man held his jaw tight, nodded briskly. "I wasn't sure who knew," he said after a minute.

"Well, on that, I can't say. Though it doesn't seem to be general knowledge...yet."

Jim sat back down, resigned. "I loved her, you know. Still do. Just want to say that. It's important to me you know that."

Max also took a seat. "Okay," he said gently, hoping to prompt him to share more.

"And it's nothing against my dear Janet. My love for my wife has nothing to do with this. I can't explain that part; I just know it's true."

Max steepled his hands, kept his tone even. "I won't pretend to know what that was like for you."

Jim leaned forward, resting his head in his hands. "But Janet found out. She was devastated—threatened to leave me. And then I had that damn heart thing..." he trailed off.

"Right," said Max. "That must have been hard."

"Son, it was the worst time of my life. I lost one of the women I loved and the only work I've ever known in a single night. I couldn't leave Janet—Anita knew that. She didn't beg me to stay. She's a helluva woman. That damn Sweetwood bastard wouldn't be where he is today without her."

"So I've heard," offered Max.

"I suppose you've heard something to the effect of Anita being Bill's right hand?"

Max nodded. "Yeah, that's pretty much what Zena said. I think she called her the family's 'everything-manager.'"

"You can say that again," said Jim with an appreciative laugh, then took a deep breath. "I've said enough. I'm going to have to ask you to leave for real now, son. Janet will be home soon, and I don't want her to have to relive any part of this whole business. She's been through enough."

Max walked out to his truck with a new outlook on Sheriff Jim Brown. What was that saying again? Never meet your heroes? Max decided it should be changed: know your heroes are only human, too.

Chapter 13

$\mathcal{H}$olly decided to give Carly a visit at the station. She could not face another day at the hunting cabin with no word from Lucas; it was frustrating and sad. At least with Carly, she could feel like she was closer to the solution instead of drowning in the sea of the problem.

She parked her rental car in a lot off the town square and walked the two blocks to the station. Walking in the door, it hit her. This was Max's domain. He was the boss here, the one responsible for the safety of the citizens of Blairsville. Holly could see what he'd been doing all these years and even lately. Max was hers—in her mind, at least. Even if she didn't consciously think that way, that was how she acted. If she needed help, he would come. If she needed an ear, he would listen.

What she didn't like admitting was that she believed this was special and specific to her. And while, yes, he probably was still in love with her, the truth was this was Max. He was someone who helped, who showed up when things got real, who made sure that everyone was safe and sound. Of course, he would end up protecting and serving the whole damn town. She was lucky to know him.

Carly perked up at her desk as soon as she saw Holly. "I was going to text you!" she said. "Max just called and told me he would be bringing in Anita Bayu for questioning. Oh, and Keith is being brought here, too. We're gonna have the two of them in separate rooms, just like they do on TV!"

Holly was confused. "Anita? What about Bill or Patricia?"

Carly shrugged. "I don't know the whole scoop yet. Max is going to take the lead, and I'm going to watch. Oh, and pray they don't ask for their lawyers."

Holly felt a rush of anxiety. "I need to get some air," she told Carly, and bolted from the building. Things were happening. They were getting closer to some kind of answer. Leaning against the brick façade, she forced herself to take deep breaths. Lucas was out there. Holly knew it. He had to be.

Just then, her cell phone rang. It was Max. She answered it straight away.

"Holly, where are you right now?" he asked calmly.

"At the station with Carly, why?"

"Good," he replied. "I need you to do me a favor and sit in the waiting room—right in the middle so that you can be seen from all angles of the station. And I want you to look calm. Can you do that for me?"

Holly stammered, unsure of what was going on and unused to this level of confidence in Max. "Y-yes, of c-course."

"Thank you, Holly. I know this has been hell for you. Just try to trust me, okay?"

Holly did trust him, and she wanted desperately to tell him so. But the words wouldn't come. There was too much going on. "Okay," she replied instead. Max was in charge. He'd given her a task. All she had to do was follow his lead.

Anita Bayu sat quiet and confident in Interview Room #1 wearing a white business suit, hands folded neatly on the desk. Max was running on instinct, taking a risk. He did not know if it would play out as he hoped, but he would have to try. If his gut was right, Anita was the key to unlocking this entire thing. She had not flinched upon seeing Holly in the waiting room as Max hoped, but she had definitely seen her. Now, he left her waiting while he questioned Keith.

Keith, on the other hand, went white as a ghost upon seeing Holly in the waiting room. In fact, he looked downright afraid. As soon as he took his seat in Interview Room #2, he asked for a diet cola and an energy bar.

"Rough night?" asked Max, sitting down across from him.

Keith was jittery and could not seem to maintain focus. "It wasn't the greatest," he said with a shrug.

Max took out his phone, hit record, and leaned in. "The cops out there tell me you had someone staying with you at the boathouse."

"Yeah," replied Keith. "I don't like to be alone."

"They said it was paid company."

Keith shrugged again, sniffed, and took a long sip of his soda. "Like I said, I don't like to be alone."

Max nodded in understanding. "They also mentioned the neighbors have complained many times about the noise coming from your family's boathouse when you're there with your...company."

"Her name is Delilah," said Keith with sudden firmness. "We like to party sometimes, yeah. No harm in it—most of the time," he said nervously making an attempt to lighten the mood.

"Yeah, these cops had a lot to say," said Max, his tone even. "Because they also mentioned you let Delilah drive your family's boat."

Keith blinked hard, clenched his fists tight. "Sometimes."

"They said Delilah does not have a boating license, that she has been caught twice at the helm and both times she was severely intoxicated."

Keith shifted in his seat and gave an anxious laugh. "You sure know a lot, Max. Anyway, she paid those fines."

Max took a pen from his shirt pocket and tapped it against his chin. "It got me thinking, Keith. Has Delilah ever visited the pool house at your family's home? And, if so, has she also been out on the water in these parts?"

"No," he replied quickly—too quickly.

"Is that so?" asked Max dubiously. "So, if I took Delilah's photo down to the marina, no one would recognize her?"

"Wait," said Keith, finally taking a deeper interest in the whole reason he was here. "What does this have to do with Lucas? I thought you wanted to talk about Lucas."

Max waved his hand dismissively. "We will get there. But I'd like you to answer the question first. Would anyone down at the marina recognize Delilah."

Keith appeared to think about how to answer for many seconds until Max could almost see the light go on in his brain. "Well, she's a lady of the night. Who knows how many boats she's been on?" He leaned back in his chair, very satisfied with his own version of quick thinking.

"That's a great point, Keith. Thank you. So, if I bring a photo of Delilah and a photo of you and ask if anyone has seen the two of you together down at the marina, how do you think that will play out?"

The smile on Keith's face disappeared. "I don't like this. I want to go. You can't keep me here."

Max took a deep breath and locked eyes with Keith. "Well, no, I can't. But before you rush outta here, I thought I should let you know that one of my officers already went down to the marina with a picture of you and a picture of Delilah. So far, we have two witnesses confirming you have both been there together. And you know what, Keith? They even remembered which day you had been there. Isn't that amazing? Any idea why they would remember the date?"

Keith was now fully agitated, squirming in his seat. "I want out of here!" he shouted.

"Now, there's no call for yelling, Keith," said Max calmly. "You haven't even been arrested. You can leave whenever you like." He watched the youngest Sweetwood carefully, gauging what to say next, planning his approach. "But see, I think you're ready to talk. I think the past year has been hard for you. You've always been a partier, Keith. But the last little while has been next level, hasn't it?"

"I-I don't know," he stammered.

Max continued. "It has, Keith. It really has been tough on you. I can see it on your face. It's aged you some. Anyone can see it." He took a pregnant pause, never taking his gaze from Keith's. "Maybe it's time to unburden yourself—get it off your chest."

Keith's breathing was rapid. "I-I didn't do anything wrong," he said.

"Okay," replied Max. "Why don't you just tell me what happened?"

What followed was a full confession. Max's instinct had been right. As soon as he had heard about Delilah and her penchant for boating while intoxicated, he got this nagging feeling to go deeper. What if Keith had been seeing the girl for a while? And what if this pattern went back for at least a year? The witnesses at the marina had been a bluff, but he was certain he could get those after the fact.

Keith confessed that on the evening the Blakes had died, he had let Delilah take the wheel. She sped up and was going much too fast, neither of them even saw the Blakes' boat. At the last minute, Mr. Blake was able to swerve to avoid them but they ended up hitting a tree.

"I wanted to just tell you guys. I swear it," said Keith emphatically, near tears now. "But Anita said not to. She said my dad would lose his mind over that kind of scandal, and it would really hurt the business."

Max perked up at the mention of Anita's name. So, he truly was on the right track. "Anita said this?" he asked. "It was Anita who told you to keep quiet?"

Keith nodded. "Well, yeah. She's done a lot of that kind of thing over the years. But I guess this was the first time people died—at least, I think so. And anyway, she had the in with the old sheriff so, a cover-up was going to be much easier to do."

Even though he had felt this was the case, the words still hit him hard. Max did his damnedest to hide his disappointment. "Sheriff Jim Brown helped you cover up what happened?"

"That's right," said Keith. "I don't really know what was involved. All Anita said was to keep quiet. And Delilah had been so wasted, she didn't even recall the accident at all."

Max pressed stop on his voice note recorder and put his phone back in his pocket. He looked at Keith. It never ceased to amaze him how confession, an unburdening of the soul, changed a person almost instantly. Keith's shoulders were more relaxed, his breathing normal, his pallor less red. *The soul craves the truth*, he thought. *It needs it like the body needs air.*

"Carly's gonna finish up with you, okay? I appreciate what you've done here today, Keith."

"My dad is going to kill me," said Keith, his tone eerily matter-of-fact. "But it was bound to happen sooner or later."

Chapter 14

Holly saw Max emerge from the interview room and give Carly a pat on the back before she headed in, seemingly to replace him. Holly guessed she was going to take over with Keith instead of tagging along with Anita. He looked pleased, confident even. It took every ounce of will Holly had not to jump out of her skin and shout out to him. What was happening? What did he know? Max appeared to read her thoughts. He blew her a sympathetic kiss, mouthed the words "trust me," and slipped into the other interview room.

It was a simple enough request, but the waiting was awful. The energy it took to keep her thoughts from coming up with worst-case scenarios was immense. Sometimes she could swear she heard Lucas calling for her. This was a feeling that had been building up over the last few days. It was hard for Holly to tell whether it was true intuition or her own wishful thinking. She wanted to trust in it. In her mind, she would answer him. She would say that everything was okay, that she would find him and bring him home.

But oh, the helplessness...

Holly took out her phone and attempted to distract herself by looking at social media. Of course, the first picture to pop up was that of Daniel and Mitzi. And they were, of course, engaged. Daniel looked happy. His eyes were lit up in a way she had to admit she'd never seen before. Holly's heart clenched a little, and she smiled. There was no jealousy, no FOMO.

Sure, she could tell some big story about how Daniel was kidding himself, how the two of them were living in a fantasy world—maybe they were. But it was no longer her business. They didn't have children together; all their ties had been cut. So, she clicked the like button and continued to scroll in an attempt to keep her mind off the bigger things going on around her.

Just then, Holly's phone rang. The screen said "Unknown Number." She assumed it was Gabe since he was always blocking his number for professional reasons.

"Hey, you," she said.

"Holly?" came a familiar voice.

Holly froze, her eyes went wide. And then coming to her senses, she squeaked out, "Lucas?"

"Oh my God, Holly! Thank God!"

Her mind was racing. It was Lucas! She had to get him. Now. Get him. Wherever he was. Right now. "Where are you? I'm coming!"

"I'm in Lula. At the pharmacy. A lady here let me use her phone," he replied. He sounded so tired, so weak.

Holly threw her purse over her shoulder and ran out the door to her rental car. "Got it. I'll be there in an hour. Hold tight. Don't move from there."

Lucas was crying. "I won't. Oh God, Holly. Thank you."

Max entered the interview room and sat across from his second witness of the day. He kept the look on his face expressionless.

"Could I have some water?" asked Anita.

"Of course," he replied, bending down to fetch a bottle of water from the small bar fridge behind him.

Anita thanked him and took a swig. "That's better."

Max sat down across from her and put his phone out on the table. "Keith is here," he said simply. Anita's face registered just the slightest hint of surprise, and then it was gone. "He had a lot to say."

Anita's mouth was tight. "Oh?"

He nodded. "Yeah, but I don't want to talk about that right now. I want to talk about Bill Sweetwood and what on earth he has on you."

Anita's entire demeanor shifted. She went from prim and polite to affected and annoyed. "I beg your pardon?" she said.

Max leaned forward. "You see, it's been bugging me. I keep hearing about you being Bill's right hand, or his fixer, or his everything-manager—what I want to know is, why?"

Anita shrugged, said nothing.

"Because I have also heard about how intelligent you are, how educated. It just doesn't add up. You don't need Bill Sweetwood. You certainly don't need him as much as he needs you. So, why? Why clean up his messes, his family's messes? Love?" he asked watching her expression for any changes. "No. We all know Bill is pretty much a robot. The kids? I mean—maybe? But they're all pretty spoiled, not especially thoughtful. So, I'm left with my original question to you: What on earth does Bill Sweetwood have on Anita Bayu?"

She took a deep breath and leaned forward, steepling her hands on the table in front of her. "Young man, this tack you are on is reckless. Do not pretend to know me nor my motivations for anything. I will not play your games. If you have an honest, serious question to ask me, then do it. Otherwise, I am gone. I am here out of courtesy. Plain and simple."

Max couldn't help it; he smirked. "You're here out of curiosity," he said. "You wanted to see what I know."

Anita sighed. "Max, there is nothing to know. As I said, I am here as a courtesy. Now, do you have a real question for me?"

"I do, yes," he replied. "Where is Lucas Blake?"

Anita rolled her eyes. "This is a waste of my time. I'm—"

"I know it was you, Anita," interrupted Max. "I know that Keith's paid companion caused the Blakes to crash their boat, killing them. I know you and Sheriff Brown covered it up. I know that Patricia Sweetwood nearly let some of this slip to Lucas one careless night, and I know that Lucas confronted Keith about it. I know that you were afraid of this getting out so, you had Lucas kidnapped—presumably because you wanted time to calm him down and bribe him into keeping quiet."

Anita's face was unreadable. She appeared to be making calculations, deciding what to reveal, if anything. "You think you know a lot."

"Well?" said Max. "Where is he?"

"You didn't let me finish, young man," she said sharply. "You think you know a lot, but I have yet to see or hear of any proof."

"I have Keith's confession, and as for the rest, I'm confident I can get it." Max's voice didn't waver. "But the thing with Lucas is timely. He needs to come home. His sister is worried sick. This is not a game, Anita."

There was a knock at the door.

"Yes," called Max. "What is it?"

Carly popped her head in. "Boss, I just got a text from Holly. She probably texted you, too. Lucas called her. He's in Lula. She's on her way to get him now."

Max immediately turned to Anita, whose mouth was wide open in shock. She checked herself within a second, but it was too late.

Chapter 15

The drive to Union General Hospital was short and did not lend near enough time for Max to clear his head. Unable to get a confession out of Anita, he felt dejected. She had demanded a lawyer and that was that—for now, at least. Of course, he was relieved and happy for Holly to have Lucas home, but he would be lying if he'd said he wasn't just the teeniest bit disappointed that he didn't get to play the hero. He chided himself for these thoughts. This wasn't about him. This was about Lucas. Max's only job now was to make sure Anita—and anyone else involved in the kidnapping—was brought to justice.

Holly was standing in the hall outside Lucas's room when Max arrived. She ran to him and jumped into his arms. He held her tight, waiting for her to loosen her grip, but she didn't let go. She kept pulling him closer and closer. And then he heard her crying, felt the rise and fall of her chest.

"Shhhh," he soothed. "No, no, no. No tears."

Holly pressed her forehead into his chest. She still could not bring herself to speak.

"I will make this right, Holly. I promise you," he told her. "I'm so sorry that I haven't done it yet, but I will. I will make sure your family gets justice."

She pulled back slightly and looked up at him with alarm. "How can you apologize to me? What are you even talking about?" she said, tears still streaming from her eyes. "My baby brother is home. He's safe. Keith and that Delilah woman are in custody for what they did to my poor parents."

Max interrupted. "I know but—"

"But what?" she said. "You did that. You figured out what Keith was hiding, and you knew that Anita was the one behind the cover-up. The rest will fall into place. I trust you, Max. And I'm not worried anymore."

He tried to process her words. There was still so much to do. How could she have all this faith in him? He hadn't even been the one to find Lucas. "I don't know that I deserve—"

Holly kissed him then, hard at first and then soft. She loosened her grip around his chest and looped her arms about his neck, gently guiding him closer. His hands instinctively went to her hips, and he let himself succumb to her. His mind blocked everything else out until there was only Holly's mouth, the curve of her back, and the lock of hair that brushed his chin.

She moaned and then pulled away. "Oh my goodness!" she exclaimed with a giggle. "Did I just do that out loud?"

Max threw his head back and laughed. "Yes, you did. Can I make you do it again?" he said, nibbling on her ear.

Holly sucked in a breath, coming to her senses. "We're in public!"

"You started it!" he replied, not ready to let her go. "I'm just... it's so good to have you in my arms again. I wasn't sure I ever would."

She dipped her head. "I know. I've been really awful and ungrateful to you. And I also just don't know what this is with us..."

Max kissed her forehead. "You have been through so much. I don't want anything from you, Holly. I'm just happy to be the man who gets to hold you right now."

He meant it. The past week, working this case, being reunited with Holly—he realized now it had taught him to enjoy the moment, to take nothing for granted. He didn't need any promises from her. He didn't need a label. All he needed was to know she was safe. The words were on the tip of his tongue: I love you, Holly. But he couldn't say them. It wouldn't be fair to her. She'd feel pressure to say them back. So instead, he just held her tighter.

"Oh!" Holly exclaimed. "I just remembered. He's asleep now, but before he was out, Lucas told me to tell you he got a first name for the guy who was holding him. It's Todd."

"Okay, great. That's a really good start. I'm so glad he's remembering things. That's going to help us a lot," said Max. "How is he?"

Holly sighed. "He's okay, considering. He needs rest and a few good meals. They drugged him, you know. I guess that was the point—to keep him out cold until after the festival, so he didn't ruin it with the truth." She said those last few words with bitter resentment.

Max shook his head. "It's so extreme... putting money before people like that."

She shuddered. "It's downright evil."

What Anita and the Sweetwoods had done was unimaginable and yet, Max saw versions of it all the time. This is what greed and desperation could look like. Where did Anita land in all of this? And did it really matter? Whatever her reasons, she was going to jail for a very long time.

Holly woke the next morning having had one of the best sleeps of her life. She didn't dream; she didn't toss and turn—she had simply rested deeply for eight straight hours. Her world was beginning to come back into balance. Lucas was coming home to the cabin today. Max was... Max. And she'd been offered a feature article in the *Times* writing about Lucas's experience. News traveled so fast. But then she knew it was probably Gabe pulling strings with the important people he hobnobbed with to help get her back in the game.

Daniel had called the previous night expressing his happiness at Lucas's return. She in turn had congratulated him on his engagement. When they hung up, she realized that could very well have been the last conversation they'd ever have. She sat with the sadness of that for a few moments and then let it go. Better things were coming. She would be okay.

She had already decided to stay with Lucas until after Christmas. Gabe would be able to find someone to sublet her tiny Brooklyn apartment in a heartbeat. There wasn't even a question. Holly belonged with Lucas right now. They had a lot of lost time to make up for. And these latest revelations about the circumstances around their parents' deaths were going to be difficult to process, much less so if they were able to do it together. The relief of Lucas's return had overshadowed the darker stuff. But Holly knew that would not last.

Max still didn't know she had decided to stay, and she was surprised that he hadn't asked her yet. Things between them were good, but far from settled. The more she thought about that, the more she liked it. Holly wanted to enjoy Max, wanted to be entirely present with him. That's how it had been when they first fell in love, before adult life came calling with its expectations and responsibilities. But how amazing would it be to just be together? To go for hikes by the lake, make love at the cabin, cozy up together at The Fox and Fig?

And then the doubt crept in. Would that be enough for him? Max was a family man. He had always been clear about that: marriage and babies were all a part of his life plan. Was it fair to ask him to settle? To wait? *Ugh*, she thought. Now she was right back to where she'd been when she broke off their engagement. It was different, but the same.

Holly walked into the kitchen and made a pot of coffee. She refused to start off this day with doubt. All she could do was be honest with Max. And the truth had been slowly rising to the surface. She still loved him, had fallen back in with all her heart, and she wanted to see him as much as possible for the next few months. If that was okay with him, then great. If not...well, she would deal with those feelings of disappointment later.

Just then, her phone buzzed. It was a text from Max: Is there enough in that pot for me?

What a freaking stalker! she thought to herself with amusement.

She poured him a cup and made the short walk across the road to deliver it personally.

"Why didn't you just stay in the cabin?" Holly asked, a gleam in her eye. "I don't bite."

"I was up late doing paperwork, so I just decided to take my usual nighttime post instead of risking waking you," he said taking the mug from her hands. He leaned forward, asking for a kiss, and she obliged. "How are you feeling, beautiful?"

Holly let out a breath. "Good, I think. I'll be better once Lucas is home."

"Would you like me to come with you to pick him up?" he asked.

She shook her head. "No, it's okay. Thank you. You have enough to deal with, and he and I have so much to catch up on. I just want to be there for him the way I should have been all this time."

Max nodded. "Okay, well, don't beat yourself up too much about that. You had your own stuff going on." His phone buzzed. "It's Carly," he said. "Just give me one second."

Holly stepped back to give him some privacy. About twenty seconds later, he banged the steering wheel with his free hand and let out a real doozy of a cuss word. "What's the matter?" she asked.

"It's Anita Bayu," he said gravely, not yet able to look her in the eye. "She's dead. And there's a note."

Chapter 16

*M*ax arrived at the Sweetwood mansion shortly after eight in the morning. Fire and ambulance were already there, as was his trusted deputy, Carly Watie.

"Pills," she said simply, knowing he wasn't in the mood for pleasantries or small talk. "The EMTs pronounced her dead on arrival. Coroner is up there now. She did it in her bedroom; Bill found her."

Max rubbed his forehead. "Damn," he said. "I hate this whole damn situation. Is Bill talking?"

"Yeah," replied Carly. "He actually seems pretty shook up—like genuinely."

"Okay, and where's the note?"

"Oh, I just bagged it. One sec, I'll grab it for you." Carly ran to a table of evidence set up in front of the main entrance to the house. She trotted back and handed the bagged letter to Max.

> *To Bill, I have failed you and I'm sorry. I tried to keep you in the dark as much as possible. In so doing, it seems I made everything worse.*
>
> *To Jim, I love you. I have taken my love for you all the way to the other side.*
>
> *To Darnell, you deserved better. I'm glad you got it. Mama loves you always.*

Goodbye,

Anita

Max handed the note back to Carly. "Who's Darnell?" he asked. "Anita had a son? Since when?"

Carly sighed. "Well, that's a long story. Do you want it from me or from Bill Sweetwood?"

"You'll do for now," he replied. "I'll talk to Bill in a minute."

"Yeah, go see him. Who knows? He may remember more by now. He's in his study just off the main entrance. I will say I think the whole thing changed her," said Carly. "From what Bill said, she had deals and contacts for years that he knew nothing about. The shadiness almost became an obsession for Anita. He admits he turned a blind eye. The company did so well, it was easier to stay ignorant."

Max considered this. Anita had clearly been Bill's superior in many ways. It was possible. His thoughts then turned back to the note and the other person mentioned therein. "Does Jim know yet?"

Carly shrugged. "Probably not. The press isn't here yet. But they will be, and soon."

"Okay. Thanks, Carly," he said. "I'll talk to Bill and then head out to Jim's."

———

Bill sat hunched behind a large oak desk, a large glass of milk in his hand. His hair was disheveled. The man looked utterly bewildered.

"May I sit?" asked Max.

Bill shrugged. "Do whatever the hell you want."

So that's where we're at, thought Max. He'd have to be gentle here. "Mr. Sweetwood, you have my condolences. Anita was a rock for this family. I know that. Zena said so many times."

The older man appeared to soften at the mention of Anita's name. "She was incredible. Y—you don't even realize."

Max took a deep breath. "So tell me," he said.

Bill took a sip of milk and sat back in his chair, slouching and keeping his eyes on his lap. "Anita was so smart," he began. "So bright and self-made. But she got pregnant during her first year of law school. She had the baby over her summer break and gave him up for adoption. The couple who took him in as their own lived in Atlanta. He was a city bus driver and she was a bookkeeper."

"This is Darnell?" asked Max.

Bill nodded. "That's right. Anyway, about a year after Anita had started working for us, she received a letter from the adoptive mother. The family had been in a terrible car accident. The father had died instantly, the mother was left paralyzed from the waist down, and little Darnell had suffered severe whiplash and broken limbs that left him in constant pain without proper treatment. The mother heard that Anita had become a lawyer and wondered if she might be able to help out with some of the bills. She enclosed photocopies." He paused as if remembering something. "Anita could not believe the cost. It was astronomical."

"That's awful," said Max.

"Yes. It was. But to Anita, this was her son. And she wanted to do what she could. And all I can think now is that she knew me. She knew how my mind worked, and my drive for more money and success. I think..." He stopped, looking up at Max. "I think she devised a plan. She would do whatever it took—legal or illegal—to get the company ahead."

"Whatever it took?" Max repeated.

Bill hung his head again, nodding. "Yeah," he replied. "In exchange, she would receive a handsome percentage of the profits."

Max sat back, considered what this meant. "This must have gone on for decades."

"It did," Bill confirmed. "Anita had gotten herself in way too deep, lost her good sense and morals. The guilt of giving up her son had morphed into a constant web of lies. Sweetwood Syrups had to maintain its good name or else she risked losing her means of supporting her son and his adoptive mother."

"Jesus," whispered Max.

Mr. Sweetwood rubbed his face that tonight looked ten years beyond his real age. "I never ever thought she'd do something like this. Not once. We are so screwed."

There it is, thought Max. *The real Bill Sweetwood.* And with that, Max stood. Tipping his hat to the older man he said, "Well, I'll leave you to it."

Chapter 17

*H*olly peered into Lucas's room to ensure he was asleep. It was only nine in the evening, but he had been exhausted. Happy to be back at the cabin, he pushed himself too hard wanting to rake leaves and trim some of the bushes. Maybe Holly shouldn't have let him do it, but she did. He needed some normalcy, and to steer his mind in a different direction than where it had been the past week. When she let herself think of all he had been through, it was too much. Her heart broke for her brother.

She went to the kitchen and poured herself a tea before plopping down in front of the fire. Checking her phone, she was disappointed but unsurprised to see there was no word yet from Max. Today would be non-stop for him. She wanted to ask him to come by when he was done, ask him to stay the night, but she decided to leave it for now. Lucas was home. She didn't need a babysitter. She was a grown woman.

There was a light knock at the door just then. Holly looked up to see the man himself at her door looking tired and in dire need of her.

"Hey, you," she said, opening the door.

Max rushed in and scooped her up into his arms. "I have been wanting this all day," he whispered. "Is Lucas asleep?"

Holly nodded.

"Good," he said pulling her close. His head dipped down to her neck, his mouth placing light kisses from behind her ear down to her collarbone. He then kissed her properly on the lips while stroking the small of her back with his thumbs. "Stay," he begged gently. "Stay for a few weeks? I'm not ready to let you go just yet."

"Yes," she promised. "I'm staying until New Year's."

He picked her up and brought her to the couch. "More good news," he said, his face close to hers. "I-I love you, Holly. I never stopped. And I...I just want to love you for as long as you'll let me. That's it."

Holly kissed him hard on the mouth, pressing herself against him as if she could not get close enough. "I love you too, Sheriff Cooper," she managed to say. "You and I have a guardian angel."

Max growled low before he kissed her again and said, "Damn, if I don't love me some Patsy Cline, too."

Chapter 17

Two Months Later

Holly tilted the seatback of the passenger chair in Max's work SUV. The snow was falling hard. They'd hit a patch of black ice and struck a small snowbank, so Max pulled over. While he went out to make sure there was no damage to the vehicle, Holly pulled out her phone and dialed Gabe's number.

"Holls!" he said instead of hello. "How are you? How's the middle of nowhere?"

She rolled her eyes. "I'm good, Gabe. And Blairsville is hardly the middle of nowhere."

"If you say so," he quipped. "What's up?"

"Well, I'm calling to ask a favor."

Gabe let out a breath. "I've been fearing this call for weeks now."

Holly sighed. "Yeah."

"You're not coming back, are you," he said as a statement, not a question.

"I'm not."

"You're ridiculously happy, in love, and you found a job," he said, mock sadness in his tone.

Holly laughed. "I am, and I did," she said. "Staff writer for the *Augusta Chronicle*. It could turn into more very soon, too."

"All right, all right," said Gabe. "I get it. No more big city escapades with your old pal, Gabe. And you're in luck. That couple is chomping at the bit to take over your lease."

She smiled. "That's great news, Gabe. Thank you."

"Yeah, yeah," he said. "I'm expecting an invite soon, you know. Christmas in the mountains is just what this lawyer needs."

"It's a date, my friend," she said.

And ending the call, Holly peered out her window to see Max looking up from the wheel well. "Just a scratch," he said. "Nothing I can't fix."

She smiled back at him, "That's great news, my love."

THE END

Sweetwood Scandal

Chapter 1

*J*acob Sweetwood hadn't worn a tuxedo in over a year. But if Instagram were correct, Ava-Rose Billings would be at the Wellington Arts Gala tonight. The website had indicated: black tie only. He had tracked her down to the New Zealand capital, the place of her birth and upbringing, using her social media as clues along the way. It had been two months since he'd seen her last. A bright August morning greeted him with his girlfriend gone. And, as it happened, two-hundred-and-fifty-thousand dollars in cash, plus his great-grandmother's antique ruby ring disappeared right along with her.

Ava-Rose had left a note, brief in its length, cold it its tone. It read:

Jacob,

I'm going bush.

Let's be honest, love. It was never gonna last.

Ta,

Aves

It was her handwriting and sounded exactly like her. She left him. "Going bush" meant she was off on an adventure, probably never to return. And as he processed that fact in his mind, it suddenly occurred to him to check his safe. What had it been? Two weeks since he whispered in her ear that the code was now her birthday and that he trusted her more than anyone? What a goddamn fool he'd been.

"You're tying it wrong, Jacob," called his mother from the doorway.

Patricia Sweetwood had shown up unannounced a week prior and insisted on having the room adjoining his. She even went so far as to pay the people who were staying in the room—a lovely couple from the Philippines in their early thirties who were on their honeymoon—to vacate immediately. At the time, his mother brushed aside his concern.

"Oh, don't make a fuss, Jacob," she said. "They'll use the money to get a better room. This way, I'm close."

All Jacob could think was: *If I wanted you close, I'd have asked you to come along.* But he didn't say that. He didn't say anything. Normally, he would have put his mother in her place. He would have gently thanked her for her concern, allowed her to stay a few days, and then insist she leave him be. But he wasn't himself. The damage done by Ava-Rose's betrayal was far greater than he wanted to admit. He prided himself on being a strong, Southern man of integrity and good manners who could read people. Ava-Rose had pulled the wool over his eyes, and it was not sitting well with him. Not well at all.

"Here," his mother said, coming up behind him and getting on her tippy-toes to adjust his bowtie. "I do this for your father all the time." She patted his shoulder, stepped back, and observed his reflection. "There," she cooed. "Much better."

Jacob cleared his throat. "Thank you," he said.

Patricia walked over to the bar and poured herself a few fingers of gin. "Are you sure you don't want me to come with you, darlin'? I don't look my age, you know. People are always telling me so. No one will think I'm your mother."

"Yes, mother," he replied. "You've mentioned that several times."

"Well, it's true!" she exclaimed. "And anyway, I don't like the idea of you confronting this charlatan alone. Who knows what she will do once backed into a corner? Who knows who she's working with?"

These were questions Jacob had weighed as well. It's incredible what you question when you find out you never really knew a person. He couldn't truly trust his memories or opinions of Ava-Rose. Everything was based on a lie. She had never loved him. No, she had been using him, and for money no less—the one thing she'd sworn up and down didn't matter to her. God, he was such a fool.

"I'll be fine, mother," he offered reassuringly. "I've handled far more frightening creatures than Ava-Rose Billings."

His mother sat in the wing-back chair beside him, swirling her drink nervously. She had that far-off look in her eye, the same one she'd worn since she arrived. Patricia Sweetwood was not one to confide in nor share her true feelings in anyway. She was forever "on," playing a part, wearing a mask.

Jacob knew what was on her mind. She'd followed him to New Zealand to escape the dogged persistence of Blairsville, Georgia's Sheriff Max Cooper and the rumors of her involvement in the disappearance of Lucas Blake. Lucas had been her part-time lover. Since her arrival, however, everything had come to a head back home. Lucas had emerged—safe and sound—and their family attorney, business manager, and long-time friend, Anita Bayu, had been named the guilty party. She had been behind Lucas's kidnapping all along. It was a stunning revelation. Soon after, Anita had tragically taken her own life.

"You're thinking about Anita, aren't you?" he asked gently.

Patricia shook her head. "No, darlin'," she said with a wave of her hand as if he'd just said the silliest thing in the world. "I'm worried about you. I told you that."

But that was a lie. Jacob knew this. It surprised him how naïve his mother could be. How could she be this cultured woman in her fifties and not know that it would never matter how far away you fled? Your problems were always right there with you. He pitied her in many ways. The manner in which she conducted her private life was such that there was no privacy at all. Her bid for his father's attention was desperate and oh-so sad.

Ava-Rose had always chided Jacob's jaded view of his mother. "You're her son, not her equal," she'd say. "You'll never be able to see your mother as an adult. Your view will always be tainted by your childish assumption that she lives for you and your siblings." In this, it seemed Ava-Rose had a point.

Jacob felt a pang of sympathy for his mother just then. These glimpses into her as an independent adult with feelings and needs—separate from her role as his mother—were rare and brief, but he could not ignore it. It occurred to him that the hurt and betrayal he was feeling right now at the hands of Ava-Rose, was more than likely a fraction of what his mother felt day-in and day-out amid the dismissal and neglect of her husband, Bill Sweetwood.

"Have you spoken to Dad?" he asked in earnest.

His mother nodded. "Yes, just once. He's devastated," she said, taking a sip of her gin. "We all knew Anita was loyal and that she handled all the dirty work, but this…" her voice trailed off.

It was true. Lord knew the Sweetwood Syrups empire was mostly built upon rigged deals and undercutting and the like, but kidnapping? Covering up manslaughter? Anita must have felt trapped. And sure, it was a trap of her own making, but who could ever know what she was grappling with? What did the kind of loss she had experienced do to a person? Bill was no angel, but he lived in a world built for him. A wealthy, white man—a big fish in a little pond—Bill Sweetwood had rarely known strife. Entitlement and ignorance ran deep in this family.

Keith, the youngest of the Sweetwood clan had taken his penchant for call girls too far one night, and allowed his date to take the wheel of the family boat after a bout of drinking. The young woman had caused an accident that ended up killing Lucas Blake's parents. Anita, in her panic and taking her role of family savior far too seriously, had covered the whole thing up.

"And Keith?" asked Jacob.

Patricia kept her gaze on her drink as she answered. "Out on bail. Lawyer says he'll most likely plead guilty to a lesser charge, pay a hefty fine and do some community service."

"But *how* is he?" Jacob persisted.

His mother looked up at him, blinked hard as if the question was totally out of left field. "Oh, I- I don't know. He's Keith. You know… He'll bounce back."

She wasn't an especially nurturing woman and not close with any of her children. Jacob was probably the closest with her. Being the oldest, he was also the most self-sufficient, and Patricia liked that. It's not that it was a trait that she admired necessarily, more that she despised being needed. It overwhelmed her, and she did one of two things: she would explode or run.

Jacob's younger sister, Zena, could not stand their mother. The two were like oil and water who could not hold a civil conversation if their lives depended on it. Zena had always blazed her own trail—even if she made a great show of doing so. He wasn't wholly buying her "independent woman" spiel and felt that deep down, she still yearned for the love and approval of their dysfunctional parents. Having said that, he loved her dearly and protectively. And he was proud of her no matter what.

And then Keith was the baby. Being not particularly bright or talented, he had floundered almost from the beginning. Luckily, he was mostly happy, and this made him easy to be around. But Jacob could not help but feel that his happiness stemmed from his being oblivious to everything going on around him.

Patricia downed the last of her drink and stood to pour herself another one. Jacob crossed to meet her and took her glass. "I'll get that, mother," he said.

She brushed her hair from her eyes and stumbled a little. "Thanks, darlin,'" she replied.

It occurred to Jacob that despite being a mostly ridiculous creature, his mother was deeply lonely. He guessed he had always known this at some level about her, but it hit him in that moment. She was like a lost little girl in many ways. Even her running out to New Zealand was about attaching herself to the most mature person she knew: her eldest boy. She was seeking comfort from him—even as he was embroiled in one of the most painful experiences of his life.

"You know, mother," he began. "Maybe it would be good if you came with me tonight after all. Having a beautiful woman on my arm will help me blend in. Bachelors stick out like a sore thumb at these things, and I don't want Ava-Rose to be tipped off in any way."

Patricia beamed. "Wonderful!" She kissed him on the cheek, taking the drink he'd made for her. "I'll help, sugar. You'll see. Leave it to your mama."

Jacob stiffened, fearing she'd misunderstood. "Mother, I only need you to come with me. In no way do I want you to help me track down or speak with Ava-Rose."

His mother frowned. "But..."

He waved his hand dismissively. "I mean it. This is my problem, and I will be the one to solve it. That woman stole from me, and she will not go unpunished."

"Fine," said Patricia sitting back down in her chair. "Will you at least show me the picture of her on Instagram? It will help to know what she's wearing. I can be another set of eyes for you."

Jacob pulled out his phone and found the picture. He wished it didn't hurt to see her but it did. Yes, she was beautiful—olive skinned with jet-black hair straight down her back, high cheekbones, and almond-shaped brown eyes. And yes, she looked incredible in the ruby red ballgown she wore. But his hurt had nothing to do with her looks. They had connected, or at least he thought they did. They had inside jokes and silly nicknames for one another (she was Kiwi and he was Cowboy). There was a history, and the future they should have had felt like a bigger loss than any amount of money she could have stolen.

Patricia took the phone and pulled out her bifocals to see the image clearly. "Always a show-off," she said.

Jacob laughed. He had not realized how much he needed to. His mother's comment, rooted in an attempt at protection, was funny. Because yes, Ava-Rose was indeed a show-off. "Yeah, she'll be in good company at this gala, that's for sure. There will be a lot of self-important, entitled people who have contributed absolutely nothing to society."

And in an act of almost unheard-of self-awareness, Patricia Sweetwood stood dramatically and proclaimed with arms wide open, "My people! I am coming. Your queen is on her way."

Mother and son enjoyed a fit of laughter and each forgot, if only for a moment, that their lives were in complete upheaval.

Chapter 2

$\mathcal{N}$ ancy Cooper surveyed the relative emptiness of her pub, The Fox and Fig, with a satisfied sigh. It was three in the afternoon. Happy hour and dinner rush were soon to come. She was grateful for the loyal patronage of the folks of Blairsville, Georgia—her beloved hometown and the only place she even considered when she decided to buy a bar.

When her parents sold their home and land and moved to a small Miami condo, they had given a sizeable share of the profits to both she and her brother, Max. Her brother had prudently put his in a high-interest savings account. Nancy bought The Fox and Fig. That was over five years ago and the blood, sweat, and tears that she had invested in transforming the place from local dive bar to hip gastro pub were, in her mind, evident.

She knew the locals were grateful. It was something she heard from them often, especially right after the re-opening. "Just because we're not Atlanta doesn't mean we don't like nice things," was a refrain she heard over and over in one form or another. The folks around here might love their lives simple, but that didn't mean things had to be plain.

The first things to go had been the rickety old tables and chairs. Nancy replaced them with cherrywood booths lined with plush forest-green velvet. Everyone wanted booths. And those who didn't could now either partake of the much more comfortable chairs and long dining tables or the high-backed pub chairs that peppered the brand new (but antique-looking) bar. The art was all Civil War era because everyone in town had a great-great grand-pappy who had served one side or the other or who had wanted freedom for themselves. There was a reverence of the Georgian experience present at the pub that Nancy was proud of. It was a warm, unassuming, and inviting place with good food, beer, and whiskey.

The door to the employee entrance off the kitchen opened, and Nancy waved to her head cook, Ashanti Ward, with a smile. She had been fortunate enough to have this skilled chef with her for three years, and the woman had never missed a shift. Finally, it had occurred to Nancy that past summer that just because she didn't take vacations did not mean her staff should follow suit. In July, she forced Ashanti to take a whole week off and had the sous chefs step up for a few days. It went fine, of course. And Nancy learned a valuable lesson about letting people help. At least, she did in theory. She still had not taken a day off herself.

"Hey, boss," greeted Ashanti. "I picked up some persimmons from the Bell sisters' farm on the way over here. Going to use them for puddings as a dessert special tonight. You okay with changing the menu or should I?"

Ashanti was a petite woman in her mid-twenties with dark skin and soulful brown eyes professing a wisdom far beyond her years. Her hair was always in long braids that reached down to her waist. She was soft-spoken but held her own in the kitchen with even the most obnoxious male employees. There would be no doubt as to who ran things. Ashanti was quick-witted and shrewd. Her smile was warm, even if she always looked as though she was keeping a secret. It made her interesting and attractive to everyone—including their clientele. Customers were always trying to sneak a peek in the kitchen to catch a glimpse of her at work.

"Oh, I'll do it, Ash," replied Nancy. "That sounds delicious."

She decided to take advantage of the mid-afternoon lull and take a seat at a booth in the far-left corner of the pub. When she had finished the changes to the menu, Nancy pulled out her phone and scrolled through Instagram while sipping a half-pint of light beer. After a minute, she stopped. Patricia Sweetwood had posted a picture of her son, Jacob, dressed to the nines in a tux. The caption read: *My son lookin' swell among Wellington's swell.*

Nancy rolled her eyes at the Sweetwood matriarch's attempt at wordplay. Of course, Jacob looked handsome. He was tall and fit and, frankly, hot. But that's not what made Nancy look at the picture again and again. Jacob Sweetwood, for all his finery, grooming and good genes, looked alarmingly sad. There was an unmistakable pain in his eyes. It caught Nancy off-guard and pulled her in. She couldn't look away. She knew that pain, had seen it in her own eyes reflected.

In high school, she had been on-again-off-again with her boyfriend, Thomas Grange. Their relationship had been tempestuous. It shamed Nancy to admit it, but she had gotten addicted to the highly-emotional fights and the makeup sex that often followed. It was a toxic pattern that her younger self had found romantic and exciting. In her freshman year of college, she had finally ended things. But last spring he had reappeared in her life, showing up at the pub unannounced, bragging about his big city job in Atlanta.

Nancy should have recoiled from him, should have known better. But she fell for him again, and she fell hard. And what was worse, she hid it from her brother, Max. That was how Nancy knew it was wrong. The fact that she could not bring herself to admit to the most important person in her life that she was seeing Thomas again told her this was a huge mistake. Thomas Grange ended up breaking her heart, and the worst part was that she should have known better.

"Damn, that Jacob Sweetwood is hot! Like H-A-W-T hot," said Ashanti from behind Nancy's right shoulder.

"Jesus, Ash!" she exclaimed. "You scared me."

Ashanti clucked her tongue. "Well, you were losing yourself in that man's dreamy blue eyes. Don't blame me. I did clear my throat first."

Nancy motioned for Ashanti to have a seat across from her at the booth. "Seriously, though. Look at his eyes. Tell me what you see."

Ashanti took the phone and sat down in front of Nancy. "Well, I'm not sure," she began with a thoughtful tone. "I mean, I don't know the man personally. Do you?"

Nancy shook her head.

"All right, so we're both out here guessing," she said. "This man looks downright sad to me. But honey, that makes sense considering what happened."

Nancy blinked and offered a blank stare. "What do you mean?" she asked innocently. "The stuff with Keith? I hardly think Jacob would be surprised about that. Keith is always messing up. Or do you mean Anita's death?"

Ashanti waved her hand. "No, not Keith. And sure, Anita's death would definitely have been a blow for that whole family. But are you telling me you haven't heard about Ava-Rose?"

"His girlfriend?" Nancy asked.

"Yes, Nancy. Oh my goodness," she rolled her eyes. "Yes! Although, she is his *ex* girlfriend now. Weren't you wondering why he's in New Zealand?"

Nancy shrugged. "I just thought he was there with Ava-Rose."

"And his mother?"

"Oh," said Nancy, scratching her head. "Good point. So, what happened? And how do you know about this and I don't?"

"Well, you don't pay enough attention in my opinion, but that's neither here nor there," said Ashanti with a dismissive wave of her hand. "Anyway, my uncle works for a car service. He drove Patricia Sweetwood to the airport; she told him everything. That woman cannot keep her mouth shut. And she had the nerve to tip my uncle two dollars. Like, honey, just keep your damn money if that's how you're going to behave."

Ashanti went on to explain the Ava-Rose debacle in vivid detail, and Nancy listened intently. It struck her—the betrayal. They say all is fair in love and war, but deceit can feel so utterly humiliating. And that's what she saw in Jacob's eyes. It was as if they were telepathically saying: *I trusted her.*

Nancy shook her head in concern. "That poor man," she said. "And it's not as if Patricia Sweetwood is the motherly type."

Ashanti laughed. "Girl, from what I hear, she's the revenge type! And my guess is that is exactly what he needs and wants right now."

"You're totally right," agreed Nancy. "I just know from experience that won't be the thing that heals."

"Maybe," said Ashanti with a shrug. "But it'll be the thing that feels good for now."

It's not as if Nancy hadn't considered some kind of revenge when she found out about Thomas. When his Atlanta girlfriend called her out of the blue to let her know he'd been playing them both, Nancy had wanted to go full Carrie Underwood from the "Before He Cheats" video. She'd wanted to burn every item of clothing, every "I love you"

Post-It that she'd foolishly saved, every Hallmark card. She'd wanted to climb to the roof of her condo building and shout out to the whole town: "Thomas Grange is a lying, cheating piece of man-trash!"

But she didn't.

Because the truth was, they'd never said they were exclusive. They had never gone deep; it was always just a fling. And she had never asked him about his life in Atlanta. Nancy had been in complete denial ever since Thomas sauntered back into her life. She ignored every red flag with total willingness. She opted for the warm body of the liar she knew instead of the cold, empty bed she'd grown tired of.

When she looked back on it, Nancy Cooper realized she wanted love but settled for so much less.

So, as much as she recognized that look in Jacob Sweetwood's eyes, she also had to admit she'd gotten herself to the other side of it. It wasn't Thomas whom she'd trusted and been betrayed by. It was herself.

Chapter 3

$\mathcal{T}$he Wellington Arts Gala was both ingenious and surprising—as if someone had plucked Emily Dickinson's bedroom and placed it in a Las Vegas art exhibit. Jacob had to admit he'd never seen anything like it. There had been no real theme, just a celebration of the thriving arts community in Wellington itself, but in all of New Zealand really. Local musicians took turns performing their music on a raised stage in the middle of the spacious ballroom. There were art installations cleverly peppered throughout, including dozens of colorful blown glass chandeliers. Hundreds of framed poems hung on the walls alongside vivid and evocative paintings. It was a visual delight without being overwhelming.

People of all ages and colors milled about the room, navigating the cocktail tables and servers carrying champagne and appetizers with ease. Despite the extravagance, the vibe was not at all stuffy. There was a true appreciation for culture—both indigenous and otherwise—in the air. Jacob loved it. It contrasted somewhat with his experience being raised in northern, small-town Georgia, but it didn't drown it out either. He liked that he could be fascinated by one corner of the world and comforted by another.

Patricia seemed enthralled, too. She kept pointing out paintings and people and dresses. She threw out her usual stance of "just one" and sampled as much food as she wanted. Jacob had not seen her like this in...well, ever. She was like a kid in a candy store—distracted and delighted by all the bright colors and treats. The two of them nearly forgot why they were there in the first place.

Servers kept coming by with trays of Pimm's Cups—an herbaceous cocktail of gin-based liquor, soda, and fruit. Jacob just waved them off as Patricia grabbed what she could before they scampered away.

"Still not drinking, honey?" she asked as she knocked one back.

Jacob winced. "Mother, I have not had a sip of alcohol since I was sixteen years old. You know this."

She did know this and yet, somehow, conveniently forgot all the time. When Jacob had been in high school, he drank...a lot. He started as a freshman and drank his way through sophomore and junior years. His parents barely noticed; his friends thought he was the life of the party, and Anita had—fruitlessly—tried to lecture him about it.

Then, one night, his sister Zena knocked on his bedroom door looking for a book she had let him borrow. Jacob had been so out of it that he'd started snapping at her to leave him alone. Zena got annoyed, and she kicked him in the shins. Unfortunately, Jacob responded by slapping her in the face.

Zena ended up with a reddened cheek and a bloody nose. And Jacob, well, he had never forgiven himself. Since that day, he had given up booze. His sister had pleaded with him one time at her twenty-first birthday that it was okay. She had forgiven him. But he would not bend. What she didn't understand was how removed a man who would slap a woman in the face, not to mention his sister, was from the man Jacob wanted to be. He would not risk being that man again, not ever.

Jacob sipped his club soda and then froze. It was out of the corner of his eye that he saw her. Well, not *her* exactly but a flash of ruby red sashaying by. His breath caught, and his heart sped up. He wanted to turn his head and look at her but found he couldn't quite move.

"What?" asked his mother, squeezing his arm tighter. "What is it, darlin'?"

He couldn't speak just then. His heart and mind flooded with competing sentiments. Ava-Rose had left him, stolen from him, betrayed him. But she also cared for him once, hadn't she? If not, she'd been a heartbreakingly good actress.

Yes, they had a lot of fun making love. But it had been more than that. She would hold his hand anytime they went out; she brought him coffee in the middle of the day, knowing he'd let his one from the morning get cold. She would rub his feet, buy the books he'd mentioned in passing, and offer to go on runs with him even though she was more of a walker. Ava-Rose had been thoughtful and kind. And right now, Jacob was finding it difficult to reconcile the two sides of the woman he had been hopelessly in love with.

Jacob swallowed hard, finally answering his mother. "I think I just saw her."

Patricia gasped, looked in every direction. "Where?"

"Mother, for love of God, chill!" whispered Jacob through gritted teeth. "She will see you."

"I'm confused, Jacob. I thought you wanted her to see us?"

It was at that exact moment that Jacob realized he did not have a plan beyond finding Ava-Rose. What was wrong with him? He was always so prepared. What had this ordeal done to his brain? He should be hell-bent on getting his money back, getting the ring back. And that commitment should be backed by a detailed plan.

"I don't know, mother. Let me think," he said, trying to rein in his irritation with her.

Patricia turned to her son and took his face in her hands, seeing that he needed someone to step in and take charge. "Jacob, I think the point tonight is you've found her. The next step is to follow her. Confronting her here will only cause her to run again, don't you think?"

Jacob nodded, appreciating his mother's uncharacteristic calm at that moment.

Patricia laid out a plan for them to wait by the entrance. They knew there was only one way out of the building because they had done security checks upon entering and exiting. Once they saw her leave, they would track her.

As it turned out, they didn't have to wait long. About an hour after he'd first spotted her, Ava-Rose made her way to the door. She looked spooked, as if someone had told her some disturbing news. Jacob wondered if she had been tipped off about his appearance there tonight, but she wasn't looking around her. She kept her head down and clutched her handbag to her chest as she navigated the other guests.

Once outside, she checked her phone, presumably to call a cab. Keeping a safe distance, Jacob and his mother did the same. Just then, out of nowhere, a tall man with broad shoulders and a shaved head approached Ava-Rose and, grasping her by the elbow, pulled her to him and dragged her into a limousine parked just ahead.

"What the hell?!" gasped Patricia. "Who on earth is that?!"

Jacob's chest tightened, and, on instinct, he ran toward the limo to confront the man and save his ex-girlfriend. The man anticipated him, though, and after shoving Ava-Rose into the car, he slammed the door and signaled for the driver to leave by banging the roof twice with his fist. Stepping back onto the sidewalk, the man stopped Jacob in his tracks with a swift punch to the gut.

"We have known you were here since the moment you landed," he sneered and spat the words. "Stay away from her," he said, mercilessly throwing Jacob to the ground. And then he ran off.

Patricia was at her son's side in an instant. Jacob heard her shout something at the man but couldn't make it out. He was still winded, trying to catch his breath and process what had just happened.

"Darlin'? Jacob? Stay with me, honey," his mother said. She had her phone in her hand trying to call an ambulance.

Jacob wriggled from his mother's grasp and wheezed. "No hospital," he said. "Just take me back to the hotel."

Patricia shook her head. "Honey, I can't carry you, and you're in no shape to walk."

"I'm just winded, mother," he said, gathering his wits and strength to stand. "I'm not a paper doll."

She continued to fuss over him as he looked up and down the street, attempting to find out which direction the limo had fled. But there was no trace. He had come so close to Ava-Rose only to have her snatched away. She looked...scared. Why did she look so scared? And who was that dude? He seemed to know her comings and goings. Were they in cahoots?

We have known you were here since the moment you landed.

Who the heck was "we"?

"Jacob? Jacob!" Patricia's voice was harsh in his ears. He turned to realize she called them a cab. "Get in, honey. We'll go back to the hotel if you promise to lie down."

Jacob nodded and sheepishly put his aching body inside the vehicle. Wherever Ava-Rose went, he wasn't going to find her tonight.

Back at the hotel, Jacob headed straight for the shower knowing it was the only way to ensure his mother would leave him alone. Minutes later though, she was knocking at the door.

"Darlin'? Jacob, honey, it's your mother."

He rolled his eyes. *Who else would it be?*

"Jacob, I'm going to head down to the hotel bar," she said from the other side of the bathroom door. "I'm all dressed up and well, I just can't stay cooped up in here all night. Are you going to be all right?"

"Yes!" he answered, probably too quickly and forcefully. He cleared his throat. "I mean, I'll be just fine, mother. I'm going to turn in early."

There was a pause and then, "Are you certain? I don't want you in here stalking that hussy's social media."

Jacob stood beneath the blast of steaming water and opened his mouth to defend himself, but no words came. He realized that was precisely what he would have ended up doing, still might. "Yes, mother," he called. "Go and have fun. I promise I won't spend the whole night obsessing over Ava-Rose."

She yelled something about fast women and never trusting anybody who wasn't blood, and then, she was gone. Jacob turned off the shower and breathed a sigh of relief. He needed some time to gather his thoughts and process what happened at the gala. More precisely, he had to run through what had not happened. And really, he needed to decide whether to stay in Wellington at all. Was any of this worthwhile? Ava-Rose kept slipping through his fingers.

Toweling himself off, Jacob put on the hotel-provided white cotton robe and went to lay down on the bed. His body still ached from the skirmish earlier. The whole thing had been so emasculating. Had she seen him get hit and fall to the ground in an undignified heap? Did he look weak to her—even more than he had before? He rubbed his face in shame. How much more could he lose?

He heard a buzzing coming from the bedside table and realized it was his phone ringing. The number started with +64—New Zealand's country code. Maybe one of the private investigators he called was finally getting back to him.

"Jacob Sweetwood," he said cautiously, deciding against a simple hello.

The caller cleared his throat. "Mr. Sweetwood, hello. How are you?"

Jacob narrowed his brow and spoke quickly, not wanting to make small talk. "Who is this?"

The man took a deep breath. "This is Ed Billings, Mr. Sweetwood. I'm Ava-Rose's father."

Jacob had to stifle a sharp intake of breath. *Her father?* She had told him her parents had died when she was a toddler. Of course, it wouldn't really be a shock to discover she had lied about that, too. But this person calling was a stranger. Who could he really trust? "I don't understand," he replied finally.

"Yes, I'm sure you're confused," said the man, his voice kind and reassuring. "No doubt she told you that her mother and I are dead. But I assure you we are very much alive, and I am indeed her father."

Jacob knit his brow. "Sorry, but I can't simply take your word for it. You're gonna have to give me something."

"Of course," the man said politely. "She was born in Auckland on November 24th, 1990. Her favorite song is 'Fix You' by Coldplay, favorite food is tuna sashimi, and favorite movie is *Clueless*."

Jacob rolled his eyes. "You could find all of that with a quick Google search."

The man laughed. "You're absolutely right," he replied. "The world these days. No privacy at all." He sighed and was quiet for a moment. "How about this? She sleepwalks. And one time, as a young girl, she sleepwalked all the way to the ravine behind our family home and nearly drowned."

Ava-Rose had indeed told him this story. And come to think of it, it was one of the few times he noticed her being vulnerable. In that moment, she had shown real fear and emotion—something she usually preferred to hide. Against his better judgment, Jacob was beginning to believe this man could be who he said he was.

"Okay," said Jacob slowly. "You have my attention, Mr. Billings."

"Call me Ed, please, son," he said. "I'd like to meet with you. I—I know that my daughter has done some awful things, and I want to help you. It's my responsibility as her father to help make this right."

Jacob hesitated. "Sir, I—"

"Please," interrupted the man. "Just...at least hear me out. Meet me tomorrow at noon at Lambton Quay Station. There's a red cable car that runs up the hill. It's a huge tourist attraction. There will be lots of people, and the ride is only five minutes long," he said reassuringly. "Five minutes of your time, Jacob...may I call you Jacob?"

"Yes."

"All right then, Jacob. Five minutes, that's all I ask."

Jacob heaved a sigh. It would have been an easy yes if he received this call when he'd first arrived in Wellington. He'd been more green and eager then. Now, he found himself weary and disillusioned. He was no longer driven purely by revenge. And if he was honest with himself, he never had been. The truth was, he wanted to see Ave-Rose again. He couldn't explain it, but it wasn't ever going to be enough to simply get the money and the ring back. No, he wanted to be face to face with Ava-Rose and to ask her, "Why?"

Maybe Mr. Billings could answer that question, but two things made Jacob question the wisdom in meeting with him. One, he could be straight-up lying, and this was all a rouse. And two, he needed and deserved to hear the truth from Ava-Rose herself.

Still, it was probably worth the risk. Meeting in a public place meant Jacob was relatively safe from harm. (He realized he had just been attacked earlier that day but decided to write it off as an isolated incident.) And some information was better than no information. This was a more productive lead than stalking her whereabouts on Instagram. And perhaps Mr. Billings would tell him where his daughter was if he demanded to know. It was worth a shot.

"Okay, Mr. Billings," he said finally. "You win. I'll meet you tomorrow."

Chapter 4

*N*ancy unscrewed the lid to her bottle of cranberry juice and chugged half of it with relish. It had been a long shift, and her thirst was off the charts. She closed the fridge door and took in the sight of her apartment for the hundredth time since the renovations were completed last month. *Not bad for a flat above a bar*, she thought to herself.

The hardwood floors had been refinished. There was exposed brick in the living room, slate counters and stainless-steel appliances in the kitchen. The bathroom was all gleaming white fixtures with a state-of-the-art shower and heated tile floors. And her bedroom finally had the pale purple and cream-colored bedding with matching curtains she'd been longing for since she was a little girl.

This was more than a renovation to Nancy, it was a reward. She had taken a risk buying the bar but with hard work and determination, that risk had paid off. The Fox and Fig was a local success and it was her baby.

Baby. The word made her wince and brought up some raw feelings. Yes, she was proud of herself and knew she had accomplished so much, but time was ticking. Nancy wanted a family; she wanted all that traditionally came before it as well—the courtship, the wedding, the settling down, and then babies. All of that took time. And she was constantly afraid she was too damaged, too used to making poor choices for any of that to happen.

Most days, Nancy tried to focus on what she did have. Her big brother, Max, was wonderful. She could always count on him for support and kindness. He knew her well, would call her on her BS, and gave good advice. Max had recently begun seeing Holly again—his ex-fiancée—and Nancy loved this development. It had been hard seeing him pine for Holly all those years they'd spent apart. But things were different now. Nancy could see how much the two of them had grown and how they were ready for each other. And all of this gave her hope.

She also loved the regulars at the bar. Most of them were extremely generous. Sure, there was the odd time where she was forced to cut a person off and call a taxi or a loved one, but those were few and far between. Nancy was acutely aware that alcohol could be the thing that made a night enjoyable or an absolute disaster. For the vast majority of her patrons, it landed somewhere in between. The bar was a place to bide time and forget worries for a while. It was more of a resting place than a refuge.

Blairsville was a beautiful town, but it was small and many of its folk worked long, hard hours. The main employer was Sweetwood Syrups and so when day shift ended at six o'clock, Nancy could pretty much time her watch to quarter past the hour and witness a good portion of those workers pile into her establishment for an after-work beer or whiskey. They were a happy bunch for the most part—always up for telling jokes, gossiping about the company, or just goodheartedly venting about their lives. It was rewarding to provide this space for them, give them a sense of community that was less about work and more about connection.

Nancy walked to her sofa and plopped down. The silence was lovely after such a long day, but it was also a reminder of her life alone—a life she had consciously built. She had chosen to settle in Blairsville. This was the town where she had grown up, and she knew practically everyone. Meeting a guy here with her lifestyle? Let's just say, the odds were against her.

Just then, the Instagram picture of Jacob Sweetwood flashed in her memory. She still could not shake what she saw in his eyes. So many people were walking around pretending to be okay in this world, and he—whether he knew it or not—had his sadness on full display. Nancy connected with that, admired it. Naked emotion—and from a man no less—was refreshing.

She opened the Instagram app on her phone and looked at the photo on Patricia Sweetwood's page again. Hovering over the image, she looked to see if he had been tagged. He had. She clicked on his name and observed his profile. It was brief, only three posts. A picture of his sister Zena from when she was in high school was posted a few years ago for National Siblings Day. One of Anita posted last year on her birthday, and lastly, one of him and Ava-Rose. It was a selfie posted two months ago with the caption: *True love found.*

She thought about the three photos Jacob had chosen to post. Zena meant a lot to Jacob; Nancy knew this without even knowing either of them particularly well. She knew that his sister was why Jacob had given up drinking, and she admired him greatly for that. Then there was Anita—the family's house manager and Bill's silent business partner who was more like family. Anytime Nancy had been to a Sweetwood party back in high school, it was Anita checking on everyone, bringing snacks and drinks and giving the Sweetwood kids kisses on the cheek. Her death must have shocked and grieved Jacob to his core.

That picture with Ava-Rose, though, was fascinating. Jacob was glowing. His smile was wide, and Nancy could read happiness clear in his eyes. His head was tilted towards her, and his body shifted protectively around her. He was head over heels. Ava-Rose, on the other hand, looked stiff. Her lips were tight, and she looked awkward and unsure beside her boyfriend. She was gorgeous, to be sure, but vapid. Nancy had to wonder what Jacob had been thinking about posting this picture. Could he not see what was so plain to her?

Of course, the answer was no. Nancy knew she had been as blind as Jacob appeared to have been. She was an expert on seeing what she wanted to see. So, the question was, where was it going to get her now? Sure, she had this experience behind her, but who was to say she wouldn't get so lonely that she would deceive herself again?

Her phone lit up just then. It was Holly. *At this hour?* That could not be a good sign.

"Holls? What is it? Is Max all right?"

Holly was sobbing. "Nancy, I'm so... I'm so sorry to b-bother you..."

Nancy's throat tightened. "Holly, what's wrong? What is it?"

She sniffed. "I tried Gabe but he's not picking up. He's probably on a date. And I just...I just need to talk to someone."

Nancy relaxed a bit. Holly sounded tipsy—not alarmed or in danger. "So, everyone is okay? You just need to talk about something."

Holly let out a wail. "Everything is changing so fast, Nancy. And I'm not good enough for Max. He's so... he's so... gooooood."

Nancy sighed inwardly. It looked like she was still on the clock after all. "Holly, slow down. Did something happen?"

"Daniel is remarrying. He called me earlier to let me know."

"Oh Holls, I'm sorry. That's a lot to process."

"That part is fine," replied Holly. "I wish him well. But I guess it was just a reminder that my life in New York is done. Gabe is there, but he'd meet me anywhere in the world at any time. I've left my job, my apartment, the life I've known for the past seven years!"

Nancy could feel the anxiety in Holly's voice, and it made her feel for her. "I know, Holly. It's a massive change."

Holly sniffed and continued. "And your brother is such a good man. I love him, Nancy. I do. And I'm glad to be back here, but it's so different than New York, so different than where I thought I was headed. I'm worried..."

"What, Holly?" Nancy asked gently. "What are you worried about?"

"I'm worried I've made the wrong decision again!" she said abruptly. "I've messed up so many times, Nancy. And I blame myself for not being here for Lucas when he needed me..."

Holly's younger brother Lucas had recently been kidnapped because he knew about the youngest Sweetwood sibling Keith's involvement in the death of their parents. Lucas was back safe and sound and seeing a counsellor to help him deal with all the trauma of what took place. But Nancy was now wondering if Holly could benefit from the same. There was no way she should be blaming herself for what happened to Lucas.

"You're worried about failing, is that it?" Nancy asked.

There was a pause. "Yes, partly," Holly replied. "I'm worried about failing and hurting the people I love. And I'm worried about losing them forever."

Nancy wished right then she could reach through the phone and hug Holly tight. Between losing her parents, the divorce, Lucas's kidnapping, and moving back to Blairsville, the girl had been through so much.

"Holly," she began. "I get it. It's understandable that after all the terrible things that have happened, you'd be on guard for more terrible things. But you'll never be able to fully prepare yourself. You'll never be able to anticipate life enough to feel completely safe. All you can do is be grateful for what and who you have, and trust that you can handle whatever comes your way. It's not that you make bad decisions, not at all. You make decisions and learn from them. That's what you've always done and will continue to do."

Holly took a deep breath. "Thank you," she said, her voice a little more steady. "Nancy?"

"Yes?"

"When did you become so wise? I admit, I've always seen you as the scrappy, outspoken little teenager who looked up to Max with such reverence. But you're a really smart woman in your own right, maybe more than you realize. Max said I should call you, and he was right. You made me feel so much better. Thank you."

Nancy heard the words and tried to take them in, but it was hard. So, she just said "no problem" instead.

"You should be a therapist," suggested Holly.

"Bartender, therapist—same thing," joked Nancy.

Holly laughed. "Okay, I'm going to let you go now. You must be exhausted. Thanks again."

After hanging up the phone, Nancy couldn't help but feel the importance of the timing of that phone call. Holly may be grappling with different events and scenarios, but her worries were not different from Nancy's, not really. So, could it be that the advice she'd given to Holly was advice she should herself be taking?

It was too late in the day for this kind of philosophizing she decided. Time for a shower and bed—especially since she was going to have to do it all again tomorrow. And if she took the image of Jacob Sweetwood's sad blue eyes with her to bed, well, no one would know but her.

———

Patricia Sweetwood wasn't answering her phone, and Jacob decided this was a good thing. His mother would be more of a distraction than anything, and he was only calling her out of courtesy. This meeting with Ava-Rose's father was one he wanted to do alone.

Jacob checked his reflection in the mirror. A fitted white t-shirt and black dress slacks were exactly what Ava-Rose would have chosen for him to wear. It bothered him only slightly that she had such good taste. He decided to look at it as something he had learned from her and tried his best to leave it at that. Snapping his watch closed on his wrist, he observed the time, eleven thirty. Jacob pulled out his phone and scheduled a cab.

He arrived at Lambton Quay ten minutes before noon and was relieved to be a bit early. Walking down the lane to the cable car itself, he took in all the buildings and restaurants in the surrounding area. The salty scent of the bay was in the breeze and mingled with the earthy smell of roasting coffee beans from a few of the open-air cafés. It was a normal-looking downtown, if not exceptionally clean. The streets were narrow and lined with chic, expensive shops. He could easily imagine Ava-Rose shopping here with the perfect handbag hanging from her arm, a floppy hat, wine-colored lips, and enormous dark sunglasses.

The day was sunny and warm, and tourists were walking leisurely about, craning their necks to take in all the sights. Jacob decided to stand by the ticket office in the hopes he would be easily spotted. Now though, he wished he'd done some reconnaissance. What did Mr. Billings look like? In the confusion of the previous twenty-four hours, he had forgotten to be the thorough man he usually was. Ava-Rose had shown him an old photo of her parents a while back, but who's to say that was real? In any case, he could barely recall the details of the couple in the photo. The only thing he remembered remarking was that she looked a lot like her father.

Just then, Mr. Billings appeared, and it was indeed the man from the photo. This man had the same eyes as Ava-Rose, black hair, and serious look. He was short—much shorter than Jacob—with a bulky build but in a way that one could tell he was still quite strong. He carried himself well and stood straight. He approached Jacob with his hand outstretched.

"Jacob Sweetwood?"

Jacob nodded and shook the man's hand. "Hello, Mr. Billings. It's a pleasure to meet you," he said.

The man smiled. "Please, son, as I said, I'd prefer you call me Ed," he said and handed Jacob a ticket. "We can board now if you like. The car leaves in two minutes."

It was clear that Ed was nervous and on edge. Somehow, this put Jacob more at ease. He followed the older man to the cable car and got on board. They found two benches near the front and sat across from one another. "I can see your daughter in you," said Jacob in earnest.

Ed smiled. "Yes," he said, clearly proud. "She and I used to hear that all the time."

"Used to?"

Ed hung his head, looking slightly uncomfortable. "I haven't seen my daughter in two years, Jacob. And so I've gotten used to referring to her in the past tense."

Now it was Jacob's turn to be uncomfortable. "I-I'm sorry. That sounds difficult."

The older man let out a heavy sigh. "It is indeed. You can't imagine."

Jacob felt for the man but had no idea what to say. Ava-Rose appeared to leave a lot of pain in her wake—perhaps especially to those she claimed to love. "So, what did you want to tell me, Ed? Why did you want to meet with me?"

Ed ran his fingers through his thinning hair and leaned back against the cable car's window. He cleared his throat. "Ava-Rose has always been... difficult. You know how beautiful she is, of course. Well, she always has been. Her mother put her into modelling at a young age, and she was very successful."

"Yes," interrupted Jacob with a nod. "She told me about that."

"Right, well, I'm not entirely sure the whole situation didn't mess with her head a bit. I mean, being adored and paid for your looks, being looked at as someone many years older than you actually are. Her personality shifted at about age eleven. She became demanding and manipulative," said Ed gravely. "Her mother and I thought it was a phase—it wasn't."

An announcement came over the PA system that the cable car required some minor maintenance, and they would be delayed by five minutes for departure.

Ed continued. "Then, when she was a teenager, the male attention started. She always dated older boys, most of whom treated her poorly but I have to admit, she often behaved badly too. It was impossible to get through to her. In my daughter's mind, her mother and I were always wrong. And after indulging her every whim for so long, we tried to introduce discipline at the age of fifteen. You can imagine how successful that was."

"She rebelled," Jacob guessed.

Ed nodded. "Big time. She ran away six times for weeks at a time before she turned eighteen. Her teen years were spent partying, never taking school seriously, and falling in and out of love with countless boys. She moved out on her nineteenth birthday, cleaned out the savings account we had set aside for her, and never looked back. We would hear from her from time to time. Her updates were always delivered with a coldness that mystified us; she never inquired as to how we were doing," said the older man with a resigned sigh. "And then, she met Dax Piper."

Dax Piper. Jacob took a sharp inhale. The name sounded familiar, but he couldn't be sure why. "Ava-Rose never mentioned him."

The car started to move, and a few tourists clapped. A father put his toddler son on his shoulders, and they both oohed and ahhed as it made its ascent up the hill.

Ed cocked his head slightly. "I can see you recognize the name and so you should. But I'll get to that in a moment." The car's interior went dark for a moment as they rode through a tunnel. "Just over three years ago, our daughter began seeing Dax and, at first, her mother and I thought it was great. Ava-Rose finally seemed to want to settle. She stopped partying and became more interested in business. She took a few classes at the local college and would call us up every few weeks to tell us how well she'd done on her tests and projects. Turns out, this was all spurred on by Dax. He told her he wanted to groom her to rise the ranks in his company."

The lightbulb went on for Jacob. He knew where he'd heard that name. Dax Piper was the Senior VP of Swansea Syrups—a major manufacturer of sugar and syrups in New Zealand, Australia and a good portion of Asia.

Ed looked Jacob straight in the eyes. "You remembered, did you?"

Jacob nodded. "Yes, I know the name, but that's it. And I know my father knew his father, Paul Piper."

"That's right," said Ed. "Paul passed away last year, and young Dax will take over once he turns thirty-five, which is still two years away."

So, Ava-Rose dated this Dax guy? What does this have to do with me? Jacob thought.

Ed read his mind. "I'm getting there, son," he said with a wink. "The ride is almost over, so listen closely. About a year into their relationship, it was clear that Dax had a hold over Ava-Rose. She seemed only concerned about him and what he would think. Her mother and I confronted her about it, and she flew into a rage. She said we were betraying her and that we would never understand the connection they had. It was a surreal experience. Ava-Rose had gone from a domineering, selfish person to someone who was at the beck and call of her boyfriend. She literally wore the clothes he picked out, bought the food he suggested. She could not make a move without him."

Jacob processed this information with some distress. It sounded familiar, way too similar to his experience. He had told himself this was what it was to be so deep in love, that it was okay to lose yourself in a way. But hearing it told back to him in this manner—it hit different. He could see how it was more toxic, more codependent and less like healthy love.

"After that confrontation, Ava-Rose cut all ties with us and we have not heard from her since. My wife cries all the time, even to this day," Ed's voice cracked with emotion. "Excuse me."

"Don't give it a second thought," said Jacob quietly, averting his eyes.

"About a year ago, I hired a private investigator to track our daughter down, and I've been having him tail her ever since. That's how I found out she was seeing you."

Jacob's eyes went wide. "That sounds expensive."

The older man shrugged. "I've done very well on the stock market. Not to mention, Ava-Rose is our only child. We are doing this to protect her and to stay sane. It's our only connection to her other than her social media, which we all believe is staged at this point."

"Staged?"

The cable car stopped at Kelburn station, but Ed pleaded with Jacob to give him a few more minutes. "They'll let us ride back down if that's okay with you."

Jacob nodded. "Yes, please continue."

"Our private investigator, my wife, and I think Ava-Rose's entire life is devoted to doing Dax's bidding. We believe she began a relationship with you in order to gain access to information—specifically on a recipe for a syrup that tastes like maple but does not affect blood sugar."

"Our Staple Syrup?"

Ed clasped his hands together. "That's the very one."

Jacob considered this. It was a huge coup. The flavor was almost identical to maple. They knew they were onto something, and the recipe was kept top-secret. But industrial espionage? Really? That seemed like something that only happened in movies, and yet, there were most definitely millions of dollars at stake with this product. How could he have been so incredibly stupid?!

"Ava-Rose is no angel, Jacob. I acknowledge that completely. But I just want you to know she is not in her right mind. It is our contention that Dax Piper has manipulated and mentally abused our daughter. She is his puppet."

"Okay, but wait, why did she steal the money and the ring? This doesn't add up."

"Yes, that," Ed acknowledged. "You're right; it doesn't add up. We think she may have done that on her own. Of course, at this point, we don't know why. But, son, I asked you to meet me because I want to help. My wife and I have been keeping an eye on you for a while now. We think you're a good guy, and it pains us to think about what you've been through."

Jacob felt a pang of sadness. It was one thing to recognize your own hurt, but to hear it acknowledged by someone else, by the father of the one who hurt you no less, was not easy to take. He also had to admit it was an eerie feeling knowing that he had been watched these past months. Jacob held his jaw tight and nodded.

Ed continued. "We want to offer you our PI's services for as long as you need. We want to help you get to the bottom of what Ava-Rose was able to uncover and how much Dax Piper knows at this point."

"I-I don't know what to say," said Jacob.

"It occurs to me that we want the same thing: answers. You've come halfway across the world and my guess is that it's not just about the money. You want to know *why* my daughter did this. Am I right?"

Jacob cleared his throat. "Yes," he replied simply.

Ed shrugged. "Well, son, you're simply outgunned here. We were, too. We had to hire a professional. Dax Piper is good at this game—too good. And our only hope to get our daughter back is to eventually confront her with the truth about who she has aligned herself with."

Jacob extended his hand to Ava-Rose's father who took it and shook in agreement. "Thank you," he said.

Ed nodded. "My advice to you, Jacob, is to catch the next flight home and try to get back to normal. My PI's name is Lex Forbes. He will contact you within forty-eight hours to set up a meeting in Blairsville."

Jacob had to admit he was relieved. He'd been running out of steam. And as much as his mother thought she was helping, she was more of an added concern. It felt right to accept Ed Billings' help. This had gone on long enough. They needed him back at work. Why had it never occurred to him to hire a private investigator of his own? Scratch that. He knew why. Jacob wanted to *see* Ava-Rose. Well, he'd seen her now and was no wiser than he had been weeks ago.

The two men exchanged contact information and when the cable car arrived back at Lambton Quay, Jacob hailed a cab and called his mother.

"Mom, it's Jacob," he said. "It's time to go home to Georgia."

Chapter 5

*N*ancy was helping the delivery guy unloading kegs from the truck when Ashanti came running up to her, face flushed with excitement. Nancy knew this look—she had gossip to share.

"Girl, put that keg down and get in the bar," she whispered with delight.

Nancy protested. "I always help Joe unload," she said out of breath. "Is something on fire? Did a pipe burst?"

"Nuh-uh," squealed Ashanti. "Better!"

Joe emerged from the truck. "I've got this, Nance," he said with a cad-like wink. "I don't think our Ms. Ward here is going to let this go."

Nancy loved to watch the sparks fly between Ashanti and Joe. Her friend would deny it to the ends of the earth, but they had chemistry. Anyone could see it. And why not? They were both young and gorgeous. Joe stood just under six feet with black hair, olive skin, and a naturally athletic physique. But it was his open, playful manner that was most attractive. And it seemed to be Joe's weekly mission to make Ashanti blush or, at the very least, smile. Unfortunately for Joe, this was not his week.

Ashanti rolled her eyes and clucked her tongue. "Anyway," she said dryly to Nancy and Nancy alone. "Like I was saying, there is something that needs your attention at the bar."

"Go ahead, Nance," repeated Joe. "Ash, can help me. Right, Ash?"

She held up her hand. "Joseph, stop. I am not your errand girl. You want help? I'll refer you to my boss for my hourly rate and benefit requirements."

"Okay, this conversation has taken a nefarious turn," said Nancy warily. "Lead the way, Ashanti. You have my curiosity now."

Ashanti clapped her hands with glee and threw one last dirty glance Joe's way, to which he promptly bowed with a flourish.

It was 10:00 a.m. The pub wasn't even officially open yet. Nancy could not guess at who or what had her friend and colleague so worked up. Ashanti led her back through the kitchen and slowed down to whisper.

"Okay, just take a peek around the corner, and you'll see what I'm talking about."

Nancy scoffed. "What on earth? You are never like this!" But she did as instructed. And as she peered into the restaurant, her eyes caught on a familiar figure sitting at the bar scrolling through his phone. Nancy did a double-take and then snapped her head back into the kitchen.

"What the heck?!" she hissed so he wouldn't hear. "What is Jacob Sweetwood doing in my bar?" She could feel heat rising to her cheeks; her pulse was racing, and her breathing was labored.

"He's having a drink," answered Ashanti with a mischievous look.

"I can see that," said Nancy through gritted teeth. "But for one, it's the morning. And for two, Jacob Sweetwood doesn't drink!"

Ashanti furrowed her brows dramatically. "Interesting you know that about him..." she teased as Nancy poked her in the ribs. "Ow!" Ashanti squealed. "Stop. First off, the door was unlocked, and he just sorta walked in, assuming we were open. And second, it's cranberry juice."

Nancy leaned back against the kitchen wall and took a deep breath in an attempt to calm herself down. Why was she reacting like this? She barely knew the guy. Sure, he was handsome. And okay, she could not stop looking at that picture of him on Patricia's Instagram, but this was silly! She was a grown woman, not some wide-eyed school girl.

She ventured another look at him. Dressed in a classic blue blazer and baby blue dress shirt with a briefcase on the bar to his right, he appeared to be on his way to work. He looked so... alone. Seeing him like this tugged at Nancy's heartstrings in the same way the photo had done. She felt a kinship, a connection she couldn't explain. Was it all in her head? Was she making up some convenient association to a super-rich, legitimately hot guy?

Now it was Ashanti's turn to poke Nancy in the ribs. "Hey!" she yelped.

"Hate to break it to you, boss," said Ashanti. "But I poured his juice because you were busy. Bartending is your job, not mine." And with that, she laughed and ran off, presumably to not-flirt with Joe some more.

Nancy steadied herself. She was a bartender. He was a customer. This was not complicated. She took another deep breath and made a slow, nonchalant meander to the bar. Jacob was so hyper-focused on his phone that he didn't see her approach. She picked up a bar towel and proceeded to wipe clean a row of freshly washed old-fashioned glasses.

"What's the good word?" she asked, instantly regretting it. *What's the good word?* Who was she? A barkeep from 19th-century Glasgow?

Jacob didn't stir, just kept scrolling.

Phew, thought Nancy. That was a narrow escape.

"Could I have another cranberry juice?" asked Jacob, pushing his glass toward her without taking his gaze from his phone.

Um, rude. Who did this guy think he was? Nancy pulled up the tall, white plastic bottle of juice and wordlessly re-filled his glass.

"Thanks," he said distractedly. He raked his fingers through his hair and bit his thumbnail.

"Is everything okay?" ventured Nancy.

"Huh?" Jacob's eyes went from the glass of juice, back to his phone, and then to Nancy. "Oh, yes. The juice is fine, thanks."

"No, I mean with you," she clarified. "Is everything okay with you?"

Jacob let out an exasperated sigh. "Yes, geez!"

Nancy threw her hands up and backed away.

He rubbed his forehead and cursed. "Shit, sorry. I-I'm not myself," he said. "You were being so nice and... Nancy?" he asked with a tone of surprise. "Nancy Cooper?"

She looked away awkwardly and offered a nervous laugh. "Yes..."

Jacob stood and outstretched his hand to her. "Oh my gosh. It's been forever! How long has it been?"

"Since Zena's college graduation bash..." she said shaking his hand. "A long time ago."

"Wow, I think you're right. That's crazy. It's not like Blairsville is a big town."

Nancy colored. "Well, I spent some time in Atlanta. And we don't exactly travel in the same circles," she added, her gaze now on her shoes.

He looked confused at her words for a moment. "I-uh, yes, I suppose you're right."

This was interesting. Could he really not see the truth of her words? He'd said it himself. Blairsville is small. They should be running into one another at fairs and concerts and the grocery store. But Jacob Sweetwood's life was bigger than that. He worked, had groceries delivered, and partied with fancy people at their lake houses. At least, that's what Nancy assumed.

"And, well," he continued. "You work in a bar and..."

"You don't drink," she said simply.

Jacob's expression turned to one of surprise. "Yes, that's right. How did you know?"

Nancy lowered her head again and shuffled her feet. "I was there that day," she said, referring to the pool party. "Max told me a few days later that you had vowed never to drink again. And, I don't know, you seem like a man who keeps his word."

He gave the slightest hint of a smile. "Thank you," he replied.

The air hung meaningfully between them. Nancy could sense she had seen him just now, in a way he wasn't used to being seen. "I don't drink either," she said quickly, breaking the tension.

Jacob laughed at this. "You? Don't drink? Bartender and purveyor of alcohol?"

She smiled widely and fiddled with her hair nervously. "I know, right?"

"Why?" he asked.

"Oh, I just never liked how it made me feel out of control and light-headed—nothing heroic like your reasoning."

Jacob's face darkened. "Oh, I'm far from heroic; I can assure you of that."

Nancy cleared her throat, unsure of whether to continue. She stepped forward again to the bar and began towel-drying more glasses. She decided a change of subject was best. "So, what is your sober self doing at my pub this early in the day anyhow?"

He looked offended, but only for a split second. Then he appeared to be amused. "If you must know, I'm meeting someone."

"Oh, and what's her name?" The words were out of her mouth before she could take them back. What was she doing? This was none of her business. Her faced turned eight shades of red; she was sure of it.

Jacob laughed again, hard. His whole face changed, and his eyes lit up. "Nancy Cooper, I wish I'd gotten to know you years ago!" he said. "I never knew you were this direct."

Nancy was a little flustered now. "Sorry, I... that's none of my business."

He looked straight at her. "No, I love it. You're hilarious," he said in earnest. "I'm not meeting a she. I'm meeting a he. It's not necessarily for business or personal reasons. It's... complicated. Anyway, this guy is from out of town, and he picked here to meet."

"Ah, I see." *Of course*, she thought. Someone else would have had to pick her pub. Why would Jacob Sweetwood ever think to come to The Fox and Fig?

Jacob observed her strangely. "Have I offended you?"

She shook her head. "No."

He tilted his head and narrowed his eyes. "Yes, I have," he countered. "Sorry, Nancy, but I've been in New Zealand for far too many weeks, back only a few days, and still fighting jet lag. You're gonna have to help a Southern gentleman out."

Nancy's stomach was now overcome with butterflies, and her legs had turned to goo. The way he said her name, his honesty—the man was effortlessly charming to say the least. "It's just... I was very surprised to see you in my restaurant after all these years and well, someone else suggesting to meet here explains it."

Jacob seemed to take this in. "I see. So, you think I have avoided your place—which looks incredible, by the way—because it was beneath me? I promise you, Nancy, it's only because I don't frequent bars. And to be honest, I don't go out much at all. I work. When I was with..." he stopped himself before saying Ava-Rose's name. "That is, I had a few months where I was going out, but it was mostly restaurants in Atlanta."

She waved her hand dismissively. "You don't owe me an explanation."

He rubbed his face with both hands and then raked his fingers through his hair. "My jet-lagged brain apparently disagrees."

Nancy poured him more cranberry juice and then poured herself a glass as well. "How was your trip?" she ventured, unsure whether this was safe territory but pushing all the same. Sometimes, she just couldn't help herself.

Jacob sighed. "Not great. It seems like you've heard rumors."

She nodded with sympathy. "I think your mom has talked about it openly, and it's spread. So... yeah."

He rubbed his temples. "That checks," he said, sighing in resignation. "I'm not exactly sure what people are saying. But I don't really want to talk about it if it's all the same to you."

"Of course," she replied. "But just so you know, no one blames you."

His face went dark again. "I understand that information should probably make me feel better, but somehow it doesn't."

Nancy recognized that look. It was the same one he wore in the Instagram pic. He was still hurting, probably still in love. She tried to put herself in his shoes but quickly realized she would just be livid. The sort of tenderness he still appeared to feel for Ava-Rose seemed so undeserved. But then, had she not let Thomas do as he pleased? Trample over her? Love was messed up. Which meant, of course, it probably wasn't love at all.

"Do you mind if I move to one of the booths?" Jacob asked kindly. "Mr. Forbes and I both have paperwork to look at."

Nancy perked up. "Lex Forbes?" she asked.

Jacob blinked. "Yes, you know him?"

"Yeah, he's Ashanti's cousin. He's the most well-known PI in Atlanta." The world was so small when you got right down to it.

"Ashanti?"

"My chef. She served you when you came in."

Jacob looked aghast. "She was your chef? Damn, I'm sorry... wait," he said, taking in the empty pub. "Are you guys even open?"

Nancy laughed. This man was so polite. "No, but don't worry."

So, he was having Ava-Rose tracked down by a pro? Good thinking. But Nancy had this nagging feeling. Did Jacob want to find his money and jewels or did he really just want to find Ava-Rose herself? Was he holding out hope that she'd been somehow coerced into these crimes? And if so, why on earth did Nancy care so much?

Chapter 6

*W*hen Jacob had awoken that morning, he'd known it was going to be a day filled with surprises, but this he could never have predicted. Nancy Cooper was a grown, intelligent woman who owned and ran her own establishment in their hometown. She also happened to be drop-dead gorgeous. Jacob tried to take all of this information in stride. Still, the fact that she was also so inquisitive meant he was trying to balance being overtired and keeping her attention by answering her questions.

He liked looking at her. She was very tall, almost his height, with sandy-blonde hair and large, keen eyes that offered so much understanding that it moved him. When she was younger, she had been all arms and legs—awkward and a bit gangly with a mouth full of braces. Now, she could grace a Parisian catwalk if she so desired. She was also incredibly down-to-earth. He hadn't wanted to end their conversation, but needed to focus on his meeting with Lex Forbes.

True to his word, Ed Billings had dispatched the infamous PI to Blairsville. And today, they would meet to discuss next steps. Jacob was grateful. He was so tired of checking Ava-Rose's social media only to see the same pictures, no new information at all. It made him feel desperate and pathetic. How unfair was that? Here he was, the one lied to and stolen from, and yet, he was feeling like a loser.

Jacob leaned back against the cherrywood banquette and pulled the files from his briefcase, leafing through them nervously. He had not known what Lex would need, so he brought everything he could think of. His head ached. Ava-Rose stealing from him was one thing, but potential industrial espionage was another. He could hear his father now berating him for being so stupid by letting a strange woman into their lives this way. This would be a tough blow considering the damage Anita had done. Of course, that wasn't really comparing apples to apples. Anita had been considered family by all of them. And it would not do any good to call Bill Sweetwood a hypocrite—he'd never see it and certainly would never admit to it.

"Jacob Sweetwood?" came a voice beside him.

Jacob turned to see the private investigator in the flesh. Lex Forbes was a Black man in his early-forties dressed in dark jeans with a black t-shirt and blazer. He was shorter in stature with broad shoulders and a shaved head. His mien was serious, but not unkind. He appeared to be the kind of no-nonsense person that his line of work demanded.

"That's me," Jacob said, standing to shake the man's hand and indicating for him to join him at the table. "It's a pleasure to meet you, Mr. Forbes."

"Please," he replied. "Call me Lex."

Lex sat down and brought out a slim file folder. Opening it to the first document, he withdrew a photograph of Ava-Rose arm in arm with a pale-faced man with thinning black hair who appeared to be in his mid-thirties. The two were both dressed in trench coats and dark sunglasses. Jacob assumed the man was Dax Piper, and Lex confirmed as much.

"I understand that Mr. Billings has filled you in a little on the nature of Dax Piper's relationship with Ava-Rose," he began.

Jacob nodded. "A little."

"Okay, we can circle back to that. Today, I want to get more information on your relationship with Ms. Billings. Is that all right with you?"

Jacob swallowed hard. "Sure."

Lex pulled out his phone and placed it on the table between them. "I'm going to record this," he said, pressing the record button. "So, Ava-Rose Billings, when did you meet her?"

Jacob recounted the brief and intense nature of his relationship with Ava-Rose. Saying it all out loud like this offered some perspective. Things had moved quickly—very quickly. He realized that she had so often said all the right things. She wore clothes that he liked, styled her hair to his preference. It was almost... studied. Jacob said so out loud.

Lex shrugged. "That's because it was. I have reason to believe she had been following your tastes on social media for months before you two even met. Your emails were probably hacked as well. I would highly recommend changing all of your passwords."

Jacob felt the sting of that. She'd been studying him? For months?

"Hey, man," said Lex with sympathy. "I know this has gotta be hard. I just... it's important that I deliver the facts to you as cleanly as possible, okay? I am not at all trying to be cruel. But it will really help the investigation if we can both be honest with one another."

Jacob nodded. "It's fine," he said. "I just can't believe what an idiot I was."

Lex shook his head. "Not at all. Dax Piper is a genius when it comes to manipulation, control, and getting what he wants. All of this only proves you're a good, trusting person. But we should keep going. How much did you tell Ava-Rose about your business?"

"I told her everything," replied Jacob. "I mean, I would tell her about my day, about meetings, new products, employee matters—you name it. She had this way of asking questions. Before I knew it, I'd told her ten times more than I had intended when the conversation began."

"Can you give me an example?" asked Lex.

Jacob nodded. "Sure. One time, I came home from work and told her about a really successful meeting I'd had with one of our product developers. She wanted to know his name so I told her. And by the end of the conversation, I had told everything I knew about the man, and Ava-Rose talked me into inviting the guy and his wife over for dinner."

Lex leaned back pensively, rubbing his chin while he jotted down some notes. "Let's fast-forward. Do you know what caused Ava-Rose to leave so suddenly?"

Jacob narrowed his eyebrows. "No, I've been wondering why since she left. Recently, I've simply assumed she'd gotten what she needed, but I don't know for sure."

Lex closed his notebook and steepled his hands on the table between them. "Anita was onto her. Did you know that?"

"What?" exclaimed Jacob. "Are you serious? How do you know this?"

Lex scratched his cheek and looked away. He appeared to be weighing whether or not to tell Jacob the truth of his methods. "Let's just say I know people in the right places who owe me favors. I was able to gain access to Anita's phone after her death. Turns out, she had software installed that noted whenever there were numerous failed password attempts. She was able to trace these to an old laptop of yours and that caused her to do even more digging on Ava-Rose."

"Even more?"

"Yes," replied Lex. "It appears Anita did background checks on all of the Sweetwood family's paramours. She—shrewdly—saw something like this coming."

"Wow," was all Jacob could utter.

"It seems her only mistake was confronting Ava-Rose when she really should have hired someone to handle an investigation."

Jacob was piecing this all together. "So, you're saying that Ava-Rose never actually got so far as to gain any information on the Staple Syrup?"

Lex shook his head. "No, I'm not saying that—not yet anyway. She did gain access to a few encrypted files. It will take my guy a day or two to tell us what's in them."

"Okay," said Jacob. "That's a start. I mean, the only people who know the process and ingredients in full are myself, my dad, and our head chemist, Bryan Ames."

"Ah, yes," Lex said, opening his notebook again and jotting down Bryan's name. "He's next on my list. I'm not sure about interviewing your father. My take on him is that he will just lie to me."

This made Jacob laugh out loud. "Yeah, that's a fair assessment. But also, he knows nothing about this. I haven't told him yet."

Lex looked confused. "You don't think Anita told him?"

"No, I don't. We learned after she passed that she kept a lot of things from him—from all of us. She took on way too much."

It was unfortunate, but Jacob wasn't going to be able to avoid it much longer. He would have to talk to his father about Ava-Rose, about the Dax Piper connection—everything. When he'd left for New Zealand, all he'd told his family was that he was going to track her down. No one cared because no one really liked her and in hindsight, this should have been a red flag. Only, he never really considered his taste the same as anyone else's in his family. And Ava-Rose had sworn that, in time, she'd charm them all. As far as Bill Sweetwood was concerned, these were personal losses for Jacob and not anything for him to worry about. Now though, the stakes were much higher, and Bill was going to lose his mind.

Jacob reached for the photo of Ava-Rose and Dax. "Do you know where they are right now?"

"As far as I know, Dax hasn't left Auckland in months," said Lex. "This photo is from last year. As for Ava-Rose, seems she's still in New Zealand, but I don't know exactly where. And I doubt she'll remain there much longer."

"Oh?"

Lex leaned forward. "Has she contacted you?"

Jacob narrowed his eyes. "I beg your pardon?" he asked incredulously.

"Sorry, man. I have to ask," said Lex. "She had a hold on you, and if Dax has decided to cut her loose, her next step will be to come running back to you. I can pretty much guarantee that."

"Well, good for her," Jacob huffed. "She stole from me! Lied to me for crying out loud! If she dared to call me or show her face, I'd be calling the cops immediately."

Lex nodded but was unconvinced. "It's easy to say that now. You're angry." He gathered all his papers together and put them back in the folders, preparing to leave. "If you want my advice, be prepared. This girl has proven she is a liar and a fairly effective manipulator. My guess is she will stop at nothing to save her skin."

"Her parents have money. She can go home to them," countered Jacob.

"Listen, man," Lex began. "Ava-Rose Billings thrives on drama. There is no drama for her in going back home, only defeat. You need to do some reading up on toxic, selfish people, my friend. It's incredible to me that you're thirty-one years old and still have such an optimistic view of the world."

The comment stung, but Jacob shook it off. "I dunno," he said wearily. "I loved her."

Lex nodded. "Of course."

Both men stood and shook hands. They agreed to meet again in two days, by which time Lex hoped to have the encrypted files opened and analyzed.

Ashanti walked up just then and embraced her cousin. "You didn't tell me you were in town! My mama's gonna have a fit. You have to come to Sunday dinner."

Lex colored. It was amusing to Jacob to see him in this light. "I'm sorry, baby cousin," he told her, kissing her temple. "It's been a busy few weeks. But yes, I will be there. Tell my auntie I can't wait to have some of her homemade biscuits."

Ashanti laughed and pulled out her phone. "Oh no, Alexander Byron Forbes. We're gonna call her right now so you can tell her yourself. You know damn well my mama doesn't take kindly to second-hand news."

Jacob watched them as they walked off and felt a pang of jealousy. He barely knew his cousins, and he felt so distant from his siblings lately. Keith had always been a mess—overly emotional and entitled. Jacob could not understand his approach to life in the least. All the partying, the women, the drinking and drugs—how was any of it not losing its lustre by now? One would hope that his recent arrest would clean up his thinking and make him reconsider his life, but Jacob sincerely doubted it.

As for Zena, he loved her more than he could possibly express. He thought of and worried about her all the time. He also kept her at arm's length. It wasn't easy to explain why except that he was afraid of hurting her. Perhaps this wasn't a reasonable fear. As Ava-Rose liked to remind him, Zena was not a child. But he had the fear all the same. And he had no idea how to undo it. He made a mental note to call his sister soon and check in on her. This wall he'd built was selfish. If he was going to move forward and ease this heartache, he would have to let someone in.

Chapter 7

*J*t was mid-afternoon before the after-work/dinner rush when Nancy decided she needed some air and to stretch her legs. Normally, she'd just head to the gym and run the treadmill or go to her apartment to do some yoga, but today she found herself wandering the small downtown of Blairsville. It was the late days of October, and the breeze had yet to turn cool. She could walk without a sweater and wouldn't work up a sweat.

The air was fresh, and she could see the mountains and woods for miles around. She took a deep breath and admired the view. Ahead, she could see vultures circling what must have been some carrion in the forest. A distant mist shrouded the trees in a comforting fog. The mixture of yellow and orange and red and green was postcard-worthy. Always lamenting a too-short summer, how did she manage to forget every year about the beauty of these months?

As she walked up Blue Ridge Street, she rounded the corner when a painting in a storefront window caught her eye. She had to do a double-take. The painting was of a man—handsome, in his thirties wearing a navy-blue suit and white dress shirt with a gold-colored tie. He was standing against a blue-green wall, looking off to his right. The cut of his jaw was severe, his look pensive, but the man's identity was unmistakable. It was Jacob.

Nancy looked up. She was standing in front of Zena Sweetwood's art gallery. *Did Zena paint this?* Nancy wondered. The painting was bold and stirred an emotion in her that she couldn't name. It made her feel like the subject of the painting was cold-hearted, haughty, and dismissive—nothing like Jacob at all. Would Zena paint something like this of her own brother?

She decided to go into the gallery and get a better look. It had been a long time since Nancy had a meaningful conversation with Zena. They were friends in their younger days but had since drifted apart. Zena came to The Fox and Fig every now and then, but they mostly exchanged pleasantries.

And then there was the brief relationship between Zena and Nancy's brother, Max. This was something that Nancy assumed neither of them talked of publicly (she knew for certain that Max didn't), though everyone knew about. She decided to act clueless. If Zena wanted to talk about it, then so be it. Otherwise, she'd rather not discuss her brother's love life.

Zena was standing on a ladder at the back of the gallery sorting through frames. She heard the bell on the front door and called out without turning around, "Hi! Begging your pardon, I'll be with you in a moment."

"Take your time," called Nancy. She wandered over to a bin of prints lined with cardboard and began to leaf through them. It seemed the gallery was lower on stock than normal, presumably because the increased traffic from the recent Sorghum Festival. Nancy was happy to see it. She was always rooting for her fellow local businesses—especially the ones owned by women.

"Nancy? Oh my gosh!" called Zena, crossing the room to see her. "It's been a minute! You, like, never come in here."

Zena looked stunning in a fitted aubergine dress and black stilettos. Her black hair was slicked into a neat bun and the only jewelry she wore was a string of pearls. Nancy sighed at the sight of her and instantly felt insecure about the blue jeans, gray t-shirt, and white sneakers she was wearing.

"Hey," Nancy replied, leaning in to give her an awkward hug. "I know, I know. I should definitely come here more, even just to browse. I love paintings, and you've got some really cool ones at the moment."

"Well, my inventory is shifting now that the festival is over," she said. "It'll be less Georgian landscape watercolors and more portraits and modern art."

Nancy rubbed her hands together, feeling out of her depth. "Cool, cool."

Zena observed her strangely. "I don't know why you're acting like you know nothing about art."

"Probably because I don't!" she laughed.

"Okay, but it's more than knowing what things are called and the various painters and eras. You have a keen eye. I absolutely love all the Civil War-era paintings of couples in love you've got at The Fox and Fig. And the way you have them lit. It's all very classic and swanky. I really couldn't have done it better myself."

Nancy colored at this praise. "Wow, thank you. That means a lot coming from you," she said. "So, um, the reason I'm here. I was walking past your shop and saw the painting in the window..."

"Oh yeah!" exclaimed Zena. "Isn't it striking? I've been getting a ton of folks walking in and asking about it. And I only just put it in the window yesterday!"

Nancy narrowed her brows. "Right, well it reminds me of someone..."

"Really?"

Was Zena being serious? Could she truly not see it? "Yes, in fact, it reminds me so much of a certain person that I was wondering if *you* painted it."

Zena laughed out loud. "Oh, wow! Nancy, you're a riot! I can paint, but nothing like that. That's not even close to my style," she said. "So, but wait... who does it remind you of?"

"Jacob!" Nancy blurted. "Your brother, Jacob! Can you really not see it?"

Zena looked confused. She started walking out the door and motioned for Nancy to follow. They both turned and stood before the storefront window. Zena clutched her pearls. "Well, I'll be damned..." she said, softly trailing off.

"Right?" exclaimed Nancy, relieved she wasn't crazy or seeing things. "How did I not see this?"

Nancy shrugged. "I don't know. Do you know the artist? Did they tell you what it's called or give you any information about it?"

Zena shook her head. "I-uh, let me think. It's from a curator in Sydney, Australia. And...well, they just sent it to me."

"Does that not happen often?"

"Maybe in New York," replied Zena. "But not in small-town Georgia. My head has been spinning since the start of the festival; I didn't even give it a second thought. Let me go pull it up in the database."

Australia, thought Nancy. That's suspiciously close to New Zealand. She followed Zena to the back of the store and waited while she pulled up the information on the painting.

"Here we go," said Zena. "It's called *After She Left Him*. The artist is anonymous, and the dealer was a gentleman named Barron Zhu."

Nancy was disappointed there wasn't more information. "And this Mr. Zhu is in Australia?"

"That's what the note said," replied Zena. "And the shipping documents say that, too."

"Hmm."

"Well, the note actually said, 'For you, Sweetwood.'"

Strange. But maybe this was what Ava-Rose did—call Jacob by his surname. "Interesting," Nancy said.

"Why? Do you think you know the artist?"

"I think I might," replied Nancy. "I think it's Ava-Rose."

Zena went white. "What? Why?"

Nancy rubbed her forehead. "I don't know. I just have this feeling. Everything around her is so sketchy and weird."

"Everything around that woman is downright criminal! She's a liar and a thief," shouted Zena who then took a deep breath. "Sorry, I have zero chill when it comes to her. And listen, I get why this is giving you a red flag, but I just don't see the motive or reasoning. First, do we even know if she paints? And second, why go to all this trouble when she could just text him some sob story?"

"She could have had it commissioned. And as for the rest, I think she's a con artist through and through. So, if she thinks something will work to her benefit—even in the long run—I see her doing it."

Zena considered this, leaning back in her desk chair. "Thank God they were only together for like eight months. I was worried they'd marry. Did you ever meet her?"

Nancy shook her head. "No. You?"

"Yeah. Once." replied Zena. "A cold shiver ran up my spine when she shook my hand. I have never felt so off-put—creeped-out even—by a person in my entire life. It was bizarre. And then to have it be someone my brother claimed to be in love with? Ugh!"

"I hear you. I love my brother's girlfriend, but when she broke his heart all those years ago, I wanted to punch her in the face." Nancy's jaw tightened even just at the memory. She never realized how protective she was of Max until someone hurt him.

"So, wait. If you've never met Ava-Rose, how do you know about her? Where are you getting this sketchy vibe?"

Nancy's stomach did a flip. She should have expected Zena to question her about this, but she hadn't. How could she tell her that she'd seen the hurt in her brother's face and known he'd been played? How could she explain that she had pieced together all the rumors and social media posts and her one conversation with Jacob to arrive at this conclusion? She felt like she was finally listening to her intuition in the way she had not with Thomas. She was at last learning to trust herself. But communicating this to Zena was a whole other thing.

Finally, Nancy decided to tell the truth, leaving out the gut instinct stuff. "Your brother was at The Fox and Fig this morning. I spoke with him a little and then with all the rumors... She sounds horrible."

Zena accepted this explanation and nodded. "She really is. So, what should we do?"

Nancy considered. "Can you get Jacob to come down here? Come up with some excuse?"

"Well, sure. I was just going to take a pic of the painting and send it to him. You think that's not enough?"

"I'm wondering if you'd learn more from seeing his reaction in real-time. He strikes me as being very protective of you, so he may not tell you the whole story if indeed this does involve Ava-Rose."

Zena gave Nancy a surprised look. "You sure seem to know my brother well. Did you guys ever...?"

"Heavens, no!" Nancy shot back. "I just have experience with liars. And I feel a kind of kinship with your brother over this, I guess."

Nancy was aware she was very attracted to Jacob. Ashanti was aware she was very attracted to Jacob. Were her feelings on full display to everyone she met? Was it as plain as day on her face? She had to try and play it cooler. Jacob was hurting and reeling from being so deeply deceived by someone claiming to have loved him. This was not a time for love connections.

"Okay, I'll text him to meet me here after work. He'll know something's up, but I suppose I'll think of something by then," said Zena. She rubbed her temples and sighed. "Man, that awful woman sure did a number on him. I can't even begin to describe how hard he fell for her. I've never seen him like that."

This hit Nancy in the gut, and she really wished it didn't. Like, yeah, okay! Ava-Rose is smokin' hot and probably super intelligent and great in bed and can balance ten textbooks on her head or something. She would never be in the same league. Message received!

"I should probably get back to work," Nancy said, slowly backing away. "You've got this all figured out, right?"

Zena nodded but looked unsure. "I think so. But, can I call you? I-it's just... you coming here has made me realize that my poor big brother is dealing with the emotional impact of all this on his own. Lord knows my mother is no help," she said, rolling her eyes. "I think I'd like to help him, but I don't know what to do. Can I reach out to you for support with that? Is that weird?"

Nancy smiled widely. This made total sense to her and was probably exactly how she was supposed to help. "Not at all. I'd love that. You've got my number. Call anytime."

"Thank you," Zena said, her voice catching in just the slightest way. "I don't talk to most of my family and sometimes I feel bad about that. But I always feel bad about the state of things with Jacob and I. He's such a good man, and he deserves better. Not just this business with Ava-Rose, but in general. I know people think he's a total snob who's obsessed with work and making money. But that's not it. He's reserved and kind, focused and driven."

"I see that," she replied softly. "There's a vulnerability to him that I..." Nancy stopped herself before she gave too much away. "That is, he and I had a nice talk today. I saw a different side to him."

Zena smiled and pulled Nancy in, hugging her tight. And this time, there was no awkwardness at all.

Chapter 8

*J*acob stood at his father's office door and felt like a child waiting to receive his punishment. He had worked for the family business since he was sixteen years old. Back then, he was running sample booths at local markets and grocery stores. Bill Sweetwood had always made it clear that Sweetwood Syrups came first and depended on his children to take it over when he retired or died—whichever came first.

Well, Bill was in his late-50s and showed no signs of retiring. Jacob's siblings, Zena and Keith, showed no signs of wanting anything to do with the company. For her part, Zena had a hate for nearly all of her family. And Keith? Keith was an absolute mess. He'd been enabled since he was born, and the expectations that he would do right in any area of his life had been almost non-existent.

So, it all fell to Jacob. He was mostly okay with this. At least, he thought so. The truth was, he'd never let himself consider anything else. He knew from an early age to not disappoint his father and that he was somehow different than his brother and sister in this sense. Though Zena was frustratingly headstrong at times, he had to admit he was envious of her independent endeavors. She was doing what she wanted to do while Jacob hadn't even considered his own desires or life purpose.

"Come in," his father beckoned from the other side of the door.

Jacob entered the room and sat down in a brown leather chair in front of the large and imposing oak desk. His father kept his gaze on his computer screen, not looking up to greet his son.

"You wanted to see me?" Jacob inquired.

Bill cleared his throat. "Yes," he answered, finally turning to face Jacob. "How was your trip to New Zealand? Did you find what you were looking for?"

This was a typically cryptic question from Bill Sweetwood. On the surface, the inquiry itself appeared to be harmless, but in actuality, the man was trying to gauge what you thought he knew and how much you were willing to disclose in an effort to unnerve you.

"It was a pleasant trip," Jacob said, leaning back in his chair and steepling his hands in front of him.

Bill smiled, not unlike the Cheshire cat. "You know, Anita was very thorough."

Jacob nodded. "She was also incredibly warm and nurturing. I miss her."

"Yes," acknowledged Bill, wincing. "I know you loved her. We all did. But what I'm referring to was her work ethic. Since her death, I've had a couple of our people in IT going through her computers and mobile devices. It seems she had a file on your girlfriend, Ava-Rose."

"Ex-girlfriend," Jacob corrected.

Bill gave a curt nod. "Right, ex-girlfriend," he said and then paused. Jacob was unmoved.

"But you don't seem surprised," he said, assessing his son. "When did you find out that Ava-Rose was working with Dax Piper to gain intel into the product development of Staple Syrup?"

Jacob swallowed, not wanting to give his dad one ounce of emotion. "Her father told me back in Wellington a few days ago. When did you find out?"

Bill tilted his head in a way that communicated his son's question was ridiculous. "Jacob, I don't answer to you."

Jacob's charade of confidence in front of his father was fading fast. Guilt rose in his gut, and he could feel his traitorous body begin to sweat. "I simply wanted to find out more details before I came to you with this," he said finally.

"Jacob, I know you've sat in board meetings and product development conferences; you've looked at charts and graphs. But do you understand the gravity of what we have here with Staple Syrup?"

"Is that a trick question?" Jacob asked weakly.

Bill let out a sarcastic laugh. "Jesus, it's worse than I thought," he spat. "I knew you were distracted by that hussy, but I didn't know she'd taken your brain along with your dignity. Staple Syrup is a goddamn gold mine, Jacob. Our last market research session showed that nine out of ten people could not tell the difference between our product and maple syrup both in its raw form and in baking."

Jacob recalled something about this revelation, but his focus was more on day-to-day operations. And yes, his mind had been distracted both upon meeting and loving Ava-Rose, and then, on losing her.

"Do you know how many diabetics there are in the world? How many everyday people there are obsessed with low-carb diets? This product will change everything. And *we* made it. *We* have the recipe. But all of this could be lost because you," he shouted, "my idiotic son, fell for a pretty face." He slammed his fist on the desk.

Jacob swallowed hard but said nothing. The sight of his father in such righteous anger made him again feel like a little child. He retreated into freeze mode, suddenly wanting only to survive this conversation.

"You've disappointed me, Jacob. And not just a little," Bill said sternly. He wasn't even looking him in the eyes at this point. "I've made a decision, and you're the first person outside of our board of directors who is hearing it, so I hope you feel the gravity of that."

Jacob looked at his father sharply. "You met with the board without me?"

Bill didn't skip a beat. "Like I said earlier, Jacob, I don't answer to you. I'm the majority shareholder. You are an employee."

"I'm your son!" shouted Jacob. "I've devoted fifteen years of my life to you and to this company. How can that not count for anything?"

His father gritted his teeth and nearly spit his words. "What counts right now is what you risked! Your actions display your selfishness, your lack of focus, and your weakness. I cannot waste any more time assuming that you will be my heir apparent. You would think having three children would increase my odds of having a lineage I can depend on, someone to take the reins. But all three of you are nothing but spoiled disappointments."

The air was tense and heavy between them. It was dawning on Jacob how toxic his father was and always had been. There was no reasoning with him. And his priorities were so clearly messed up. Money, power, image—these were what mattered. No wonder his mother acted the way she did. Who could thrive in an environment like that? At least he, Zena, and Keith had had Anita for love and emotional support. Patricia had no one.

Bill took a deep breath and leaned back in his chair. "I've decided to sell the company as a whole to Swansea Syrups. To me, there is no point continuing if I cannot depend on my legacy. Best to go out on a high note."

Jacob's eyes flared. "You can't be serious."

"I'm perfectly serious. And the board agrees. We will be making a formal announcement in the coming days. The company will be up for grabs to the highest bidder, and we all suspect that to be Swansea."

Bill's words felt like a punch to the gut, and Jacob knew he was finally seeing his father for who he had always been. There had never been love, closeness, or even respect—only expectation. It was incredible the void that Anita's absence had left. She had been the link between him and his parents—a nurturing presence always ready with a smile, a hug, and a reassuring word. It pained Jacob to think of all that she had been hiding, all that she'd had to navigate for her entire life. He had been so narrow is his view of her, such a child thinking she existed only for him and his family. He kicked himself for not helping her, for not seeing how deep she had sunk to protect all that she loved.

Somehow, the contrast of his father and this incredible woman who not only cared for his family but was also responsible for so much of the success of Sweetwood Syrups gave him pause. So much had changed. Did he really want to follow his father into this line of work? And how could it be that this was the first time he asked that question? Bill Sweetwood was cold and calculating. Not only had he clearly made up his mind, but he had not even wanted Jacob's input or opinion. What was left for him in this company but money? And how much did he even care about that at this point?

Jacob looked his father in the eye. His chest was tight, and his pulse raced. It occurred to him in that moment that he could not recall ever telling his father how he really felt or what he actually thought. He had always chosen his words carefully, had observed his father closely trying to suss out what would gain his approval. Knowing this made Jacob feel nauseous, but it also offered him a temporary kind of bravery. He stood to his full height.

"Good," he said. "Sell it. Sell the company that Anita built. She's not here anymore and nothing is the same without her—especially this goddamned place! You are a sad, shallow old man with no love in your life. I don't want that for myself. So, thank you, father," he spat. "Thank you for helping me see where my career was headed so that I can know this moment for what it really is: the day my life became my own again."

Bill Sweetwood scoffed. "Pretty speech, Jacob. Well done," he said and gave a slow golf clap for three beats. "Now, get out of my office."

Jacob turned and left with his heart in his throat. Sure, his father had mocked him, but there was no mistaking the look on his face. Jacob hit a nerve; he spoke the truth. And that triumph was so much more satisfying than any kind of succession could have ever been.

It had taken Jacob twenty minutes to pack up his office into two legal boxes. He left the large tropical plant for whatever poor sap would end up moving in. As he passed by his secretary Glenda's desk, he stopped. Reaching into his wallet, he pulled out four-hundred-dollar bills and handed them to her.

"Thank you for everything," he said, looking at her shocked and slightly worried face. "You have my personal cell. Feel free to use it anytime."

"Uh, Mr. Sweetwood, is everything okay?" she asked, her voice unsteady.

"Everything is great, Glenda," he replied. "Never better!"

And with that, he turned and walked out of the building. His mind and body were buzzing. He was a mixture of panic, relief, elation, and fear. Each emotion volleyed for his attention, and it was dizzying. What had he done? Did he really just leave the only job he had ever known? Yes. And did this mean he walked out on any kind of inheritance? Maybe. He would have to think about all of that later.

Just then, Jacob's phone buzzed. He looked at the screen; it was Zena.

"Hey," he said, surprise clear in his voice. She rarely called. "Everything okay?"

"Hey!" Zena replied, a pep in her voice that Jacob found unnerving. Did she know about their dad selling the company? "Yeah, for sure. Everything is totally fine. I was wondering if you could come down to the gallery after you're done work. I, uh, I just wanted to talk. Maybe see how your trip to New Zealand was."

"Oh, um, sure," he said, raking his fingers through his hair. "I'm actually done now so, I'll head over."

He hung up the phone feeling like there was no way this day could get any weirder.

Chapter 9

*N*ancy stooped and leaned over the bar. Drumming her fingers on the smooth cherrywood surface, she felt both bored (the bar was absolutely dead) and anxious (had Jacob seen the painting?). She had forgotten the Baptist church down the road was having a spaghetti dinner to raise money for the local food bank. It was going to be dead all night. Nancy could hear Ashanti in the kitchen laughing and singing with her staff, and it made her smile. At least someone was enjoying the lack of customers. She would most likely end up sending them all home early and closing up.

By six o'clock, Nancy had finished polishing the bar, wiping down all the tables, toweling off the glasses, and cleaning the menus. It was time to call it a night.

"We're gonna head out, boss!" called Ashanti from the front door, reading Nancy's mind. "I'm taking these boys here to my mama's for dinner. You wanna join us?"

"No, thank you," she said graciously. "I think I'm just gonna close up here and head home to have a nice, long bath."

Ashanti told her friends to wait and walked toward Nancy. "You okay?" she asked with a genuine look of concern.

"I'm good, Ash," she said. "I promise."

She watched the group of them leave, all joyful and excited, and wished she'd been more in the mood for a family dinner like that. As it was, she felt like she'd only bring them down. And thirty minutes later, she was slipping off her shoes in her apartment about to flop herself down onto the sofa when she heard someone tapping on the door to the pub downstairs. Nancy rolled her eyes. *Of course*, she thought. *Not a soul all evening and now the people would start to pour in.*

Except that it wasn't people; it was one person. When Nancy went to her window to call down to the knocker, she was surprised to see Jacob peering in the glass door, his hands cupped around his eyes to get a better look.

"Hey!" she called from above. "Back again so soon?"

Jacob looked up and waved. "Hi!" he said. "Did you guys close early?"

"Yeah, First Baptist is having its annual spaghetti dinner. The whole town is there."

"Oh," Jacob replied, looking somewhat deflated.

Nancy felt a pang in her gut and immediately wanted to make things better for him. "Why don't you come up? I've got a slow cooker of pulled pork and can fry up some green tomatoes."

Jacob nodded, and she made her way downstairs to meet him.

"Thank you for this, Nancy," he said as he followed her up the stairs. "I'm not particularly hungry, but I just couldn't be alone tonight."

She led Jacob into her place and motioned for him to take a seat at her breakfast bar. "No problem. I'm happy to keep you company." It was humbling to notice her body's reaction to his presence. Her stomach was doing flips and her pulse raced. Could he tell? Was she radiating her ridiculous crush outwards and obviously?

He threw up his hands as he sat down. "I'm a Southern gentleman through and through. Honest. This was not a play or a trick to be alone with you. I thought I'd be drowning my sorrows in a tall glass of cranberry juice served by a pretty bartender alongside half of Blairsville."

Nancy blushed in spite of herself and smiled ear to ear. He called her pretty! "Well, now you can have that same cranberry juice served to you by a bar *owner* in sweats who needs a haircut."

Jacob laughed. "I'll take it," he said. "And don't think I didn't catch your correction. You're absolutely right. You are the owner of my new favorite pub."

She smiled widely and poured them each a glass of cranberry juice. "Cheers to that!" she said, clinking his glass. "So, do you feel like telling me why you don't want to be alone tonight?"

He lowered his head into his hands and rubbed his temples as he let out an exhausted sigh. "Nancy, I've had the strangest day."

She stood in front of him as the picture of patience and ease, but within she only wanted to fly across the bar and hold him tight, kiss his forehead, and tell him everything was going to be all right. The feeling came upon her so fast and furious that it startled her. Nancy Cooper was one-hundred-percent falling for Jacob Sweetwood. In the end, she merely uttered: "Okay, tell me more."

Jacob took a long sip of his drink and began. "Well, it started with my father telling me that he is selling Sweetwood Syrups."

"Holy crap!" Nancy blurted. "Wait, can he do that? Don't you guys have a board of directors?"

He nodded. "Yes, we do. And they're all for it, apparently. My darling dad explained that he told them how weak and stupid I was to fall in love with someone who was only with me to spy on the company."

Nancy's jaw dropped.

"I know," he acknowledged with a wink. "And we still don't know how far she got, or how much she knows. My father blames me for the entire thing. But instead of coming to me and talking to me about it, he went behind my back and did this," he tapped his index finger to the bar for emphasis. "The company that has been promised to me since I was a teenager—gone. And there is nothing I can do about it," Jacob said.

"Wow," managed Nancy, still in shock.

"Yes, wow. So, I quit. I walked right out the door without even looking back. And it feels... liberating."

Nancy smiled, reassured by his apparent confidence. "Okay! Well, that's good!"

A look of worry washed over Jacob. "I think it must be, but I also have nothing to fall back on. This was my life path. This was my big plan. I've lost so much in the past few months that I'm...I'm spinning a bit," he said, his voice cracking.

Her heart sank. So he wasn't that confident after all—not yet at least. "Jacob, I'm so sorry. You don't deserve this."

"I don't know if that's true, but I really appreciate you saying so."

Nancy leaned down and reached out for his hand. He gave it to her and let out a long-held breath. "You deserve better," she repeated.

"I'm naïve," he countered.

"You were deceived, possibly by an expert," she said.

Jacob spoke as though he hadn't heard her. "You know, what? It actually helps knowing Ava-Rose is a liar and a cheat. It helps in the sense that getting over her has been much easier than I feared it would be. But the blow is still huge," he admitted with a shrug. "It makes a man question everything to be so deluded, so deceived. I thought I was smart and that I could read people well. You really wouldn't believe how many times I've pat myself on the back for knowing whether I could trust someone or not. You know who they came to when it was time to interview job applicants? Me. Because I could suss out a faker no problem. Well," he laughed harshly. "That's all a bunch of garbage now."

Nancy stroked his hand with her thumb. It was a small gesture, yet so intimate. She surprised herself at how forward she was being. But it was what she wanted to do, how she wanted to comfort him. She needed him to understand that he was seen and cared for. So, if he wouldn't *hear* her, maybe she would have to *show* him.

Slowly, she could sense his body rise and fall with a breath that was warm and wanting more. He began to draw tiny circles in her palm, raising his eyes to hers with a look that said at once, "Thank you," and "Where have you been my entire life?"

Jacob stood and walked slowly around the breakfast bar to meet her. His hands reached tentatively for her waist, and he pulled her to him. Nancy arched her neck to look at him. Her lips parted slightly as an invitation, and he moved his hands to the small of her back.

"I'm going to kiss you now," he said.

She nodded slowly, pressing herself into him, wanting to be as close to him as possible. He smelled incredible—like earl gray tea wrapped in leather and smoke. He was muscled and firm, but his touch was tender. And the kiss... Nancy felt a sigh leave her body as she allowed his mouth to claim hers. The circles he had been drawing in her palm he now drew on her back, and the sensation was overwhelming.

Jacob drew back from her slightly. "You don't drink, so I'll never see you actually drunk. But I think the look in your eyes right now is pretty close."

Nancy giggled. "You got your confidence back pretty quick."

He shrugged. "It's you," he said, his voice heavy. "You remind me of the man I am, I think."

She wrapped her arms around his neck and pulled him down, kissing him full and soft. It was her answer. *Not I think; I know*, she was saying.

Jacob shifted to look at her. "I love this, and I don't want to stop, but I should," he said with a note of apology in his voice.

Nancy untethered her arms from him and took a step back. "Of course," she whispered, unable to hide her disappointment.

"My mind is a mess today," he muttered, shuffling his feet.

"It's fine," assured Nancy. "I get it. And I love this, too."

Jacob smiled. "You do, don't you? Get it, I mean. I feel like I can tell you anything. The fact that you're gorgeous is just an awesome bonus."

Nancy laughed and blushed. "Okay, you sit back down while I cook. I'm listening though. Tell me more about your dad," she said as she brought out the cutting board.

"Oh God," he grimaced. "He is the last person I want to talk about. What a waste of my life trying to get approval from that man. I didn't even think about another career. How pathetic is that? I put my head down and set to doing whatever he wanted from the time I was sixteen years old."

"We all do this, Jacob," she said, cutting thick slices of tomato. "We're all trying to get our parents' attention in some way, either by trying to please them or trying to piss them off. You're not that special." This last bit she said while winking pointedly at him.

He chuckled.

"Seriously though," she continued. "I took nutrition classes in my early twenties, not because I had an interest, but because my parents were starting to eat healthy. They were taking all kinds of supplements, juicing, trying different diets. And I wanted to be an expert. I wanted them to come to me for answers."

Jacob smiled. "That's actually really sweet."

"I mean, I guess so," Nancy shrugged. "But it was not something I wanted to do or was interested in at all, so it didn't last."

He nodded, fiddling with his glass of juice. "Well, I'm happy you found your true calling. I hope I can find mine."

She let that sentiment hang in the air. It seemed obvious to her that he would find his calling. Jacob was so clearly smart and talented and capable. But just as he had admitted earlier, his mind was a muddle right now. It would take some time clearing out the cobwebs of old alliances and spoiled hopes to settle into this new life and awareness.

After a moment, Nancy asked, "Anything else strange happen today?" Zena was supposed to have called him down to the gallery, but he hadn't mentioned it yet, and she'd had no word from Zena. Maybe the whole thing had been a coincidence. Was it possible that painting had nothing to do with Ava-Rose at all?

"Oh! Yes. This was so weird," he said. "My sister Zena called the second I walked out of Sweetwood Syrups. She asked me to come down to the gallery. She never does that."

Nancy made her best attempt at pretending she had no idea what he was talking about. "Oh?"

"So, I get down there, and you know what's in the front window?"

"What was it?"

"My painting!" he exclaimed.

Nancy stopped chopping the peppers for the garden salad and looked at him in complete surprise. "Wait, what? What do you mean by *your* painting?"

"I mean *my* painting—you know, a piece of art that I made by using paints and a brush on a canvas," he replied drily.

"That's what I figured you meant, but I had no idea you could paint! And so well!"

"So well? How do you know I paint well?" he asked.

Nancy froze for a second and then recovered. "Well, it's in the front window of your sister's gallery. It has to be good."

Now it was his turn to wink at her. "Nice save," he said, grabbing a piece of avocado from her chopping board and popping it into his mouth. "Zena told me all about your little meeting today. It's okay, really. I appreciate the concern."

She let out a sigh of relief. "Thank you," she said offering him another slice of avocado from the side of her knife. "So, what happened? How did your painting make it to Zena's gallery? Why all the mystery?"

Jacob pushed back from the breakfast bar and sat up straight. "When I left Blairsville, I didn't go directly to Wellington. I stopped in Sydney for a few days," he said, his voice now more serious. "Remember, I was devastated but also hell-bent on revenge. Still, this voice in the back of my head kept telling me to slow down, to collect my thoughts. The only way for me to do that is to paint. Anita signed me up for classes when I was seven, and it's just always worked."

"That is so sweet," Nancy said softly.

He smiled and continued. "Yeah, she was complicated; I know that. I know she has done horrible things. But the side of her that I knew was so incredibly kind."

Nancy said nothing, only offered a knowing smile.

"Anyway, I knew I couldn't paint here, and once I got to Wellington, I knew I'd want to hit the ground running. So, I booked myself a hotel room by the harbor and had some paints and canvas sent before I arrived. My intention was to paint the skyline. But somehow, it wasn't what I felt moved to do. Somehow, when I stood there and caught a glimpse of myself in the mirror on the far side of the wall, I knew I had to paint what I saw. It was a way to let the inside out—a way to feel better, if only for a moment."

Nancy reached across the space between them and caressed his cheek. Her throat was tight with emotion. She could feel so viscerally what must have come over him in that moment.

Jacob tilted his face to her touch and took a deep breath. "I loved the painting but hated it too. In my mind, it was the picture of a specific space and time—one I did not particularly ever want to see again. So, I left it there. And apparently, the maid thought I had forgotten it. She gave it to the hotel manager, but I had booked the room under a pseudonym."

"So how did they know it was you?"

He shook his head. "They didn't. The hotel manager's husband is a curator. I include my last name in everything I paint, but I make it very difficult to see. Well, he was able to see it with his special magnifier. And the two of them, now feeling so invested in getting the painting back to its mystery painter, googled 'Sweetwood' and 'paintings.'"

"And came up with Zena's gallery," said Nancy.

Jacob smiled. "Precisely."

Nancy felt a pang of disappointment. She had to admit to herself that she'd wanted Ava-Rose to somehow be involved in this, to be even more guilty. She wanted to outshine this woman in every way, and it was ridiculous. Ava-Rose had zero integrity and had so clearly treated Jacob abhorrently. Nancy needed to get her shit together and let the woman take herself down like the Hindenburg she already was.

Chapter 10

Jacob left Nancy's apartment feeling so much better. Not only was he full from an incredible meal (Nancy was a total chef in disguise), but he also found himself feeling hopeful for the first time in forever. They had kissed some more (*God, she was hot*) and that had been awesome, but it was more than that. She listened to him and genuinely seemed to care. After his disclosure about his father and then the business with the mystery artwork, she had taken the opportunity to point out to him that perhaps this hobby of painting could be more.

She was so generous with her praise; it moved him. Painting had been this secret thing, more like a coping mechanism. It never occurred to Jacob that it could be more. Of course, his sister Zena had been encouraging as well. And she had chided him for not telling her that he was still painting after all these years and had become quite good at it. For Jacob, this potential move to making money at something he loved was exciting. And if it was supported by two women he cared about, even better.

That was the truth. He had come to really care for Nancy is this short period of time. Everything about her fascinated him. From the turn of her lips when she smiled to her opinions on pretty much anything—he was riveted. Jacob was shocked at how she had been right there in his own hometown for decades and yet, he was just finally *seeing* her. He felt as though he were discovering a hidden treasure. But she wasn't gold and jewels. She was a woman. She was flesh and blood, intelligence and grace.

Jacob sat in his car outside The Fox and Fig and took a moment to calm himself down, breathe in and out. The past few days had brought a lot of news and even more change. He knew that it had not all hit him yet. But these glimpses of goodness—of Nancy and embracing the art that he loved as a possible career—this could be *why* everything came crashing down. This could be a divine intervention of sorts.

Just then, Jacob opened his eyes to the most astonishing sight.

"There you are!" mouthed Ava-Rose beyond the windshield as she smacked the hood of his car. She was smiling widely at him as if this was the best reunion either of them could ask for. Dressed in a black tube dress, a denim jacket and cowboy boots, she was a Georgian boy's dream. For Jacob though, she was a nightmare. *What on earth could she be doing here?*

He got out of the car and slammed the door shut. "What the hell, Ava-Rose?" he shouted. "How dare you show your face in this town after all you've done?"

She feigned confusion as she walked gracefully toward him, her head held high. "Babe, what do you mean? Didn't you get my note?"

Jacob was reeling. "Um, the one where you told me you were going bush and it was never going to last? Yeah, Ava, I got that note," he spat. "Of course, you didn't explain why that meant you had to steal my money and Granny Sweetwood's ruby ring, but these were details you understandably had to leave out when writing to your fake boyfriend!"

He was shaking with anger and the shock of seeing her in person. His words surprised him. He wasn't fumbling or holding back. No. He was saying exactly what was on his mind.

Ava-Rose was in front of him now and unnervingly close. He didn't like that he could smell her perfume, and he especially didn't like how the scent reminded him of kissing her neck.

"Babe, oh my goodness! I can explain everything. Let's go back to your pla—"

"No!" he shouted. "Absolutely not."

She gritted her teeth in a smile that didn't reach her eyes. "Okay," she said slowly, attempting to keep calm. "But you're going to at least let me tell you my side of the story, right?"

Jacob's veins were flush with adrenaline. He was taken aback by the fact that the woman he'd been searching for all this time was now standing in front of him, but that wasn't the whole of it. She was here, and she was calling him "babe" as if nothing had happened. He could sense the lies that she wanted to tell all around her like a cape of deception. She was here to convince him of *something*, but it was damn sure not the truth.

"Why should I?!" he demanded.

Ava-Rose took this as an invitation and stepped closer to him. "Because what we have is real. We're in love. And we owe one another the truth."

Jacob had to stifle the instinct to laugh out loud. How could she be serious? But of course, she wasn't. This was all a game to her. God, it was so good to be able to see that now! He felt as if he had woken up from a deep and ignorant sleep.

"All right, Ava," he said. "I'll bite. What is the truth?"

She smiled, a self-satisfied smile that she tried to hide by tilting her head innocently. "Can't we go somewhere and sit?" she asked. "I don't want all of Blairsville knowing our business."

This time he did laugh. "All of Blairsville already knows our business! This is a very small town, Ava-Rose. Everyone here knows you left me and stole from me."

"But I didn't steal from you, babe! You have to believe me. It was Dax. He made me take the money and the ring. He's blackmailing me."

This was such a predictable move. Jacob wanted to roll his eyes. "Oh, really?"

"Yes! Oh, my goodness, he is the worst! So mean. You wouldn't believe it, babe. He somehow got pictures of me with a married man from like over a year ago, and he's threatening to show the guy's wife!" Ava-Rose threw her hands up for emphasis. "Normally, I'd be like 'whatever,' but his wife is like super sick with cancer or something, and it just wouldn't be a good scene at all."

Jacob observed her closely. She was a good liar, that was certain. But why was she really back? What could she possibly want from him now? "So, you're not with Dax?"

She cocked an eyebrow. "Like *with* him, with him?"

He nodded.

"God, no!" she exclaimed. "Babe, he's like part of some syrup empire or something and wanted to use me to get to you. When I made it clear I wouldn't betray you like that, he demanded money. I know I should have just asked you but I panicked. I took everything in the safe. Of course, I know how smart and successful you are. You'll totally make it back. So, all in all, no harm done. Right, babe?"

Jacob stood there, speechless. She was unreal—no self-awareness, no dignity at all.

Ava-Rose stepped to him and tugged at his shirt, fluttering her eyes at him like some doe-eyed schoolgirl. "Maybe you could have me work it off?" she asked in her flirtiest voice.

Just then, Jacob heard a window shut from high above them. *Nancy. Damnit!* He tried to extricate himself from her grip. "I have to go," he said. But she wouldn't let go.

"Wait! What do you mean? We have to work this out, Jacob."

"No, we actually don't," he said.

She scoffed. "Is this because of your new girlfriend? That pale, awkward blonde? Are you for real with her, Jacob? I can't even..."

How did she even know about Nancy? He turned serious just then. "Ava-Rose, none of what you have told me changes the fact that you are a liar and a thief. You stole from me. You stole a helluva lot of money, not to mention a family heirloom. So, you will either give those things back to me, or I will have you arrested."

She pouted as if she didn't believe him. "But babe, I had to! It's like I said. And anyway, you'll make it all back."

Jacob shook his head. "Hate to break it to you, sweetheart, but I'm no longer wealthy. I quit my position at Sweetwood Syrups, and my father is most likely now taking the steps to disinherit me. Soon, I'll be flat broke."

Ava-Rose stepped back. "You what?"

"Yeah, that's right. I quit. No more money, honey. Nothing left for you to take from me. And I'm thinking of taking up painting full-time," he said, reveling in the look of complete shock on her face.

Her face went white, and her eyes turned cold. All semblance of sweetness was gone. This was the real Ava-Rose in front of him now. This was the woman he had failed to see all the months they had been together. "What the hell, Jacob?" she shouted. "Do you have any idea what you've done?"

He pulled back from her in impatience and disgust. "I don't have time for your games," he said and took his phone from his pocket. But Ava-Rose was quick. She lunged for his hand and grabbed the phone, wrestling it from his grip. They were tangled like this for a few seconds until she bent down and bit his arm. "Ahh!" he cried, finally letting go.

"You never appreciated me and never once trusted me!" she shouted backing away, holding the phone above her head. "Do you know how exhausting it was being treated like that? Well, no more, Jacob. I am out of your life forever. Don't follow me like you did in Wellington. What a psycho stalker you are. And you wanna make *me* look like the bad guy?!"

"Ava, don't!" he shouted shuffling toward her.

She was now standing over a sewer grate, and it was clear what her next move was. "You always underestimated me, Jacob. That was your biggest mistake." And with that, she dropped the phone into the sewer and ran off.

Chapter 11

*N*ancy had been all right with the shouting, but once that stopped and she saw the two of them close and the look in Jacob's eyes, she was done. She shut the window with a thud and fled to the back stairs out to where her car was parked at the rear of The Fox and Fig. How could she have done it again? How could she have seen what she wanted to see in yet another guy whose eyes and heart were elsewhere? Just when she was feeling like she had made progress, she messed up all over again.

Now, in her car driving out of the center of town, all she could think was that she had to get away. She could not face Jacob, and she certainly could not face Jacob and Ava-Rose together. That was the height of humiliation. Nancy knew she would not be able to avoid it forever, but she could at least avoid it tonight.

God, to think that only an hour ago she and Jacob had been so close—their eyes hungry for one another as they tried their best to keep their hands to themselves. But it was more than attraction, at least it had been for Nancy. And she really felt it was for Jacob, too. Just then a song came on the radio and her eyes filled with tears as she heard the familiar refrain.

"Bad Timing" by Blue Rodeo, thought Nancy. The heavens must be playing a cruel joke because the potential truth of this sentiment in her life was just a little too accurate. She knew it. She'd known it flirting with him at The Fox and Fig. It was too soon. Jacob had too much unresolved stuff with Ava-Rose, and Nancy had no business expecting anything from him.

But the way he'd looked at her...

No. She had to shake that off. Thoughts like this were not going to help her extricate Jacob Sweetwood from her heart or mind. The road ahead was dark; she was out of Blairsville now, but her eyes were fogging up with unshed tears. Damn her foolish heart. It was no use; she was too emotional to drive.

Looking about her, she noticed she wasn't far from Holly's family cabin. There was a good chance that Max would be there, so she decided to head their way. Sure enough, Max's truck was parked in the driveway. Hopefully, they weren't having a romantic evening.

Nancy knocked on the front door, and Max answered almost immediately.

"Hey, sis!" he said, his arms wide open pulling her in for a hug. "I was just about to head out for a late-evening walk. Holly's in bed with a cold, but I can wake her if you want?"

She sniffed, wiped at her eyes, and shook her head. "No, it's okay. I actually wanted to see you."

"Oh hey, are you crying?" he asked with concern, finally registering her tears and the overall state of her. "Shoot, I'm sorry, Nancy. Of course. Come on in."

Max led her to the small table in the kitchen and put the kettle on. "Chamomile?" he asked, remembering her preference for it since high school. She used to get the worst migraine headaches, and it always seemed to help ease the pain.

"Thank you," she replied.

He waited for the kettle to boil and then poured them both a cup. As he sat down across from her, it struck Nancy how calm and kind he was. Of course, he'd always been like this—a tall, handsome man with the most caring brown eyes. But he was also her big brother, and she had to admit that she took many of his good traits for granted. Now though, as she took a careful sip of the tea he prepared, she said a silent prayer of thanks for another good man in her life.

"So, what's going on?"

Nancy took a deep breath and told him as much as she could about all that had transpired in the last few days. She made an effort to reel in the details of her feelings for Jacob and how far they'd let those feelings go. To be honest, she was embarrassed about that part. And as much as she loved her brother, she didn't want to hear any form of 'I told you so,' no matter how well-intentioned it may be.

Max listened intently to her story, edited though it was, and leaned back in his chair observing her kindly. "You're worried about Jacob," he said.

She nodded. "Well, yes. I think he's really vulnerable right now and Ava-Rose is like—"

"A vulture," Max finished.

"That's exactly it."

Max shook his head, apparently recalling a memory. "I pulled her over once. She'd been speeding. And she honest to God tried to get out of the ticket by offering to give me a massage," he said. "She said I looked stressed out. The whole thing was nuts."

Nancy rolled her eyes in disbelief. "See! This is what I mean. The problem is he still has feelings for her. She's tricked him before, and I don't put it past her to trick him again."

Max tilted his head in consideration. "Well, sure. I don't put it past her either. But, Nance, he's spent a lot of time with you in the last few days. You couldn't be more different than a woman like Ava-Rose. And once a man has met a good woman, been cared for by one, it's hard to go back to anything less. In fact, I'd say it's downright impossible."

Nancy smiled at her big brother, flecks of tears in her eyes. "That's really nice to hear," she said softly.

Her big brother shrugged. "I expect it is, but it's also the truth," he said. "Give him some time. What you saw—it was out of context, right? I mean, you couldn't hear exactly what they said."

She shook her head. "No, but... the way he looked at her."

"Listen, sis. Ava-Rose is a beautiful woman," he said in a lowered voice, presumably so Holly wouldn't hear him from all the way upstairs in her bedroom with the door closed while she lay asleep. "I'm not gonna sit here and deny that. And, for Jacob, she's his ex—an ex whom he had not seen in a long time...since she left, in fact. He's gonna have some kind of look on his face. Let him process all that's happened. He'll come around."

Nancy brought her knees to her chest, resting her chin between them. "I'm not sure it's good for my heart to hold onto that."

Max stood and kissed her temple. "Well, I'm not sure it's good for your heart to take to runnin' at the slightest hint of trouble either."

"I guess," she said.

"Nancy, you've done a lot of growing since Thomas Grange. It would do you some good to acknowledge that. You are a strong, capable, intelligent woman. Even if it's not Jacob Sweetwood, it'll be a good man who wins your heart, mark my words. You won't settle for less."

It helped to hear this; she had to admit it. She found it comforting to think that Max saw something in her that she wasn't aware of yet. Nancy trusted him, so maybe, one day, she'd see what he was seeing.

Jacob woke the next morning with a terrible headache. He'd spent two hours trying to track down Ava-Rose with Carly, the Deputy Sheriff of Blairsville, then another two trying to get ahold of Nancy using his tablet, but she clearly had her phone off and was not at her apartment.

Carly had advised him to let the police handle the Ava-Rose matter as soon as he called it in, but he'd been determined to track her down.

"Listen," she said on the phone. "I know you pulled a one-man manhunt in the land of *Lord of the Rings*, but that doesn't qualify you to be involved in a car chase in the middle of the night on the backroads of Georgia. If we've learned anything about this Billings chick, Jacob, it's that when she wants to disappear, she disappears."

Carly had been right, of course. And this was yet another blow to his ego. He had driven around aimlessly and with no idea what he would even do if he found Ava-Rose. Then, when he switched to looking for Nancy, he eventually realized he didn't know what he would say or do with her either. The sudden appearance of his ex-girlfriend had reduced his clarity of mind to a Smokey Mountain fog.

Reaching into his side table drawer for aspirin, Jacob opened the bottle, threw two pills into the back of his throat, and downed three gulps of water. His iPad rang, and he answered it as soon as he saw Carly's name.

"Hey, Jacob," she said brightly. "Good news! We fished your phone out of the sewer. The bad news is, it's toast. You'll have to get another one."

Jacob rolled his eyes, thinking this was the least of his issues right now. "Okay, I figured," he said. "But what about Ava-Rose? Did you find her?"

Carly let out a sigh. "No, Jacob. I'm sorry. We did receive a lead that she was at your family's home, but by the time we got there, she was nowhere to be seen. Your parents denied she'd been there and refused to let us look at the security cameras without a warrant. I assume you want to press charges? If so, we will get that warrant on Monday."

Jacob said nothing. He thought about pressing charges, about how that was the right thing to do. He should receive justice. He should want it! But somehow, the thought of being entangled with Ava-Rose in any way any longer was repugnant to him. His whole being rejected it.

"Jacob? You there?"

He cleared his throat. "Yeah, I'm here."

Carly paused for a moment before speaking. "Listen, it's okay if you don't want to go down this rabbit hole with her. From what the town is saying, this woman is toxic to say the least."

Jacob winced at that. The whole town? Lord only knew what they were saying about him. "She stole a quarter of a million dollars from me and a precious family heirloom," he said.

"Yes, Jacob. There is no denying she's a thief," she said patiently. "I understand wanting justice. I also understand wanting peace and to move forward. Ava-Rose is an extremely resourceful, deceitful person. She's proven herself an escape artist. This could go on for years."

"I know."

Carly cleared her throat and continued. "There's another option."

"I'm listening," replied Jacob.

"We could wait a few days before pressing charges and putting a warrant out for her arrest. This would give her a head start and prevent you from having to deal with it right now. The charges would be hanging over her head, following her all around the world. So, even if you don't get your stuff back, you can know that she's not separated from what she did to you. It's stuck to her like fleas to a dog's behind."

Jacob considered this. It was a very attractive offer. To not have to think about Ava-Rose or the money or their sham of a relationship—at least for now—would be a welcome relief. He could focus on better things like his painting and Nancy.

"Okay," he said. "Let's do that. And Carly?"

"Yeah?"

"Thank you."

"You bet," said Carly, her voice full of understanding.

Chapter 12

*N*ancy stood in the middle of her pub feeling frozen in place and numb. She had barely slept—the sofa at Holly's cabin not being her bed and all—and was still feeling shaken by the whole Jacob and Ava-Rose spectacle. Her phone was still off and, if it weren't for having to run a restaurant, she'd be under the covers all day, hiding from the world.

Max's pep talk had been good, but the truth was her wounds had been triggered and that wouldn't just magically disappear. Besides, Max was crazy cuckoo in love and hardly seeing straight when it came to relationships. She needed a dose of reality. She needed Ashanti.

Nancy walked into the kitchen to find her favorite chef in the world bent over a platter of whole chickens, rubbing them with herbs and oil.

"Whatever it is, honey, you're right and they're wrong, and you deserve better," she called without even looking up.

"How did you..."

Ashanti clucked her tongue and rolled her eyes. "Nancy, your vibes are so freaking heavy and sad, you may as well be walking around with a ball and chain like that Jacob Marley in *A Christmas Carol*."

Nancy gave a half-laugh feeling a little less inclined to open her heart now. She sniffed the air. "What's that smell?" she asked, attempting to distract from her obvious low mood. "It's divine."

Ashanti stood and quirked an eyebrow at her. "I'm roasting garlic cloves," she said. "I'm glad you're here; I wanted to talk to you."

Nancy leaned back against one of the prepping tables. "Okay, what about?"

"You remember Joe, right?"

Nancy offered a smile. "Did you and he finally profess your undying love for one another?"

But Ashanti was unmoved, looking far more serious than the conversation should call for. "No, Nancy. But he did send me something I think you should see," she said, pulling her phone from her apron pocket. "Joe received a message last night on a dating app he's been using. The message is from you."

Nancy took the phone and looked at the screen. It was her all right. The picture was a few years old, but all the information on the profile was eerily correct—her height, where she went to college, her likes, and dislikes. "What the hell?" she whispered in disbelief. "I didn't do this, Ash. Someone set this up. Someone is using me to catfish."

Ashanti nodded. "I figured you'd say that. It's just—"

"Just what?!" she heard herself shout. "You don't actually believe it's me?"

"Hey, there's no call for yelling," Ashanti admonished. "I wondered if it might be a move to make Jacob jealous is all. Or maybe to distract yourself."

Nancy's mind was racing. Who would do this? And how many men had they messaged as her? Was it a bot? Some kind of dumb foreign espionage? Or was there a real person messing with her? Just then, Max's words flashed through her mind: *She's a vulture.*

"Ava-Rose Billings," said Nancy through gritted teeth. "Ava-Rose is back in town. I saw her with Jacob last night."

Ashanti's jaw dropped. "What? Are you serious? And what do you mean you saw her *with* Jacob?"

Nancy paced a few feet of the kitchen, her thoughts running miles a minute. "I, they, I don't know. They were arguing, I think, and then they made up. They were in the parking lot and I watched them from my room upstairs, but only for a little bit. It started to feel intrusive. But anyway, she must have figured out Jacob had been there to see me, and she decided to get revenge."

"You think Ava-Rose put this profile together hoping it would get back to Jacob?"

Nancy nodded. "It wasn't me, Ash. And I can't think of anyone else who would attempt something like this, not to mention the timing. Everything points to her."

"So, are you going to talk to Jacob when he gets here?" asked Ashanti.

"Wait. What?"

"Jacob," she repeated. "Lex told me they're meeting here this afternoon. Well, soon actually. He's giving him an update on the investigation. Though, from what you're saying, maybe Jacob has more to tell Lex than vice versa."

Nancy needed to pull herself together. She was planning to avoid him today, and maybe even tomorrow. God, what was she wearing? One of Max's huge t-shirts from the police academy? Yoga pants with flecks of flour on them? Ugh. She was utterly disheveled. She checked her watch. It was two forty-five. They were most likely meeting at three. She had fifteen minutes to look like a normal person.

She bolted out of the kitchen without so much as a goodbye. Even if Jacob had decided to go back to the nasty claws of Ava-Rose Billings, she could at least appear confident. She would look hot and breezy and unbothered. Because who was to say this kind of drama would stop at a catfish post on a dating app? If Nancy pursued Jacob, would this bizarre woman always be messing with them? And if so, did Nancy want any part of that?

Clambering up the stairs to her apartment, she headed straight for the bathroom for a thirty-second shower, leaving her hair untouched by the water. Then, she grabbed a bottle of dry shampoo and went to town over her entire scalp until every ounce of moisture was gone. She ran her fingers through it over and over until she achieved the texture and look she wanted.

Next, Nancy ran to her closet, put on a black lace bra and matching thong because—why not? And then pulled on a simple black fitted cotton dress with spaghetti straps. Rummaging through the floor of her closet, she finally found a pair of classic black stilettos and wedged her feet into them. Lastly, she put on her mother's pearl earrings and lathered her lips in cherry red lipstick.

She observed herself in the mirror, satisfied. It was always empowering to dress up a little and throw on some lipstick, she thought to herself. She really should do it more often. The Fox and Fig was like her baby and she the frazzled mom—complete with the messy bun, sneakers, and yoga pants. But it didn't have to be like that. She could take better care of herself, feel better about herself. And that was heartening to know.

Nancy looked at the time: two fifty-eight. Perfect. She threw back a glass a water, reapplied a layer of lipstick for good measure, smacked her lips together, and walked purposefully down the stairs to the pub. She was met at the door by the most incredible pair of blue eyes wearing that same, sad look from the picture.

"Nancy," said Jacob somewhat startled. "You look incredible."

She shot him a smile and thanked him, hoping she appeared to be calmer than she felt.

"I've been calling," he said. "Did you turn your phone off?"

"Yeah, I just needed some peace and quiet after last night. I haven't looked at it yet today."

Jacob nodded. "I see." He looked nervously from her to the ground to the open space of the restaurant and then back to her. "I have something to tell you," he uttered.

Nancy's stomach did an uncomfortable flip. She couldn't hear what he had to say right now—no matter what it was. She had customers to serve, a restaurant to run. As much as she had tried to steel herself for this moment, as soon as the words left his mouth, she was left panicked and wanting only to flee.

"Can it wait? I have to talk to Ash about tonight's menu," she said.

Jacob looked at her in mild confusion. "Are you upset with me? When I left last night..."

"Yes, when you left last night things were one way, and then minutes later I see you up close and personal with Ava-Rose, and so things are now a completely different way," she blurted, her voice hot with emotion.

Jacob blinked hard. "That's what I was calling about," he said, jarred by her anger. "That's what I was going to tell you."

Nancy bolted from him. "I don't have time for this right now, Jacob."

He called after her, but Lex Forbes walked in the door just then. If Nancy had to busy herself in the kitchen and behind the bar to avoid talking to Jacob today, she would do just that. A voice in her head told her she was being immature and avoiding him was a defense mechanism, but she didn't care. Right now, it felt like she needed defending.

Chapter 13

"*H*ey, Jacob," Lex called from behind him. "Good to see you, man."
Jacob turned and shook Lex's hand, trying to pull himself
together after a disastrous exchange with Nancy. She saw him with
Ava-Rose from up above and shut the window, just as he worried she
had. *Damnit.* Damn Ava and her conniving tricks. That woman ruined
everything she touched, and he was sick to death of it. He held his jaw
tight and shook off the feeling of disgust. He would get through this
meeting with Lex and then clear everything up with Nancy. That's all
he could do right now.

He led Lex to a booth in the back corner of the restaurant and
flagged a young server whom he'd never seen. Both men ordered club
sodas and then turned back to the business at hand.

"So, I'm guessing you know Ava-Rose was in town?" Jacob said,
trying his best to focus on the P.I. in front of him and not scan the
room for Nancy.

Lex cleared his throat and brought out his phone to look at his
notes. "Yes," he answered. "I had a feeling she'd show her face here, but
I only saw her in the flesh once."

"Me, too," said Jacob with a sarcastic laugh.

Lex offered a look of sympathy. "You want to tell me about
that meeting?"

Jacob nodded and proceeded to tell Lex about how she accosted
him in the parking lot of The Fox and Fig. "I don't get it. How did she
even know to find me here?"

Lex shrugged. "She most likely tracked your location with a third-
party app."

"Yeah, but she knew about... she knew I'd been hanging out with Nancy," Jacob said in hushed tones.

"Oh," replied Lex. "Well, that one might be on me. I took a picture of you and Nancy together the other day, and asked my cousin to post it on her social media with a hashtag of #JacobSweetwood. Seems Ms. Billings took the bait."

Jacob recoiled. "Dude, is there no such thing as privacy?"

Lex shook his head without apology. "Nope."

"Right, well, anyway... she was all over the place. She said that Dax was blackmailing her because he was threatening to expose an affair she'd had with a married man. She was claiming she really did love me but that Dax was using her."

Lex nodded. "She's desperate," he affirmed.

Jacob had to agree. "That was exactly the feeling I got, too. She seemed like she was running out of options. And her whole devoted lover act turned completely sour the minute I told her I had quit the family business and would most likely be disinherited by my father."

"Damn, son," said Lex, clearly surprised. "Your dad never mentioned that."

This amused Jacob. "Oh, so you spoke to old Bill, did you?"

"Yeah, for what good it did me. The interview served more or less as a distraction as I had my guy sneak in and look at the house's security footage"

"Oh," Jacob said. He was beginning to see that Lex knew much more now than he did when they were last together just a few short days ago. "You look as though you've got a lot to share, Mr. Forbes."

Lex leaned back. "I hope you'll forgive me, Jacob. I have definitely learned a lot these past few days and felt my loyalty was with Mr. Billings, so I've been keeping him abreast. Knowing, of course, that I would be meeting with you today."

The young server dropped off their club sodas and hurried away.

"Understood," he replied, crossing his arms in front of his chest. "So, what have you got?" Jacob was starting to catch on to life with Ava-Rose, now that he knew who she really was. The key was to brace yourself for the worst.

"Well, I don't know about the married man bit. That sounds like a load of garbage. But the part about Ava-Rose and Dax Piper working together was and still is true. He used her and, I mean, she let him. That seems to be their vibe. So, whatever she told you about him blackmailing her or whatever, I'm telling you that is not what I'm seeing or hearing. All evidence points to the two of them being in this together through and through."

Jacob swallowed. The sting was light, and that felt good to know. Ava was a crappy person who did crappy things. Losing her was really no loss at all. The truth of that was sinking in.

Lex continued. "It does get worse though. Seems Ava-Rose hit a wall trying to get the recipe for Staple Syrup. I'm not sure what happened—whether it was Anita's interference or what. All I know is Dax gave Ava-Rose instructions to get the recipe out of you. When it became clear you weren't involved enough with that project, she was instructed to move onto your father."

Jacob felt all the color drain from his face. "What do you mean by 'move onto'?" he asked with no small amount of dread in his voice.

"Ava-Rose seduced your father, Jacob. They were...together...at least twice." Lex cleared his throat.

"When?" Jacob asked, his body stone still.

"I'm sorry, man. This is straight-up cold."

"When?!" Jacob insisted, his tone serious and his hands gripping the edges of the table.

Lex took a deep breath. "Both times that I know of took place while you and Ava-Rose were together," he said. "Once at the office."

"And the other time?"

Lex shifted in his seat, but he looked Jacob in the eye. "The other time was at your place."

Jacob clenched his jaw and fists tightly. "That son of a bitch," he seethed. "That lying, cheating piece of trash who dared to come at *me!*" He slammed his fist on the table. "He dared to come at me when he had done the exact same thing, only worse!"

There were only a few patrons and the young server in the pub, but all eyes were on Jacob. He didn't care, except he realized he may be embarrassing Nancy by putting his temper on display. Taking a deep breath, he leaned back and mumbled an apology to Lex.

Lex waved his hand dismissively. "Jacob, man, don't sweat it. I know this has gotta be a blow."

"Thanks. Please, go on."

"Your dad is terrible at security, by the way. Maybe he thinks he's clever by emailing himself text messages and then deleting them off his phone, but when your email address password has been the same for over ten years, you're not even close to secure. Besides, email is the easiest to hack by far," said Lex shaking his head. "But I digress. From what I have gathered, they exchanged flirty texts for a few weeks. Then, Dax's guys moved in for the bribe. They demanded the recipe, or they would publish pictures of your dad and Ava-Rose together."

"Pictures? That's it?"

Lex rubbed his chin. "Yeah, but these pictures showcase your father's...tastes. And let's just say BDSM exists on a spectrum, right? Well, your dad is at the far left of center."

Jacob raised an eyebrow. "Oh, wow. The untouchable Bill Sweetwood," he said with a sardonic laugh. "Looks good on him."

Lex nodded in agreement. "Your dad is not without protection of his own. Before she passed, Anita was involved, too. There were threats thrown back and forth. In the end, Bill decided to tell Ava-Rose about the money and the ring in your safe. He told her to take it to Dax and make a deal—tell him that was all he would get."

"But she had to know Dax wouldn't settle for that? I mean, my dad is arrogant and can convince himself of almost anything. But Ava-Rose?"

"Yeah, I'm with you," said Lex. I think she took the money because why not? But I don't think she counted on Dax's anger. The cash and jewels weren't nearly enough, and because she should have known better, Dax couldn't count on her. He washed his hands of her when she was in Wellington. Apparently, he confronted her after the gala—you were there. This all happened behind the scenes. Anyway, he cut her off that night—the deals, the relationship, everything."

"And that's why she came crawling back to me," Jacob deduced.

"Probably," he affirmed. "I think maybe a last-ditch effort to get the recipe from you, or at least get back with you to have some financial security. And when you told her no, my guess is her next move will be to reach out to your dad again."

Jacob ran his hands threw his hair. "Sweet Jesus, what a mess."

Lex continued. "Problem is, with Anita gone, Bill was starting to panic and grew desperate. Dax had upped the ante. He didn't just want the recipe, he wanted the whole damn company. And well, looks like Bill will give it to him. So, Ava-Rose didn't have a leg to stand on. If she wanted to go public with the photos of her and your dad, she would now have to deal with Dax Piper and his thugs."

This was almost too much for Jacob to process at once. Of course, he had always known that Anita was the brains of the operation when it came to Sweetwood Syrups—when it came to anything Sweetwood-related, to be fair. But for his father to feel so lost and backed into a corner over a simple scandal? Geez, the man really was weak. It shook Jacob. This man he had so feared all these years was just a bunch of gusto in an expensive suit. There was so little substance there, so little worthy of his respect.

And then Ava-Rose going from man to man like some lost puppy looking for its true home. All the while, she had loving parents who wanted her and cared for her. But Jacob had to admit, there was something self-destructive about her. Anytime he got too close or said something just a little too vulnerable, she would pull back. She would make a joke or change the subject or even chastise him for being too cheesy. Now, she was on her own and would be on the run for God knows how long. Jacob felt bad, but mostly for her parents.

"What did Mr. Billings have to say?" Jacob asked.

Lex looked down at his hands. "Not much, but I could hear the hurt and disappointment in his voice when he thanked me for the work I had done."

"Are you quitting?"

Lex nodded. "Yeah, man. I'm not built for this world travel stuff. I like Georgia too much. Ava-Rose has fled North, probably heading for Montreal. If the Blairsville Sheriff's Department doesn't actively pursue this—and I suspect they won't—I could be chasing this girl for months, maybe years. And yeah, the Billings family is paying good money, but it doesn't feel right." He paused, trying to get a read on Jacob. "You okay? I laid a lot out just now."

"I know," replied Jacob. "I'm taking it all in. Part of me is surprised, part of me is disgusted, and a big part of me is disappointed in myself for trusting in such bad people."

"Well, you're not the first guy to fall for a pretty face with a cold heart. And as far as Bill goes... Jacob, man, Bill is your dad for crying out loud. You're supposed to be able to trust him," said Lex in sympathy.

Jacob thanked him. He could sense the truth of his words, but it would be a while before he could accept it. The feeling of being duped over and over again was like a punch to the temple. It made him dizzy and forgetful of who he really was. It made him question his own strength and intelligence. He would have to channel this frustration somehow. There was no way he could let Ava-Rose or his jerk of a father get the better of him. He had to rise above.

Chapter 14

*N*ancy watched as both Lex Forbes and Jacob exited The Fox and Fig, got into their separate cars, and drove away. Her stomach sank. So, he wasn't even going to fight for her? He wasn't going to try to talk to her again? Yes, she had made it clear that she didn't want to talk to him, but it disappointed her that he had given up so easily.

Luckily, she barely had time to ruminate on any of it. Business picked up at around four, and it didn't let up until close to midnight. She was on her feet all night and sincerely regretted her choice of footwear. She ended up borrowing a pair of Crocs from Ashanti halfway through the evening.

As she was closing up, Ashanti came up behind her and gave her an uncharacteristic embrace. "You've been through a lot, Nance," she said. "I hope you're being easy on yourself."

"Thank you," Nancy replied, soaking up the affection. "What are you up to now? Heading home?"

Ashanti gave a wicked smile. "Actually, Joe is picking me up in a few minutes. We're going to hit a house party at his sister's place. That is, unless you have a problem with that, PubGirl92?" joked Ashanti, referencing the fake profile name.

"Stop! I'm still reeling thinking about how many men she's messaged using my name and image."

"Joe reported the profile. I asked him to. He's a good guy like that," said Ashanti, her cheeks coloring.

"I knew it!" exclaimed Nancy. "You are the worst at hiding when you like a guy. And you tried to make me think I was crazy."

"Girl, you *are* crazy. And I don't owe you a damn thing," she said with a wink. "Now, get some rest. Treat yourself to a bubble bath or something. You're looking tired as heck."

"Thanks?" said Nancy, taking the tough love that Ashanti offered with grateful humor. Even if she wanted to lay awake and stew about Jacob Sweetwood, she simply didn't have the energy. And maybe, just maybe, that was a blessing.

She made her way up to her apartment and heard her landline ringing as she reached her door. No one except telemarketers ever called. Normally, Nancy would let it go to voicemail. But something made her want to answer. Things hadn't been normal lately, so it seemed right to not do the normal thing.

Nancy put her key in the door, walked into her apartment, and picked up the phone. "Hello?" she said softly, her pulse racing just a little.

But there was no response, only breathing.

"Hello?" she repeated. "Is someone there?"

A deep breath came, but no words.

Nancy grew impatient. She knew now who it was and suspected she knew subconsciously as soon as her phone had rung. "Ava-Rose," she began. "I know it's you. If you're calling to talk, I'm listening."

Still nothing.

Nancy plopped down on the sofa. "Should I speak first?" Of course, she knew she should just hang up. Ava-Rose was unstable, chaotic, and unpredictable. But something in her told her to stay on the line. "Listen, we don't know each other. And even though you've scoured my social media to come up with a plausible dating profile for me, that does not equal familiarity. And you're probably the absolute last person I should be vulnerable with but, you know what? I have something to say."

More breathing, though it had slowed somewhat.

"I think I've been beating myself up for falling for a charming guy. And I suspect that Jacob is doing the same about you," she said, putting her feet up on the coffee table. "So, if he decides to go back to you, all I can say is I get it. I get it, because I've done it."

The caller cleared their throat, but said nothing.

"That's it, Ava-Rose," said Nancy. "That's all I got. But thank you for helping me arrive at this conclusion. I hope you have a good day." And with that, she ended the call.

The Sweetwood mansion always looked so pretty at night. The grounds were elegantly lit and the façade of the house itself seemed even grander against the backdrop of the nighttime sky and full moon. Sometimes, Jacob missed living here. But it was mostly because of Anita and Zena. Any good memories he had were because of those two women.

Losing Anita had changed Jacob. He no longer felt a naïve sense of forever when it came to his life and relationships. No one was guaranteed to stay. He had to make the most of the good things now, today. And anything that pained him or sucked the energy out of him, well, there was no sense dwelling on it. His new outlook would stick with him. There was no going back.

As he pulled up to the front door of the house, he noticed his mother in her dressing gown sitting by the pool. She had a drink in her hand and sat slightly slumped with her feet in the water. Jacob parked and walked over to her. He had intended to speak to his father, but something was clearly wrong with Patricia.

"Mother?" he called, walking toward her.

She looked up, and he could see she had been crying, her eyes smudged with black mascara. "Jacob? Oh, darlin.' How are you? I've missed you, my boy."

"I'm okay, but how are you?" he asked, his voice full of concern. "What are you doing out here?"

Patricia was clearly three sheets to the wind, but had the presence of mind to answer him truthfully. "Baby, I can't stand being in that house since she died," she croaked out. "I miss her."

Jacob sighed and sat down by his mother. He removed his shoes and socks, rolled up his pant legs, and put his feet in the water. "I miss her, too," he said softly. "Anita was incredible."

"She had the mind of a tactician and the heart of a saint. And all I've ever been is selfish."

"Mother..."

"We ruined her," said Patricia flatly. "We took a good woman and made her bad, Jacob. That's what this family does. Well, you and Zena are good eggs. But the rest of us..."

Jacob observed her keenly just then. She rarely spoke this kind of truth, at least to him. "She made her own decisions, mother. But I think I know what you mean. There's a toxic sort of focus on money and power in this house that can be poisonous if you let it."

Patricia took a sip of her drink. "Yes, exactly. And I think that focus is gonna kill us all—slowly."

Jacob reached out and touched her knee gently. His heart was racing. It pierced him to hear her talk with such resignation about her life. He wanted her to see there was a way out, that he had found that way. "Mother, it doesn't have to be like that," he said. "You can leave. He can't make you stay. You can make your own way in the world. I can help you. You can even come live with me for a while, if you like. You don't have to live under his thumb."

His mother brushed a lock of hair from her eyes and stared at the water. It occurred to Jacob how beautiful she was and how young still. She could claim a new life and have decades of happiness ahead of her. She had time.

Patricia turned to him, held her hand to his cheek. "My sweet boy. You were always so good, so kind. I often wondered where you had come from."

He smiled at her. "Thank you," he said.

"I'm sorry for what your father did, Jacob," she said softly. "I know you had strong feelings for that girl. Sometimes...sometimes I think that's why he did it."

Jacob furrowed his brow. "I beg your pardon?"

Patricia turned her gaze back to the sparkling blue of the pool water. "He has been jealous of you since day one. As much as Bill Sweetwood crowed on and on about wanting an heir, he sure backed off of that once you were born. It was as if he could sense from the get-go that you were better than him."

This was certainly news to Jacob. His father had never indicated any kind of jealousy or envy, only a disinterestedness.

"I felt for you as you grew up," his mother continued. "You so badly wanted his approval, and he withheld it on purpose, knowing exactly how it would hurt you, over and over. And me? I did nothing to stop it."

Jacob felt the truth of this in his gut, and it pained him.

"So, when the woman you loved showed up here dressed head to toe in Chanel and cruel intentions, he fell for it. The man couldn't help himself. It was twisted and sick—I told him so. But he just called me a drunk and told me to be quiet."

He swallowed hard. God, there was so much hurt in his family. How had he not seen it before? The things we think we can hide when we have nice homes and cars and clothes. But it all comes out. It all finds its way out.

"It's all right, mother. Ava-Rose is not a good person. I'll find a way to work through this. I've quit my job; I'm going to try painting for a living and see how that goes. And, I met an incredible woman."

Patricia Sweetwood turned to her oldest boy and smiled. "Oh, Jacob. That's wonderful. Your sister can help you with the painting stuff, can't she? You were always so talented. Anita would show me your pictures."

"Thank you," he uttered.

"Who is this lucky woman? Do I know her?"

Jacob blushed slightly. "Nancy Cooper."

His mother nodded. "Oh yes, the sheriff's sister," she said. "She owns that little bar near the courthouse."

"Yes, that's the one."

She reached out for his cheek again and stroked it lightly. "Well, good, darlin.' I'm happy for you. I know you'll be good to her. And I just hope she'll be good to you, too." Patricia took another sip of her drink and looked up at the moon overhead. "I used to love a full moon. When I was a teenager, I had a whole ritual. I'd set up my crystals and light candles, and I'd pray. I'd pray for a rich man and a big house. What a laugh."

"I didn't know that," said Jacob.

"Yeah, big cosmic joke," she said.

"Mother, please remember what I said. You don't have to stay with him. There is life beyond Bill Sweetwood."

Patricia looked at him, despair clear in her eyes. "Baby, I wouldn't even know where to start. He would make my life even more of a living hell than it already is. At least this way, I have some freedom. If I left him, he'd never quit. Infidelity is one thing, but divorce? He would never accept it."

He took her hand and squeezed it. "Okay," he said. "I understand. And I'm sorry."

"Don't you ever say sorry to me, Jacob Sweetwood," she said with sudden conviction. "I want to watch you live a life of love and hope and happiness. I want to see you embrace everything that you deserve. Because I'm the one who is sorry. I failed you."

"Mother, I—"

Patricia raised a hand, cutting him off. "We will say no more of what we both know is true," she said. "Now, I have had more than enough to drink as usual. It's time for me to head to bed."

Jacob stood and helped his mother to her feet. They had never had a night like this together, and he suspected they may never again. He bent to kiss her forehead. "I love you," he said.

"And I love you, darlin'," she whispered. "Word of advice?"

"Of course," he answered.

"If you're here to speak to your father, don't bother. He will never give you what you want. He was never going to and never will. Be satisfied with breaking from him. Live a good life. That's the best revenge on a man like him," she said. And then she blew him a kiss and walked back into the house.

Chapter 15

*N*ancy awoke with sore feet and a heavy heart. Before bed, she had finally turned on her phone and read all of the messages from Jacob. He had asked where she was, if she was okay, told her he missed her, that he could not wait to see her again, had thanked her again for the food. She was overwhelmed by him in the best way. But he had made no mention of Ava-Rose, and she did not yet know if that was a good thing or a bad thing.

When she had checked her Instagram, Nancy noted there had not been a post in four days. Well, that was unprecedented. Ava-Rose was constantly posting mirror selfies. Something wasn't right, and she could only hope that Jacob wasn't involved.

She got out of bed and padded towards her kitchen to make some coffee and toast. The rye bread from the bakery down the street was heavenly with black coffee. She'd have to tell Jacob about it—as long as he wasn't back with the worst woman alive. He was missing out on so much local goodness by having his groceries delivered from some warehouse in Atlanta.

The truth was, she could not stop thinking of him, considering him, wondering about him. It wasn't obsessive, not really, it was genuine regard. She was drawn to him as an equal—like he was her person, and she was his. That's how it felt. And so, Nancy had to admit, even if Ava-Rose might always be in the background with her drama and her tricks, Jacob was worth it. He was worth everything.

Just then, there was a knock at her door. Nancy looked at the clock on the wall. It was barely nine o'clock. She was dressed in an oversized Falcons t-shirt and white cotton underwear, but decided whoever was calling on her this early deserved such punishment.

Nancy peered through the peephole, but no one was there. She opened the door and looked down. It was a painting. Not just any painting, it was a painting of her. In it, she was standing by the kitchen door of The Fox and Fig. Her hair was tied back in a loose ponytail. She wore a gray t-shirt and black yoga pants, and her face was lit by the mid-afternoon sun as it streamed through the glass of the front door.

This was her—yesterday. This was her fifteen minutes before she had bolted upstairs to transform herself into a sexy goddess. Nancy studied the painting. He had seen her. The look on her face was thoughtful and shrewd—as if she had been weighing her options. And this was juxtaposed with the softness of her hair framing her face with delicate blond wisps. Her mouth was pouty, her eyes wide and attentive. Jacob had seen Nancy in all her unstudied glory, and this was the woman he had decided to paint.

Nancy's eyes filled with grateful tears. Every hue, every brushstroke was beautiful. She was in awe of his talent. "Jacob?" she called, putting it down. "Are you here?"

He emerged from the fire exit and smiled hesitantly. "Do you like it?"

Her heart burst at the sight of him. She had missed him, had missed the ease between them. "Like it? I absolutely love it. Jacob, it's incredible."

He put his hand to his chest. "Phew!" he said. "I just—I saw you yesterday before my meeting with Lex as I was coming up to the door, and you were there. You were standing right there in front of me, and you looked other-worldly, ethereal. You didn't see me, but I saw you, and I... I don't know. I just had to paint you. I made sure to burn that image of you into my brain, and that's what I did last night."

She stepped closer to him. "I was rude to you yesterday."

Jacob shrugged, his face colored. "I understand," he said.

"Please, tell me now," she pleaded. "Tell me before I fall any further. Are you with her? Are you considering being with her in any way?"

Now, he stepped closer, placing his hands on her hips and pulling her in. "No," he said succinctly. "Never again."

She liked that, the finality of it, and how it meant she could potentially see him as hers. "Good," she uttered.

"That chapter of my life is closed forever. I'll tell you more another day, but today... Can today just be for you and me?" he asked, his breath hot near her lips.

Nancy arched herself toward him, begging to be kissed. "Yes," she said. "I would like that."

Jacob's hand moved to the small of her back, and he pressed her to him as he touched his mouth to hers. Nancy reached up and raked her fingers through his hair, pulling him closer and parting her lips. They remained that way until they had to come up for air.

"You want to come in," asked Nancy laughing. "Or do you wanna stay out here in the hallway?"

He smiled and flashed his blue eyes. "Nancy Cooper, I want to be wherever you are. Just lead the way."

THE END

Sweetwood Christmas

Prologue

McCaysville, Georgia, Christmas Eve 1999

Seven-year-old Zena Sweetwood escaped the living room of her Uncle Octavius's estate and hid out among a pile of dusty, old paintings in a room that was called the attic but was, in fact, the same size as her school gym. She found an old bedsheet and wrapped herself in it, gaining refuge in a corner beside a painting of three pretty ballerinas.

The adults, about twelve in total, were drinking gin and tonics by the pitcher, and the living room conversation had turned into something she found both boring and uncomfortable. Adults sounded funny when they drank gin. Their words were blurry, they talked over each other, and their voices would get louder.

Her older brother Jacob sat in the family Volvo wagon listening to CDs with the heat blaring. There was no way he would let her join him. And her other brother Keith was down by the creek hunting for snakes. Zena had briefly considered going down to meet him, but he was always too rough about his hunts. To her, it seemed that animals who could be caught should be treated with care, but Keith saw it more as a competition—like only the strong survived.

The day was kind of a big mess. Her mom and dad yelled at each other that morning and were silent the whole car ride. She and her brothers had been too afraid to speak, choosing instead to hope it all got better by the time they arrived.

Now, as Zena lay back among the paintings, bits of the adults' living room conversation played around in her head.

"Jacob will be fine," Bill Sweetwood had said to his captive audience. "He has intelligence and discipline. He's too soft, but that's something I can work on. Keith will always be a concern. He's too much like his mother."

Those last words had been said with what Zena thought was disgust and a glance cast towards her mother. But Patricia Sweetwood didn't blink an eye, nor did her expression change. "Our Zena, though," Bill continued. "She's a wild card. She will either take over the family business with a skilled and confident hand, or she will disown us altogether."

Her Uncle Octavius clucked his tongue at this. "Jesus, Bill. You're cut off," he said, taking his brother's glass—half joking, but really not. "These kids have minds and lives of their own. Don't limit their existence like this."

And that's when the shouting started.

"Whatcha doin', sugar?" called Adora Sweetwood, interrupting her thoughts. Auntie A was one of Zena's favorite people in the whole wide world.

Zena shrugged wordlessly and wished she could smile for her aunt, but faking feelings was hard.

"Yeah, I hear you." Auntie A offered Zena a comforting smile and sat down, smoothing the pleats of her cream-colored silk skirt and tucking her legs up beneath her. "Adults sure are loud when they drink, aren't they?"

Zena nodded, keeping her gaze down at her lap. She allowed herself a brief glance at her aunt. The woman was impeccably dressed, her white-blonde hair always curled and her lips always the perfect shade of peach. She'd told Zena once that her mouth was her homage to her beloved state of Georgia—the very color of a Georgia peach.

"Zena, darlin'?" Auntie A began.

"Yes?" she croaked. It had been many hours since she had said a word.

"You do know that you are the only one who gets to decide who you are, right?" she asked, brushing a lock of hair from her eyes. "I mean, that's between you and the Lord," offered Auntie A.

Zena nodded her head fervently, both with emotion and understanding.

"Honey, you're just so dang smart, and I want you to hear from a different adult who loves you and sees how special you are... You can be anything you want. And your mom and dad will just have to deal with it. You know?"

Zena's eyes filled with tears, but no words would come. She tried so hard to think of something to say, to tell her aunt how much that meant, but her mind was too crowded by feelings.

"Aw, sugar, don't cry. I didn't mean to make you sad," said Auntie A, pulling a handkerchief from her pocket and offering it to Zena.

"You didn't," managed Zena. "I just..."

"Just what, honey?"

Zena wiped her eyes and took a deep breath. "I just sometimes wish you were my mom and Uncle O was my dad. And I wish I could live here with you."

Her aunt pressed her hand to her heart, clearly moved by Zena's sentiment. "Now, I do believe that is the sweetest thing anyone has ever said to me, Zena Millicent Sweetwood."

Zena smiled then, finally feeling like she could. It made her happy to make her aunt happy.

"I wonder," Adora began. "Since I am not your mama, but I am your auntie, maybe I could ask your folks if you could stay here a few weeks each summer. That way, you always know when you'll be comin.' It'll be a guarantee. And I'll make sure it's just you for those weeks, not the boys, and no adults. How would that sound, honey? Would you like that?"

Zena nodded emphatically, her heart feeling like it might burst from her chest. She bridged the distance between them by doing a half-crawl, half-leap into her arms. She buried her face in the honeyed vanilla scent of her aunt's long blonde hair and allowed herself to cry happy tears. Auntie A cared. She cared about her and her feelings, and that realization was almost overwhelming.

Adora offered soothing, hushed tones and rocked Zena back and forth. "Shhhh, baby girl. It's all all right," she said. "We're gonna have lots of fun together, so no more tears, okay?" She pulled back, grasping Zena's chin gently. "There are good days ahead, honey. I promise you. Lots of good days ahead."

Chapter 1

*J*t was the perfect night for a drive out on the outskirts of town. Snow fell in tiny flakes, peppering the weary green with white. Zena Sweetwood had finished a long week at her art gallery and wanted nothing more than to belt out the Christmas carols of her youth with no direction in mind.

Yet in thy dark streets shineth,

the everlasting light

The hopes and fears of all the years

are met in thee tonight.

Emmylou Harris's rich, angelic voice filled the interior of Zena's car. It catapulted her back to the Christmases of her youth. She'd grown up privileged, to say the least, and Christmas was another opportunity for her parents to show everyone in Blairsville they were the best. Their home was professionally decorated inside and out—a Scotch pine from one of the finest tree farms in Ohio and an outdoor light show to rival Clark Griswald's. The kids would wear matching outfits and be paraded like prize hogs at the Christmas Eve church service.

Looking back, Zena could barely believe that people bought into this dog and pony show. Her parents, Bill and Patricia, were so

191

blatantly splashy—how could anyone not wonder if they were hiding anything? Behind the scenes, her parents fought constantly, and Zena, Jacob, and Keith were ignored. Care was taken, but not on anything intrinsic or meaningful. Instead, their lives were carefully curated to appear enviable and perfect.

Of course, somewhere along the way, her parents had given up investing in appearing the ideal family. Her mother started to stray as soon as Keith graduated high school, and her father buried himself in the business until he got in too deep. Then, last year, he'd sold his beloved company, Sweetwood Syrups, to a rival and had spent the time since convincing himself he loved golf.

And last year also saw the death of her beloved Anita—an "employee" of her father's who was more like family in Zena's eyes. She still wasn't over the loss, and, considering how painful it was to even think of her, it looked as though she may never be. The ache in her chest at missing Anita was too much, and Zena knew there was guilt mixed in there, too.

Anita had been carrying a lot, and it never occurred to Zena to ask her how she was. Granted, she'd known Anita her whole life and looked to her as a surrogate parent, but she had grown up. And maturity meant that you showed some interest in the people you loved, not just looking to them as support systems and bringers of snacks.

Now the playlist shifted to Kenny Rogers, and she thought of her mother, who had often described him as a teddy bear with a voice like sweet rum who'd always win a bar fight. This had been a terrifyingly confusing image as a child. Still, she enjoyed his rendition of "God Rest Ye Merry Gentlemen" all the same.

Zena had not spoken to her mother in years. And it wasn't due to one singular event, though there had been enough terrible things that would have justified Zena's walking away right then and there. Instead, it had been a slow growing apart.

In college, she had played the dutiful daughter and called her mother every Monday night. After graduation, however, she'd stopped. At first, it had been a test to see if her mom would miss her. Then, it turned into a game to see if she'd ever be the one to reach out to her own daughter. Eventually, Zena gave up and made a conscious effort to move on with her life and not share any of it with her family.

Her mother's answer to this was apparently silence. At times, she would use Jacob as a messenger for family events and celebrations, but Zena always had an excuse not to attend. Finally, she told her brother flat-out, "I don't want to see mom and dad. You can stop asking." And he'd agreed. He shrugged and nodded, saying he would respect that.

That's when the loneliness hit her like an unexpected wave. Zena wiped at her eyes that had filled with tears. Her whole body went tight, and the heaviness in her chest was unbearable. She breathed deep in an attempt to gather herself.

She knew she needed to reach out more and isolate less. It had been nearly two years since she'd dated, and the pathetic thing of it was she was still hung up on the last guy—Max. Zena sighed. She had been way more into him than he had been into her. For crying out loud, the whole town knew he was still in love with Holly Blake.

Luckily, Zena had shut herself off through most of their brief affair. If Max knew how hard she had fallen, she would be feeling so much worse. But he'd been convinced of her only casual interest in him—so much so that they hadn't even really broken up. The whole thing just fizzled. Zena could feel him pulling away, and so she let him.

He would never know the effect he had had on her. There had been close calls when they made love. She was drawn to him, his body, his scent—just him. But she figured he simply assumed she was a passionate lover. The pain of opening herself up to him physically only to shut down emotionally was deep. But the impulse to self-protect was far stronger than to show any real vulnerability.

And it wasn't just physical for Zena. Max was kind. He was clever and cared about important things like justice, community, and searching for the truth. He didn't back down from something because it was hard. He was committed. Unfortunately, his commitment to Holly was etched in stone. It was admirable and endlessly frustrating.

Zena didn't know Holly well at all. They had never traveled in the same circles. Still, she disliked her. She seemed to be flighty and entitled. Her automatic reach for Max when her brother Lucas had gone missing was, to Zena, presumptuous. But there was nothing to be done now. Max and Holly were engaged. And Zena was alone—again—in a small town where her chances of meeting someone new were about the same as the Falcons finally winning a Super Bowl.

Taking a deep breath, she looked out her window, noticing the road was already covered with a light dusting of snow. Her gaze traveled further along and she rolled her eyes once she realized where she was. Not more than fifteen feet to her left was the Blake family cabin complete with Max's SUV in the driveway.

The tightness in her chest intensified, but Zena knew she had to get the heck out of there. The last thing she needed was to be spotted by the happy couple. They were both so goddamned nice, they'd probably invite her in for hot cocoa. Zena shuddered at the thought.

Just then, her phone rang over Bluetooth. It was her Uncle Octavius, so she answered right away. He didn't even let her say hello.

"She's shut the door, Zena," her uncle said, his voice fevered and rushed. "She's shut the door and will not let me in."

Zena pulled her car over, sensing this conversation was going to require her full attention. "Who?" she asked.

"...and she'd been in her painting room. You know the one, darlin'? Her painting room where I'd tried for years to fill every nook and cranny with the portraits she loved most," Octavius continued on, not hearing her apparently.

Zena did know the portrait hall very well. She would hide out there as a kid when her brothers got too mean and the adults got too loud. Inevitably, it was Adora who would seek her out. And she'd start the process of coaxing Zena back by explaining the origins of one of the paintings.

"Uncle O, you're going to have to slow down. I can barely understand you," said Zena patiently over the phone. "Maybe just start from the beginning?"

He let out a strangled cry. It hurt her heart to hear it. "I don't know what the beginning is, Zena. I've never felt so helpless in my life. Your aunt she... she won't speak to me. I've tried begging, pleading, yelling, banging on the door, calling her cell phone a hundred times—nothing works. I swear I've tried everything except removing the goddamn door from its hinges."

"I'm so sorry," said Zena. She waited a beat before asking her questions as gently as she could. "Did you say something to her? Did you two argue?"

Chapter 1

The truth was, Zena had never known her aunt and uncle to argue. They seemed to genuinely like each other, and she noticed this because it was the opposite of her parents who shot put-downs back and forth like arrows and played bizarre mind games. No, Auntie A and Uncle O smiled at each other from across rooms. She would kiss his cheek at random moments in full view of everyone, and he often placed his hand at the small of her back in the sweetest gesture of protection.

Octavius sniffled and cleared his throat. "Her moods have been up and down the past few weeks. She went to the doctor the other day, and I'm not sure what came of that but she's been subdued. When I asked her about it, she said everything was fine and normal. But Zena, the way she said normal..."

"Yes?"

"I don't know... it's as if she was disappointed about it."

Zena's mind flashed in remembrance. "Doesn't breast cancer run in her family? Could she mean that? That it was normal somehow because it had happened to her aunt and grandmother?"

His voice was tight with emotion. "I don't think so. She would tell me something like that. She's had unclear mammograms before, and she's always told me about them."

"Okay."

"I know it sounds ridiculous, Zena. But something in that painting room of hers set her off. I can feel it in my bones. And you know her. You know her and you know art, so maybe you can piece together what happened?"

Zena paused, not knowing what to say. None of it made sense. And because her uncle was so in the dark, she clearly had to speak to her Aunt Adora. "Okay, don't worry. I can come there tomorrow and see if she'll speak to me. Would you like me to do that?"

"Y-yes," he replied. "I'm sorry, Zena darlin.' I know you're grown with a life of your own. I just don't know what else to do. You two always had a bond, and if she won't speak to me, you're the only other person I can think of who she will."

Zena felt a rush of appreciation run right through her that almost instantly eased the ache of loneliness she'd been feeling. How could she forget how loved she was by her uncle? By her aunt? And by Jacob, too? "Don't give it a second thought," she said soothingly. "Go pour yourself a strong glass of bourbon and get some sleep. I'll be there in the morning. We'll sort everything out."

Octavius sighed with audible relief. "Thank you," he replied, his voice cracking slightly. "This means a lot to me."

But as she said goodbye to her beloved uncle, Zena had to admit she felt out of her depth. Here was the only couple she'd ever known who truly loved each other, were devoted to one another for decades, and now they were falling apart.

Chapter 2

Gabe Da Silva sat across the long boardroom-style table from his newest client. The meeting rooms of the law firm Spitz, Elba, and Kerr were all opulent and tastefully-appointed, but this one was particularly posh. Fuchsia-colored orchids lined the walls at eye-level sitting atop floating ebony shelves. There were portraits of select clientele—all recognizable—shot by the one and only Annie Leibovitz. And the views of Central Park were second to none.

Priya Jolly and her boyfriend, Arman Nicol, had hand-picked Gabe as their legal representative. Priya was a famous mommy blogger and influencer from Manhattan, now living in White Plains and wanting a divorce from her husband, Dev Jolly. Gabe had met Dev a few times at some high-class, high-stakes poker games he'd sometimes play in Midtown. He seemed like a good guy, if not a bit shy and nervous. His vibe was almost out of place among the sharks of Manhattan. As it turned out, he was Arman Nicol's business manager. And Arman? Well, let's just say Arman was in real estate and leave it at that.

Gabe had also seen Mr. Nicol at the poker games, but never actually approached him. He knew that whatever the business really was that he engaged in, it was not anything he wanted to touch with a ten-foot pole. Guys like Arman find out you're a lawyer, and they take note. So, Gabe chose to lay low. Apparently, he hadn't laid low enough because it had been less than twenty-four hours since Arman's assistant had called to set up the meeting for Priya, and here they were. Gabe's new clients normally had a waiting period of at least two weeks before he could see them. Such rules, however, did not apply to men like Arman Nicol.

"He just can't accept it," said Priya. "Arman and I fell in love. We didn't mean for it to happen. But we were clearly meant to be, and Dev needs to get that through his head."

Gabe cleared his throat, cast a quick glance to his assistant, Cherry, who was seated beside him, and addressed Arman, "Is he still working for you, Mr. Nicol?"

Arman sat back in his chair, relaxed and one step away from crossing his legs up on the table like he owned the place. He shook his head. "No," he replied after a beat. "The quitter quit."

Gabe made a note on the legal pad in front of him and, keeping his expression professional, turned back to Priya. "So, Ms. Jolly, you have already filed for divorce. I take it you're here to draw up a parenting plan regarding your twin boys?"

Priya grasped the tiny gold medallion at her throat, running it through her fingers. She looked confused for a moment and then righted herself. "Oh, yes, we're here about custody and laying down some ground rules."

"The moron showed up to our house unannounced," Arman interjected. "That can't happen."

"Oh? And so, there has been no real schedule or parameters until now?" asked Gabe.

Priya huffed. "Dev has been too busy looking for a job, so he's basically been seeing the boys when he can. I've been more than charitable that way, and it may have been sending the wrong message. And now, after he had the nerve to pop by their birthday party, I'm done."

Gabe furrowed his brow. "He popped by your house to see his sons on their birthday?"

"Yes," she replied.

"Did he know you were having a party?"

Priya crossed her arms and sat back in her chair. "Well, no. He wasn't invited."

Gabe shook his head. "Ms. Jolly, I'm confused. Are you saying that Mr. Jolly was using the boys' birthday as an excuse to see you? Because you stated earlier that he cannot accept the separation."

Cherry kicked Gabe under the table just then and gave him a look that said, "What the heck are you doing?"

Arman took a deep breath and offered calmly, "She's saying Dev believes he still has full access to Priya and the boys. That's not what she wants. We're here to make it official."

Gabe looked at Arman in challenge. "So, there was no clear directive for visitation on the boys' actual birthday? And you are telling me you were surprised when their father showed up on that day to see them?"

Cherry cleared her throat and stood abruptly. "Boss, sorry, can I see you out in the hall for a moment?" She offered a look of sympathy to Arman and Priya and motioned for Gabe to leave with her. Once in the hall, she whispered through gritted teeth. "What the heck are you doing? Do you understand who these people are? Are you purposely trying to mess this up?"

Cherry Gill was sharp. And their relationship was congenial. He gave her a lot of free rein. Gabe had long-felt she should pursue being a lawyer, but she was in her mid-twenties and had lots of time. Being nearly a foot taller than her and her employer, you'd think he would feel in control, superior. He did not. And the truth was, she was right. "No," he said weakly. "I dunno, Cherry. These people are shady."

She observed him dubiously. "You are a divorce lawyer practicing in Manhattan. Your entire clientele is shady."

He let out a laugh. "Yeah," he said. "Good point."

Cherry paused, clearly mulling a thought over. "What's this really about, Gabe?"

Gabe let out a breath he'd been holding. "I think you better give these folks to Rob. I'm too amped up."

"They asked for you specifically," she said. "If I give them to Rob, who's to say they won't walk?"

"Didn't he just finish up the mayor's divorce? Tell them that. They're the kind of people who will care about that," he said. "Trust me."

Cherry shrugged. "You're the boss," she said. "I'll do it now. Luckily, Rob's free until lunch. But Gabe?"

"Yeah?"

"Whatever this is, you need to get a handle on it. You work with custody cases all the time and frankly, I didn't hear anything out of the ordinary just now. So, deal with this. Like, yesterday," she said.

Gabe nodded solemnly and watched her head back into the meeting room. He rubbed his temples and shook his head, attempting to clear his mind. Whatever that just was, he didn't like it. And yeah, he would have to deal with it.

Holly Blake sat curled up in front of a blazing fire, wool blanket around her shoulders, as her best friend from college, Gabe, recounted his day.

"Geez, that's not like you," she said. "Something triggered you, for sure. You want my guess?"

Gabe sighed heavily. "Not right now, Holls. Just telling you this happened is making me tired. I need a drink or a vacation—preferably both."

She pictured him alone in his gorgeous home in Harlem. He was most likely stretched out on his antique black leather sofa, staring up at his crystal chandelier, tie loosened and shoes off, trying to shake off a bad day.

All she wanted was to make him feel better. "You can come here and spend Christmas with us! Oh my gosh, I would love that! You could stay here at the cabin! Or, wait..." she stopped, suddenly remembering key information that Gabe may be less than pleased to hear.

"What?" asked Gabe.

"Well..."

"Holly, what is it?" he demanded.

"I just remembered something."

Gabe made a dramatic inhale and exhale. "Holly Meredith Blake. For the love of God—"

"All right, all right!" she exclaimed. "It's Adora Sweetwood."

"Who?"

"Jacob's aunt. You remember Jacob; he's Nancy's beau. Anyway, Adora is in my book club. Well, it's more like a wine club," she laughed.

"Holly, focus!"

"Right! Anyway, we all met up last week to discuss *The Paris Apartment*—it's so good—but I could tell Adora was upset, so I approached her after the meeting to see what was wrong. And Gabe, she was beside herself. She was almost incoherent. Something big had happened earlier that day—I still don't know what—and it was major enough that she told me she was going home and asking her husband of nearly thirty years for a divorce."

Gabe sighed. "I'm sorry to hear that."

"So was I! And because she seemed so devastated, I may or may not have volunteered your services…"

Gabe went silent.

"Are you still there?"

He sighed. "Yeah, I'm here."

"Are you mad?" asked Holly in her smallest most apologetic voice.

Even if he was mad, her heart was in the right place. Also, Gabe was always working, nearly incapable of relaxing. Working while in a different environment could prove to be a good distraction, the kind of the thing to put his head back on straight.

"No," he replied flatly. "So, this vacation is gonna be more like a working vacation?"

She squealed again. "Does that mean you're coming? And you'll help her?"

"Yeah, yeah," he answered. "I'm coming. I'll get the first flight into Atlanta tomorrow."

"Yay!" said Holly. "Stay with us tomorrow night, and then I'll drive you up to Adora's place. She and her husband have a huge house near the Tennessee border. She hosted book club a few months ago, and we were all floored. She has an art collection like you wouldn't believe. The whole place looks like some kind of fancy museum on the inside."

Gabe chuckled. "As opposed to a non-fancy museum?"

"You know what I mean!" she chided. "Anyway, just text me your flight details, and I will be there to pick you up. We're making paper snowflakes tomorrow night, and I'm cookin' up a batch of my famous hot cocoa." Holly lowered her voice to a whisper. "The secret is melting Belgian chocolate and adding just a touch of Madagascar vanilla extract."

"It sounds delicious," he said, sounding tired.

Holly's stomach clenched with concern. This was not the Gabe she'd known and loved since college. He was perpetually optimistic, the man with the plan, forever having solutions to any problem. He was cool and wry and honest. Whatever was bothering Gabe seemed to have come out of nowhere for him and yet, being caught off guard had never fazed him before.

Holly knew his parents had a messy divorce and an epic custody battle. It was the reason Gabe became a divorce lawyer in the first place. But what she had not considered was if he processed any of the emotions related to this massive part of his upbringing. She assumed his work ethic and mission had replaced any childhood pain, but was beginning to see that was naïve on her part.

"Okay, Gabe. I'll let you go. But don't worry. Whatever this is, we will work through it—together."

"Who was that?" asked Max, coming into their bedroom dressed only in a towel after his shower.

"Gabe," answered Holly. "He's flying in tomorrow, and he does not sound himself. I invited him to stay with us over Christmas—well, us and Adora Sweetwood."

"Wait, what? Adora Sweetwood?"

Holly ran her hands through her hair. "Oh, right. I forgot to tell you, too. She is asking her husband for a divorce. When she asked me for the name of a good divorce lawyer, I obviously recommended Gabe."

Max nodded. "Gabe is the best," he said. "Are you okay with all of this though? Are you afraid of being dragged into this?"

Holly knit her brow in confusion. "Not at all, why?"

He shrugged. "You barely know this woman. Why did she ask you? It seems odd to me."

"Max Cooper, can you stop being sheriff for even one second? The woman needed some advice. Me being in New York for ten years has rendered me an out-of-towner, and I think she wanted a recommendation of someone who is not local and, therefore, not gossipy."

He stepped toward the corner of the bed where she sat, leaned down and kissed the top of her head. "Just please stay out of it, Holly. We've had enough drama these past few years, you especially."

"I agree. Though, I do like a little drama..."

Max pulled her up to standing and dropped his towel to the floor. "No," he protested. "You like distraction." He placed a hand behind her head, as the other traced her jawline with his thumb and tipped her mouth to his.

"Mmmm," moaned Holly involuntarily. How gosh darn annoying it was to be wrong and yet enjoy it so very much.

Chapter 3

*T*he two-hour drive from Atlanta to Blairsville was blissfully wholesome with Holly at the wheel and classic country music playing quietly in the background. Even though she and Gabe texted nearly every day and had bi-weekly phone calls, there was apparently something to being live and in person that drove her to repeat all the news of her life that he was already aware of. It didn't bother him one bit. Holly's excitement was the perfect diversion from his inexplicably dark mood.

She updated him on her new job as the social justice reporter for the *Augusta Chronicle*, as well as her and Max's engagement (the wedding date still TBA), and her excitement over Nancy's imminent engagement to Jacob Sweetwood.

"And you're certain Jacob is going to ask her this Christmas?"

"Yes!" she affirmed. "It's been a year, Gabe. He has to lock it down. Nancy is a total catch, and I'm not just saying that because she's my future sister-in-law."

"How's her pub doing? And how's Jacob doing without daddy's business?"

"The Fox and Fig is thriving," she said. "They even have a karaoke night on Tuesdays. And Jacob is an actual human being now that he's not working for that awful Bill Sweetwood. He's sold a couple paintings for big money and teaches painting to kids at the community center on weekends."

Gabe rolled his eyes. "He sounds like a saint."

Holly cast him a wary glance. "What's with the sarcasm?"

He hadn't meant to say those words out loud, so her question caught him off guard. The annoying thing was, he didn't know why he'd said it. He didn't know why, all of a sudden, everything seemed bleak and irritating. Did he really have anything to complain about? He was a successful lawyer with a steady client roster of the rich and famous, and he lived in a beautiful Harlem brownstone in the greatest city in the world.

In fact, he'd felt almost unshakeable since he graduated high school, leaving his boring home town and even more boring home life. His parents had split when he was ten but remained in the same neighborhood even to this day—as if pursuing something bigger or even different was a pipe dream. And Gabe knew what they told themselves. They were both convinced their sacrifice was for their son, but it wasn't. He knew they were too scared to change. He'd been practicing law for years now, free of debt, living large. And yet, they remained the same.

Last year, Gabe had sent them each ten thousand dollars. His dad used it to build a bomb shelter. His mom donated it all to the local food bank. At the time, he'd told himself it was a gift; it was their money, and so he had no right to an opinion on how they spent it. Now, though, anger bubbled up. What about investing? Or a vacation? Or going back to school? Nope. They wasted it.

"Sorry," said Gabe. "Jet lag."

"From a two-hour flight?" asked Holly, dubiously.

He rubbed his forehead and reclined the car seat a few inches. "Yeah, I don't know what to tell you."

Holly nodded sympathetically. "Okay, okay. Have you spoken with Adora Sweetwood?"

Gabe had in fact spoken with her, and she insisted on calling him Gabriel, despite him correcting her twice. Adora was also insistent that he stay at the house until her husband signed the divorce papers. She meant it as a show of defiance and determination, that she had no intention of changing her mind. Gabe had not yet attempted to garner any details from her. He knew it was best done in person.

"Yes, I'll head up to the house tomorrow afternoon," he replied. "Looks like I'll be staying there until Christmas Eve unless Octavius signs the papers before that."

"I'll drive you," offered Holly. "Did Adora tell you what happened?"

Gabe shook his head. "Nope, she just kept saying there was no point."

"What a crappy way to spend Christmas," she said. "I didn't think this through, Gabe. Look at what I'm subjecting you to!"

"Don't worry about that," he replied. "I'll get it done. This is what I do. I'll be spending Christmas with you and Max and Lucas, I promise. Octavius will see reason. These things are never fun, but it's better to pull the bandage off quickly."

"I have no doubt in your abilities as a lawyer," said Holly. "But it's draining being dragged into someone else's drama."

Gabe laughed out loud. "Holly, are you high? It's literally what I do for a living."

Holly pulled to a stop at the traffic light and lightly banged her head on the steering wheel. "I'm sorry, Gabe. My head is a mess. I have a deadline for this story I'm doing on the new mayor of Augusta," she sighed and made a left turn onto the road leading to the cabin. "You're absolutely right. This is what you do for a living, and I know you're the best person for the job. Adora is really going through it, and you're the one to help her with the legal stuff."

They pulled into the driveway, and Gabe immediately noticed the absence of Max's truck. "Where's my favorite small-town sheriff at?"

Holly frowned. "Working," she said. "He'll be home late, too. But I've got beef stew in the slow cooker, so we can make our snowflakes with full bellies!"

Gabe smiled widely. She was like a balm for his soul. And it was heartwarming to see how easily she'd shaken off New York City to embrace a renewed version of her old small-town life. He had been missing her, hated not having her to meet up with at a moment's notice. But she belonged here in these northern Georgia woods. She needed Max's steadiness, and he needed her effortless joy. "Sounds perfect," he said.

The next day, Gabe and Holly were off early to avoid a storm that was moving in by late afternoon. Throughout the quiet car ride, Gabe attempted to push everything about his life in New York out of his mind. The past few weeks had been jarring. Never was he not on his best game until recently. It annoyed and scared him. And the only thing he could think to do was to take a break and immerse himself in something new in a place with a much easier pace.

He couldn't believe the number of trees lining the backroads to McCaysville. It reminded him of upstate, but everything seemed denser and more untouched. He wondered what sort of people Octavius and Adora Sweetwood would be. His knowledge of the family was limited to Keith Sweetwood—the moronic ne'er-do-well. His idiocy led to the death of Holly's dear parents and, subsequently, her brother's kidnapping.

If Holly could muster the kindness to see Adora as separate from all of that, then Gabe would as well. But, really, this whole thing should be a piece of cake. Adora wanted a divorce, and Gabe's job was to make sure she got it—plus whatever else she was entitled to. And he hazarded to guess that was a lot.

"Wow," said Gabe, a note of awe in his voice. "I don't know what I was expecting, but it wasn't this."

"Told you," replied Holly. "Wait'll you see the inside."

She pulled into the half-moon drive of Octavius and Adora Sweetwood's home, and Gabe attempted to take in the whole of the house and its grounds. One thing was sure, this was more than a house, in truth. It was a proper Georgian mansion. The cream-painted brick was fading in spots, revealing the age and splendor beneath. A broad chimney separated the two wings of the home. Tall, sashed windows were accented with black shutters. The grounds were extensive and lightly covered with snow. And a sprawling mini-forest of indigenous trees surrounded the home leading to a breathtaking hilltop view.

"I have to head back, Gabe. You okay to face these Sweetwoods on your own?"

He laughed. "If I can handle the divorce of a known gangster and a railroad company heiress, then I'm pretty sure I can handle a rural Georgian domestic dispute."

Chapter 4

A man no taller than five feet dressed in a black dress shirt and blue jeans answered the door with a dignified smile. "You must be Mr. DaSilva," he said coolly, his blue eyes expertly assessing Gabe. "I'm Joseph, the house manager. Ms. Adora is expecting you. Leave your things by the door and come with me. I'll bring them to your room later."

Joseph left no room for debate and began walking ahead without another glance. The man had established dominance immediately, and Gabe gave him nothing but silent props for it.

The interior of the Sweetwood home was somehow glamorous and tasteful. Everything was high quality and well built.

"Like what you see?" asked Joseph, a knowing smile on his face.

"Very much so."

"The floors were flown in from Bulgaria. They're from a church that was torn down in Sofia. The walls you see here," said Joseph, gesturing to a narrow hallway. "Are covered in silk tapestries from a weaver in Croatia."

Gabe looked as directed, and it occurred to him that some people simply had a natural sense of aesthetics and when that sense was married to a lot of money, a house like this was born.

Joseph continued. "And the grand chandeliers lining the main foyer and each hallway were made by a local glassblower."

But it was the paintings that stood out to Gabe. There were Rothkos, Basquiats, and a Kandinsky. And they looked like originals. His jaw was on the floor thinking of the cost. He dated an art curator a few years ago and picked up a few things. There were more paintings he recognized and simply couldn't place the painter's name, but one thing was for sure: someone had impeccable and very expensive taste.

"It's Ms. Adora who has the eye for art," said Joseph, reading his mind. "And if you think these are spectacular, there is a room on the fourth floor that will blow your mind."

"Damn," Gabe replied under his breath.

"Indeed."

They were climbing a set of stairs now that were to the right of the main foyer. Gabe was going to need a map to navigate this place.

"Don't worry," said Joseph. "There is a map you may download on your phone that will help you. I believe Octavius uploaded the floor-plans or something like that. I'll text you that information shortly. Now, follow me. Ms. Adora's rooms are at the end of this hall."

The man had to be psychic. Or perhaps simply good at his job? He led Gabe to what appeared to be a sitting room with a door to the left that he knocked quietly.

"Adora?" Joseph called softly. "Your lawyer is here." And with that, he bowed his head curtly in Gabe's general direction and left.

The silence in the room was unnerving, and Gabe realized he had no idea what to expect. Mrs. Sweetwood was going through a hard time Holly had said, but was she emotionally stable? Was she in a state to see reason if need be? Gabe was experiencing a panic that was normally uncharacteristic of him, but that had lately become more normal than he cared to admit.

The worst part was that it was now interfering with his career. His thoughts drifted back to his last client meeting where he'd lost control. Was he going to do that today? What had he signed up for here? *Leave it to Holly to get me into such a bizarre situation*, he thought to himself. Who were these people?

"Gabriel?" Gabe looked up to see an attractive woman in her late-forties with platinum blonde hair dressed in a black velvet track-suit smiling half-heartedly at him. She was put together to be sure, but her sadness and exhaustion were clear.

He walked over to her and offered his hand. "Yes, Mrs. Sweetwood. It's a pleasure to meet you."

Adora nodded slowly, observing him. "Are you nervous, sweetheart?"

Gabe blinked hard and cleared his throat, taken aback by her gentle, yet direct question. "I-uh, I'm all right, Mrs. Sweetwood—"

"Call me Adora, honey," she said, walking over to sit on one of the two plush white loveseats and directing him to be seated on the other. The room was warm in both temperature and décor. Wine-colored walls boasted cream sconces, all adorned with lit candles. A grand mirror edged in black, at least six feet by six feet, stood at opposite end from where he stood. There was a glass and copper bar cart with bottles of liquors, an ice bucket, and highballs. And in the corner, an old record player.

Gabe did as he was bid and continued. "As you wish, Adora," he said with a wink. "I was saying that I am all right. Thank you for asking." Those last few words came out colder than he'd intended though, and internally he scolded himself.

Adora smiled sweetly. "Of course," she said. "Did Joseph offer you any refreshment? It is colder than a polar bear's bottom out there. Would you like some coffee? Hot cocoa?"

"I'm fine, Adora. But thank you."

"Now, I am very sorry you and I are meeting under such unfortunate circumstances, Gabriel. But I suspect that is an occupational hazard. Now, has Holly told you my wishes?"

"I believe so," answered Gabe. "She stated you would like to file a complaint and begin the process for a no-fault divorce. In Georgia, as I'm sure you're aware, that means you have a mandatory thirty-day waiting period after which it should only take a few weeks for the divorce to be final. Holly did mention you wanted this done as soon as possible."

Her eyes appeared to tear up just then, but her face remained fixed. "That's right. No fuss. I have a home in Chattanooga I inherited from my mama and daddy, and they left me with more than enough to live on. I don't need anything from Octavius and Lord knows, he doesn't need anything from me."

The way she said those last words hit Gabe. Something wasn't right here. Adora Sweetwood had all the appearance of a woman who knew what she wanted, but underneath the façade she was so clearly hurt and sad. Gabe didn't know what to do. His job was to do as his client instructed and yet...

Adora continued. "So, what I need from you, Gabriel, is to get Octavius to sign the papers without delay. Convey to him that I will not be swayed; there is nothing he can do."

Gabe cleared his throat. "Do you have any reason to believe your husband will contest this?"

She shrugged, tears now plain in her eyes. "It's the way it has to be. And I know you will make him see my side of things."

Gabe doubted this without even having met the man himself. "I think you need to prepare yourself, Adora. This may not go as smoothly as you want it to. For instance, your husband may hire an attorney of his own, and then I won't be able to speak to him directly."

Adora shook her head. "He won't, Gabriel. I can assure you. Once Octavius understands this is what I want, he will not stand in my way."

Her voice took on a tenderness when she said this. As if their love and respect for one another were so fixed, it could not be moved. This then only further begged the question: why the heck did Adora Sweetwood want to divorce her husband?

Chapter 5

*E*ven though her Aunt and Uncle's home was only thirty miles away, it always seemed colder and stormier during the winter. And the roads were often more unpredictable. But, Zena made it without a hitch and breathed a huge sigh of relief as she crossed the threshold of her favorite childhood home.

Joseph greeted Zena with the slightest smirk. "It's good to see you, Miss Sweetwood," he said.

"Are you sure?" Zena asked with a side-eye glance cast in his direction. "What's got you looking like the cat who caught the canary? Especially considering what your employers are going through? And stop calling me Miss Sweetwood. It's creepy."

He rolled his eyes at this and took her black wool coat. "Those two will be just fine. This is nothing more than a rough patch, and they have simply never seen one before."

"Joseph, Uncle Octavius was beside himself when he called me. I've never heard him like that before. How can you be so casual?" asked Zena.

"Zena, sweetheart, you still see through the eyes of a child when it comes to your aunt and uncle. If there was ever any drama between them before this, you wouldn't have seen it."

She considered his words and decided he could have a point. "Okay, but you haven't answered my question. What's got you so amused?"

He sucked his lips in and made a gesture like he was closing a zipper. "Oh, you'll see. It would be unprofessional of me to say more. But I'm tickled for you."

Zena narrowed her brow. "You're what?"

"Tickled," he repeated. "The universe has brought you quite the gift."

"You're so weird, Joseph. Where is my uncle?"

"Maybe, maybe not," he said with a shrug. "Octavius is downstairs in his man cave drowning himself in bourbon and old home movies."

Zena made a face that said, 'help me,' but Joseph only whispered sarcastically, "Enjoy!"

Octavius's study was in the basement of the east wing of their house. Adora had it constructed for his 45th birthday five years ago. It was her way of reciprocating for the portrait hall he had gifted her all those years back. She'd had it tastefully decorated in the style of an upscale mountain lodge complete with elk horns, Georgia pine wood paneling, old school movie projector, and a full bar with bourbon dispensers instead of beer kegs.

At first, Octavius had balked. "Are you trying to get rid of me?" he'd asked at the family birthday party. The question had been put forth as a jest, but Zena saw the genuine concern in his eyes. And she witnessed her aunt's kind response. Adora had stroked his cheek with her thumb and leaned in to place a kiss on his lips. "Never," she said.

Now, here was her uncle slumped in a leather armchair alongside a sad-looking fake Christmas tree with slow-blinking red lights. He had his phone in one hand, a generous glass of bourbon in the other, and was dressed in a tartan-blue velvet smoking jacket with matching silk pants and brown leather slippers. Even in his sorrow, he was the picture of elegance.

"Sixty-two," he said absentmindedly, staring at the ceiling.

Zena took a seat in the armchair opposite her uncle and looked up to see if she could figure out what he meant. She only saw solid wood beams and drywall. "I beg your pardon?"

Octavius coughed and wiped his mouth with his sleeve. "That's how many times I have texted your aunt without a reply. Sixty-two," he said. "I believe I am officially what you kids would call a simp."

Zena gave a short, amused laugh. "How on earth do you know that term?"

He shrugged. "TikTok."

"Of course," Zena replied with a smile, deciding not to inquire any further. It was jarring to see her uncle in this state. She was so used to him being calm, capable—the perfect foil to her self-absorbed father, his brother. She felt totally unprepared for the role she'd been asked to play. "Are you all right? You sounded so upset on the phone."

Octavius sat up at this and looked Zena in the eye. "Am I all right? How can you ask me that?" She started to reply but he cut her off. "Did Joseph not tell you who your Aunt Adora has invited to stay with us?"

Zena shook her head. "No, he just made some innocuous joke about the universe bringing me a gift."

Her uncle laughed sardonically and took a gulp of bourbon. "A gift, huh? Well, maybe. But to me, he's my worst nightmare."

"He?"

"Yes," Octavius replied. "Your aunt has hired a divorce lawyer from New York City and invited him to stay in our home."

"What?" she proclaimed. "That doesn't make any sense. Auntie A has never even been to New York City. What on earth is going on here?"

Octavius stood up suddenly, losing his balance momentarily, but quickly regaining it. "Right? You see? I feel like I'm taking crazy pills, Zena! It's like your aunt has been inhabited by a stranger—a stonewalling, mean and spiteful stranger who locks doors, doesn't reply to messages, and hires lawyers who look like underwear models!"

"I-I'm sorry...did you say underwear model?" asked Zena, a slight quiver of curiosity in her voice.

"He's handsome, okay? But all this is beside the point, Zena. Your aunt is serious. She wants a divorce, and I have no idea why!"

Zena shook herself back to reality. She got up, poured herself a glass of water from the bar, and paced the hardwood floors of her uncle's study in an attempt to focus. "So, you said that Auntie A went to the doctor's, and then later, she was in her portrait hall. And after these two things happened she decided she wanted a divorce?"

"Well, I think so," he said. "She did leave at one point to go to her book club meeting. I only know that because Joseph told me. He's been my eyes and ears with your aunt this past week."

"Book club meeting? Is that where she met this underwear lawyer?"

Octavius sighed, opting to ignore her comment. "Joseph said Adora spoke to someone named Holly. She's the one who told her about the lawyer, said he'd fly in and help her. So now some slick divorce expert from the Big Apple is helping the love of my life leave me without even so much as an explanation!"

"Holly?" asked Zena, with an edge to her voice. "Holly Blake?"

"That's the one," he replied. "You know her?"

Zena gritted her teeth and crossed her arms tight about her chest. "Oh, I most certainly do," she said. It was amazing what a shift Holly's name caused in her. Zena felt a rage she'd never experienced before, and she wasn't sure why.

Maybe it was because Holly's involvement felt intrusive. This was *her* family. Who was she to be recommending lawyers and flying them in? Who did she think she was? Wasn't it enough she was the one Max wanted? Now she was coming for Zena's own loved ones? "Where is underwear lawyer now?" she asked.

Octavius shrugged. "The west wing of the house, I assume. You know where the guest rooms are."

She nodded. "Don't worry, Uncle O," said Zena. "This will all work out. I'm here now."

Chapter 6

*Z*ena needed to splash some cold water on her face before she met with this guy. She made her way to the bedroom that was always reserved for her. The nerve of Holly Blake! And how come Miss Divorced from NYC knew about her aunt and uncle before Zena did? It was maddening.

She rounded the corner at the top of the stairs and headed down the hall leading to the set of rooms that were designated for Zena and her brothers. Ever since she was little, it was a source of pride that she had a bedroom to herself while Jacob and Keith had to share. Auntie A was a fierce defender of the decision. "A girl needs a space of her own," she'd said.

But as she approached the doorway of her room, she was horrified to find it occupied—so horrified that she let out a shriek.

"Ah!" shouted a tall, dark-haired man in his thirties. He recovered quickly, more quickly than Zena. "I'm so sorry," he said. "You startled me."

She could not help the expression her face made at that. "I startled you? This is my room!"

The man looked confused. Zena put together that this was underwear lawyer and yes, he was good-looking. And well-dressed. And smelled like leather, lemons, and smoke. He pointed to a suitcase on the floor, then to himself. "I—uh, this is where Joseph left my things but I can absolutely move if this is your room, Ms.?"

"Sweetwood," she said. "And I think I see what has happened. Joseph thinks he's hilarious."

He stepped toward her, his hand outstretched. "Ms. Sweetwood, I am Gabe Da Silva, and I'm very sorry for the mix-up. I'll gather my things at once if you can point me to a different room."

Zena shook his hand and sighed. "Yeah, come on," she said, already hating that he was being nice and so, she had to be nice in return. "You can sleep in my brothers' room next door."

"They won't be needing it in the coming days?" Gabe asked.

She laughed. "God, no. They haven't set foot in this house since we were all kids. I'm the only one who is still in regular contact with our aunt and uncle."

"Ah, so you're the niece."

"And you must be the smart lawyer, because you put that together so quickly," she said, regretting the sarcasm almost immediately. Why could she never play it cool in these situations? Her emotions always seemed to get the better of her.

But Gabe let the comment go as he grabbed his things and followed her to Jacob and Keith's room. "Thank you for this," he said curtly.

He was clearly waiting for her to leave, and she realized that she had probably offended him. Well, too bad. She wasn't apologizing. This guy was literally here to break up her Auntie A and Uncle O. Who cared if he looked like he belonged on a billboard in Times Square? She wasn't going to go out of her way for him. No way. She was going to break him, make him feel like garbage for what he was doing to her family.

"You're welcome," she uttered in spite of herself.

Chapter 7

*G*abe closed the door and swallowed hard. The niece was here! And she was beautiful... and kinda mean. He really should be accustomed to being automatically disliked based on his line of work, but this felt different. She seemed genuinely hurt by his presence.

Even now he was picturing how tightly she'd held her red lips and how her dark hair kept getting in her eyes the more frustrated she became. And the way his body reacted to her—as if she glowed with both excitement and warmth. He felt instinctively drawn to her, which was confusing considering the circumstances.

In fact, his thoughts were going against every cutthroat lawyer instinct he normally had. He found himself mentally researching ways to help her. But maybe it wasn't just the beautiful niece inspiring these ideas. Adora had seemed so sad and almost... dissociated. Gabe didn't know her, of course. But that didn't change the fact that something was off.

So, what was he going to do about it? As Adora's lawyer, he was meant to be working on her behalf. Of course, she hadn't officially hired him yet. Cherry was on vacation for a few days, not back until the day after tomorrow so Gabe was waiting on the papers to be drawn up. No money had been exchanged. Nothing had been signed. This meant he had some time to help the niece. Was it a sketchy, unprofessional move? You betcha.

After a hot shower, shave, re-application of cologne, a fresh suit change, and one last look in the mirror, Gabe was ready to knock on her door. And a minute later, they were face to face.

He was slightly nervous and hated that. Was this part of the new, annoying series of feelings that had been descending upon him the past few weeks? Or was it something else? Was it her?

"Oh, hello," she said, her pale face coloring. "If you need something, you can just text Joseph. Do you need his number?"

Gabe smiled tightly, trying hard not to give the impression that she affected him. "No, no. I have that, thanks. I wanted to ask you something."

"All right," she said.

"Well, first. What is your name? I realized I'm a total jerk for not even asking you that when we met."

She cocked an eyebrow and crossed her arms about her chest. "Yes, you did, and I answered you."

Gabe inhaled. This woman was not going to make anything easy. "Touché, Ms. Sweetwood. You got me there. Would it be permissible to ask for your given name?" asked Gabe, pulling out all the stops and offering up his most diplomatic, polite tone of voice.

After a beat, she replied, "My name is Zena."

He immediately wanted to call her the Warrior Princess—based on the old TV show his father loved so much, but stopped himself. She had heard that ten thousand times throughout her life, without a doubt. So instead he said, "That's a beautiful name. And my name is Gabe Da Silva. It's a pleasure to formally meet you."

Zena appeared to relax a little, but her raised chin told Gabe that her guard was still up. "Mr. Da Silva. I am a Southern lady and so of course, I will say the pleasure is all mine. But you must see how your presence here is problematic for me and my uncle."

Gabe nodded. "I appreciate your candor, Zena. And I do see how my presence would be uncomfortable, but I'm here to try and remedy that."

"Really?" she replied, recrossing her arms about her chest.

"Do you, Zena, want to form an alliance with me?" he asked, punctuating each word.

She looked briefly amused and then shifted back to skepticism. "Did you just quote *The Office* to me?"

"Maybe."

Zena rolled her eyes. "What are you talking about?"

"I spoke to your aunt this morning, and I'm not convinced she really wants a divorce. Something happened to trigger this. She seems more spaced out and hurt than angry—at least to me."

"Yes, yes! This is what Uncle O has been saying! So, you see it too?"

Gabe nodded. "I think so. I mean, I don't know your aunt. But something isn't right."

"Okay," said Zena. "So, what's your plan?"

"Well, what do you know about how this all started?" asked Gabe.

"Apparently, Auntie A had a doctor's appointment but my uncle said she was fine afterwards, maybe a little off. The thing that changed her though was spending time in her beloved portrait hall. Something in there upset her and caused all of this—my uncle swears it."

Gabe was encouraged by this. "And you're an art collector?"

She laughed. "I can't afford that. But I am a curator with a degree in art history and my own gallery."

"Perfect," said Gabe. He stood tall, puffed up his chest, and raised his chin. "So, I'll ask you again: do you want to form an alliance with me?"

Zena blushed and tucked a lock of hair behind her ear. In her most contrived and serious voice she replied, "Absolutely, I do."

Chapter 8

*Z*ena stood before her aunt's doorway and paused before knocking. Her cheeks were still warm from the exchange with Gabe. There was no lie about his looks. He really could have been an underwear model. But she could still hate a good-looking man. She'd done it before.

Unfortunately, he also seemed to be genuinely kind, intelligent, and even had a sense of humor. This was not good. This, in fact, was a recipe for disaster. Because if she were to follow through with the plan Gabe had suggested, Zena was slated to spend a lot of time alone with him in the next day or so.

He wasn't at all what she'd expected. She had anticipated someone slick, arrogant, and totally lacking in empathy or morals. But Gabe Da Silva didn't appear to be like that at all. There was something about his eyes—something vulnerable and honest. He looked as though he were going through a tough time but doing his damnedest to remain in control of himself. Or maybe she was projecting that last part.

Still, here he was at her aunt and uncle's home with the sole mission of facilitating a divorce, and yet he was helping her to hopefully undo the whole thing.

"I have seen it before, Zena," he'd said. "As a divorce lawyer, trust me, it's rare but it happens. Your aunt is conflicted. She's being rash. If we had time on our hands, I'd say she would eventually see reason. But we don't."

The plan was for Zena to speak to her Aunt Adora and see if she would divulge what happened. And if that didn't work, she and Gabe would go through the portrait hall and attempt to discover what on earth could have spooked her so. In the meantime, Gabe would sit down with her uncle and let him know they were both now on his side.

Now, as Zena was about to speak to her aunt for the first time since this whole mess had started, she wasn't sure what to wish for. It was possible Auntie A would confess everything, and it all got resolved. Would that mean Gabe would leave?

Of course, she was being ridiculous. She'd only just met him. And even though his effect on her was clear (blushing, playing with her hair, sweaty palms and the kind of laugh she hadn't made since she was fifteen years old), they were strangers. It was cruel to want to prolong all of this just so she could spend time with him. And yet...

Just then, the door opened and Aunt Adora stood before her with a hand on her hip.

"Zena Millicent Sweetwood! Where are your manners? You have been standing outside my door a good two-and-a-half minutes. I could see your shadow. What are you doing eavesdropping on an old lady?"

Adora Sweetwood was almost fifty years old. "Old lady" was a bit of a stretch. "I-I'm so sorry, Auntie A. I was just... I was nervous is all. But it's so good to see you," said Zena as she stepped forward to embrace her aunt.

"My goodness, child. Why would you be nervous? You're my favorite, and you know it. Just don't tell your brothers," she said with a wink. And she was smiling, but Zena noticed the smile did not reach her eyes.

"You're my favorite, too," she said. "But feel free to tell my mother."

Auntie A laughed at that. "Okay, darlin.' Now, tell me what you're doin' here, for goodness sake!"

Zena made a face. "Really? You're going to play dumb? I'm not ten years old anymore, Auntie A. You can't keep things from me."

Adora clucked her tongue and turned on her heel, motioning for Zena to follow her and have a seat on her sofa. "Honey, I can keep whatever I like from you. I am my own woman. But I can tell this is about your uncle and me."

It was then Zena realized what was playing on the record player. Dolly Parton was belted out "I Believe in Santa Claus." A memory flashed in her mind. Her Uncle O dressed as Kenny Rogers and Auntie A as Dolly Parton at the family Christmas when Zena would have been about twelve. The two of them lip-synching to this very song, and her brother Jacob doing a terrible air guitar.

They had heard a rumor that Zena no longer believed that Santa was real, and this was their response. It had made her feel so loved and special. Like they cared, they actually cared what she thought and how she felt. When she told her parents about her skepticism, they laughed. Her dad said, "Took you long enough."

"Divorce?!" cried Zena as she sat down across from her aunt. "You're divorcing the love of your life? Uncle O! My Uncle O. What is going on?"

Adora didn't say a word. She sat still and looked at Zena with a frozen expression, as if keeping her cards close to her chest. Zena studied her. She held herself tightly, primly, as a Southern lady should. But she wasn't just a Southern lady. She was her aunt, the closest she had to a mother figure. Damn this imaginary hierarchy she had created. This was too important.

"Auntie A, I'm not leaving until you give something, anything. He is beside himself with sadness and worry. What did he do to you? What did he do to create this?" Zena demanded, gesturing about the room.

"Nothing," uttered Adora finally, her voice tight with emotion. "He's done nothing."

Zena was surprised and relieved at the words. She threw up her hands. "Okay, then. So, call this off."

Adora's eyes flashed with rage. "Zena, you will not come into my home and speak to me this way about things you are too young and inexperienced to understand. I have made up my mind. It is much too late. And as much as I love you, I will have to ask you to leave now."

Zena felt her aunt's words like a blow. It was clear she was angry and hurting. But why? There was no answer, not yet, but she was in no state to open up to her niece.

Reluctantly, Zena stood up and went to the door. As she did, she looked back and said, "I love you, and I promise you all I want is to understand."

She left the room with Dolly's words playing in her head like a message of love and a reminder that all could still be well, the part where she sings about there being hope even when everything seems lost.

Zena looked down at her phone to see a text message from Gabe.

Gabe: Your Uncle Octavius was indisposed.

Zena was impressed. One would almost mistake Gabe Da Silva for a Southerner. Clearly, he meant "drunk and passed out in his wing-back," but the diplomacy was appreciated regardless. Their plan was now to meet up in the portrait hall after dinner. Joseph left for his home at 7:00 p.m. Lord knew Adora wouldn't dare leave her room for fear of running into her husband, and Octavius was in no state to leave his.

It was best that their investigations were performed in private—at least for now.

Chapter 9

$\mathcal{G}$abe had to admit the portrait hall was stunning. Most would not even know it existed by looking at the exterior of the home. It was an attic of sorts, but enormous in size with impossibly high ceilings, gold filigree walls, a narrow sky light, and literally hundreds of paintings hung throughout. Add to this though, hundreds more in piles like dominoes lining the floors.

All of this to take in, and he couldn't take his eyes off of Zena. It was as if she'd been transported. She was physically present and in the room with him, but her face said she was lost in whatever the room represented for her. Maybe it was memories, or the art itself, or both—he wasn't sure. But she seemed more at ease.

"How long has it been since you were in here last?" he asked her.

Zena scrunched her nose, considering. "Gosh, it's probably been five years. I did my master's thesis on Hilma af Klint—my aunt's favorite painter. And I came here for research."

"Klint," said Gabe. "That's the guy who did *The Kiss*, right? The poster that like every girl I knew in college had in her dorm room?"

Zena giggled. "You're thinking of Gustav Klimt," she corrected. "No, no. Hilma af Klint was a visionary, a genius. She's thought by many to have been among the first entirely abstract painters of the Western world."

She led him to a nook on the other side of the room, and Gabe was in awe of what he saw. Paintings, four of them, large and colorful with a kind of sacred-looking geometry, hung purposefully two-by-two. The shapes the artist had created seemed like a code to Gabe. He was transfixed. And they were placed on a wall that was clearly a special space for Adora Sweetwood. Across from them was a pink velvet chaise longue where Gabe imagined she sat with a drink and stared.

"What are these?" he asked. "I mean, I can see why your aunt loves them. But have they been decoded?"

Zena looked pleased. "That's an interesting choice of words," she said. "Decoded. Because they were like a message. The artist was a Spiritualist. She and some of her friends used to hold seances and some of her paintings, including these, became kind of like spiritual downloads—messages for us from the beyond.

Gabe nodded, still admiring the works.

"Personally, I'm not interested in decoding them. I just love her use of color and light," said Zena. "And I think she's one of the bravest painters to have ever lived."

"Did your aunt instill in you this love of art?" he asked.

"Oh yes, absolutely. Auntie A was my emotional refuge as a child, and I think I instinctively trusted anything she loved. Art and my uncle were at the top of her list, and so they moved quickly to the top of mine."

Gabe took a step closer to her, feeling encouraged in getting to know her better and not wanting to lose any momentum there. "Do you not get along with your parents?"

Zena glared at him. "If you know Holly Blake, then I suspect you know about my family, particularly my parents. But to answer your question, no. I do not get along with my parents. They are selfish and toxic with no self-awareness. The number of people they have hurt over the years... Well, it's staggering. And I made a decision to keep my distance."

"I understand, in my way. My parents are difficult, too. They refuse to speak to one another. And guess who they've used as a go-between?"

She looked at him pointedly. "You don't still do that for them, do you?"

He shrugged, noticing how uncomfortable it felt to be called out in that way. "I've cut back. Old habits die hard. And nothing is straightforward when it comes to family."

Zena nodded. "Ain't that the truth."

"You mentioned Holly Blake. How did you know I knew her?"

Zena was still staring at the paintings when she answered him. "My Uncle O told me. And to be honest, your connection with her was one of the reasons I was determined not to like you."

Gabe was confounded. "Really? But Holly is so...vanilla. I mean that in the nicest way, don't get me wrong. She just has a way of suiting herself to anybody's tastes. What could she have done to offend you?"

She didn't answer, kept her eyes fixed on the wall. It took Gabe a moment, but he put it together. "Oh, wait a second... Zena Sweetwood." Saying her name triggered a memory. "You dated Max for a while," he said, pleased with himself. But the look on her face worried him. "Hold on, you're not still hung up on him, are you? Is that why you don't like Holly?"

Zena's face went red, and she stepped back with a huff. "We'd better get looking. We're not here to chat."

Gabe had struck a nerve, and it occurred to him that he should leave her alone, but his ego was hurt, and it spoke first. "Geez, what is it about Max that has all the ladies swooning? Is it the uniform?" She ignored him, and he couldn't help but add, "And what did Holly do to you? It's not her fault Max never stopped loving her."

"Jesus, Gabe," said Zena annoyed. "I never said it was. Holly just rubs me the wrong way, always has. And yeah, Max always loved her, but she didn't do a whole lot to deserve it in my opinion. She simply existed, and he pined for her. Does it make me kinda jealous? It did at the time, for sure! But the fact of the matter is, Holly Blake is not my cup of tea. She's boring, predictable, and whiny—has been since high school. And I understand that you two are good friends, but I don't think this is something we need to agree on to complete the task at hand, do you?"

He blinked, stupefied. "I, uh, no. I guess not."

"Great," she said, and walked to the other end of the hall to start sifting through some of the old prints and paintings.

It was weird to meet someone who disliked your best friend. That's all Gabe could think as he watched Zena. Like here they were, two educated people of similar ages who knew Holly and had such different takes on her. Gabe wanted to tell himself Zena's view was all rooted in jealousy, but he could tell it wasn't. She straight-up did not like Holly. So that was that.

It occurred to him that Holly had lived a whole life here in Georgia he didn't know much about. Holly talked about Max and her brother, that was it. And after what happened to her parents, Gabe decided not to push for more. Zena Sweetwood, on the other hand, was a mystery he was interested in solving.

Chapter 10

Zena could feel Gabe watching her as she flipped through a box of art prints on the floor. She was glad she'd had the foresight to wear yoga pants, sneakers and a comfortable t-shirt instead of her usual uniform of a black mini-dress and heels. It was much easier to sit on the floor cross-legged this way. And she wasn't self-conscious as underwear lawyer stared. The guy thought he knew everything. It was annoying, and it felt good to prove to him that he didn't.

If only he wasn't so damn good-looking. That part of him was the hardest to take. She found it difficult to face him without staring at his mouth like she was drawn to it. Of course, that all vanished at the mention of Holly Blake, so maybe she should be grateful for the switch in conversation. It saved her from thoughts of just impulsively kissing him, pressing her body urgently against his.

Whew.

Concentrate, Zena, she told herself as she tried to focus on what her hands were doing. *Uncle O needs you.*

And just like that, her thoughts were transported to another Christmas memory from childhood. This time, she and her brothers were exploring the woods beyond her aunt and uncle's home on the hunt for the perfect Christmas tree.

Keith spent the entire time making snowballs and hurling them at her until she ran up and kicked him in the shins. "Stop it, you idiot! We're here to find a tree."

He winced in pain and swore at her before running back to the house.

"Ugh, good riddance," she said, adjusting her cream-colored wool hat.

Jacob was twenty paces in front her, taking his time observing each evergreen he passed. Zena ran to catch up to him.

"How tall should it be?" she asked her big brother. "How wide?"

Jacob shrugged. "Well, it's for the front hall, so we have a lot of room to play with. But I don't think our father will want to hire anyone to help get it home, so it's gonna have to fit in the truck."

Zena nodded in agreement with his assessment. He wasn't treating her like a baby for once, and she wanted to make sure she didn't make a stupid mistake that would change his mind. "The smaller trees are this way," she said, pointing up ahead.

"Good eye, Zena," he said. And she melted inside. Having her older brother's approval was a big deal. He was smart and nice, but not a pushover. His respect had to be earned.

The memory made Zena ache a little. And she wanted reassurance of her brother's love right then and there. She could feel tears coming to her eyes, and the thought of getting emotional in front of Gabe made her nauseous.

"I'm just gonna zip out for a moment," she called to him without looking up. She made her way out of the portrait hall and headed for the nearest restroom.

Zena rounded the corner at the end of the hallway and darted inside the first door on the right. Her heart was beating fast and loud, and it took her a second to realize she was close to panic. She put her hand on her chest and forced herself to breathe slow and deep as she sat down on the edge of the bath tub. The knot in her stomach was so tight, and the fact that it had appeared seemingly out of nowhere was confusing.

But had it? She had been thrust in the middle of a family drama and was handling it alone while Keith and Jacob were just skating along, not even aware of all that was happening. Of course, Keith was useless, but Jacob...

Zena pulled out her phone and clicked on his number. After two rings, he picked up.

"Zena?" he asked, surprise clear in his tone. "Is everything okay?"

The sound of his voice made her body relax just a little and sent a wave right through her. Jacob was one of the good ones. "Yeah," she replied. "I just needed to hear you, I guess."

"I see," he said. "Is this about our aunt and uncle?"

"How did you—?"

"Nancy heard gossip down at the pub. Something about Aunt Adora filing for divorce. I told her there had to be some mistake but now you're calling…"

Zena took a deep breath again and rubbed her temple with her free hand. "No mistake," she said. "But I do think it's a load of BS. I'm here at the house trying to figure out what happened. Something made Auntie A freak out, and I'm going to figure out what it is."

There was silence for a few beats, and then Jacob said softly, "You know, it's not up to you to save them, Zena."

Her jaw tightened at his words. "Uncle O called me, Jacob. You should have heard how distraught he was! How desperate!"

His tone remained gentle. "I'm not surprised he called you. You've always had such a strong connection to the two of them. And I know how much their marriage means to you."

Their marriage? What the heck was he talking about? She was helping her uncle. She was doing as she'd been asked. She was a helpful person who cared about her family. "I don't know what you mean."

Her brother sighed as if struggling to deliver an uncomfortable truth. "Zena, you've always idolized Auntie A and Uncle O. You've put their relationship on a kind of pedestal ever since we were little. You didn't have Barbie and Ken dolls, you had Adora and Octavius. And I get it. Truly, I do. Mom and Dad were—are—so messed up and toxic. It's no wonder you latched onto a couple who actually love each other."

"Well, I…" she trailed off, not knowing what to say.

"Look, all I'm trying to do here is let you off the hook. Maybe something big has happened, you know? And maybe they won't be able to recover. That's between them, Zena. Just try and remember that. They're only human. And so are you."

Zena rolled into the giant soaker tub with a thud and stared up at the painted ceiling. The overjoyed cherubs featured in the frescos seemed to mock her. She felt her throat tighten up at Jacob's words. He was right. She couldn't save her aunt and uncle. She couldn't save their marriage. This was a childish thing she was doing, and all at the bidding of her sad, drunken uncle.

"What was that noise?" asked Jacob. "Are you okay?"

Now it was Zena's turn to sigh. "Yeah, I'm fine. Listen, I should go, okay?"

"I've upset you."

She shrugged—a silly thing to do considering he couldn't see her, but the words just wouldn't come. "I've upset myself, I guess."

"Zena, listen to me. You are a beautiful person with an enormous heart. I love you. Nancy loves you. And our aunt and uncle both love you, too. Just go easy, okay?"

"Okay," she said noncommittally and hung up without saying goodbye. He knew her enough to know she meant no harm. She simply had to move on quickly.

There was a knock on the door.

"Zena?" called Gabe. "Are you in there? Are you okay?"

She rolled her eyes. "Yes and yes," she replied, getting up from the tub to open the door. There he stood, the solid stance of him paired with the look of concern on his handsome face was almost too much. "I just needed a minute," she said.

"Your brother isn't all the way right, you know," he said, taking a step toward her.

"Huh?"

He swallowed. "Your call...he was on speakerphone."

"You mean you eavesdropped," she clarified.

He made a vague gesture. "Well, one could argue I overheard. But that's neither here nor there. What I mean to say is that your brother is right in that it's not up to you to save them. But that doesn't mean you can't try to help them."

Gabe seemed sincere. And Zena noticed how much she wanted to believe him. Not just because she had already promised her uncle she would try to help, and not just because she was invested in this as a loving niece. But also, because, for whatever reason, she wanted to work more with Gabe, get closer to him. She didn't want to lose this opportunity to know him better. And for him to know her.

It occurred to Zena now, right now at this moment, Max had never seemed to want to know her. He was a gentleman—thoughtful, strong, and kind—but he was also perennially distracted. It was almost as if throughout the entire time they dated, Max was comparing her to Holly.

Zena never had a chance. She could see that clearly now. Their relationship was never going to go anywhere, and it had been unfair of him to pretend otherwise. Anything beyond casual dating would have been out of the question. And he must have known that all along. It all made her feel naïve and stupid.

Gabe appeared to be reading her thoughts. "Hey, there's nothing wrong with you. You're a good person."

"You barely know me," she shot back.

He studied her and shook his head. "How well do I have to know someone who would go out of their way like you are for your family to know you're a good person? It's not complicated, Zena. You're doing a good thing...because you're good."

Just then, they heard shouting coming from the main entrance to the home. Zena recognized the voices immediately. The first was her Uncle Octavius. But the second? For the love of all that was holy, it was none other than Sheriff Max Cooper.

Chapter 11

*O*ctavius was not okay. Gabe could see that clear as day. He sat on the floor of his grand foyer dressed in a Santa suit that was one size too small and yelled for everyone to leave him the hell alone. It would border on humorous if it wasn't so damn sad. The scene reminded Gabe of his father.

Johnny Da Silva hated Christmas. And no matter what his wife Maria did to try and make the holiday fun or even palatable, he revolted. Johnny would start drinking at the crack of dawn and do his best to make noise, stick his finger in cooling pies, open presents before it was time, and generally make an ass of himself.

This behavior didn't change after the divorce. If anything, it got worse. He'd invite himself to Gabe's mom's house with promises of being fine this time and beseeching how un-Catholic it was to leave a man alone at Christmas. The whole day was poisoned with noise and unpredictability.

As an adult, Gabe didn't really have to deal with the holidays. He could make up excuses about having to work and avoid the whole hot mess. But watching Octavius now—so broken and angry and sad, it hurt Gabe's heart. It triggered something raw in him, something he could normally push aside.

His instinct was to yell at Octavius and tell him to get up and stop being such a whiny baby. But he couldn't do that to Zena. He did not want her to feel any more uncomfortable than she already must have felt. Here was her drunken uncle being escorted home by her sheriff ex-boyfriend. Gabe watched her walk over to him and struggle to try and pull him up. Octavius was having none of it, and it was only giving Gabe more painful flashbacks. He had to do something.

With deliberate strides, he crossed the front entrance and knelt beside Octavius. The man reeked of booze and urine. He whispered curtly in his ear, "You need to stand. If Adora sees you, that will be it." He could hear Zena apologizing to Max for the trouble and could see Max, hat in hand, saying it was no trouble at all. Finally, Octavius seemed to hear him, and the man tried to stand.

Immediately, Max rushed to help. "Whoa there, Mr. Sweetwood. Not so steady yet, are you? Perhaps this gentleman can help you to your room?"

It was at that moment it dawned on Gabe that Max assumed he was "the help."

Zena spoke up. "Oh, no. That's not Gabe's job," she said, clearly embarrassed by everything now.

Max narrowed his eyes, observing him. Then realization dawned. "Oh shoot. Gabe, I'm so sorry. I didn't recognize you at first. And I completely forgot you were in town."

"No worries, man," said Gabe kindly. But he could not help but feel weirded out by the whole exchange. Where was the guy's head at? Was he distracted by Zena?

Joseph appeared just then carrying a blanket. "Mr. Sweetwood," he exclaimed as he wrapped the blanket around his employer. "I have a strong cup of coffee and a cold shower waiting for you upstairs. You've caused enough chaos for one day, wouldn't you say?"

Remarkably, Octavius stood up to his full height and allowed himself to be helped by the much shorter man. "I'm broken, Joe," he said.

Joseph shook his head. "Never Joe, sir. You know that."

"S-sorry, Joseph," he uttered as the two headed to Octavius's man cave. They clearly had a bond that the rest of them knew nothing about. And it got Gabe wondering, why wasn't Joseph as worried about the fate of Octavius and Adora's marriage as everyone else seemed to be?

After a moment, Zena broke the silence. "Max, I'm so sorry about my uncle. What even happened out there? We didn't know he'd left the house!"

Max waved off her concern. "Don't give it a second thought, Z."

Z? Gabe found himself crossing his arms in front of his chest and widening his stance hearing this informal version of Zena's name.

"But you may want to consider some increased security measures while your uncle is...going through this," he continued. "Just some kind of camera system that allows you to see when someone tries to leave, not simply when someone tries to enter."

Gabe noticed that Max only addressed Zena. He also noticed the color rising in her cheeks as the sheriff spoke, and he wanted to roll his eyes. It was annoying to see them both like this. Was Max aware of Zena's feelings for him? He had to be, right? And yet, he didn't appear to be doing much to assuage them. Sure, he and Holly were a confirmed item, but that didn't prevent a guy from getting some attention from a girl he knew full well still pined for him.

"That's a good idea," replied Zena finally. She shifted her weight awkwardly, running a shaky hand through her dark hair. And Max just stood there as if he had no idea he was the cause.

"I think we can take it from here, Sheriff Cooper," Gabe heard himself say. He kept his tone light and friendly, trying not to give away the irritation he felt.

"Oh! Right," said Max. "Yeah, I should get home to Holly. I've been on shift for too long. I'm starting to space out."

And with that, Gabe clapped him on the back, thanked him, and sent him on his way. As he shut the door and turned around to face Zena, he could see she'd been watching him carefully.

"What was that about?" she asked, cocking her head slightly in question.

Gabe narrowed his eyes. "I don't know what you mean. Did you want him to stay for dinner or something?"

Zena made a face that said she didn't believe him. "I thought you liked Max. That's all."

"Max is a great guy, Zena. But we have work to do. Am I wrong?" asked Gabe. "Your uncle is in terrible shape. I don't want to lose our momentum."

Zena yawned and shrugged. "To be honest, I need a break. I think I'm gonna turn in for the night."

Gabe felt a mini-panic in his chest. "Already? We haven't had dinner yet. I think Joseph mentioned something about home-made chicken noodle soup."

She shook her head. "I'm not hungry, Gabe—just tired."

Chapter 11

Except she looked more than tired. She looked sad and frustrated, embarrassed and exhausted. And as much as he wanted to convince her to keep going, he knew it would be a selfish move.

"Oh, okay," he replied, pretending so hard to be cool. "Just text me if you need anything. I'm gonna pick up where we left off."

Zena smiled weakly. "Thank you," she said.

Gabe sorted through another box of prints and set a few aside that had notes from Octavius on the back. The latest one was of a couple walking in the rain—a piece by Gustave Caillebotte. The inscription read, "Will you always take my arm? For I will always keep you safe." And the one before that was a self-portrait by Egon Schiele where Octavius wrote, "The way you are able to see the beauty of this world is so beautiful to me."

There had to be hundreds of these. It was incredible. Each piece was clearly special, and yet they were all so different from each other. It was evident that she adored art. He indulged her adoration. It was how he loved her. So, what could make Adora pull away like this? It had to be something only she was seeing, something only she understood to be true.

Gabe's mind drifted back to Zena and how affected she'd been by Max. It occurred to him how painful it is when love is one-sided. His mother had always told him, "One of you's gotta love the other more. And when it's a man and a woman, it should be the man. A man has to be aware, constantly, of what he stands to lose."

It would be hard for Gabe to believe that Zena actually loved Max at any point. From what he'd heard, both parties admitted it had been a casual thing. Still, she'd been hurt, and that hurt remained, though how much of it he couldn't be sure.

Just then, Gabe's phone buzzed. It was Cherry calling.

"Hey Gabe," she said. "I've got good news and bad news. I'll start with the bad, okay?"

Gabe groaned. "Is it the Jollys?" he asked.

"No, no," she said. "We've got them taken care of. It's your dad, Gabe. He came by the office today unannounced. He was looking for you."

235

"Jesus Christ," he swore. "Was he in a Santa suit, too?"

"Was he what?" asked Cherry.

"Never mind," said Gabe. "What did he want?

Cherry sighed. "He seemed...inebriated."

Gabe let out an annoyed sigh. "Yeah."

"But he was okay. He said he just needed to talk to you." Cherry paused then continued. "Gabe, he said he has a diagnosis he needs to tell you about. I think he was a bit shaken up. I was able to sit him down, and he had a cup of coffee. He's in a lot of emotional pain."

Gabe swallowed. "I know," he said. "I know he is."

"Anyway, he's going to give you a call in the morning. I told him I'm a "friend of Bill's" and slipped the info for an AA meeting into his hand. He didn't get upset, thank goodness. He even promised to think about going."

The lump of feeling that Gabe had just swallowed was now a full-blown ache in his throat that threatened to bring on more emotion than he was prepared to show right now. "Oh, Cherry. Wow," he managed to get out. "You have no idea how much..."

"Don't sweat it, Gabe. Really," she said, gracefully cutting him off. "I'll let you two talk out the rest. That's really all I had to share. And don't worry, he didn't make it past reception so this all stays between you and me."

That brought on a massive wave of relief. His dad had embarrassed him so many times. Gabe was certain he had a kind of PTSD from it. And if that had happened at work after all the mess-ups Gabe himself had made? Well, let's just say he didn't need any of that right now.

"Cherry, you're the best," he said, his voice tight with emotion. "Merry Christmas."

Gabe swore he could actually hear her smiling through the phone. "Merry Christmas, boss!"

Chapter 12

Seeing Max Cooper just so happened to be the absolute last thing Zena Sweetwood needed.

"I should head home to Holly."

Yeah, you go do that, Max, thought Zena. *Head on home to the only woman you ever loved and leave me in peace.*

Of course, this house was far from a place of peace.

Zena walked to her bed and plopped down face first, burying her head in the pillows. Why did he have to look and smell so good? Damn, damn, damn, damn, damnit! Tears pooled in her eyes, and she let them go. There was too much going on at once, and Jacob's words from earlier kept running through her mind. "I know how much their marriage means to you."

He'd never said this to her before. And it was strange to think of him knowing this about her and keeping it to himself all this time. Because he was right. The thought of her aunt and uncle falling out of love, ending their marriage, and moving on without each other was devastating to Zena. They were her fairy tale within reach. They were proof positive that not everyone was selfish, toxic, and cruel.

But Auntie A was being distant and cold. And Max was with someone else. And underwear lawyer was being so kind.

What was going on?

Zena had to get ahold of herself. She felt the very core of her drifting away, leaving nothing but the shell of someone who simply exists for the whims of others. No. That may have been the person her parents wanted her to be, but she promised herself long ago to not let that happen.

Uncle O wanted her to save him. Auntie A wanted her to ignore everything that was going on. Max wanted her to be okay without him. And Gabe? Well, she couldn't yet tell what he wanted.

But Zena wanted Anita. She wanted her warm hug and her "Child, shush" so badly that her chest ached. The mixture of love and longing and guilt were overwhelming, and she forced herself to focus on the love. What would Anita tell her to do right now, feeling how she was in this moment? What would she say? Zena could hear the words like a whisper, and they would be something to the effect of: What could she focus on right now for herself? What could she do to shut out all the noise and listen only to her own heart?

The answer was to draw herself a bath and listen to Christmas Carols.

Before she could do that, there was a knock at her door.

"Miss Sweetwood?" called a voice from the hallway. It was Joseph. She called to him to come in.

"Your uncle is asleep," he told her, clasping his hands in front of him. "There's a pot of soup on the stove, and I do believe your lawyer fellow is up in the portrait hall continuing his investigations."

Zena offered a weak smile. "Thanks, Joseph."

"My pleasure. If there's nothing else, I'll head home to Barry."

She nodded. "I'm certain you more than earned your wages today, Joseph. Have a great night. Say hi to that husband of yours whom I've never met and suspect I never will."

"That's right, Zena Sweetwood," said Joseph with a wink and smile. "You never will. Sleep well."

Zena had to laugh and then lament... what was it like to have such ironclad boundaries? She felt like she was barely holding up the paper walls she'd erected. It helped that her parents were inherently self-focused.

I will never be enough for them, she thought to herself, feeling so tired she could cry. It was not a new thought, but it was one she had recently come to accept. And even though it still made her sad, there was freedom in letting it be what it was. She could stop expecting Bill and Patricia Sweetwood to be anything other than what they were.

She filled the tub with warm water and lavender Epsom salts and played "O Holy Night."

Long lay the world in sin and error pining

'Til He appeared and the soul felt its worth

Zena sank into the bath and closed her eyes. She allowed herself to breathe into those words: He appeared and the soul felt its worth. It occurred to her that the kind of peace and acceptance she'd reached regarding her parents was so much bigger than what she was facing with Max.

If she was honest, he'd been a crush—nothing more. And so, maybe she was making this all a bigger deal than it was. Maybe she was just a little sad and lonely, a little jealous. That didn't mean that real love couldn't be right around the corner for her. And what was more, Zena was beginning to admit she may be worthy of it.

Zena awoke at midnight feeling hungry. She'd passed out so quickly earlier that evening, she had skipped dinner altogether. Remembering Joseph saying he would leave a pot of soup out for them, she threw on one of Jacob's giant college hoodies and made her way to the kitchen.

The house felt empty and quiet, but there were nightlights lining the floors of the hallways, so it wasn't hard to navigate in the dark. She decided to check in on her uncle quickly and, as she thought, he was sleeping soundly on a sofa in his man cave—the right side of his body hanging off the edge. Hopefully, his hangover would be significant tomorrow. The drinking really had to stop. His pain was understandable, but getting this wasted day in and day out only made things worse.

Zena padded back up the stairs, making her way to the kitchen. As promised, there was a pot of chicken noodle soup on the stove, and it was still warm. She took a ladle, poured herself a bowl, and dug in. The broth was perfect—slightly salty, aromatic, and just rich enough to taste like a hug feels. Joseph nailed it.

Just then, she heard a rustling behind her and turned to see Gabe standing in the doorway.

"I'd say I didn't mean to scare you, but that's pretty impossible in the middle of the night," he said. His smile was warm, slightly self-deprecating. He wore grey flannel pants and a Led Zeppelin t-shirt. He noticed her staring at it and pulled at the collar. "My dad," he said. "Huge Jimmy Page fan."

Zena put her soup down on the counter and hopped up to sit on top. Legs swinging beneath her, she patted the space next to her and invited Gabe to join her. "Tell me about your dad," she said.

Gabe let out a breath. "That won't make for light conversation," he said, taking his place beside her. "My dad is not an easy man. He left my mom and me when I was ten, but then he fought her for custody. The whole thing was awful. I got dragged into every bitter little feud. Until one day, he gave up. He let mom have me. And that's when he picked up the bottle."

Zena's heart clenched. "I'm so sorry," she said. "I'd always wished my parents had gotten divorced, but I guess neither side is ideal."

"I guess having parents who aren't selfish is the ideal," he quipped.

She nodded. "Yeah, that would have been awesome. How about your mom?"

Gabe shrugged. "I love my mom. But she got caught up in my dad's storms. She still does. I think she spent most of my childhood trying to prove to me she was a better parent than he was. She liked to point out his shortcomings whenever she could. His house was around the corner from ours, and we'd drive past it every day on the way to school. She'd often have something to say—his shutters needed painting, his grass was too long. And this was just the mild stuff. She also liked telling me about arguments they'd had when I was little."

"Really?" asked Zena. "Why?"

"I didn't really think about the why until I was an adult. When I was a kid, it was just how she talked, you know? Like I just knew if the subject of my dad came up, she'd have something bad to say. Unless she wanted time to herself," he said with a sardonic laugh. "Then it became really important I spend time with him."

Zena laughed. "Got it."

"She was a good mom at heart, don't get me wrong. But she shared way too much with me. And I'm still learning to see my dad through my own lens without her view coloring it—even to this day."

"And they still don't speak?" asked Zena.

Gabe shrugged. "Not really. They talk about one another. And I suppose they do talk when my dad inevitably crashes Christmas every year, but I don't think that really counts."

He looked sad just then. Zena could sense the helplessness and grief beneath the throwaway comments about his family. She knew how deep it cut when the ones who were meant to love you most were caught up in their own dramas,

"I've given up on either of my parents ever changing. It's just not in them, and they aren't interested." She took Gabe's hand in hers. "I wish we could bond over something more joyful, but I get it, Gabe. I understand what you're going through."

He tightened his hand around hers, gratefully. "They're just... they're so afraid of life, Zena. It drives me nuts. And I refuse to be like them."

"I get the feeling you are nothing like them," she said quietly.

This made him smile, the kind of smile that made Zena's stomach do a little flip. Like she'd really made him happy. "What other feelings do you get about me?" he said. "Can I ask that? Too cheesy?"

She laughed nervously, tucked a lock of hair behind her ear. Why was everything he was doing suddenly so attractive? "You can ask, sure," she said, trying desperately to keep her voice steady. "I-uh, I think you're good at your job, and you're good at reading people."

He was rubbing her knuckle with his thumb, and she could sense his breathing growing heavy. "I am good at my job," he said softly. "But I've been tanking lately. And I—." He stopped suddenly, unsure if he should say more.

Zena looked up at him from beneath hooded eyes. "You?"

Gabe brought both hands to her face, stroking her cheeks lightly and looking for permission in her eyes. She gave it. She parted her lips and pulled him to her as he answered with a kiss, soft and warm and slow. "This is okay?" he asked, more a Southern gentleman now than an entitled Yankee.

Zena nodded and inched closer to him, and Gabe's hand slid down to her neck, pulling her more deeply into their kiss. She felt his thumb linger over the pulse point beneath her chin, stroking lightly as it raced. His body was tense, as if he was holding himself back from lifting her off that counter and carrying her away. The thought was intoxicating, and she offered him silent permission.

Instead, he moved himself to stand in front of her, his mouth leaving hers for mere seconds. Expertly, he spread her knees apart and stepped between them. Holding her close now with both arms, his hands moved to her hips, kneading her flesh and relieving an ache she didn't know was there.

Zena arched herself against his chest and crossed her arms behind his neck. She gasped softly as he deepened the kiss. Her breath as heavy as his now, she bit his lip gently and matched his hunger with her own. She wrapped her legs around his hips, drawing him in. But for some reason, this sobered him. He pulled back, his breath hard on her forehead.

"That escalated quickly," he said, his characteristic charm replacing his apparent desire for her almost instantly.

"Oh," she said nervously. She pulled away from him and crossed her arms over her chest protectively. "Yeah, I should be getting to bed anyway."

"I didn't mean—"

She waved him off. "It's fine," she said, gathering her bowl and spoon, and placing them in the sink. "It was nothing. Let's just forget it."

The rejection was like a punch to the gut, and she hated how casual she was being when all she wanted to do was cry or scream or yell at him and say, "How dare you?" But of course, she'd been stupid. Gabe was like cover-of-GQ good-looking. He would be dating the most beautiful women in the country back in New York. And here she was just a new-money Southern girl from northern Georgia who got crushes on men in love with other women. What a fool she was.

"Zena," he said, running his hand through his hair. "I don't want to forget it. It's just—"

"Gabe, please. Stop," she said, cutting him off before he could say something that might hurt her more. The truth was he owed her nothing. She was overtired, overwhelmed, and it had been so long since she'd kissed a man. That's all this had been—a mistake. And the fact that she felt rejected was nothing more than a bruised ego.

"Okay," he said, sounding defeated. He turned to her just before he left the kitchen and added, "I'm sorry."

Chapter 13

*G*abe left the kitchen feeling like he made yet another grave error in judgment. Zena was goddamn gorgeous, and she'd been so willing. But for God's sake, she was also vulnerable to the max. Pun intended! The last thing Gabe wanted was to be some rebound guy for her. He liked Zena—a lot. He was drawn to her in a way that felt different. She wasn't a hookup or a coffee date or a "fine for now." She was someone he wanted to know deeply, and he wanted her to know him in return.

But now she was angry. She felt rejected and wouldn't let him explain. Gabe had been trying to tell her the things she was awakening in him. He wanted to say he knew he had stuff to process—stuff from when his parents split. He was going to tell her he realized that to be good man he needed to get this right. And that he couldn't skate by on his smarts alone.

Maybe it was for the best that she cut him off when she did. There was almost zero chance he'd have been able to resist her doe eyes and lips just begging to be kissed anyway. And the words he had almost said were… kind of a lot—probably premature. But she was worth the risk. In fact, he had a feeling she was worth everything.

Here was a woman who, on the surface, appeared to have everything. She came from money, was well-educated, owned her own gallery. She had unmistakable style and grace. And yet, she was hung up on a small-town sheriff while idolizing her aunt and uncle's secretly messed-up marriage. Zena Sweetwood had been sad for far too long.

Gabe knew he couldn't fix her, but he wanted to. Oh, how he wanted to. He had seen the relief in her eyes after they'd kissed, and it relieved something in him, too. It told him he had an effect on her, that shifting her mood was possible and it pushed him to want more. Not more as in more making out, though he was down for that too, but more as in being her boyfriend, her man, her confidante, her partner.

He had to repair the damage done just now in the kitchen. She needed to know how much he had wanted to continue what they'd started. But first, he would have to prove himself. Zena Sweetwood needed to forget about the sheriff of Blairsville and see him, see Gabe Da Silva.

Gabe stood on the balcony of his bedroom. The air was cold, but the morning sun was bright, and it was enough to keep him warm in his wool sweater. He'd waited until a reasonable hour to call Holly. He needed to talk out all that was going on.

"Gabe! Oh, my gosh," she said, not even giving him the chance to say hello. "I've been wanting to text you so badly but Max advised me not to. He said you and Zena had your hands full with Octavius Sweetwood over there. But I've been bursting at the seams! Is everything okay? Did he sign? Did Adora change her mind?"

Gabe rubbed his temple, wishing he'd texted instead of called. It would take Holly a full five minutes to match his energy, and he wasn't sure he could wait that long. "Holly, honey. I can't do this so early in the day."

"Sorry," she said immediately. He could hear the tiny hurt in her voice, but she moved right past it. "Go ahead. I'll just listen. Whatever you need."

"Thank you," he said. "I appreciate that. It's been a week and I..." Gabe trailed off and went silent. Suddenly, he didn't have the words.

"What's going on, Gabe?" asked Holly softly. "Something happened, didn't it? Something that's not really to do with this case."

His throat was tight with emotion once again. He tried to move past it, to say something...anything. But all he could get out was, "Yeah."

"Okay," said Holly. "If you're this upset, it has to be your mom, your dad, or a woman."

This was silly. Why were his chest and throat so constricted right now? His body was being melodramatic, and he was wasting poor

Holly's time. He clenched his teeth and pushed out some words. "It's all of the above, I guess."

"All right, well, I'm gonna use my women's intuition and say it's mostly the last two, am I right?"

Gabe nodded and said, "Yeah."

Holly continued. "And it's close to Christmas, so your dad is probably drinking again. That sucks, and I'm sorry. I really hope he gets his shit together, Gabe."

"Yeah."

"And if we're talking about a woman, I'm guessing it has to be Zena."

Gabe cleared his throat, but said nothing. Holly was smiling; he knew it. She did love being right.

"You know, I always felt like one day you were going to meet someone who was going to figuratively knock you over and literally change everything. And here we are," she said laughing. "Tell me about her, Gabe. Tell me what happened between you two."

So, he did. He told Holly about first meeting Zena, working with her, watching her with her family, listening to her. And then he told her about being close to Zena, kissing her, holding her. It felt good to say it all out loud and to stop keeping it locked up inside of him.

"Gabe! This is incredible! You're falling for her. I can hear it in your voice," said Holly.

Gabe swallowed hard. "But that doesn't matter. I've got too much work to do to fix myself, to deal with all the dad and mom stuff—past and present. My confidence is shot, Holly. I've been dropping the ball at work and then that meeting with the Jollys and being unceremoniously taken off that case... I'm not myself."

"Okay," Holly said. "So, you're going through a rough patch, acknowledging some stuff. That doesn't mean you can't date!"

"But I don't want to just date her, Holly."

Holly paused, took a breath. "Honey, I get it. I do. You're feeling something real for the first time, and it's scary. It's disorienting even. But she's not some angel dropped from the sky. She's a human being with messed-up parents and messed-up coping mechanisms just like you. She's scared, too. And I can guarantee she's into you."

Gabe ran a hand through his hair and kicked at some pebbles on the balcony floor. "I don't know," he said. "I hate to say it, but I'm pretty sure she's still into Max. And I think Max knows it, too."

"What? No way. Those two are ancient history."

"Holly, I'm telling you, something is up with Max. He's been weird around me. When he first saw me at the Sweetwood home, he didn't even recognize me. He mistook me for a house cleaner or butler or something."

"Heaven forbid," said Holly drily.

Gabe ignored her comment. "Then he acted like I wasn't even there. He kept his attention solely on Zena and didn't even address me. I've been a big supporter of you and Max. So, I don't get it. Something doesn't add up."

Holly sighed. "Gabriel, stop. Not everything is about you," she said. "Before Max picked up Octavius, as a favor, keep in mind, he'd just come from a serious car crash where a teenaged girl died. He was totally shaken."

"Damn," whispered Gabe.

"As for only addressing Zena about the state of her uncle, you are Adora's lawyer! Do you really need reminding of that? Max assumed you were not involved in the care of the husband your client is trying to divorce. He was being polite."

Gabe looked skyward and took a deep breath. Reflecting on that night, he realized he may have misconstrued some things. "I'm sorry," he said simply.

"Gabe, honey, I think you need a proper vacation—as in no work, no contact with the office at all. You deserve a break," said Holly. "Promise me, once this business with the Sweetwoods is done, you'll just rest. I don't care where it is as long as you're devoted to relaxing and taking care of yourself."

"Yeah," he agreed reluctantly. "You're probably right. I've been around bickering couples in some way since I was a child. A break is a good idea."

"Yikes, that's true," said Holly.

Gabe felt better. As difficult as it was to admit he needed time off to deal with stuff that he'd been avoiding for too long, he knew it had to happen. And he knew it because he suddenly had the motivation.

Zena represented hope. Even if she didn't end up being the right girl or the timing didn't work out, she stood for the kind of person he wanted to be around—to learn from and support.

New York City divorce court was an endlessly disappointing place to be. People were petty and cruel, and they were this way because they were hurting. Gabe knew that. And yet, it didn't make being in that kind of environment any easier. If he was going to continue in this career, he would have to learn to take time away to recharge. He deserved that, so did his clients. And so did his future family.

Chapter 14

Zena was back in the portrait hall early the next day with coffee and a headache. She had barely slept and ended up giving up at six in the morning. The kiss with Gabe replayed in her brain over and over. She'd tried to get it to stop by playing games on her phone, reading a book, but nothing worked. Of course, the truth was she liked replaying it. She liked reliving it. But she hated admitting she was weak for him in this way. Zena pictured him congratulating himself on making yet another woman moan, and it got her mad all over again.

What a mess she'd made. She didn't want to see him again, but she had to. He was Aunt Adora's lawyer, and she did need his help. He was going to want to talk about last night, but there was no way she was picking up that conversation. The thought of it annoyed her. She didn't want to hear his polite excuses. They had to keep it all above board moving forward. No talking about family or exes or anything personal. The focus had to stay on discovering what had made her aunt so upset.

Two hours into looking through the prints, paintings, and letters though, Zena was becoming more and more discouraged. She was clearly missing something.

"Goodness, how long have you been at this?"

Zena turned around, startled. But it was only Joseph. "Jesus, Joseph."

"And Mary?" he quipped.

"Ugh," she groaned. "I did not have enough sleep to deal with you this morning." Zena stretched out her legs in a vee and sat back against the wall. She'd been kneeling for what felt like ages, and her entire lower body hurt.

Joseph clucked his tongue. "It's fine. I know I'm funny," he said taking a sip of his takeout coffee cup. "Making progress?"

"Not really," said Zena.

"And what about with underwear lawyer?"

Zena felt her face go red. "Uncle O cannot keep a secret to save his life."

"Well, to be fair, he only told me that's what you call Mr. Da Silva. But I want to know what has made you go the color of Scarlett O'Hara's revenge dress!"

She shook her head. "Nooooo way, Joseph. Nope. I have work to do."

He smiled, looking pleased with himself. "I called this, you know. He is your type to a tee, and I told Barry, 'Those two are gonna end up in the sheets before Baby Jesus's birthday!'"

Zena tossed a pen at him. "Oh, my goodness! Stop! Nothing like that happened."

Joseph rolled his eyes. "If you say so," he said. "Miss Sweetwood... Zena, don't make this complicated. If you like him, and you're attracted to him, and he's into it, just enjoy. It's not like every encounter needs to be a match made in heaven."

"You sound like Jacob," she said, rolling her eyes dramatically.

Joseph perked up at the mention of her brother's name. "How is the firstborn son? I haven't seen him in forever."

Zena shrugged. "He's good, teaching art and painting. He and Nancy are ridiculously happy. They live together in the apartment over The Fox and Fig."

"Mm-hm," said Joseph. "And how about Miss Chaos herself...Betty-Daisy? They find her?"

She laughed. "Ava-Rose, you mean?"

"Po-tay-to, po-tah-to."

"Well, to answer your question, no. She has not been found, and Jacob doesn't think she will be. She has the resources to stay gone. But he also isn't convinced she won't pop up in some strange, covert way. Every time he gets a friend request or a follow request from someone he doesn't know, he's on alert."

Joseph looked unconvinced. "I don't know, Zena. If she's as crafty as she's made out to be, she's already in."

Zena sat with that statement for a moment. He was right. Ava-Rose didn't do anything by halves. But she couldn't think about any of that right now. Jacob was his own man with support from Nancy. She had enough on her plate.

"Have you seen my uncle today? Is he okay?"

He nodded. "Yes, he is fine. I gave him an aspirin and an electrolyte drink and advised him to walk out to the stables. It always makes him feel better to see the horses."

"Good idea," said Zena. "You know what? I think I'll walk out there myself, see if I run into him. I could use the fresh air."

Chapter 15

*G*abe spotted her from fifty yards away. She wore a black wool coat with an oversized gray scarf and matching hat. Her movements were slow, and her eyes were fixed on the ground as she walked, as if she was deep in thought.

Instantly, he pictured himself beside her, their arms linked together. He'd pull her closer, protectively, and help her avoid an icy patch on the ground. She'd nuzzle his chest and tell him every little thing on her mind. And he'd listen, just listen, until she said, "What do you think, babe?"

The image of the two of them was so strong, it was like a premonition. He could feel her body beside his, the softness and warmth of her. He could hear the sweet timbre of her voice, the inherent trust in it. The bridge between the present moment and this dream of his... how far? How long could it be? Because it felt as close as his next breath.

Zena looked up just then and waved awkwardly to him. The sight of it was deflating. He wished their last moments together hadn't been so filled with misunderstanding. Gabe waved back and quickened his pace to meet her.

"I didn't realize Georgia could get this cold," he said, hoping to break the ice. "I should have packed my parka."

She smiled. "That might be over the top. Though you would look like the New Yorker you clearly are," she said. "I was walking to the stables. Would you like to join me?"

Gabe nodded and let her lead the way through the powder-fresh snow and mid-December chill.

Zena was quiet for a moment and then asked, "Are you a native New Yorker? I never asked you."

For so long, it was all he wanted—for people to assume he was a big city guy with an ivy league degree and the whole world at his feet, not the lower-middle-class boy from Elmont he really was. But with Zena, he wanted to be honest. He wanted to present the truth of his life to her without shame.

"I'm from Long Island," he told her. "A town called Elmont. My parents never had a lot of money. I was very aware from an early age that if I wanted to go to college, I'd be on my own. I'd need a scholarship."

"And?"

Gabe shrugged and offered a humble smile. "I got one," he said. "And then Columbia Law after that."

Zena shook her head in amazement. "Do you know how rare you are? At least, in my world you are. Everyone I knew had a trust fund. I think it's difficult to feel grounded or even challenged when you know you've got that much money just waiting for you."

"But I'm sure most people still go into careers like law or business."

"Yeah, but they have a parent who paves the way," she said. "Nepotism and grandfathering are standard practices around here."

Gabe lowered his head. "I guess every station in life has its downfalls. Most of my friends had deadbeat dads or alcoholic moms or both."

Zena nodded. "I don't think money can save you from everything. I have friends who have similar stories. It just looks better, you know?" She paused and then continued. "My parents have money to be sure, but they are miserable on the inside. As their daughter, it's meant a long road trying to remind myself that the acquisition of things does not equal love or contentment."

"No truer words…" he said softly.

She took her gloved hand and placed it on his arm for the briefest of moments. But it happened. Gabe felt every millisecond. "And what about your parents? I know they were divorced. But were they there for you?"

"My mom did all of the day-to-day parenting. She took me to school, little league games, made dinner—all the things moms typically do, I guess. But I always felt secondary to her. It was like the most important thing to my mom was that she appear to be good. I don't mean physically, though she is beautiful. I mean she wants people to believe she is a stand-up citizen. So, she volunteered a lot, served on the PTA, baked for the church bazaar, that kind of thing. And as a kid, I mean, I knew she was there in body. But she was often distracted, almost like she was adding up the selfless deeds in her head to make sure they came out to a certain result. And like, then she'd finally be good enough."

Gabe said the words with such fluid honesty it stunned him. These were things he'd thought on his own for years, but never dared express. Who would he even tell? Holly, maybe. But there never seemed to be a good moment. And yet, with Zena, it had been automatic.

She nodded in understanding. "My mom is similar, but she doesn't really care what people think. She has a very transactional approach to life—she does things to get things. Actually," Zena laughed, "my dad does that, too."

Gabe let the words hang for a moment. "Your dad sounds intimidating," he offered.

Zena let out a sardonic laugh again. "He does sound that way, doesn't he? And that is the reputation he wants, trust me. The sad truth is, I don't really know him. What's worse is, I've accepted I never will. Bill Sweetwood has no interest in being genuine with anyone, let alone his own daughter."

"So, you cut your ties?"

She nodded. "Not officially, but yes. It's not like I came to them and said, 'I'm done.' I just don't visit. I don't take money or anything anymore. The thought of being indebted to them makes me ill. And ultimately, I simply want my relationships to be real and honest. This is something Bill and Patricia can't offer. So, I'm in the process of accepting that."

Gabe tried to catch her eye. "And how's that going?"

Zena scrunched up her face. "Horribly," she said, then waved her hand dismissively. "No, it's fine. Some days I get sad thinking about what I missed out on, but then, I get so much out of my relationship with my aunt and uncle. I always have. I'm blessed in that."

Gabe offered a reassuring smile. "You are, Zena. You definitely are," he said. "Adora has a lot to do with your love of art, right? Did you always want to own your own gallery?"

"Believe it or not my childhood dreams did not involve paperwork, haggling with artists and agents, and never leaving my hometown," she said with an edge of snark.

He gave her a look that said he knew that wasn't what he meant. Zena relented.

"Okay, okay," she said. "Yes, when I went to college to study art history, that was the goal. Mind you, I would have preferred the gallery to have been in Atlanta, but I can't afford the rent. So, Blairsville it is. But when I was a kid, I wanted to be an artist. I wanted my paintings hung in the gallery. Unfortunately, I just didn't get the gift. Jacob did though."

Gabe studied her face and didn't detect any jealousy, simply acceptance. "Do you like his work?"

She nodded. "I do. It sucks that it took him so long to embrace his talents, but I'm glad he did."

They reached the stables, and Gabe made an attempt to casually look at his watch. Just as he thought, it had gotten late. He was meant to meet with Adora in ten minutes.

Zena appeared to notice his distraction. "You've got to be somewhere?"

He nodded. "Your aunt. She asked to meet with me."

Zena stepped back, almost imperceptibly, but Gabe noticed. It was as if their little bubble had been burst. "You should go then."

Gabe took a deep breath and searched her face for just a little hint of encouragement. He wanted to talk to her about what happened in the kitchen, but he didn't want to make her angry again if she wasn't ready. "I will, but first... Zena, can I just say that I didn't mean to pull away like that last night."

Her eyes flashed. "I thought we weren't going to talk about that," she said.

This wasn't going the way he wanted. Feeling pressed for time and wanting to do some damage control, he blurted, "I'm going away."

Zena blinked in surprise. "You're going away? Like today?"

Gabe cursed his impulsive mouth. "No, not today. When we're done here. When we fix this."

"I see," she replied and started walking for the stables. "I'm happy for you, Gabe. And you should really go to my aunt now. She hates when people are late."

"I—I didn't mean... what I'm trying to say..."

But she was gone.

Chapter 16

Zena was somewhat relieved that the next few days in the portrait hall were spent in silence. Gabe tried one more time to bring up the night of the kiss, but she cut him off instantly. She wanted to say, "I get it. You're important—a big-time lawyer with big-time clients and places to be." But she didn't. Instead, she stuffed her feelings down and soldiered on. She stole glances at him multiple times a day and relived the feel of his mouth warm and soft on hers—she'd be lying if she said she didn't.

Today though, Zena focused on sorting through the many boxes in a storage room off the main hall. This was it, the last place to look through. She'd texted Gabe earlier to say she'd handle this herself. He could sleep in. He had apparently read the text as soon as he received it, but didn't reply. Whatever. She knew he was disappointed. He made it clear that he liked spending time with her, but all Zena could think was: to what end?

Her phone lit up; Zena looked at the screen and saw that it was Jacob video-calling her.

"Isn't it too early for video?" she said, angling the phone to show her face.

"Probably, but you look beautiful, don't worry," Jacob said with a smile. She had to admit it was good to see his face, to see the face of someone she loved who was happy. "Listen, Nancy and I were talking. We'd like to head up there on Christmas Eve to see you all. We thought we'd bring a few roast chickens, a couple salads—keep it simple. Give Joseph the night off. And hopefully relieve some of the tension there."

Zena felt her entire body sigh with relief. "Jacob, yes. Oh my goodness, yes. I would love to see you guys," she said, a slight crack in her voice. "I'm hoping everything is resolved by then, but either way, please come." She set the phone down to stand up, but as she did, she knocked a manila file folder to the ground.

"Zena?" called Jacob, not able to see his sister's face. "Where'd you go?"

But she barely heard him. Three things fell from the file folder she had dropped: a print, a letter, and a receipt. Zena's heart sped up, her breath catching as her mind raced. She picked up each piece and then read the letter. The words confirmed her thoughts, and she let out a small cry. This was it. This was the thing.

Oh, Auntie A...

Christmas break when Zena was twelve meant a week away at her aunt and uncle's home all by herself. Jacob considered himself too grown up to go, and Keith just wanted to be home with his friends. This didn't bother Zena one bit. She was sick of her brothers, truth be told. They were mean and smelled bad and left their socks everywhere. Let them stay home and do what they always did. Zena was getting the heck out and spending time with normal people.

"Your Aunt Adora called this morning," said Patricia Sweetwood from the driver's seat of the family's Range Rover. She had agreed to take Zena to her brother-in-law's home and use the drive as some mother-daughter bonding time. Zena was dubious but said nothing. As long as she had this week away, she could tolerate her mom for the forty-five-minute drive north from Blairsville up through North Carolina and back down to McCaysville, Georgia.

"Oh?" said Zena out of politeness. Patricia Sweetwood may not have taught her much for life out in the world, but she did often refer back to the importance of manners. As an adult, Zena couldn't help but wonder about the irony of being polite but also generally a crappy person.

"She said there's snow where they are. You two can make some forts and snowmen if you like. She said Uncle Octavius would be working this week, so it'll be the two of you most of the time," said Patricia.

Zena knew this already. Her aunt had sent her a message on MSN. But she didn't want to fight. "Okay," she said simply.

Patricia looked at her reflection in the rearview mirror and adjusted her lipstick. "The reason your aunt called was to apologize to me," she said carefully, pronouncing each word slowly and with purpose.

This got Zena's attention because, well, it seemed preposterous. Why would Auntie A ever apologize to her mother? "How come?" she asked.

Patricia cleared her throat. "Well, she said some nasty things about me the other day at a doctor's office, and a friend of mine was there. You remember Kimmy Lacroix, sweetie? Anyway, she overheard the whole thing."

"And you told Auntie A what Kimmy told you?"

Her mother shook her head. "Your father did," she said. "He saw how upset I was. He was being protective."

Zena knit her brown in confusion. "Dad did that?"

"Uh-huh," said her mom.

This didn't make any sense to Zena. Her dad was not the protective type and usually couldn't care less what people said about his wife. Besides, he liked Auntie A. If anything, he'd side with her. But why would her mother lie? Especially about something Zena could just ask her aunt about.

"What did she say?" asked Zena.

Patricia bit her lip and gripped the steering wheel tighter. "She said I was a bad mother. She said it wasn't fair that women like me got to have three kids while she couldn't even have one."

It took a minute for Zena to process what her mother was saying. "Auntie A can't get pregnant?"

Patricia shrugged. "I don't think she knows that for sure. She's being dramatic, darlin.' One miscarriage doesn't mean you can never have a child. Sheesh."

"Miscarriage?" asked Zena. "You mean she lost her baby?"

"Yes, yes. It happens all the time. No need to get all upset. Your aunt is young. It'll happen."

Zena looked out the window, watching the trees whiz by and felt a pang of sadness for her aunt. "It sounds like she's scared it won't."

Patricia clenched her jaw. "That doesn't make what she said okay."

Zena's head zipped back, and she looked at her mother, feeling suddenly guilty that she hadn't acknowledged her pain. "I know, mama," she said, leaning forward to place her hand on her mother's arm. "I'm sorry your feelings got hurt."

Patricia smiled, and Zena felt relief at being good in the eyes of her mother once more.

The memory of that car ride was fresh in Zena's mind as she walked to her Aunt Adora's room. She had spent all these years believing she was her aunt and uncle's favorite child, their joy. The feelings Zena had brought forth from that conversation with her mother were all about Patricia Sweetwood—how she'd been treated, how she'd been affected. And it occurred to Zena now that that had been the entire point.

Her mother may as well have said, "Listen, your aunt may be sad this week about this super tragic thing, but I want you to know that she said some shitty things about me to strangers when she was upset, and that is way worse."

Zena had not even questioned Adora and Octavius's lack of children. That would have distracted from her haven there and favorite kid status. She didn't even let her mind go there. She had stayed focused on her own needs. Granted, she'd been a child, but she was an adult now. And this was her chance to make things right for the people who had been so kind and generous to her. They'd been surrogate parents. And Zena had needed that so badly.

She checked her armpits with a sniff test and decided they were a pass. Her hair though? That was another matter. Zena stopped in front of a hallway mirror putting the file folder between her teeth as she fixed a messy bun. As she was doing this, Gabe appeared behind her.

"Shit," she exclaimed, dropping the file folder to the ground.

"We've gotta stop meeting this way," he joked weakly.

Zena was impatient. "Gabe, can you not do this right now? I need to see my aunt."

He bent to pick up the papers. "What's this?" he asked looking at each piece. "Zena. Did you figure it out?"

She grabbed everything out of his hands in frustration. "I don't know!" she shouted. And then more calmly, "I think so. Sorry, I'm just on edge. And I really need to talk to my aunt."

Gabe reached out and gently touched her arm. "Let's do it together," he said. "I'll be there for moral support. And I'll advise Adora that it's in her best interest to listen to you."

His face was so sincere. Again, he was being kind and thoughtful. Technically, Adora was still his client, and this conversation probably should not be taking place. Was it possible this was who he truly was and not some act? Was he more interested in humanity than money and rules?

"Okay," Zena said, nodding her head in agreement. "That sounds like a good plan."

Chapter 17

Gabe kept a respectful distance in the corner of the room as Zena sat down with Adora. The connection between them was clear. Blood or no, these women loved one another deeply. Adora was still checked out, but attempting to look perfectly fine. Zena held her aunt's hand in her lap and quietly told her that she had something to share. The look in Adora's eyes was one of barely holding it together, almost begging Zena to give her something to cry about.

"Gabe and I have been doing some digging," she began, her knees angled toward Adora as a symbol of closeness and support. "Octavius told us about the circumstances of you asking for a divorce, as you know. So, we knew about the doctor's appointment, and we knew about you seeing something in the portrait hall—something deeply unsettling that set you off."

"Okay," said Adora, slightly unsteady.

Zena paused as if she knew the words she was going to say next would be hard to hear. "And we've spent many hours looking through the portrait hall, sorting through all your paintings and prints and letters. But it wasn't until I remembered two things," she said offering Gabe a sidelong glance. "One was how often people mistake af Klint for Klimt. And two, the terrible ordeal you had before I came to stay with you the Christmas after I turned twelve."

Gabe noticed that Adora remained statue-still. Zena was clearly onto something. She presented the file folder she'd been sitting on and opened it on the coffee table in front of them. She spread out the letter, the sonogram photo, and the receipt.

"It all clicked when I saw the receipt. That painting by Gustav Klimt—*The Three Ages of Women*. I know you. I know you would have no interest in that. It's too commercialized, too misinterpreted. Klimt is beneath your notice. But a man who knows nothing about art, who simply loves a woman who loves art—he may hear the name 'af Klint' and then go buy a Klimt. And a man who loves a woman so deeply, will more than likely want to have children with her. And so, he demonstrates this by—with good intentions—buying a famous painting by the wrong artist, and writing a letter telling the woman he loves how he can't wait for their future and all it will bring."

Adora was silently weeping now, tears streaming down her face, but she still held steady.

"My mother told me about the miscarriage, Aunt Adora. All those years ago, she told me a secret about you that she never should have. But in a way, I'm glad she did. I'm glad she's the selfish person she is because it made the picture clearer. You are forty-nine years old. When my mother was forty-nine, she made a point of telling us she was going through the change of life—menopause."

Gabe mentally put the pieces together, and his heart wrenched. The pressure Adora must have been putting on herself all these years, the suffering in silence, the avoiding of questions. It was a lot. It was too much.

Adora let out a cry now, a strangled, heavy cry that she had been holding in for far too long. "I felt like I'd failed him," she sobbed. "Like I'd never be able to give him what he wanted. Every year passed, and I just put thoughts of my age aside. I denied it all and held out hope. I can't believe I did that."

Zena was crying now, too, holding her aunt close, the two women finding relief and comfort in one another.

"We all do it," Gabe heard himself say. "We all cling to some kind of denial or hope at some point. The pain is too much otherwise."

Adora pulled back and nodded. "Yes," she said through her tears. "It was overwhelming."

"But you were always enough," said a voice from the doorway. The three of them looked up to see Octavius standing there tall and sober with complete love and acceptance in his eyes. "I'm sorry I didn't say that. Because you were."

"We didn't talk about it," said Adora. "I never let you talk about it. I was too ashamed and kept thinking, maybe next year. It was ridiculous denial. I was so obtuse."

Octavius crossed the room with purpose. Zena rose and made way for him. "I love our life, Adora," he said, voice full of emotion. "I love you!"

Gabe inched his way out of the corner towards the door and, as he did, he tried to catch Zena's eye. She was transfixed by her aunt and uncle but soon began to feel like a third wheel and followed him.

Out in the hallway, she reached for Gabe and let him hold her. He kissed the top of her head and squeezed her gently as she cried softly. It was not lost on him the honor it was to be a comfort for her, to be allowed into this private family moment. Yes, it was often part of the gig but not like this, never like this. Reconciliations and acts of love were rare. And when they did happen, he usually found out via email.

"I texted Octavius and asked him to meet us here," Gabe whispered to her. "I hope that was the right thing."

Zena pulled back and nodded. "Yes," she said. "It was the perfect thing. Thank you."

Gabe looked at her tear-filled, puffy eyes and wanted to tell her so many things. He wanted to say how beautiful she was, how strong. He wanted to tell her how she'd affected him these past few days— both physically and emotionally. But all the times she'd respectfully asked that he not mention anything to do with their kiss or beyond ran through his mind at that moment, and he simply took her hand, kissed her knuckles, and told her, "Anything for you, Zena. Always."

Chapter 18

McCaysville, Georgia, Christmas Eve – Present Day

*J*acob and Nancy were in the kitchen chopping vegetables and stealing kisses. Zena loved to see it. Jacob deserved every second of happiness and from what Max had told her, Nancy did, too. Zena walked to the butcher's block, pulled up a stool, and sat down.

"Oh," said Nancy turning to Zena. "I almost forgot to mention. We invited Max and Holly to come up tonight."

Zena blinked in slight surprise but was pleased to notice she had no bodily reaction to this statement—no tightness in her chest or butterflies in her stomach. It was as if letting go of the idea of Max also meant letting Holly off the hook for being...well, for being Holly. "That's great," she said in all honesty. "What time are they getting here?"

"Max has to work. But Holly will be here around six after she drops Gabe off at the airport."

Zena didn't risk saying anything, simply offered a tight-lipped nod. She didn't want any questions about her and Gabe. And anyway, he'd left the night her aunt and uncle reconciled—went straight back to Holly's. She knew he probably did it out of respect for her, but it still stung.

Jacob looked at Zena but said nothing. Instead, he turned to Nancy. "Where's he off to?"

Nancy expertly carved a radish rose as she answered. "I think Max said he was going to see his parents tomorrow, and then he was off to Italy for a week by himself, and then to Tunisia where he will stay with a cousin for a few months."

Zena knew Jacob asked this for her benefit. She wasn't sure how many details he had, but Holly had most likely told everyone what she knew. And judging by how close Gabe and Holly were, that was probably everything.

"Are Adora and Octavius still upstairs?" Zena asked, changing the subject.

Jacob rolled his eyes. "Yes," he answered. "And I won't dare knock on their door. But Uncle O did promise to break out the Santa suit after dinner so we have that to look forward to."

Zena smiled. "Good. I'm glad. We need a bit of normalcy," she said. Clearing her throat, she ventured a question about the rest of the Sweetwood family. "What are Mom and Dad doing for Christmas? Keith?"

"That's big of you to ask, Zena," Jacob said, bending to plant a quick kiss on her head. "Mom and Dad are in Miami. They rented a boat and are sailing between Christmas and New Years with a bunch of Dad's old business contacts."

"Sounds shady," said Nancy.

"Right?" said Jacob. "It's Bill Sweetwood, so it's safe to assume it's shady. And as for Keith, I'm not sure. Last I heard, he was chasing some model down in Houston. I sent him a text this morning but no response."

Zena nodded. None of this was surprising, and it affirmed her choice to keep her distance. The people she loved, the people who mattered, were here in this house. But as that thought settled in her mind, she realized it felt incomplete. Gabe's face flashed in her mind. The truth was, she missed him. She had been missing him ever since he left.

But that didn't change anything. He had his life in New York, and she had her gallery here in Georgia. Zena was in her thirties now. She had no interest in being Gabe's "girl in Blairsville." He'd never said it like that, and Zena figured she was probably being presumptuous, but she also knew her heart needed protecting. She'd had to sever enough ties these past few years.

As promised, at six o'clock, Holly bounced into the Sweetwood home armed with a magnum of red wine, a baguette, and candy canes. "Merry Christmas!" she squealed as she greeted everyone with a hug and a kiss on each cheek. "Thank you so much for inviting me tonight, you guys. I would have been home alone otherwise."

Zena stood off to the side of the living room unsure of how to greet the embodiment of sunshine and gumdrops that was Holly Blake. But Holly made the decision for her by attacking her with the same hug she'd given everyone else. "It's so good to see you, Zena," she said. "And I have something for you from Gabe."

Zena stepped back, her heart racing just a little. "From Gabe?" she asked, trying to sound nonchalant and failing miserably.

Holly smiled warmly. "Yes," she said handing Zena an envelope. "He insisted I hand-deliver this."

Zena gave an awkward smile and sauntered back to lean against the wall and read her letter.

Dear Zena,

I haven't handwritten something this long in probably ten years so forgive my chicken scratch. Hopefully, you're reading this, and it's not burning in one of the Sweetwoods' giant fireplaces.

Maybe I'm selfish, but I could not leave Georgia... I could not leave you without saying the words I've been wanting to say. It's understandable that you'd assume certain things about me and that you would want to protect yourself. I haven't had a steady girlfriend since college. But that's not because I prefer casual relationships. It's because I have been so laser-focused on my career, I've had very little time for anything else.

Truth be told, I've been so focused on being the kind of lawyer I wanted to be, I haven't even thought about the kind of man I want to be. I'm ashamed to admit that. But since meeting you, it's all I can think about.

I've been unraveling at work. And yeah, I need a vacation. But I also need to look at some things from my past—some of these I shared with you—and process them. These are things that can't be ignored. I need to accept who my parents are so that I can move forward.

What I'm trying to say, what I've been trying to say but failing at, is that you are the woman I want to be with. You are who I see building a life with. But I know that's a lot. It's too soon. So, I'm not asking that of you right now. But I am letting you know my most pressing work is to become the man that a woman like you deserves. My deepest hope is that you'll be there when I'm ready, and that you'll want to be together, too. What can I say? I'm an optimist.

You once said how rare I was. I wonder, do you realize how rare you are? To be so kind-hearted, so loving and open, but to also know how to protect yourself from being hurt.

Zena, you are beautiful—like smoking hot. That's not in doubt. But what makes you a woman to strive for goes way beyond all that. It's your nobility, your strength, your intelligence, and your capacity for compassion. Add all these things up, and I'm running to be your equal.

That's where I am right now. I'm not running away. I'm doing what needs to be done.

In the meantime, I know you'll be living your life, as you should.

Can I call you in the spring?

Yours,

Gabe

Zena finished reading and realized she'd been clutching the paper so tightly, she crumpled the edges. Who was this man? How had she not seen this was what he had been trying to say all along? He wanted to be her equal? He thought she was noble? And smoking hot?

The kiss had been good, really good. And if he hadn't stopped them, they would have ended up in bed. Their chemistry wasn't in question. But if Zena was reading this letter correctly, he knew that, and yet, wanted more. Gabriel Da Silva wanted her, Zena. But more than this, he wanted to be good enough for her.

Her eyes welled up with emotion. She realized in that moment all that she'd been holding in. Gabe wasn't just some good-looking, big-shot lawyer. He was deep and caring. He paid attention to people, to how they felt. He listened. And he only wanted to do better, to be better. She had to stop walling herself off and take a chance. If she'd learned anything from her aunt and uncle this past week, it was that.

These realizations colored every interaction they'd had. She could see now that he had been playing the long game. But it wasn't calculated. It was...pretty damn romantic.

"Where is he?" she demanded loudly to no one in particular, finally looking up from the letter. "Where's Gabe?" The urgency in her voice surprised even her.

"He's at the airport, honey. Chattanooga," said Holly. "Are you all right?"

Zena made for the stairs to grab her coat and purse from her room. "I've gotta go. I've gotta see him before he leaves."

"His flight leaves in an hour, Zena! You'll never make it on time."

She heard Holly's voice, but ignored it. All she knew was she wanted to see him, kiss him. And whatever came after that, she'd let it be.

The highway was covered in a fresh layer of snow, and there were barely any drivers on the road. Zena was driving slightly faster than maybe she should, but her mind was set. Before she left her aunt and uncle's house, she checked the flight app. Sure enough, Gabe's flight was delayed by forty-five minutes. This meant Zena had a tiny window of catching him.

Music. She needed some music. The silence was starting to unnerve her, so she turned the radio on. The local station was taking listener requests, and of course, it was mostly Christmas carols—people dedicating their favorite songs to their loved ones. But Zena was shocked when ten minutes later, she heard Adora's voice coming through her speakers.

"Can you please play 'I Believe in Santa Claus' for my darling niece, Zena Millicent Sweetwood? I want to tell her to believe there's always hope when all seems lost. There are good days ahead, baby girl. Lots of good days ahead."

That did it. The tears started, and they didn't stop until she pulled into the airport parking lot. She took five deep breaths and looked at herself in the mirror: her mascara was smudged, but it wasn't too bad. Zena took a tissue, wiped the bottoms of her eyes, and put on a little lipstick. Staring at her reflection, she said, *You've got this. He laid his heart on the line. It's safe for you to do the same.*

The interior airport lighting was harsh, and the red metallic garlands strewn randomly didn't help. But it was an attempt at holiday cheer, so Zena appreciated it. The snow still fell gently; she could see it float like feathers down the windows overlooking the tarmac. She'd bought a ninety-dollar ticket to Newark in order to make it past security to the gates where Gabe would be.

She was running now. Past the overpowering smell of the perfume from the duty-free shop, past the popcorn stand, and past the long-bearded guy cleaning the floors near the bathrooms who yelled, "Slow down, lady!"

Her breath caught when she spotted him, and she stopped suddenly. He was on his phone showing a picture to a couple of women in their seventies.

"She owns her own gallery in Georgia," he was telling them.

"Well, she's quite pretty," said one woman.

The other looked up and said, "I think she's standing right there, Gabriel."

Gabe's head shot up, and his eyes met hers. "Zena," he said in surprise. "You're here."

Zena nodded and stepped closer to him. "Can we talk?" she asked. "Somewhere private?"

He stood. "Of course," he said. But first he introduced the ladies he'd been speaking with. "This is Linda and Sharon. Ladies, this is Zena."

The woman named Linda spoke. "Lovely to meet you, Zena. Sharon and I have heard a lot about you." Her smile was warm and encouraging. "You've got a nice young man here."

Zena's eyes didn't leave Gabe's. "I know," she replied. "I'm a lucky girl."

Gabe stepped to her, grabbed her by the hand, and led her to a small meeting room that said "Private" on the door. There was no way they were allowed to be in there, but she didn't protest.

"You got the letter," he said, pulling her tight to him. "It was okay? You understand what I meant? What I have to do?"

She nodded. "Yes, I think so."

Gabe cupped her face in his hands and bent to kiss her. His lips were hot on hers, his hands demanding as they moved around her waist and pulled her even closer. "You have no idea what it means to me that you're here. You came all this way for me. And you get it."

Zena was breathless against him. "I have some idea," she said. "I know we've had a lot of misunderstandings because I wouldn't listen."

He swallowed hard. "Well, I know Max hurt you. I understand that whole thing may be difficult to get over."

She shook her head. "He never stopped loving Holly. I know that. I think I even knew it then, but I was so lonely, and he was so kind. Anyway, that's not what it was about. I was worried that you... I want to be taken seriously."

"I know and I—"

Zena pressed a finger to his lips, silencing him. "I know you do. Thank you for your letter. No one has ever seen me the way you do."

Gabe ran his thumbs down the curve of her waist and kissed her again, hungrily this time, making a low growl noise and then forcing himself to pull away. "Leaving you is not easy, Zena."

"I have a flight booked to Newark that leaves in two hours," she said locking her arms around his neck.

He lowered his mouth to the tender spot beneath her ear and tasted her skin. Planting kisses slow and soft down her neck, he breathed her in—his desire for her laid bare. "Are you saying you will come to New York tonight? You'll stay with me?"

"Yes," Zena replied. "If you'll have me."

Gabe lifted her up and placed her on top of the desk they'd been standing in front of. "You know exactly what you're saying, don't you?" he said, his eyebrow raised teasingly. He bit her lip gently.

She smiled and stroked his cheek with her hand. "I'm saying I want you, Gabriel Da Silva. I want you in every way."

He bowed, touching his forehead to hers. "Finally," he said. "A Christmas worth remembering."

THE END

Book Club Discussion Questions

Sweetwood Secret

1. If this were a movie, who would play Holly and Max on the big screen?
2. Were you surprised by the identity of Lucas' kidnapper?
3. What do you think of Bill Sweetwood as a patriarch and businessman?
4. This story features a few interesting side characters, who was your favorite and why?
5. Anita appears to be the backbone of the Sweetwood family and empire. What do you think of her choice to stay with them through the years?

Sweetwood Scandal

6. This story bounces from New Zealand back to small-town Georgia. Which places in the book would you most like to visit?
7. We get a better sense of Patricia Sweetwood as a mother in this story, what did you think of her character development?
8. What did you think of Ava-Rose? Have you ever met anyone like her?
9. Do Jacob and Nancy have what it takes to last as a couple? Was their growth believable?
10. If you could hear Sweetwood Scandal told from another character's point of view, who would you choose?

Sweetwood Christmas

11. Was this story Christmas-y enough?
12. What did you think of Gabe's backstory? Did it shed some light on the life choices he's made?
13. Zena makes brief appearances in the previous two stories. Did you enjoy learning more about her?
14. What did you think of Adora and Octavius as a couple compared to the other Sweetwoods, Bill and Patricia?
15. Art plays a significant role in this story. If you could have a painting of one of the scenes in Sweetwood Christmas, which one would it be?

Acknowledgements

Writing can feel like a solitary process, but I'm blessed to have the support of many.

Big thanks to Arielle and Tonya at Orange Blossom. Your feedback and belief in Sweetwood have meant the world to me.

To all of my friends—especially Corinne, Hannah, Uchechi, Elise, and Kimmy—your kindness, cheerleading, and expertise keep me writing.

To the inaugural members of my writing group—Mark, Macha, Cindy, Shana, and Margaret—thank you all for showing up and sharing your beautiful work.

Thank you to my parents, my mother-in-law, and family for the unending support.

To my girls, Noelle and Ariel—thank you for your ideas, opinions, and ex-boyfriends' names. And thanks to Jelissa as well. Our group chat is a continual source of inspiration.

To my son, Ivan, who always asks about my writing.

And to my husband, Robert, who reads when he can, always shows interest, always cheers me on, and shows me the kind of love a girl just has to write about.

About the Author

D anielle Hines grew up reading by a flashlight under blankets way past her bedtime and has been writing stories about imperfect people finding their perfect love since 2013. Danielle edits books, coaches aspiring writers, and infrequently podcasts at Little Love Stories. She makes her home with her husband and their three kids just outside of Toronto, Canada. The Sweetwood series is her second published work. You can learn more about Danielle at her website, http://writingmiracles.me.

More from
Orange Blossom Publishing

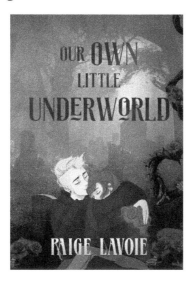

Our Own Little Underworld by Paige Lavoie

After getting dragged out of her school's winter formal, seventeen-year-old Percy Bloom needs to escape her controlling mother. Fleeing into the cold night, she's lost, alone, and freezing.

Ditched by his date and attacked by bullies, Hayden Addams wants nothing more than to be done with high school forever. He finds Percy shivering in the woods and brings her back to the first place he can think of—his family's funeral parlor.

Percy is charmed by Hayden and his usual family. Eager to help her get away from her problems and forget his own, Hayden offers Percy everything she needs: a truck, a destination, and the prettiest blue eyes she's ever seen.

Together, the two hit the road, letting their hopes, dreams, and sparks fly along the way. But can the two arrive at a future without confronting their pasts?